MAYFLOWER
DREAMS

Karen Petit

MAYFLOWER
DREAMS

KAREN PETIT

TATE PUBLISHING
AND **ENTERPRISES**, LLC

Published by Tate Publishing & Enterprises, LLC
127 E. Trade Center Terrace | Mustang, Oklahoma 73064 USA
1.888.361.9473 | www.tatepublishing.com

Tate Publishing is committed to excellence in the publishing industry. The company reflects the philosophy established by the founders, based on Psalm 68:11,
"The Lord gave the word and great was the company of those who published it."

Book design copyright © 2014 by Tate Publishing, LLC. All rights reserved.
Cover design by Rodrigo Adolfo
Interior design by Jomar Ouano

Published in the United States of America

ISBN: 978-1-62994-293-3
1. Fiction / General
2. Fiction / Historical
13.01.27

ACKNOWLEDGMENTS

I am thankful to my children, Chris and Cathy, and to my daughter's husband, Chris, for their loving support. They have encouraged me to keep writing, even during those times when I was working more than sixty hours a week.

My thanks also go out to my family members, including my brothers and sisters—Ray, Rick, Margaret, Carl, Bill, Sam, Dan, and Anne. Their love and support have helped to make my life into a wonderful journey.

Additionally, my thanks are extended to my many friends, including those at Phillips Memorial Baptist Church, the Dancin' Feelin', and the Fitness Studio.

I am thankful for the opportunities I have had to grow as a writer through my interactions with my students and colleagues (present and past) at the following colleges: the Community College of Rhode Island, Bristol Community College, Bryant University, Massasoit Community College, New England Institute of Technology, Quinsigamond Community College, Rhode Island College, Roger Williams University, the University of Massachusetts at Dartmouth, the University of Rhode Island, and Worcester State University.

My thanks are extended to the historians and museum personnel at Plimoth Plantation, *Mayflower II*, Plymouth Rock, and Pilgrim Hall Museum. They have helped me and many other people to learn about our ancestors.

I am thankful to the Pilgrims and their descendants, as well as to their economic, emotional, and religious supporters, for helping to create a country where people can enjoy their freedom. The name of the United States, in and of itself, is a symbol of what humans can achieve with courage, love, and God's help: the co-existence of unity and diversity at one time in one place.

I also thank Tate Publishing for helping me to enhance my writing enjoyment and skills.

Finally, I am thankful to my Lord and Savior, Jesus Christ, who has blessed me with many gifts, including my loved ones, my life, and my abilities. Additionally, he has helped me to understand the historical, linguistic, and personal connections between myself and my loved ones.

CONTENTS

PREFACE

We are descendants of our ancestors, and their history is a part of our modern society. The connections between our Pilgrim ancestors and our current culture are depicted in *Mayflower Dreams* through the use of dream chapters, reality sequences, and the actions and dialogue of the novel's characters.

The dream chapters in *Mayflower Dreams* are based on historically accurate events. While illustrating accurate historic events, these dream chapters have fictional sequences intended to show realistic aspects of Pilgrim culture, including religious beliefs, settings, personalities, language, and viewpoints. For example, the "Feather-hat Lady" is a fictional character who speaks, acts, and makes the *Mayflower* voyage as if she were a real Pilgrim. Within the dream and reality sequences of this novel are actual words spoken and written by some real Pilgrims and Puritans, such as William Bradford and the Reverend John Robinson. Endnote documentation in *Mayflower Dreams* explains the source for each real quotation.

In addition to the dream sections are "reality" chapters, in which the protagonist, Rose Hopkins, is awake. She learns about the Pilgrims' history while interacting with other characters in the twenty-first century. Some of the modern fictional characters in this novel have been given the same names as *Mayflower* and Leiden Puritans in order to show that a large number of people who are alive today are descended from the Pilgrims. According to *Ancestry.org,* about "10 percent of Americans today can trace their ancestry back to the Mayflower."[1]

In *Mayflower Dreams,* realistic historic actions and dialogue confront Rose and help her to find herself, as well as her ancestors. Not only do these historic components connect to Rose psychologically throughout her dreams, but also through her reality. There are some twenty-first century scenes that take place in Plymouth, Massachusetts. These Plymouth scenes are set in real tourist attractions that people can actually visit. The *Mayflower II* and the Plimoth Plantation are examples of present-day living museums: people can go to these places and interact with actors who depict seventeenth-century American Pilgrims with historical accuracy.

A Broken Watch

A bolt of lightning shot across the night sky so quickly that it was almost invisible. A loud thundering noise followed. The noise wobbled so slowly within its own time frame that it soon was too far behind the lightening to ever catch up. Was the wobbling noise being made by thunder or gunshots? Rose moved her left knee and rubbed the scar, but her knee was fine; it wasn't bleeding or painful. Since it was the Fourth of July, the wobbly thundering noise was probably just some fireworks.

A man's voice shouted: "This is a robbery, and this gun is not a dream."[2]

With her eyes still closed, Rose whispered, half to herself and half out loud, "Am I awake or asleep?"

When no one answered her question, she opened her eyes and looked around. She found herself at work in the First National Consumer Bank in Warwick, Rhode Island. There was a man in a mask standing nearby. She asked him, "Am I dreaming again? Is this last winter's bank robbery?"

Even though the mouth area of the robber's mask did not seem to move, he still said, "No."

Rose decided to try a reality check to see if she was awake or lucid dreaming. She looked at her watch. It read 2:30 a.m. After shifting her eyes off into a different direction for a few seconds, she looked again at her watch. It now read 11:00 p.m. She knew immediately that she was lucid dreaming. Some people could control elements of their lucid dreams; Rose sometimes could and sometimes could not. Either way, while lucid dreaming, she was at least conscious of herself and could better remember her dreams.

The robber raised his gun toward the bank's ceiling, where heavy glass panels enclosed the fluorescent lights. An explosion of sounds erupted. Rose closed her eyes and covered her ears. After a few seconds, she opened her eyes again. Hundreds of pieces of broken light bulbs and ceiling panels were flying around the room. She stood quietly in the same spot, hoping that no one would get hurt by the flying glass. Suddenly, the glass pieces went back up into their correct places in the ceiling. Rose sighed in relief, happy that perhaps she was able to change something within this lucid dream.

With a surprised look on his face, the robber stared at the ceiling. Then he moved his gun upwards and shot more bullets into the glass panels. Pieces of glass began to fly around the room again; the robber glared at Rose before saying, "You can't change the past."

Rose sighed again as she remembered that no one in the initial bank robbery had been hurt by the flying bits of glass. Within her dream tonight, some of the glass was bouncing off of the floor and hitting people, but no one was getting hurt.

The robber's mask moved slightly so that a part of the mask slid into his mouth. He began to chew on that section of his mask. Behind the mask, his chin appeared huge as it moved up and down. Finally, the robber stopped chewing and moved the mouth hole over to the left side of his face. He then said, "Okay. Put all of the money in these bags. And I'll kill someone if I see any dye packs or sensors."

Rose began putting money from her teller drawer into the bag. When she was finished, the robber gestured toward several other teller drawers. Rose moved to the next drawer. The robber kept glaring at her and then yelled, "What's taking you so long?"

"I was shot once before in a bank robbery. It's tough for me to move fast." Limping, Rose walked over to the last teller drawer.

"What bank robbery was that?"

"I think it was the same one as tonight's."

"You're not making any sense. The past and the present cannot be the same." The robber watched her legs, waved his gun at her knees, and said, "You can go faster than that! Speed it up!"

Rose's voice quivered as she murmured, "Okay."

When she was done with the teller drawers, the robber waved his gun toward the other people in the bank. "All of you. Go into the vault. And help to fill up this last bag." He moved his gun to his left, pointing into the center of the open vault door. Everyone just looked at him.

The robber aimed his gun toward the center of the round opening of the vault. Then a shot rang out; the bullet moved slowly through the center of the vault's doorway, made a black line as it skidded across a table, knocked several stacks of bills to the ground, and landed in the back of the vault, where it hit a giant stack of gold bars. The dark bullet disappeared into the brightness of the bars.

Rose kept watching the stack of gold in the vault. The golden color gradually became brighter until it looked like the brightest rays of a summer's sun. Rose turned her head and looked out a window; she could see the light of the sun as it moved into position for what was sure to be a fantastic sunset. Then she realized she was outside, speeding along in someone's car.

The robber grunted. Rose turned to look at him and saw glints of reflected light bouncing off of the gun's barrel. She and the robber were in the back seat of a getaway car. A shadowy-looking masked man was driving. There was a large bag of money sitting in front of them in the passenger seat. The other bags of money were probably in the trunk.

The car was travelling north on Route 2, going at least seventy miles an hour, and passing other vehicles. Police cars with blazing sirens were somewhere behind them.

"All of these stupid drivers should pull their cars over," the masked driver said. "We all know they can hear the cops' sirens."

The robber in the back seat with Rose smirked. He then looked closely at her quivering face and asked, "What do you think? Are we good, law-abiding citizens? We could be the first car to pull over."

His breath smelled like old fish. Rose tried to turn away, but his hand grabbed onto her chin and stopped her from moving. Her eyes looked down at the floor of the car. The black mat had brownish stains. Were the stains from someone's blood? Rose looked down at her own feet and legs, but she couldn't see any injuries. Possibly the stains were from someone else's blood, or maybe the robbers had just spilled coffee. An empty, squished coffee cup suddenly appeared on the floor, partially hiding the stain.

The robber asked again, "Should we be the first car to pull over?"

Rose remembered what had happened during the first robbery. As soon as the bank robber's car had pulled over, he had pushed her out and then shot her. She tried not to swallow, but she did anyway. Her stomach felt funny as she told the robber, "Whatever you think."

Waving his gun slightly forward and to the right, the robber said to the driver, "The entrance to route 95 is up here. Slow down so we can turn."

"Yeah, let's do that. The cops will think we're pulling over."

"Once we're at the entrance, we *are* pulling over." The robber looked at Rose and continued, "But just for a second."

Rose started to shake. She had been in this same car and had dreamed this same dream many times before. She knew how the dream would end. However, this was a lucid dream, so maybe—just this one time—she could change the outcome.

The driver said, "No, I won't stop. You promised not to hurt her."

"She'll be fine. We just need a diversion to keep the cops busy."

Rose looked at the bank robber's cold face. In a stuttering voice, she said, "So, do you want me to jump out? I could lie in the road and start yelling. That'll make the cops stop."

The robber stared at her. The frozen pupils of his eyes were blank, as if they were only looking through Rose, rather than at her. He then started to laugh, which made the next words that he spoke seem to be a lie: "All right. I'll be a good guy and won't shoot you, but you must promise to yell a lot."

Rose shook her head in agreement. "That's something I can do really well. My parents are always telling me about when I was a kid. I was a great screamer. I'm even better now."

The driver and the robber ignored her; both of them were looking out the front window at the road.

"Good screaming runs in my family," Rose added as the car slowed down and turned onto the Route 95 entrance. "My family, my family, my family," she said softly as the car stopped on the right side of the road. The robber reached behind Rose, opened the door, and shoved her out onto the roadway.

When Rose landed on the road, her left forearm hit the ground first. Then her elbow and knee made noises as they slid across the pavement, but the sound of her watch breaking was much louder than the sounds of her scraping limbs. The broken timepiece disturbed a flock of birds, making them fly out of a nearby tree. Rose looked at the tree; its leaves were oval-shaped, looking like a face. As she watched, the face's features became more definite. A branch with leaves looked like a nose—a very familiar one. It appeared bony but of a correct size to fit in with the rest of the face. The mouth was formed by a frown-shaped line of red berries. The eyes became the same shade of blue as her husband's. The leaves at the top of the tree changed colors, eventually becoming a reddish brown like the color of her husband's hair. Rose yelled, "Travis! Don't get mad at me! It's not my fault! This time, I'll yell at the right time. I won't be late! I'll stop the bank robbers from shooting me!"

Rose's left forearm, elbow, and knee hurt in the places where they had struck the pavement. Rubbing her eyes, she tried to wake herself up, but it didn't work. She rolled over to see if the car was still on the road next to her. It was, and both of the robbers were watching her. The robber in the back seat put his hand to his ear, acting as if he wanted Rose to say something. Then she realized that she was supposed to scream. She opened her mouth, but no sound came out. She closed her eyes, hoping the robber would be invisible, but he wasn't. She could still see him. He was holding the gun and turned it in her direction. A loud sound was followed by her left knee feeling strange. Was that from a bullet or just from another scrape?

Without even realizing what she was doing, Rose started to scream. As the getaway car sped off onto the highway, several police cars moved to the beginning of the highway entrance, which was only forty feet behind Rose. Two of the cars stopped so fast that a third car behind them was unable to stop; it slammed into one of the already-stopped patrol cars, shoving it toward Rose. She screamed even louder as the car moved toward her injured knee. Within inches of hitting her bleeding knee, the car stopped. For a few seconds, bits of gravel hit her knee and slid down her leg, mixing in with her blood.

Police officers came running up to Rose. She looked over at the broken pieces of her watch; she couldn't tell what time it was. Parts of her husband's face briefly appeared in the face of her broken watch. He said, "It's your own fault you were shot." He then took Rose's wedding and engagement rings off, put them in his pocket, and stomped off. The broken pieces of Rose's watch were all that remained next to her left hand.

Rose heard the sound of an ambulance's siren, but she kept watching the small broken glass pieces from her watch. The pieces moved around, trying to connect with each other into a complete face. Rose sighed, uncertain about whether or not she wanted to see her husband's face again. As she watched, the pieces formed into a twirling circle. They kept on moving and growing in size until they had taken on the form of a single piece of glass that was several feet high and about a foot wide. With the setting sun, the glass piece changed some more; it looked thicker and darker. Antique-looking wood began to grow around the glass. Clock hands and Roman numerals were now visible. A pendulum went down from the clock's face toward the bottom of the timepiece. The clock was now a grandfather clock, and its parts began to move. It was keeping time, but its hands were moving backwards.

The metallic hands on the clock's face pointed toward the Roman numerals, which changed into pictures of people. Rose saw herself at the "twelve" position. She was alone; her husband Travis was nowhere to be seen. The clock's hands moved backwards to the "eleven o'clock" position, where Rose's parents, Joe and Linda Bradford, were holding hands and staring lovingly into each other's eyes. The clock's hands moved backwards again until they reached the ten o'clock position; the names and pictures of Rose's four grandparents were there. At the nine o'clock position, she saw multiple people; one of them was her great grandfather, John H. Robinson. He had lived from 1908-88. Rose had met him a couple of times when she was young. He loved cheese. As Rose watched, a piece of cheese appeared in the clock's hand next to Grandpa Robinson; the hand moved the cheese up to his mouth, and he ate it.

The hands on the grandfather clock kept moving backwards in time, pausing briefly at each numeral on the clock's face. There were many people and words, but the faces and names were not clear enough for Rose to know who most of the people were. The clock itself gradually faded out, being replaced by a sundial and then by the light of a rising sun. It was morning; under the slowly shifting time displayed by the sun's movements appeared the Reverend John Robinson, the pastor of the Pilgrims. Within his hands appeared a bible: the *1599 Geneva Bible* that was used by the Pilgrims before, during, and after their 1620 voyage on the *Mayflower*. As the Reverend Robinson opened the bible, his hand moved in the wind, looking almost as if it was waving at Rose. Pages in the bible fluttered until the wind stopped. John Robinson turned the bible around and pointed at two verses. Rose took several steps forward and then read:

> Blessed be God, even the Father of our Lord Jesus Christ, which according to his abundant mercy hath begotten us again unto a lively hope by the resurrection of Jesus Christ from the dead, / To an inheritance immortal and undefiled, and that withereth not, reserved in heaven for us.
>
> (1st Peter 1:3-4 GNV)

Rose asked, "Is my inheritance really immortality?"

The Reverend Robinson responded by waving his hand back and forth. His hand then began to turn around in a circle against the bright yellow of the sun. The hand and the sun together looked like a clock. The hand kept moving, faster and faster with the sun's light; the moving hand started to make swishing noises. The noises became louder and louder until Rose realized that one of her alarm clocks was ringing.

BANKING REALITY

Rose's hand reached out and hit the snooze button on her alarm clock. Within what seemed like seconds, a different alarm clock sounded. This one was further away. To turn it off, Rose would have to get up and walk across the room to her bureau. Sighing, she pulled a blanket over her head, but the sound continued.

When an even louder alarm clock joined in with the other sounds, Rose finally got up. She limped slightly as she moved to turn off the two alarm clocks on her bureau, as well as the one on her bedside table that was sounding off again.

Before leaving her bedroom, Rose stretched out her left leg and looked at her knee. The scar from the bank robbery was still visible, despite all of the scar-removal lotions she had been using. At least the pain in her knee was better; sometimes, it even felt good enough for her to go to work without taking any pain medication.

By the time Rose had showered and dressed, it was already after seven fifteen, and she needed to be to work by seven forty-five. Looking at herself in the mirror on the back of her bedroom door, she realized that the skirt she was wearing might be too short. She sat down on her bed and looked at her knee in the mirror again. The scar on her knee was partially visible. Despite the too-quickly moving hands on her bedroom clocks, she changed into a longer skirt; she then grabbed a couple of protein bars and her lunch tote bag as she headed out of her apartment.

Rose frowned as she looked at her wrist watch and frowned some more as she looked at the clock in her car—she was going to be at least ten minutes late for work again. Ever since being injured in the bank robbery seven months ago, she had been having problems getting to work on time. Setting three alarm clocks for earlier and earlier times did not seem to be helping much.

When Rose finally reached the parking lot of the First National Consumer Bank in Warwick, Rhode Island, she saw another teller—her friend Kate Odyssey—through one of the windows. Rose sighed with relief; she knew that Kate was all set up and ready to start helping customers. On the days when Rose was really late, Kate would wait on customers at Rose's drive-through window, which was supposed to be open at eight o'clock.

Kate let Rose in the front door of the bank. Rose looked around to see if the boss was in his office yet. He was. Rose sighed and then said to Kate, "Thanks."

"You're welcome," her friend replied as she closed and locked the bank's front door. Early customers would have to go to one of the drive-through windows or wait for more than an hour to come into the lobby. While the bank's drive-through windows were open at eight o'clock, the lobby was not open until nine.

"You're almost on time today," Harry Walker, the bank's vice president, said to Rose as she walked past his office. His voice was not sarcastic; he actually sounded happy that Rose was nearly on time. Since her injury in the bank robbery, everyone in the bank had been very supportive of her attempts to get back to her former self.

Rose looked at her watch and blushed before replying, "I'm sorry. I promise to set my alarm clock earlier."

After Harry turned his attention to some papers on his desk, Rose quickly walked into the break room in the far right corner of the bank, put her purse and lunch away, and then came back into the main part of the bank. She set up her teller drawer in front of one of the drive-through windows. At eight o'clock, she was ready to begin helping customers. Kate went back to her own teller window and started to credit accounts with deposits and payments from the overnight deposit box.

Around ten o-clock, there were no customers in the bank lobby or at the drive-through windows. All of the night deposits were finished. Kate glanced around the bank's lobby and then walked over to where Rose was seated on a tall stool in front of one of the drive-through windows. "How's your knee feeling?"

Rose had been watching the cars in the street on the side of the bank's parking lot. She turned around, smiled at Kate, and then looked down at her knee. Her skirt was covering it up. She stretched out her leg, held it up for a few seconds, and rubbed it slightly before saying, "Right now, it's okay. A few nights ago, though, it was really bothering me."

"Have you asked your doctor about some more prescription pain medication?"

"No, I haven't bothered. Most of the time, my knee's okay."

"Do you need more physical therapy?"

"My doctor keeps telling me to just exercise. Any kind of exercise is supposed to be good."

"Have you been going to your Zumba classes?"

Rose sighed. "I haven't gone since before the bank robbery."

"Really?"

"I just don't seem to have enough time or energy anymore."

Kate hesitated, looked at the sad expression on Rose's face, and then finally said, "I always wanted to try some Zumba classes. Can I go with you one day?"

Rose laughed. "You're taking ballroom dance lessons. You have even less time than I do."

"No, really. I would love to go to a few Zumba classes. My Latin motion isn't too good, and I sometimes have problems if the ballroom dance music is really fast. I think Zumba classes will help me to be a better ballroom dancer."

"Can I go, too?" Lisa Reilly Davidson, another bank teller, asked. She had walked up to them and was standing next to Kate with a big smile on her face.

Rose looked at Lisa's excited face. "Oh, you're a newlywed. You're busier than both of us."

"I've been married for more than three months now." Lisa looked down at her engagement and wedding rings before adding, "See? Doesn't my hand look really great now?" She raised her hand up. Sunlight from the large drive-through window made the diamond sparkle.

Rose smiled at Lisa's joyful face and then looked down at her own left hand. There was an indentation—but no rings—on her ring finger. She had separated from her husband Travis just a week after Lisa's wedding.

Noticing Rose's expression, Lisa and Kate were both silent for a moment. Then Kate asked, "So when's the next Zumba lesson?"

"There's one at six o'clock on Saturday morning," Rose said as her eyes moved from looking down at her hand up toward the front door of the bank. A customer had just entered; he walked over to one of the tables and began filling in some paperwork. Kate and Lisa walked back to their teller stations.

About twelve noon, the lobby was empty again. Lisa said to Kate, "Why don't you and Rose go have lunch together? If it gets too busy, Ed and I will call you back to the lobby by turning the lollipop trees around."

"Okay," Kate said. She and Rose closed their windows, walked past the vice president's office, and went down a short corridor into the break room. They left the door open, so they would be able to see if the bank tellers in the lobby needed their help.

"Is your knee feeling well enough to go to Zumba again?" Kate asked as she got sodas for both of them from the refrigerator.

"Yeah, I think so. Whenever it bothers me, I just take some Ibuprofen, which usually helps." Rose sat down in one of the chairs and kicked her foot up and down, bending her knee several times. "It doesn't hurt even a little bit right now."

Kate grabbed a bright yellow lunch tote bag from the refrigerator and then asked, "The blue bag with flowers is yours, right?"

"Yeah, it is."

Kate brought both of the bags over to the table, handed the blue flowered one to Rose, and then sat down. "Are you still having nightmares about the bank robbery?"

"I had one last night."

"Was it the same dream as the other ones?"

"Yeah, it was mostly the same. I was kidnapped. And then because I couldn't scream, I was shot, just like in the real robbery."

"Was there anything new in your dream last night?"

"Yeah. My watch was broken."

"Didn't that happen in the bank robbery?"

"It did, but my broken watch was never in my other dreams."

"So what happened?"

"When I was thrown from the car, my wrist hit the road. Then my watch broke."

"Did the broken watch hurt your arm?"

"No, but it got me all upset. The face on the broken watch was Travis's." The volume of Rose's voice increased as she continued, "And he yelled at me for getting shot."

"Really?"

"Yeah, there I was, shot in the knee and lying in the road. Travis yelled at me. Then he just left me there. He didn't try to help me. He didn't call 911. He didn't do anything at all." Without realizing what she was doing, Rose stood up. Her whole body looked tense from her anger. After a few seconds, she sat back down again.

Kate looked at the table and then back at Rose's anxious face. "Do you think the broken watch is symbolic of your separation with Travis? A watch and a wedding ring are both round."

"Possibly. But Travis was never that mean to me in real life. He never really yelled at me for not screaming during that bank robbery." Rose opened up a protein bar and took a bite before continuing, "I think the yelling part of my dream means that we were fighting a lot."

"What were you fighting about?"

"Oh, the usual thing: money." Rose hesitated and then added, "After my injury, we kept on fighting over other things, too, like who should be doing what."

"Well, because of your injury, he should've been doing most of the household tasks."

"He should have, but he wasn't. Some things, he just didn't want to do. Like he wouldn't vacuum. He kept on saying that the rugs were clean enough. And he didn't understand that I couldn't move a vacuum cleaner while I was on crutches."

"So are you two getting divorced?"

"I don't know." Rose sighed. "We separated so that we could stop yelling at each other. I really couldn't take the fights, especially when my knee hurt all the time. Even with pain medication."

"I'm so glad your knee is feeling better, Rose."

"So am I." Rose sighed. "I just wish my marriage were better, too."

Kate had finished most of her sandwich. She opened up a bag of chips and offered some to Rose, who ate one before saying, "Thanks. I was in a hurry this morning. I was trying to get to work on time and just grabbed a couple of protein bars again."

"Do you want the rest of my sandwich?"

"No, I'm okay."

"How about some chocolate?"

"Did you say 'chocolate'?"

Kate pulled out a Dove dark chocolate candy bar from her yellow lunch bag. Smiling broadly, she offered half of the bar to Rose, whose smile became even larger as she accepted it.

After they had eaten most of the candy, Rose said, "I wonder if my broken watch during the bank robbery means something about time. Possibly there's a psychological connection between my broken watch and my being late all the time."

Kate smiled. "Well, you have been almost on time now for quite a while."

"Yeah, for the past month, I've often been just five to fifteen minutes late. But I really want to be on time."

"I know you've tried setting your alarm clock earlier, but when was the last time you tried it?"

"At least two months ago. When I finally climbed out of bed, my knee hurt a lot, and I got an awful headache. So I was even later for work."

"Maybe you could set your clock just a minute early. Then in a week or two, after you got used to the one minute earlier time, you could try two minutes."

Rose's face looked thoughtful as she responded, "That's a good idea. It would be like going backwards in time, which is actually what the hands on the clock did in my dream last night. They went backwards in time."

"So the hands on your broken watch went backwards?"

"No, the backwards hands were on a grandfather clock with my relatives on it. When my great grandfather appeared, I think I was able to give him a piece of cheese. Even though I can't remember everything from that dream, I think I was still having a lucid dream."

"Yeah, I think you were, too. You and Lisa are both so good at lucid dreaming techniques." Kate sighed.

"I thought you had a lucid dream before. You said that you knew you were dreaming during one of your dreams."

"Yeah, I did, but just that one time. I know lucid dreams can happen when you are conscious of yourself while dreaming or when you change things in a dream."

"I wish I could make things happen more often in my dreams, but just knowing I'm dreaming while I'm dreaming is sort of nice." Rose paused for a few seconds before adding, "Anyway, the Reverend John Robinson was in my dream last night."

"That name sounds familiar."

"He was the pastor to the Pilgrims, and he's one of my ancestors."

"Really?" Kate asked.

"Yeah. In my dream, first there was a clock with my great grandfather, John H. Robinson, on the clock. Then there were other relatives and a sundial. I think the Reverend John Robinson was at the end after the sundial disappeared, but he could have been on the sundial or on the clock. I can't remember. He also could have just been in the sunshine. Anyway, back in the seventeenth century, clocks were handmade. They were very expensive, so not too many people owned them."

"How about watches?"

"The earliest watches were expensive, too. Back then, most of the people just used the sun as a clock. So if they were five or ten minutes late, they wouldn't have known about it." Rose's eyes brightened as she said, "If we were living four hundred years ago, when I came to work this morning, everyone would have thought that I was on time."

Kate laughed. "You're right. But I think you've been doing great in the last month. You've been getting to work most mornings before eight o'clock."

"Thanks. You're always so nice to me." Rose looked up at the clock on the wall. It was after twelve thirty. "So anyway, we should get back to work."

"Yeah, we should. Lisa and Ed are probably getting hungry."

Rose and Kate went back into the main part of the bank. There were no customers in line, but Lisa was making a deposit for a young man, and Ed appeared to be waiting on a drive-through customer. After Lisa and Ed finished helping their customers, they put closed signs up in front of their windows and left for the break room.

The next couple of hours were slow; only ten customers came into the lobby for help. At two forty-five, Rose glanced up at the clock on the wall. In fifteen or twenty minutes, she would be able to close out her cash drawer. She looked out the drive-through window—no cars were in line, but she could see a customer who had left the bank a few minutes earlier. The customer was searching in her purse and finally pulled out her keys, got into her car, and drove away.

Rose heard the front door of the bank open, but she didn't bother to turn around; Lisa or Kate would be helping customers in the bank lobby.

"Good afternoon."

Recognizing the voice of Travis, her husband, Rose spun around. He was standing in front of Kate's window with a check in his hand. His sky blue eyes and reddish brown hair initially appeared to be just like in Rose's dream, but as she watched, his features seemed to brighten up and to become more alive. His medium-length hair moved slightly as he turned his head to look at the lady who was with him. She was about four inches shorter than Travis, so she was the same height as Rose was. Her red blouse was low cut, but not showing any cleavage. She looked into Travis's eyes, lightly touched his elbow, smiled, and then said, "Whatever you want is okay with me."

Travis's eyes lingered for a moment, looking at her expressive face, before turning his head back to look at Kate. "Twenties are fine."

Kate hit a few keys on her computer, counted out ten twenties for Travis, entered some more information into her computer, put the check into her drawer, and said, "Have a good day."

"Thanks." Travis and the woman were about to leave the bank when he paused and looked in Rose's direction.

"Hi," Rose said. The right side of her mouth moved up slightly as she tried to smile, but her face was otherwise completely blank as she looked at Travis.

Travis gazed intently at Rose. She looked back at him and was still unable to smile. She did, however, stand up and walk over to Kate's window. As she walked, she limped slightly. "It's nice of you to stop by."

"I needed to cash a check, but I also wanted to see how you're doing."

"I'm fine." Rose's face appeared frozen in the same blank expression.

"That's good. Give me a call if you need anything." Travis and the lady walked out of the bank. They were standing very close together.

Kate put her left hand on Rose's elbow. "Are you okay?"

"Yeah, I am."

"Who was that with your husband?"

"I don't know." Rose inhaled sharply, sounding as if she were trying to stop herself from talking. After a few seconds, she said, "I should get back to my window." She turned around, limped over to her stool, and sat down. After a minute, she realized that it was after three o'clock, so she began the process of closing out her cash drawer. She stood up, stretched out her left leg, and then bent her knee. After straightening and bending her left knee a couple more times, she sat down again and began to count up the money in her teller drawer. As she was in the middle of a calculation, she felt her cell phone buzzing in her pocket. No customers were in the bank, so she answered the phone.

"Hello, mom."

"Hi, Rose. I know you're at work, but I thought you might be able to talk for a minute."

"Yeah, I can."

"Oh, good. I was worried that I was interrupting something."

"No, mom, you're never an interruption. Besides, I'm only counting up my money."

"Okay. Hopefully, it'll all be there." Rose's mother paused before continuing, "Anyway, the grandfather clock is broken."

"Did the hands stop moving?"

"Actually, I couldn't wind it up again, so the hands stopped moving."

"I'd love to look at it."

"Thanks, Rose. You're so good with clocks."

"Should I stop by tonight, or do you want me to come by on the weekend?"

"Tonight will be great, especially since I'm planning on making something special for dinner."

"Okay. What time should I come over?"

"Whatever time you want to."

"How about if I stop by right after work? Then I'll be able to look at the clock before dinner."

"That's a good plan. I'll see you when you get here."

"Okay, mom. Bye."

Rose went back to counting up her money. She then compared her computer's figures with the actual money amount before sighing and making a face.

Kate walked over to her. "How much is it off today?"

"Only four dollars, but I'd prefer it to be four dollars the other way."

"So you have four dollars extra?"

"Yeah. That means some customer is missing four dollars," Rose frowned before adding, "Unless I messed up two or more times to equal the four dollars."

Kate looked down at Rose's teller drawer. "Have you double-checked everything?"

"Not yet, but I will."

"Yeah, you're good at counting the money."

"Well, at least all of my errors are usually found and fixed." Rose counted up her money again and looked at some computer print-outs, but she was unable to find any problems. She wrote on a form that her teller drawer had four extra dollars; she then left the form for Harry Walker, the vice-president of the bank. After waving at Kate and Lisa, she left the bank, got into her car, and drove away.

THE MAYFLOWER
ON A SAMPLER

When Rose arrived at her parents' house, she parked in the driveway behind her mother's car. Without limping, she walked quickly up the sidewalk and paused to look at the rose bush. The bush had been planted by Rose's parents, right after they had bought the house and a year before Rose herself was born. The bush now was about thirty-three years old and very healthy. It was over five feet tall and four feet wide. Rose reached out and touched one of the leaves. A bead of sweat fell off of her chin and landed on the leaf. The small drop of moisture made the leaf feel crisper. As Rose stepped back, she noticed that the one leaf she had touched looked greener than the other leaves. It was supposed to rain over night, so the whole bush would soon have enough moisture to keep it healthy in the summer heat.

After turning around, Rose moved up the front stairs and knocked on the door. Her mother immediately opened it up.

Rose walked into the living room, hugged her mom, and asked, "Is that your lasagna?"

"Yes, it is. Supper will be ready in about a half an hour."

As Rose's mother went into the kitchen, Rose's father came into the living room. Rose hugged her father. Then she looked at the grandfather clock in the far corner of the room. The clock was exactly like the one in her dream. It was made of cherry wood and had Roman numerals on its face.

"Go right ahead, Rose, and get started. I know you love playing with that clock." Rose's father gestured with his hand at a table next to the clock, "I left you some tools over there. Let me know if you need anything else."

Rose walked up to the clock. She looked at its decorated face and hands before opening up the long rectangular trunk door below the clock's face; she then examined the interior. The pendulum and metallic wheels were not moving. "The motion train looks funny," she said.

"What's the motion train?"

"It's the series of wheels behind the clock's face; they work together to make the hands keep time." Rose waved her own hands in circles, mimicking the motion of several of the wheels, showing how they worked together. "Did you or mom move the clock at all?"

"Yeah, we did. Last Saturday, your mom wanted to clean under the furniture in here, so I helped her to move everything. The clock stopped after that. And she couldn't wind it up again. The parts were stuck."

"Maybe the problem has to do with the wheels sliding into wrong positions."

"That makes sense. We did tilt the clock over partially in order to move it."

"Some of the parts might have been broken when mom tried to rewind the clock."

Rose's father looked toward the doorway leading into the dining room and then called out to his wife: "Hey, Linda." When she appeared in the doorway, he asked, "Did you hear any strange noises when you tried to rewind the clock?"

"Possibly," Linda said. She thought for a few seconds before adding, "I don't know for sure. The stereo was on."

Rose said, "Hopefully, the problem is minor. Replacement parts might have to be custom-made."

"You're the clock expert in our family. Whatever you say must be true," Rose's mother said with a smile as she went back into the kitchen.

Rose had the trunk door of the clock open. Her father said, "We have plenty of clocks in the house. There's no reason why the grandfather clock has to be repaired right now. We can wait on taking it apart until after supper tonight, unless you have other plans."

"My only plans were visiting with you and mom tonight."

Rose and her father smiled at each other. Then Rose looked back at the clock, started to close its trunk door, and stopped. "There's something attached inside, up against the back wall."

"Oh, really?" Rose's father got up from his chair and walked over to stand beside his daughter; they both looked at the interior of the clock.

Rose reached her hand inside of the rectangular case; she felt around on the wall behind the pendulum. "It feels like paper, but I don't know if it's glued or taped onto the back wall."

"I'll go and get a flashlight," her father said as he walked out of the living room.

"Thanks, Dad." While Rose waited for her father to return, she continued to feel along the inside of the clock.

"I'll hold the light for you," Rose's father said as he came back into the living room; he walked over to the corner where she still had her hand inside of the clock.

"Thanks, Dad." They both watched as Rose's hand moved behind the pendulum. Using the fingernail on her index finger, she pulled the top half of a piece of thick paper forward. The color of the paper closely matched the color of the clock's wooden frame. Carefully, Rose pulled the whole paper off of the clock's wall and handed it to her father. The old glue on the paper's edges looked almost like a shiny frame.

"There's something else in here," Rose said as her hand reached up against the far wall of the clock's case. "It feels like cloth."

Her father moved the flashlight close to the pendulum so that Rose had enough light to see. "It is some kind of cloth." She pulled out a rectangular piece of linen from the clock's case.

"Where'd you get the sampler?" Rose's mother asked as she suddenly appeared behind Rose and her father. All three of them were quiet for a moment as they stared at the piece of cloth with its small designs.

Rose's father asked, "Is a sampler some kind of a sample?"

"In a way," Rose's mother replied. "A sampler is made by stitching onto a cloth. Samplers often have different needlework patterns, pictures, colors, words, and sometimes even the creator's name. By sewing a nice-looking sampler, someone can show off different stitching skills. In the old days, a sampler also used to be a way to educate girls."

"I think whoever sewed this one was very creative. I love the colors and the different stitches," Rose looked more closely at the sampler. It had the months of the year spelled out; each month was stitched with the use of a different color. A bible verse about treasure and hearts was at the bottom part of the sampler. Some small pictures were sewn into the sampler; different kinds of stitches were used for flowers, suns, stars, a moon, and other shapes. The most interesting images were narrow triangles with lines coming out of their tops.

"So, do you think these triangles are arrows?" Rose asked her mother.

Rose's parents both moved closer to the sampler. Rose placed it on the table so that all three of them could see it at the same time.

Rose's mother reached out and touched one of the triangles. "I don't know. The triangles do seem to be pointing toward some of the other shapes."

Rose said, "Some of the triangles are pointing toward lines, rather than shapes."

"Maybe it's a map," Rose's father said. He, his wife, and Rose were all silent for a minute while they looked at the narrow triangles and other shapes. Rose turned the sampler around several times, so they could see the artwork from different angles. Her father ran his finger between each triangle and the line or shape that each "arrow" pointed toward.

"I think you're right, dad. It's some kind of a map."

Her father moved the sampler so that the words were upside down. "The terrain looks familiar, but I can't figure out what it is."

Rose's mother asked, "Where did you find it?"

"It was inside the clock behind a piece of paper. Do you have the paper, Dad?"

Rose's father went over to the coffee table and brought back the piece of paper. "Here it is." He gave the paper to Rose.

The smoke alarm in the kitchen suddenly went off. "I think supper's ready," Rose's mom said as she walked quickly toward the kitchen.

Rose and her father went into the dining room, where the table was already set. A vase of flowers with a red rose in the center stood at the head of the table. Rose's father got some sodas from the refrigerator; Rose helped her mother to bring the lasagna, rolls, and salad into the dining room.

They sat down in their usual chairs, said a prayer, and began to eat. Rose's mother asked her, "How was work today?"

"Like most Thursdays, it was just busy enough to keep us from getting bored. How was your day?"

"It was great." Rose's mother smiled broadly. "Even though I love teaching history to high school kids, having some time off in the summer is so wonderful."

Rose's father said, "Yeah, you deserve some time off. Teaching is something I would never have the patience for."

"Working with numbers all day like you do, dad, is also a tough job. It requires a lot of patience, too."

"My job working as a financial analyst is more similar to your bank job than it is to your mom's teaching position. Except I don't usually communicate with the public like you do."

Rose put her fork down before saying, "Speaking of communication, that sampler is really interesting. Should I go and get it?"

Her parents looked at each other; their eyes lit up, and they both smiled, showing their desire to see the sampler again.

Rose went into the living room and quickly returned with the sampler. She set it down in the middle of the table so that she and her parents could all see it at the same time. As soon as Rose sat down and glanced at the sampler, she noticed that it was placed so that her parents had an upside down view of its words and pictures. Quickly, she swiveled it around; the front of the sampler was now turned toward her parents.

"That makes your view upside down," Rose's mother said.

Rose stopped her mom's hand from turning the sampler around again by saying, "I think it's a good idea if we all look at it from different angles, just to see if the letters and pictures say anything different when they're sideways or upside down."

Rose's parents nodded their heads in agreement.

A minute later, Rose said, "I can't find anything different with the pictures upside down." She turned the sampler ninety-five degrees so that its sides were in front of herself and her parents.

Soon after, Rose's mother turned the sampler again so that she and her husband were looking at it upside down. "I don't see anything here."

Rose turned the sampler again; they continued to stare at it while quietly eating their food.

Rose finally said, "What do you think this stream of dots is?"

Her father said, "If the spots were yellow, I would think they're the tail of a comet." He pointed toward a circle at the beginning of the dots. "If it were the right color, this could be an actual comet."

Rose and her mother looked at the sampler's circle with a series of dots flowing out behind it.

"I don't think a comet would be greenish blue. Wouldn't it be yellow?" Rose asked.

Her mother said, "Comets are not all yellow. In November or December of 1618, there was a comet, possibly of that color. Nick Bunker's novel, *Making Haste from Babylon*, mentions a comet and the different ways that people reacted to it. Wait a minute, let me get the book." She got up, went into the living room, and brought back the book.

After looking in the "Index," Rose's mother turned to a page in Bunker's book. She silently read several paragraphs before saying: "The comet was seen by many people, and there were different reactions to it. Right here is one person's depiction of the comet's significance." She read out loud: "According to Johnson, the comet prophesied not only the arrival of the *Mayflower* bringing the light of salvation to the new continent, but also God's intervention to clear a space for his emissaries."[3]

"It sounds like at least one person thought the comet symbolized the future arrival of the Pilgrims in America," Rose's father commented.

"Perhaps the sampler is trying to say something about the Pilgrims."

"You could be right, Rose. What do you think these other things mean?"

"The Bible verse at the bottom of the sampler is talking about treasure and hearts." Rose paused and then read the verse out loud: "For where your treasure is, there will your hearts be also" (Luke 12:34 GNV).

"It's probably a reference to treasuring one's family," Rose's mother said.

After smiling at each other, Rose and her parents looked back at the sampler. They were all quiet for a few seconds. Suddenly, Rose's mother said, "I know what it is!"

"What?" Rose and her father asked at the same time.

Rose's mother picked up the sampler and pointed to the flower that was stitched next to the month of May. "This white flower looks like a 'Trailing Arbutus.'"

Rose asked, "Does that have anything to do with the comet?"

Her mother explained, "No, actually, 'Trailing Arbutus' is another name for a 'mayflower.'"

"Do you mean the Pilgrims' *Mayflower*?" Rose's father asked.

"The Pilgrims' *Mayflower* was named after a mayflower, which is a beautiful wild flower often seen in the Eastern part of the United States. It is supposedly difficult to grow in a garden because it needs acid soil."[4]

Rose said, "The mayflower does have a pretty pink center."

Her mother shook her head up and down, agreeing with her. "Do you see how this flower is right next to the 'y' in 'May'? It almost looks like the flower is the ending of a word beginning with 'May.' Plus, the flower looks like a real mayflower."

"So you think it means 'Mayflower'?" Rose asked.

"It's more than that." Rose's mother appeared excited as she asked, "Do you remember that watch case my mother has?"

"You're talking about my grandmother in Albany, New York, right?"

"Yes." After a pause, Rose's mother continued, "She has a watch case from one of our ancestors. I think the watch case has some similar things on it."

"Exactly what do you mean by 'similar'?" Rose's father asked. "Does it have a flower joined with the word 'May'?"

"I think so. I don't remember exactly what all of the designs look like, but I remember we thought the word 'May' with a flower next to it was a little strange. It looked almost like some kind of code."

"The month of May might not be a reference to a month. It could be a reference to the owner's name."

"I'm fairly certain the same flower was carved into the watch case. It was right next to the word 'May.'"

Rose's father picked up the sampler; he shifted it closer and then further away from his face, squinting his eyes as he tried to see the designs better. "Look here, right next to this gold circle." He moved his finger to the left of a three-inch circle that was beneath the word "May" and its flower. "The flowers here are in a triangle. They look sort of like letters. Maybe the word is 'maq' or 'map.'"

Rose's mother said, "If you read the letters counter-clockwise, the word will be 'pam.' Many women used to stitch their names on their samplers."

Rose said, "The 'm' is at the top of the triangle; if we read the triangle of letters in a clockwise order, then it clearly says 'map.'"

Rose's parents shook their heads in agreement. Her father then set the sampler down on the table. "I like maps."

Rose sighed. "I know. You especially like large paper maps. You always use one instead of your GPS."

Rose's father smiled as he said, "That's because I like maps." He stood up and stretched before looking down at the sampler on the table before him. After a few seconds, he stretched his head backwards. "You know, looking at the sampler from this distance, it actually could be a map."

"Really?" Rose stood up and walked over to be next to her dad. "What do you think this little symbol next to the flower is?"

"It looks like a bell."

"Yeah. These vines even look like a musical note."

Rose's father ran his finger around the sampler's vines. "If you focus just on these stems and vines, the design looks like Cape Cod over here on the right and Plymouth on the left."

"The Cape Cod Bay area is a little skinny, but I think you're right, Dad. A part of the Plymouth section is covered by the light gold circle."

"What about the watch case? If the watch case and this sampler have the same *Mayflower* code, they might have been made at the same time. Linda, do you know how old your mother's watch case is?"

"No, I don't think my mom ever told me, but I think it's at least a hundred years old."

Rose said, "The watch case probably was made after conductors started using pocket watches on trains. Before that time, only rich people had watches, and I don't think any of our ancestors were rich."

Rose's father laughed before picking up the sampler. He pointed at the light gold circle beneath the *Mayflower* code. "The flower designs inside this circle also look strange. The design looks like a compass. And this arrow is pointing toward the Southwest."

Rose's mother reached over and touched the gold circle. "These stitches definitely are different from the other ones in the sampler."

Rose was still staring at the lines inside and outside of the golden circle. "If we can see Granny's watch case, then this part of the sampler might make more sense."

"Linda, do you think your mom will let us borrow the watch case?"

"Oh, Joe, there's no way she will ever part with that case."

"Do you have any pictures of it?"

"No, but now I wish I did."

Rose looked over at her mom. "Maybe Granny can take a picture of the case and send us the picture."

Her father said, "It's probably a better idea if someone goes in person and looks directly at the case. There could be a message inside of it, or there might be a hidden panel."

"You're right, Dad. There could be a message in the way the designs are carved into the case."

"Also, the pictures on the sampler might be connected to the pictures on the watch case. Looking at the watch case and the sampler together could be important."

Rose's mother got up from the table and went into the kitchen. She brought back a plate of brownies. "I made these from scratch. I have some ice cream, too."

Rose helped herself to one of the brownies. "I love your brownies just as they are, but Dad always wants some ice cream. On second thought, I want some ice cream, too."

Rose's mother went into the kitchen and came back with three bowls and some ice cream. Her face became thoughtful. "I think we're all forgetting something."

"Whipped cream?" Rose asked.

"No, I was thinking about something else."

"Chocolate sauce?" Rose's father asked.

"No. I'm sorry. I didn't buy any whipped cream or chocolate sauce. I'll plan on doing that for your next visit, Rose."

"Oh, no, Mom. I was just kidding. This dessert is perfect just the way it is."

"Thanks. Anyway, I was thinking about what you found in the clock. Did you say there was a piece of paper?"

Rose got up, went into the living room, and brought back the piece of paper.

Her mother took the paper, looked at the painted side, and then turned it over. "It's blank."

"Yeah, Rose and I noticed that, too. The paper was probably glued inside the clock just to cover up and hide the sampler."

Rose's mother held the paper over her head, right below the ceiling light. She frowned and then walked into the living room. Her husband and Rose followed her as she went over to one of the end-table lamps. Rose took the lamp shade off, and her mother put the paper up close to the 150-watt light bulb.

Rose's father walked up closer to the lamp. "There's something written on the paper." He moved closer to the lamp and read: "There is no creature so perfect in wisdom and knowledge but may learn something for time present and to come by times past."[5]

Rose's mom said, "Joe, that sounds like one of John Robinson's famous sayings." She walked over to the bookcase, took out a book, looked at the "Contents" section, and turned some of the pages. "Yes. It's from his 'Observations Divine and Moral.'"

Rose's father again read the saying from John Robinson before saying, "He's talking about learning from the past."

"You could be right. He might be talking about learning. But 'to come by times past' also could mean something about the watch case that Granny has," Rose said. "Just how old is the case?"

Her mother replied, "I don't know, but I'm fairly certain it's not from the time of the Pilgrims. I think the case was made for a railroad watch."

Rose said, "Railroad chronometer watches weren't made until the middle of the nineteenth century. So Granny's watch case is less than two hundred years old."

Her mother looked at John Robinson's words on the paper. "John Robinson lived in the late sixteenth and early seventeenth centuries. He wouldn't have had a watch."

Joe said, "Then the words on this paper probably weren't written by John Robinson himself."

"You're right," Linda said. "The grandfather clock is a little less than a hundred years old. My great grandfather—the one who worked in a bank—was the one who bought it."

Rose smiled. "Really? I never knew that I had a relative who worked in a bank."

"The next time you talk with Granny, ask her about your great grandfather. She has some interesting stories."

"Okay." Rose paused and then continued, "The Bible verse on the sampler mentions 'treasure.' Do you think John Robinson's words and the Bible verse say something about the watch being a treasure? Maybe there's a treasure hidden somewhere that one of our ancestors hid."

Her parents looked at her and laughed. Her father then said, "I don't think any of our relatives had a treasure."

Rose smiled. "Even if our relatives had no money, they still could have had some small treasures."

"Okay, I'm sure we all have some treasures, like our families, friends, and homes."

Rose shook her head in agreement. "You're right about that, Dad." After a moment of silence, she said, "I think the word 'treasure' could be a reference to a treasure. We should look around inside of the grandfather clock."

Rose's father walked over to the clock. He was followed by his wife and daughter. He asked, "Where would a treasure be?"

"I don't know," Rose said. "Maybe there's a hollow section somewhere."

Her father asked, "Rose, can you hand me those pliers? The ones with the bright yellow handles?"

"You're not going to break open the clock, are you?"

"No, of course not. I'm going to very softly hit parts of the clock with the pliers' handles."

Rose handed the pliers to her father. He hit the clock multiple times with the rubber handles, moving methodically up and down the front, sides, and back of the clock. Everything seemed solid.

Rose tilted the clock about forty-five degrees and pointed to the wooden section that was underneath the clock's bottom section. Her father sat down on the floor and tried hitting the bottom of the clock. Again, the clock seemed solid. He shrugged his shoulders before commenting, "The word 'treasure' on the piece of paper might be referring to another grandfather clock."

"Perhaps it's a reference to my mother's watch case or to the watch that used to be in it."

"Did you ever see a watch in the case?" Rose asked as she put the clock back into its normal position.

"No, I never did. I only remember my mom saying something about a railroad pocket watch a couple of times." Rose's mother walked back into the dining room. Her husband and daughter followed her.

"Well, the ice cream is melted." Rose went into the kitchen, took some vanilla ice cream out of the freezer, and put it into clean bowls for herself and her parents. Her mother then placed fresh brownies next to the ice cream.

Once seated at the table, they began eating dessert in silence. Rose then said, "This is the best dessert I've had all week."

"We always have great desserts. You should come visit us more often," her mother said.

"You know I'd love to come over more often. We're all working too many hours, though."

Her father said, "Even if we're all busy, one of us should take a short vacation and go visit Granny in New York."

Rose smiled. "I have some vacation time, and I haven't seen Granny in a few years."

Her parents looked at her, exchanged glances with each other, and then shook their heads in agreement. Her mother said, "How about if I call Granny later tonight? I can tell her about the sampler and send her a picture of it on *Facebook*."

"That's a great idea, Mom. I'll check with my boss tomorrow to see if I can take a few days off."

"I'm guessing you don't want to drive your car all the way to Albany, New York." Rose's father looked at Rose, who quickly shook her head side to side. He then said, "I'll check out the plane, train, and bus ticket prices."

Rose said, "I'd rather not fly, and the bus will probably be cheaper than the train."

"I'll check out the prices. Then your Mom and I will buy you a round-trip ticket." When Rose tried to disagree with her father, he just waved his hand at her and continued, "We'll drop you off and pick you up from the train or bus station in Providence. Just call us tomorrow night, after you talk to your boss, and let us know when you can go and return."

After they had finished dessert, they went into the living room. Rose's parents sat on the couch; their eyes gazed down at the sampler that had been placed on the coffee table in front of them. After sitting across from her parents in a rocking chair, Rose looked over at the grandfather clock. "Last night, I had a dream. That grandfather clock was in it."

Her mother looked up. "Really?"

"Yeah, the clock had some of our ancestors on it. John Robinson was at the number one position on the face of the clock."

Rose's father said, "Well, he was the pastor to the Pilgrims, and he's your most famous ancestor."

"In my dream, he looked just like his pictures. He's actually depicted with the Pilgrims on the back of the 1918 series of $10,000. bills."

"You don't have any actual $10,000. bills at work, do you?" her father asked.

"No, they haven't been made since 1946. I've only seen pictures of them."

Rose's mother said, "I wonder if your great great grandfather—the one who worked in the bank—ever had the chance to touch any of the $10,000. bills."

Rose looked thoughtful for a few seconds. "He might have."

"So, did John Robinson do anything in your dream?"

"He only waved at me, and then I woke up. For some reason, I thought his appearance was a symbol for my separation from my husband."

Rose's mother said, "That actually makes sense. John Robinson was one of the religious leaders who fled from England because of persecution. He and other Puritans were called the 'separatists.'"

"I must have read about the separatists somewhere. Then my subconscious connected my separation to the separatists."

Rose's father said, "Dreams are like that. They sometimes show us things we haven't thought about."

Rose shook her head in agreement before saying, "So, the separatists left England and then came to America."

Her mother said, "What actually happened was the separatists spent some time in Amsterdam and Leiden before some of them came over on the *Mayflower* in 1620."

"Our ancestor, Reverend John Robinson, stayed in England, right?" Rose asked. "So he became separated from the 'separatists.'"

"Yeah, in a way, he did, but he only was separated from some of the separatists. He was the minister of the Leiden church; there were 473 men, women, and children in the Pilgrim Leiden colony between 1609-1620.[6]"

"Oh, with so many Pilgrims in Leiden, some of them probably had to stay behind."

"Yes, and they needed some of their leaders to stay with them. There were only 102 passengers who began the 1620 trip on the Mayflower, and fewer than half of them were from Leiden. Some were from England."

"That's interesting. The passengers from England must have also been unhappy with King James or had some other reason to join the Puritans. Otherwise, they wouldn't have left England on a possibly dangerous journey into a new land."

"I think the Leiden Pilgrims were admired by some people because they were printing some stuff that King James didn't like."

"Really?"

"Yes. Back in the time of the Pilgrims, there was freedom of the press in Holland, but not in England."

"I can see why some people would want to leave England."

"Yes. Even though John Robinson was well liked and highly respected by everyone who knew him, he spent time in prison while in England. Bradford also was put in prison and heavily fined."

"So, once Robinson left England, he stayed in Amsterdam and then in Leiden."

"Yes. Even after the Mayflower left, though, he maintained contact with the Pilgrims in the new world. He wrote them letters and hoped to join them in Plymouth, Massachusetts. He died, though, before he was able to make the trip to the new world."

"His son came over, right?"

"Yes, you're directly descended from John Robinson's son Isaac. There's a Web site, *www.revjohnrobinson.com*, which lists many of John Robinson's descendants."

"Did Isaac Robinson come over on the *Mayflower?*"

"No, Isaac came over on a later ship. He didn't arrive in Plymouth until 1631. In 1660, he and thirteen other colonists founded Falmouth." Rose's mother got up off of the couch and walked over to the bookcase. "Here's our copy of William Bradford's *Of Plymouth Plantation.*" She brought the book over to Rose.

Rose looked at the back cover of the book, silently reading some of the notes from the book's editor, Samuel Eliot Morison.

She then read some of the words out loud to her parents: "Bradford was the principal leader of the Pilgrim Fathers."[7] Rose looked over at her father before continuing, "Wouldn't it be interesting if you're descended from William Bradford, Dad? That would mean I'm a descendant of both John Robinson and William Bradford."

"Yeah, I wish I had more direct information about my ancestors. I've even checked *www.ancestry.com,* but so far, I've only been able to trace my roots back through four generations."

Rose's mother said, "Whether they know it or not, a lot of people in this country are direct descendants of the Pilgrims. According to *Ancestry.org,* around '10 percent of Americans today can trace their ancestry back to the Mayflower.'"[8]

Rose silently started to read *Of Plymouth Plantation.* After about ten minutes, she said to her parents. "This footnote by Morison, the editor of the Bradford book, says, 'The term *Puritan,* like *Quaker,* was originally one of reproach, not accepted until nearly the close of the 17th century by the people to whom it was applied. The Puritans called themselves 'God's people.'"[9]

Her mom agreed with the statement. "Yeah, they didn't like being called 'Puritans,' but people called them by that name anyway. The Puritans were persecuted in other ways, too. Some of the Puritans were put in prison for no reason, and some were watched so closely that they were too scared to even leave their homes."

Rose went back to reading the book while her parents read the newspaper. After about fifteen minutes, Rose noticed that her mother was yawning.

"I think I should get going," Rose said as she stood up. After looking over at the grandfather clock, she added, "I'll have to fix the clock after visiting Granny."

"That sounds like a plan," her father said.

Rose put the Bradford book back in the bookcase, hugged her parents, and picked up her purse.

Her mother said, "Rose, you have to take the Bradford book with you. I know you'll love to read it on the train or bus."

"Okay." After retrieving the book and saying good-bye, Rose went out the front door. Once outside, she paused for a few seconds. Even in the evening, the rose bush was beautiful. Rose slowly walked over to her car and then drove to her apartment. It really was her apartment—and only her apartment. When she and Travis had separated, they had both gotten their own apartments. Sighing, Rose walked up the front steps and unlocked the door. Her apartment was small, but at least it was peaceful.

For an hour, Rose read some sections from the William Bradford book *Of Plymouth Plantation*. She then checked her *Facebook* account. Her mom had already uploaded a picture of the sampler. Rose printed a copy of the photo so that she could take it with her to work tomorrow. After looking at the picture for a few minutes, she said out loud, "I'll keep thinking about this sampler as I fall asleep. Maybe I'll be able to dream about it." She then set all three of her alarm clocks to go off one minute earlier than usual.

PERSECUTION

As Rose fell asleep, her thoughts were still focused on the sampler. She had several dreams, but they were not lucid dreams, so she did not realize that she was dreaming. When the darkness of the night was beginning to fade away into the light of another day, Rose sat up. She found herself to be staring at the sampler; it was resting in her right hand and looked a little bit different. The colors seemed too bright, and the threads were moving. They appeared to be running away from each other, rather than combining into pictures. Rose stood up and tried to remember if she had been holding onto the sampler when she went to sleep last night.

"Perhaps I'm lucid dreaming," Rose said out loud. She looked around, but no one had heard her words. To see if she was awake or asleep, she tried a reality check about the time. She looked at her left wrist, trying to find her watch, but it was not there. Then she felt circular movements within the pocket of her long skirt. She was still holding onto the sampler with her right hand, so she placed the sampler on her shoulder. Then she used her right hand to take a pocket watch out of her pocket; she opened up the case to see the time. The hands of the watch indicated the time was eight o'clock. Rose closed the case, concealing the watch, and then opened up the case again. Now the time was eleven o'clock.

"I'm lucid dreaming about the sampler," Rose said in a happy voice; her joyful face showed her pleasure at being able to dream about something she had planned ahead of time.

As Rose put the gold pocket watch back into one of the pockets of her skirt, she noticed that the pockets were really large. "I don't have any skirts with pockets like these," she said as she pulled outwards on both of the pockets. Her skirt was heavy. She looked down at her almost ground-length tan skirt. It was covering her shoes, so she could not see what they looked like. However, they felt more like heavy boots than shoes. She kicked one of her feet forward quickly and was able to see the front part of a pale black boot with a buckle on it. As the boot was covered up again with the fluttering motion of her long skirt, Rose realized that her skirt had taken too long to fall back down to the ground; she was wearing multiple layers of clothing under her skirt; there were also multiple layers of clothing under her blouse. Even the socks on her feet felt layered—as if she were wearing more than one pair of socks, or perhaps they just felt really thick because they were made of wool.

When Rose's right hand went up to her shoulder to retrieve the sampler, her fingers paused at the giant off-white collar at the top part of her blouse. She then reached higher and touched her hat, which had a large round rim on it. Her hand moved downwards and wiped the small beads of sweat off of her forehead. Since it was July, it was obviously too hot to be dressed in such warm layers of clothing. She took off her hat, felt a linen cap still perched on her head, took off the cap, and tossed both the hat and the cap onto the ground.

Rose looked at the sampler that was in her right hand again. The pictures now appeared normal. She looked at the map portion; as she focused intently on that part of the sampler, the map became larger until it took over the whole area of the sampler. There were no longer any words or flowers; only the map was visible. The cloth of the sampler then changed into a paper version so that it more closely resembled a map. As she looked at one of the arrows on the map, her feet automatically started to propel her in the same direction. Almost immediately, she tripped, staggered forward, and then regained her footing. After another few steps, she staggered again. She nearly tripped a third time before realizing that the problem was not with her knee—the problem was with the uneven pathway beneath her feet. Her eyes turned away from the map and looked at the ground upon which she was walking. It appeared to be a narrow cobblestone roadway; the stones beneath her feet were not lined up to be exactly even with each other, resulting in an uneven surface.

Rose began to pick up her feet higher and to carefully place them on the road. Her eyes went back to the map; the arrow curved slightly to the right, so Rose veered in the same direction. The map said, "30," so she started to count each of her steps: "One, two, three, four..."

Before Rose even came close to reaching the thirtieth step, she had to suddenly stop. A lady's voice with a British accent said, "You are not watching at all in the direction where you think you are going. Are you reading the paper at the same time, which maketh more difficult your walking?"

Rose looked up and realized she was about to bump into the lady. "Oh, I'm really sorry. I was acting like someone who was texting."

"What dost thou mean by the word 'texting'? Art thou reading a single paper, which thou toredst out of a book?" The tone of the lady's voice showed that she was unhappy with people who tore pages out of books. She now sounded more British than she had at first.

"I don't have a book."

"Then why art thou texting?"

Rose frowned, uncertain about what to say. She then asked, "Why did you first call me 'you,' and now you're calling me 'thou'? You changed your pronouns."

"I do not recall which pronouns I was saying to thee. 'Thou' is a pronoun that is used when friends are speaking to friends."

"We're not friends yet." Rose's brows furrowed, showing her confusion. "I don't even know your name."

"'Thou' is also spoken when people talk to someone like thee."

"What do you mean by 'someone like me?'"

"Someone like thee, which art in a lower social class."

Rose bit her lower lip as she tried to force herself to remain silent. She then whispered, "If I say anything to this lady, I might start screaming at her."

The British lady asked, "What sayest thou?"

Rose looked down at the ground, forcing herself to be quiet.

After a minute of awkward silence, the British lady started to speak again: "Thou art correct to be quiet. Thou dost not speak in a goodly fashion."

Rose's face showed her anger. She opened her mouth to scream a four-letter word at the lady, but no sound came out. She slowly inhaled and exhaled, trying to relax. Then she said in a whisper, "This is a lucid dream. If I want to scream at you, I should be able to scream!"

"What sayest thou?"

Rose opened her mouth, trying to scream again. All she could do was to ask a question in a barely audible, scratchy voice, "Why can't I scream?"

"I can not hear thee. Art thou texting again, instead of talking with me?"

Rose looked at the lady's face, which did not appear to be too mean. Sighing, Rose said in her normal voice, "'Texting' means to write a message on a phone."

"What doth the word 'phone' mean?"

"It's a metal tool. I use it when I talk to people."

"Words move through the air; they do not never go into tools."

"Yes, they do go into tools. Phones are modern tools."

"Doth thy phone make thy words fly, like a bird flieth?"

Rose shook her head, but before she could say anything, the British lady was speaking again: "Thou canst not mean 'flown.' Thou canst not be writing on a bird before it hath flown up into the sky. It will be higher in the sky than thine arm can reach." The British lady frowned in confusion and then laughed. "I now understand why the bird hath flown away from thee. The bird thought thou wast most strange because thou likest to ruin books. Even a Puritan would be a better friend for a bird than thou art."

"Do you dislike Puritans?"

"Of course I do." The lady laughed again; then her eyes and face moved up and down, showing that she was stating something so obvious that Rose should be agreeing with her. "Even Puritans dislike Puritans."

"Why don't you like Puritans?"

"They do too many wicked things. The one Puritan which I knew was placed in prison."

"What did the Puritan do?"

"He refused to go to an English church, like our Sovereign Lord King James requireth." The lady looked at Rose's head. "Thou needest to be more modest with thy hair. All of thy hairs are showing, so thou dost not look like a good person."

Another woman, with older-looking clothing, walked up to Rose and the British lady. The new woman said, "Maybe her cap be lost." Her accent was less British than the first lady's accent. After pausing for a few seconds, this Less-British woman added, "How now, good woman?"

Rose smiled. "So, at least you like me."

The Less-British Woman frowned. "I just met thee. I do not know if thou art good or wicked."

"Then why did you call me 'good woman'?"

The Less-British Woman's eyes dropped down to her apron. She looked like she was trying to hide. After a few seconds, her eyes shyly looked back up at Rose. "I always say that. 'Tis a greeting for all women."

The British Lady asked the Less-British Woman, "How now?"

The Less-British Woman bowed her head before saying, "I am blest."

The British Lady looked up at the sky and then said, "The moon is very bright for being in the last part of its arc."

Rose looked up at the sky. The lady had been referring to the moon's arc across the sky, which is how people without clocks could tell time. The smaller lights from the stars were twinkling within the deep blue of the sky, looking like they were ships sailing upon an ocean. Were these ships symbolic of future voyages to America?

Rose said, "The moon and the sky are pretty tonight, but it's a little warm." She wiped a strand of hair off of her sweating forehead before asking, "Why are we wearing so many layers of clothing?"

The British Lady and the Less-British Woman exchanged looks that showed they thought Rose was dumb. The Less-British Woman spoke to Rose with a touch of sarcasm in her voice: "We be wearing clothing to be modest."

The other lady said, "We understand why thou art in the street by thyself."

Rose glanced briefly at the ladies. They were both looking at her as she said, "We're all strangers. How can you know anything about me?"

The Less-British Woman said, "Ay, we really do know what thy problem is."

"With no cap to cover thy head, thou dost not look very pretty. So no one careth for thee."

Rose said, "This is a lucid dream. Perhaps I can make my husband Travis appear." She then looked beyond the two ladies, trying to find him, but he did not appear. She was all by herself.

"My parents love me."

The British Lady stared at Rose for a few seconds before asking, "Dost thou have a husband?"

Rose turned around several times in a circle, looking in all directions for Travis. When she started to feel dizzy, she stopped turning and said, "We're separated."

The British Lady and the Less-British Woman looked knowingly at each other. The lady said, "We know why he left thee."

The Less-British Woman said, "Always, he wanted thee to wear thy cap; he did not want to see thy hair, especially when thou turnedst in circles."

Rose said, "You're kidding! You're not really saying my hair is ugly, are you?"

The British Lady glanced sideways at the Less-British woman's smirking face and then said, "Of course not. We are good people and would not tell thee about thy bad looks." She moved one of her hands forward as if she was going to place it on Rose's shoulder and then stopped herself. "We are trying to help thee to have a more better life."

Rose moved back a step so that the lady's hand was no longer close to her. "No matter what you think, I look fine. Just because I have a scar on my knee is no reason for you to be so mean to me. I haven't done anything to you."

"Dost thou have a scar on thy knee?"

"How wast thou hurt?"

Rose partially pulled up her skirt, as well as the layers beneath it, and tried to show her scar to the ladies.

Both of them looked horrified. They then turned their heads away and stared at the ground. The British Lady, with her eyes still on the ground, said, "There be some things which thou canst not do. Being modest and wearing thy clothing is the law!"

The Less-British Woman nodded her head in agreement. "Ay, thou must behave thyself."

The two ladies stepped close to each other. Rose heard one of them whisper, "If we stand near this whore, we also may be put into prison!"

Rose looked closely at the lady with the British accent. She was now running her hands along the top of her apron. She seemed to be trying to find something. Her clothing not only was multi-layered but also made from strange material. Her long green skirt appeared to be a combination of silk and wool. A long cotton apron was on top of her skirt. As Rose watched, the lady's hand grabbed onto a large pair of scissors that was attached to a ribbon streaming from the top of her apron. The lady gripped the scissors, opening and closing them as if they were a weapon. After she noticed that Rose was scared of the scissors, she took a step backwards. The scissors fell out of the lady's hand; the heavy metal blades were still open as they swung down to lie in wait against her apron.

Rose's eyes moved down the row of stone houses along the edges of the street. A sign suddenly appeared in front of one of the houses. It said, "Scrooby, England." Rose asked the ladies, "What year is it?"

"Tis 1607."

Rose's eyes lit up. "Really?" she asked.

"Ay."

"Well, that explains a few things." Rose pulled at her skirt, making certain that it entirely covered her legs, ankles, and shoes. "Do you know the Reverend John Robinson?"

The British Lady and Less-British Woman exchanged looks of surprise with each other.

The Less-British Woman said to Rose, "Thou art not acting like a Puritan."

The British Lady said, "Thou canst not be friends with those Puritans. Though they do not act according to the laws of our great King James, they are more modest than thou art."

"Most of the time, I am modest. I'm really sorry about showing you my scar."

Both of the ladies were quiet.

Rose said, "I usually am a good person. My family brought me up correctly, and I'm a descendant of the Reverend John Robinson."

"Oh, thou sayest the word 'Robinson' like thou art proud of thyself and thy family! Thou needest to know what thy station is in our country," the British Lady said.

"What do you think my station is in your country?" The tone of Rose's voice showed her anger.

"Why art thou speaking like that?" the Less-British Woman asked. Her face looked pale.

The British Lady looked even more upset. Her face was red.

"Do you have high blood pressure?" Rose asked.

"What? Art thou threatening to make me bleed?"

"No, your face looks all red. I'm just worried that you're sick or hurt. Do you put a lot of salt on your meat?"

"All meat hath salt on it, which maketh it safe to eat. It also tasteth better," the British Lady said.

"Too much salt can make you sick." Rose noticed their strange expressions; she said, "I'm just trying to keep you healthy."

The Less-British Woman said, "Nay, thou art lying to us."

The British Lady said, "Thou art a wicked person."

The Less-British Woman waved her hand at the British Lady before saying to Rose, "Thou hast seen how good this here lady doth look. And now, thou art staring some more at her pretty clothing."

Rose realized that she really was staring at the British Lady's clothing. The lacey threads on her blouse and apron were especially interesting. They looked as beautiful as the threads of the sampler that Rose was still holding in her right hand.

The British lady tilted her head, acting as if she were trying to show off her fur and linen hat.

Rose laughed. "Most of your clothing is pretty, but I think your hat is ugly."

The British Lady looked shocked. After turning red again, she said, "Nay, 'tis pretty."

"It doesn't match your other clothes."

"Match? What dost thou mean? I can no longer speak with someone like thee. And we need to report thee, so the magistrate can put thee into prison."

Rose took a step backwards. "Look, lady, you're spitting at me, and there's a lot of sickness in Europe right now."

"I am not sick. I attend the Church of England on every Sabbath."

The British Lady said, "I always go to worship our God at our Sovereign King's Church. As a Puritan, thou art the one who dost not go to a good church. On the Sabbath, rather than going to church, thou goest to the house of a man."

The Less-British Woman said, "And then thou, with Robinson and other criminals, worship using thine own ways!"

Chimes began to sound; they seemed very loud, sounding as if they were nearby. Rose looked at the surrounding buildings, but she saw no bell towers. The chimes gradually became softer; they were moving away into the distance.

Rose said to the two ladies, "The Puritans did follow God." The chimes became louder again, gradually increasing even more in strength.

Rose spoke louder, trying to be louder than the chimes. "Right now in 1607, the Puritans are not just doing their own thing. They're following God! And the Reverend John Robinson is not just any man. He's one of God's ministers." The chimes became even louder.

"Thou canst be punished for saying such things!" The Less-British Woman took off her hat and hit Rose's hand with it, knocking the map part of the sampler out of her hand; it fluttered slowly to the ground. The Less-British Woman then rubbed the section of her hat that had come into contact with Rose. The woman looked like she was trying to clean her hat before putting it back onto the white linen cap that was still on her head. Without saying anything else, she and the British lady turned their backs to Rose and began walking away. After they had travelled about ten feet, they stopped. A gentleman was standing in front of them.

In a negative tone, the Less-British Woman said to the man, "Thou art holding onto the bible which is from Geneva. Art thou another Puritan?"

Before he could reply, the British Lady asked the Less-British Woman: "Dost thou not know this man?"

"Nay, I do not."

"He is the Reverend John Robinson."

In a sarcastic tone, the Less-British Woman said, "Then he is one of those Puritans."

Rose yelled, "Stop attacking the minister! He's a good man."

The Reverend John Robinson walked over to Rose, opened up his bible, and read the following verse out loud: "But I say unto you, Love your enemies: bless them that curse you: do good to them that hate you, and pray for them which hurt you, and persecute you" (Matt. 5:44 GNV).

Rose sighed. "Okay, I'll pray for these women."

John Robinson said, "May God bless thee." He then walked away from Rose, disappearing as he moved up a dirt pathway.

The British Lady and Less-British Woman muttered "Puritan" several times as they walked up the same dirt pathway and then disappeared.

Rose realized that the chimes were still making noises. Their sounds became louder and louder until a cement tower began to grow up out of the cobblestone road. The tower had bells rocking back and forth inside of it. Rose tried to see the bells better and then opened her eyes to the sounds of two of her alarm clocks going off at the same time. She said out loud, "I think I prefer my alarm clocks to those two British ladies—or were they women?"

Plans for a
Dream Story

By the time Rose woke up, got ready for work, and drove to the bank, she was more than fifteen minutes late. Kate saw her come into the bank and immediately moved back to her own teller window.

Rose walked up to her friend and said. "Thanks so much, Kate. I tried setting all of my alarm clocks a minute earlier last night, but I somehow wound up getting here five minutes later than yesterday."

"You're still a lot better than you were several months ago."

"Even so, I keep worrying that Harry will fire me."

"He would never do that. You were injured while doing your job. Plus, any of us could have been shot by those robbers."

"Several years ago, Harry fired Leslie for being late all of the time."

"Well, Leslie was new. Plus, she was often absent."

By the time Rose had set up her teller drawer, there were already two cars waiting in line at her drive-through window. She glanced up at the clock. It was one minute after eight; she began waiting on the customers.

After a couple of hours, Rose found herself looking around the bank's lobby—there was only one customer, and he was making out a deposit ticket. She walked over to Kate. "I'm going to take a short break while it's slow."

"Okay. I'll cover the drive-through window for you."

"Thanks." Rose left the lobby, went into the break room for a few minutes, and then came back out into the lobby again. The same customer was still in the bank—he was being helped by Lisa.

Rose went over to her own teller window. Kate was still standing there, waiting patiently for drive-through customers. Rose asked, "Do you know anything about samplers?"

"Do you mean those people who give out samples in stores?"

"No. I was thinking about a piece of cloth with stitches in it."

"Oh," Kate said with a slightly confused look on her face. "I don't think I've ever seen a sampler."

"During lunch, remind me to show you a picture of one. We found it last night inside of my parents' grandfather clock."

"Really?"

"Yeah. One of my ancestors might have made it."

"How old is it?"

"I think it's at least a hundred years old."

The customer at Lisa's window was still standing there. He was looking at Rose and had probably heard all of their conversation about the sampler. Lisa counted out some fifty-dollar bills for him. He scooped up his money and then looked at Rose again. His eyes seemed crooked. After staring at Rose for another few seconds, he said, "I know something about samplers. Do you want to show me that picture? I'll let you know if it's worth anything."

"No, thanks. The sampler is a family heirloom, so whether it's worth something or not doesn't really matter. We wouldn't want to sell it."

The customer stood there, shuffling around the fifties that Lisa had just given to him. His hands moved forward and backwards a few times. He then counted out ten of the bills, gave them to Lisa, and asked her for twenties. As Lisa finished the transaction, he slowly turned around and walked toward one of the tables in the bank's lobby, where he stopped to count and shuffle his bills again.

Lisa asked Rose, "Is your knee feeling good enough so you can go to your Zumba class tomorrow morning?"

"Yeah, it is. Are you coming?"

"I'll be there. It's at the Fitness Studio, right?"

"Yeah, it is. Do you need directions?"

"No, I know where it is—on Warwick Avenue in Warwick."

"I'll bring the sampler. The picture doesn't really look as nice as the real thing." Rose went back to her window; the customer with the crooked eyes was still standing in the bank lobby. He was writing something down on a piece of paper, which he placed with his stack of bills. He then turned around and left the bank.

At eleven thirty, there was a lull in the customers, so Rose and Kate went into the break room together. They took their lunch bags out of the refrigerator and sat down to eat at the round wooden table. Rose took the picture of the sampler out of her purse, passed it across the table to Kate, and asked, "What do you think?"

"Is the month of 'May' supposed to connect to the flower?"

"Yeah, I think so. The flower is a 'mayflower.'"

"That's interesting." Kate glanced up at Rose and then looked back at the picture of the sampler. "What do you think this shovel near the flower means?"

"Is that a shovel? I thought it was a bell." Rose looked closely at the paper. "I'll have to look at the actual sampler again. On this paper version, it's tough to figure out what all of the little symbols are."

"This line here could be a coastline or a river, but then the *Mayflower* is above the line, so it means the *Mayflower* is on land."

"I think the *Mayflower* is just in a different section of the sampler and was not intended to be on land. Many samplers have different sections." Rose pointed to the round part of the sampler. "For example, look at this round section. It doesn't seem to be connected to the other sections around it."

"Yeah, I see what you mean by different sections."

"Even though that round circle section looks different, it actually might be connected to the rest of the sampler. I just don't know for sure until I look at my grandmother's watch case."

"Why is the watch case connected to the sampler?"

"It might not be, but I'm guessing that it's connected. My mom thinks some of the case's pictures are the same as the ones in the round section of the sampler."

After Kate was finished looking at the picture of the sampler, she passed it back to Rose, who put it into her purse.

Rose and Kate were quiet for a few minutes, and then Rose asked, "Did you have any interesting dreams last night?"

"Probably, but I don't know for sure. I'm not good at remembering my dreams, like you and Lisa can do." Kate thought for a moment and then added, "I think I had a dream about being at work, but I don't remember exactly what it was."

"I think everyone dreams about work."

"Why do you think that happens so much?"

"If someone's thinking about work and then falls asleep, it's very possible the first dream will be about work."

"I should try to think about more interesting things, then, like going out on a date. Hopefully, it'll be with someone cute."

Rose laughed and then sighed. "I can't think about anyone else besides Travis."

"Are you still in love with him, or do you just miss his company?"

"I know I have feelings for him, but I don't know if I'm still in love with him."

"Are you having dreams about him?"

"Yeah, I just can't seem to control his actions. He's always controlling mine, especially when I'm lucid dreaming."

"Maybe you subconsciously want him to control you."

"No, I don't think so. He asks me to make him dinner. So I cook for him, even when I work as many hours as he does, am not feeling good, am on crutches,..." Rose's voice trailed off.

"Your dreams sound a little too close to reality."

"Our dreams are connected to our reality. We just don't always know exactly what the connections are."

Kate retrieved her purse and took out some papers. "Here, I looked up dreams again and printed these for you. They might give you some ideas about more lucid dreaming techniques."

Rose looked at one of the papers. "This one's a definition from the *Columbia Electronic Encyclopedia*. It defines a 'dream' as being 'a number of visual images, scenes, or thoughts expressed in terms of seeing.'"[10]

"That's why there are so many symbols in dreams. The focus is on visual stuff."

Rose shook her head in agreement, looked at the definition silently for another minute, and then added, "This encyclopedia's definition also mentions lucid dreaming: 'Studies have demonstrated the existence of lucid dreaming, where the individual is aware that he is dreaming and has a degree of control over his dream.'"[11]

"The other pages are an article with some lucid dreaming tips. I've tried a few of them, but I haven't been able to lucid dream like you can."

Rose smiled and then turned to one of the other pages. Before she began reading the page, though, she asked, "Would you like some chocolate?" She moved her lunch tote bag over in front of Kate.

"Thanks, you know I love chocolate."

Rose silently read one of the pages from the article and then said, "It took me months of practice before I could do things like a reality test in my dreams."

"I can't remember ever doing a reality check in my dreams, but I'll keep trying."

"This idea about planning a fantasy is something that I've tried before. It has sometimes worked."

"How do you plan a fantasy?"

"I do it just like the article says: 'Before you go to bed, think about what you want to dream lucidly about, in as much detail as possible.'"[12]

"Planning a fantasy sounds like fun."

"It is." Rose looked off into space for a moment before adding, "I wonder if I could do a dream story."

"What's a dream story?"

"It's something I've been thinking of trying for a while. Logically, if I can concentrate on one idea, plan out what I want to dream, and then dream about it, I should be able to do something more. I could try one part of a story on one night and then the next part of the story on the next night."

"So you would dream about different events or scenes of a story over several nights."

"Yeah. I dreamed about the Pilgrims last night, so I was thinking about finishing my dream on another night."

"Tonight, you could dream about them landing in the new world."

"Well, I probably should dream about their journey across the ocean first."

At twelve noon, Rose and Kate were finished with their lunch and went back to work. A couple of hours later, Lisa said out loud, "Oh, no!"

Rose looked over at her. "What's wrong?"

Lisa had a stack of fifty-dollar bills in front of her. She was holding onto one of the bills. She squeezed it between her thumb and forefinger, moved it upwards closer to her eyes, and then put it down on the counter. "This one feels funny. It's not printed on the right paper." She marked it to see if it was counterfeit and then closely looked at it again. Sighing, she said, "I'll have to tell Harry, our boss, about this."

"Do you know who gave you the bill?" Rose asked.

"It could have been that guy who was interested in your sampler, but I don't know for sure. Harry and I might be able to figure out who it was by looking at some of today's pictures." Lisa's eyes blinked as they focused on one of the bank's cameras.

Lisa went to see Harry in his office. About twenty minutes later, a detective came into the bank. The detective spoke briefly with all of the bank's employees; he then made a few phone calls and left.

When there were no customers at her drive-through window, Rose walked over to Lisa's teller station and asked her, "Does the detective know anything yet about who the counterfeiter is?"

"No, I don't think so. If the detective suspected someone, though, he probably wouldn't tell us anything."

"The counterfeiter could also be a woman."

"You're right, but the detective asked us about the people we saw today who were not regular customers. That must mean that counterfeiters are more likely to be strangers—or at least people who don't have accounts at our bank." Lisa turned her head to look at a customer who had just walked into the bank. The customer went over to one of the counters and began to make out a deposit ticket.

Rose said, "That's one negative thing about working at the drive-through—I don't see the customers as well as when they walk into the bank's lobby."

Lisa shook her head in agreement. "I like the regular teller windows better. I get to interact with the customers a little more."

"The drive-through customers often have their radios on, so they sometimes don't even hear me when I ask them questions."

"The only people I saw today who weren't regular customers were men. How about your customers, Rose? Could you see them well enough to know if there were any new ones?"

"Well, I told the detective that I couldn't remember any non-customers. I think they were all our regular customers, but I'm not completely certain."

The bank began to get busy, and Rose was tied up at her window for the rest of the afternoon. After she closed out her teller drawer, she went home and called her mom's cell phone. "How was your day, mom?"

"It was really great. How was yours?"

"Okay, except for the counterfeiter."

"What happened?"

"A customer gave Lisa some counterfeit money."

"Is Lisa one of the tellers?"

"Yeah."

"That's too bad. Do they know who did it?"

"Not yet, but the pictures from the cameras will help the cops to find him."

"Well, I think you deserve a vacation in Albany with Granny for a day or two."

"Yeah, I think I do, too. When's a good time to visit her?"

"She's free this weekend and Monday. Possibly also on Tuesday."

"I'll check with my boss tomorrow. I might be able to go and see her as early as Sunday."

"Okay. I e-mailed Granny a picture of the sampler, and she's excited about seeing the real thing."

"I'll bring it with me."

Rose paused and then asked, "Are you sure you don't want to go to Albany with me? Granny would love seeing both of us."

"I have to go to some meetings at work this week, so I'll be tied up. I'll visit Granny sometime next month."

"Okay."

"You'll have to give her an extra hug for me."

"I will." Rose smiled before asking, "Guess what?"

"What?"

"Lisa thought there was a shovel on the sampler. It's near the word 'May' and the flower."

"Oh, that would be interesting. I'll go and get my picture of the sampler. Can you hang on for a moment?"

"Of course."

Almost immediately, Rose's mom was speaking into her phone again: "I have the picture of the sampler right here. The thing you're talking about could be a shovel, or it could be a bell."

"When I looked at the real sampler, that little design looked more like a bell. However, on the paper version of the sampler, that bell looks more like a shovel."

"One of the nearby vines looks like a musical note, Rose, so I think this line with the nearly-oval shape is really a bell."

"Maybe the vine is a vine; then that oval-shaped thing would have to be a shovel."

"If it's actually a shovel, then the sampler really has code about a treasure."

"You're right, mom. If there's a real treasure involved, we'll have to find it."

"The treasure hunt is about to start. Your dad will buy your train tickets, so you can visit Granny."

"Oh, mom, that's so wonderful of you. Thanks."

"There will be two trains to get you to Albany. The first train is the Northeast Regional. Then you'll have to switch to a different train in the New York Penn Station." Rose's mother continued talking, explaining to Rose about some of the dates and times for the trains.

"Thanks for looking up those times, mom. I'm guessing I'll be able to leave here early Sunday morning and return on Monday afternoon. But I'll have to check with my boss tomorrow before I can let you know for sure."

"Okay. Granny already said that she'll be picking you up and dropping you off at the train station near her home."

"That's so wonderful of her."

"She's very happy to be seeing you again, Rose."

"I'm looking forward to seeing Granny, too."

"Don't forget to bring your camera; you'll have to take lots of pictures."

"Okay, I will."

"Your grandmother has a computer, so you can even e-mail me copies of the pictures you take."

"All right. I might even take a few of Granny."

"Yes, please do. I know your pictures will come out great because Granny always smiles whenever she's near you."

"Oh, thanks, mom."

"Did you check out the link that I e-mailed to you?"

"No, I didn't have a chance yet. The URL looked like it belonged to a Pilgrim Website."

"Some of the pages refer to Pilgrims. The name of the whole Website is *ancestry.com*. There's a lot of information about the activities of the English Separatists while they were in Leiden."

"So they didn't go straight from England to Plymouth, Massachusetts?"

"No, Rose. They first went to Amsterdam for a year and then to Leiden for the next eleven years."

"They must have been a very closely knit community in Leiden."

"Yes, they were. They obviously had similar religious beliefs and were very supportive of each other. However, they were not as conservative or closed-minded as some people today might think."

"Oh, really? I'll have to read about their life in Leiden tonight."

"The stay in Leiden gave the English Separatists a lot more freedom to worship God in their own way. However, instead of being primarily in a rural community, like they were in England, the Pilgrims in Leiden found themselves in an industrial city. They had to work hard. Because they were mostly laborers in the clothing industry, they were poorly paid. Even their children had to work a lot of hours."

"Really?"

"Yeah. Bradford was one of the exceptions. He did well enough as a weaver that he was able to buy a house.[13]"

"Now I'm curious about the life of the Pilgrims in Leiden."

"I think everyone enjoys learning about the Pilgrims."

"You're right. Learning about the history of our country and our ancestors is so much fun. I'll have to look at that Website as soon as we get off the phone. In fact, I should be going right now. I'm getting up early tomorrow morning to go to my Zumba class again."

"That sounds so great!"

"It should be fun."

"I'll let you go. You can call me sometime tomorrow."

"Okay. Bye, mom. I love you."

"I love you, too. Bye for now."

Rose got ready for bed; she then turned on her computer and went to the Website that her mom had mentioned. There was a "Leiden American Pilgrim Museum" page that was especially interesting. One section stated that "contact with Dutch Memmonites and with other groups of refugees... expanded the Pilgrims' horizons and led to the development of a uniquely cosmopolitan, relatively tolerant view of the world."[14]

Before Rose fell asleep, she thought about the Pilgrims in Leiden. She remembered the cobblestone road that she had walked on during her previous night's dream about the Pilgrims. As she fell asleep, she concentrated on picturing the same cobblestone road.

THE SEPARATISTS

When Rose found herself walking on the cobblestone road from her previous night's dream, she immediately knew she was lucid dreaming. She also realized that dreaming about this road might be okay, but she didn't want to dream about the two anti-Puritan women. She tried to move herself into one of the houses. However, nothing happened. She then tried to turn around and walk away into a different neighborhood, but the two anti-Puritan women suddenly appeared in front of her.

Without speaking to either one of them, Rose looked down at the ground and walked quickly past the two women. A few steps after she had passed them, they flew over her head and re-appeared in front of her. They bowed their heads to Rose as a way of showing her respect. Rose had to stop walking. One of the women opened her mouth, which grew and grew until it was larger than Rose's face. The woman then said, "Good morrow to you."

Rose frowned. "I think you mean 'good morning.' But even so, it's not morning. It's evening. You're only supposed to say 'good morning' in the morning."

The other woman asked, "Art thou often confused about the time?"

Rose replied, "No, I'm only confused when I'm late."

"Thou must be late, which is why thou thinkest 'tis the evening."

Rose said, "Well, it isn't the 'morrow,' either. It's the morning."

The British Lady raised her chin high, looked above Rose's head, and then said sarcastically, "Thou sayest 'morrow' badly. Art thou a Puritan?"

Rose tried to say "No, I'm a Baptist," but the words would not come out. After shaking her head sideways, she took a step backwards and said, "Yes! My ancestors are Puritans, and so am I!"

Both of the anti-Puritan women began to laugh. Then the Less-British Woman looked at Rose while muttering the word "Puritan" in a negative way.

Rose stared at the woman and remained quiet for a few seconds. She then said, "Let's not fight. Does it really matter to you if I'm a Puritan or not?"

The Less-British Woman said, "Ay, it doth matter very much."

Rose's eyes shifted back and forth between the two women. "Which one of you hates Puritans the most?"

The women stood still and did not answer her. As Rose's eyes kept moving back and forth between them, a third woman walked up and stood next to her. The new woman's bodice was light brown, and her skirt was dark gray. Her hat seemed to match her skirt, but her clothing looked old and tattered in places. She was probably a lower-class lady. In a sweet voice, the third woman asked Rose, "Are these women being mean to you?"

Rose's eyes stopped moving between the two anti-Puritan women and turned to her right. She bowed her head to the Sweet-voiced Lady, who bowed back at her. Rose then said, "I think so. They called me 'Puritan' again."

The Sweet-voiced Lady said, "I saw them looking at you in a very mean way. One of the verses in our Bible saith, 'A haughty look, and a proud heart *which is* the light of the wicked, *is* sin'" (Prov. 21:4 GNV).

Rose smiled. "God is so right. Last night and tonight, those ladies were really mean to me. They looked down on me and called me 'Puritan' because I'm related to the Reverend John Robinson."

"Noone doth never like to be called 'Puritan.'" After pausing for a few seconds, she added, "How are you related to our Reverend Robinson?"

"He's one of my ancestors."

"Then thou art invited to be with me and my friends for dinner."

"Oh, I would love to go to your home. You're so wonderful."

"And I do love this meeting with thee. Thou art not a Puritan, but art one of God's people."

"So do you also call yourself one of God's people, rather than a Puritan?"

"Ay, thou art correct. We do like being called 'God's people.'"

"Are you also a Separatist?"

"What dost thou mean by 'Separatist'?"

"Someone who is separate from the Church of England."

The Sweet-voiced Lady thought for a moment before saying, "Yes, for some months now, I have been separate from the people who follow the Church of England, which is the religion of King James."

"Do you go to a separate church building from the Church of England?"

"Oh, we still go to Church of England churches, but sometimes, our men do not remove their hats."

"Do you get into trouble for that?"

The Sweet-voiced Lady laughed. Her laugh sounded like a series of musical notes that were even sweeter than her regular voice. "Whether we wear our hats or not, everyone already knoweth that we're 'God's People.'" Her voice became serious and almost lost its sweetness as she said, "But we sometimes do get into real trouble. If we do not attend one of the churches of King James, then we are fined or placed into prison, which is our punishment for doing what is right."

"I'm so sorry about the problems you're having." Rose looked at the spot where the anti-Puritan women had been standing; they were no longer there. The Sweet-voiced Lady was still nearby, and she asked, "What is thy name?"

"Rose. What's your name?"

"People call me by the name of Mary."

Rose followed Mary into a stone building. The windows were all open, and there were no screens. A large number of flies and mosquitos were present. Some were flying around, and some were interested in the food sitting on the wooden table. There was meat that looked like chicken or turkey. Wooden bowls in the middle of the table contained pieces of flattened bread, a salad, and a cheesecake. The table was set with cloth napkins, spoons, and knives; there were no forks.

The floor under the table had a beautiful handmade rug with flowers, leaves, and other designs. In the middle of the rug's designs appeared some words from the Lord's Prayer: "Give us this day our daily bread" (Matt. 6:11 GNV).

Rose stared at the bible verse and then asked Mary, "Are those words actually knit into the rug, or did my mind add them into the designs?"

Mary had walked over to the fireplace and begun to stir a pot of soup. She was humming a song and didn't seem to have heard Rose's question.

Rose looked back at the rug; the designs started to change. To the left of the words were some flowers that were too straight. The flowers became even straighter, lost their leaves and blossoms, and changed to a dark gray color. The stiff-looking flowers now looked like the bars of a prison cell. A lock appeared, stretching its way around some of the gray bars. Then some gnarled ropes flew onto the bars; the ropes tied themselves into twisting knots. Finally, a picture of King James I appeared. He was standing atop the prison bars with a strong stance, as if he were showing everyone that he was in charge of who would be put into the prison and who would be let out. His crown had white pearls embedded in the gold metallic structure; a red cap that was inside the crown was partially visible, and a gold cross sat on top of the crown. His clothing was red, white, silver, and gold. His golden shoes had wide ribbons on them, and between his feet and the tops of the prison bars was a thick rug with bright flowers, leaves, and other designs on it. The rug beneath his feet looked like the same rug that he was a part of.

Rose looked at the right side of the rug. The pictures began to change. A key and an open door appeared. Then straight ropes made of bright yellow sunlight created a path from the open door toward a field of flowers, bushes, and trees. Some Puritans began to walk joyfully along the pathway, and King James disappeared. Rose jumped onto the path and ran after the Puritans. The path went past a sign that said "Amsterdam" and then went past another sign that said "Leiden."

Mary walked over to where Rose was standing on the rug and looked down at the floor. "Didst thou change the rug?"

Rose stepped off of the rug before saying, "I didn't mean to, but I might have changed it by mistake. This is a lucid dream, so I might be changing some things."

Mary laughed. "Methinks I saw King James on my rug, but I very much enjoy this version with no picture of him. I will be so happy to never not see his picture no more. He hath done so many bad things."

"What has he done?"

"He putteth many of us separatists into his prisons. We did only want to leave England, but we could not get approval for our papers. Therefore, we could not leave, except in secret."

"So you left England in secret?"

"Ah. Some of us sold everything and secretly paid for tickets to sail away from England. Then our money was stolen by the captain of the ship."

"That's awful."

"Then some of us were put in jail for trying to leave the country without the proper paperwork."

"What happened to the captain who stole your money?"

"Nothing."

"So a thief was not put into jail, but some of God's people were?"

"Ay."

"That's too bad."

"Robinson, Bradstreet, and others were put into prison. Eventually, they were let out. As thou hast discovered, we left England secretly."

"Why did you leave England? Was it for religious reasons?"

"Ay. I did leave so that I could be free to worship God with other people who followed the word of God. Some people left England for other reasons."

"Really?"

"Ay. Outside of England, there is more freedom to print writings on a printing press."

"So, are you happy here?"

"We have more jobs here in Leiden than we did in Amsterdam. And we have more freedom than we did in England."

Rose started to sit down on one of the chairs in front of the table, until she saw that Mary was frowning at her. Mary had her hands clasped in front of her apron as she said in a polite tone, "We should wait to rest until my husband returneth."

Rose smiled and stood up. "Oh, I'm sorry. I didn't realize that you have a husband who will return."

Mary looked down at the rug again. "I truly like the pictures that thou hath made on top of my rug. The pictures show our life to be separate from the King of England."

"In a way, the pictures symbolize my life, also, because I'm separated from my husband."

"Oh, what dost thou mean by separated from thy husband? Hath he joined our Lord in heaven?"

"No, he and I may be getting a divorce."

"Oh, I am very sorry for thee. Will thy husband be punished for adultery?"

"No, he has done other things wrong, but not adultery."

"Then thou can not never have a divorce."

Rose paused for a few seconds as she tried to figure out how to respond. As soon as she said, "I'm from a different time and place than you," the room became dark. She felt herself being moved away from Mary and toward the door.

Rose said, "Mary," but her word was not heard. While she could no longer speak to Mary, Rose could still see and hear what was happening in Mary's home.

Mary went over to the table and lit the candles. Then she spun around the room several times, looking for Rose, before asking, "Where art thou, Rose?"

"I'm here, right in front of you."

Mary walked over to the front door of her home and looked outside, but she still couldn't see Rose anywhere.

Rose said, "I'm invisible, and my voice is not being heard." She went over to the doorway and stood next to Mary. A man was outside and walking toward them. He asked, "Art thou looking for me or for someone else?"

"Ah, I always look for thee whenever thou art not here." Mary stepped backwards so that her husband could walk through the door. They both started to walk toward the wooden table. Rose followed them and then looked down at the rug. Mary also was looking at the rug. Rose and Mary both frowned at the same time. The rug underneath the table had reverted to its original flowery designs.

"Dost thou not like the rug anymore?" her husband asked as he sat down. He placed his feet on top of the spot where the

Puritans had been walking joyfully onto the pathway just a few minutes ago. Now there were flowers in the same spot.

"I really love our rug. It is one of the most nicest things that thy family hath given to us." Mary poured some wine into a mug for her husband and then politely stepped backwards, smiling the whole time.

Rose looked at the rug again. Even with its original almost too-flowery artwork, she still liked it. The rug looked like a large, thick sampler that was lying on the floor, rather than being in an important position on a wall. As Rose thought about people with dirty, wet boots stepping onto this beautiful creation, she sighed, but no one heard her. Mary and her husband were busy talking to each other. Rose heard Mary's husband say, "Marriage." In her sweet voice, Mary said, "Forever."

Rose's eyes went back to the rug underneath the table. She wished that she could do something to help its existence. As she continued to look at the rug, it began to slide out from under the table. Like a magic carpet, the rug then lifted itself up off of the floor, gracefully flew across the room, and carefully positioned itself in a place of honor in the middle of the wall.

"To what place hath our rug gone?" a voice asked, sounding as if it was alarmed at the missing item.

Before Rose had a chance to respond, the alarmed voice was being drowned out by an alarm clock going off.

Zumba

With the alarm clock near her bed making noise, Rose automatically hit the snooze button. Then she glanced over at the work-out clothes that she had placed on her bureau the previous evening. She smiled, got out of bed, and shut off her series of alarm clocks before another one of them could sound off. She didn't limp at all as she got ready for her Zumba class. By five thirty, she was running out the front door of her apartment and heading for her car.

Early on a Saturday morning, driving along Warwick Avenue was fairly easy. Rose soon arrived at the Fitness Studio. She parked next to Lisa's car and glanced over at Kate's car. After she looked down at her watch, she smiled. She was only five minutes late.

Once inside the gym, Rose paused for a moment to look at the decorations. Nancy, the owner of The Fitness Studio, always decorated the gym for the season. Even though it was a few days after the Fourth of July, the room still had a lot of red, white, and blue decorations, including flags, banners, ribbons, and lights.

Rose walked over to a bench that had sign-in sheets on it. There were at least thirty other people who had signed in for this one class. As Rose wrote down her name, she noticed Kate's and Lisa's names were near the top of the page. Her friends had arrived early, possibly at the same time.

Rose sat down on a chair, changed into her Zumba aerobic sneakers, and began humming along with the music. One of her favorite Spanish Salsa songs was playing. Moving her feet in time to the music, she walked from the carpeted area up onto the gym's wooden floor.

Usually, there were only women in the class, but this morning, there was a single man. He was wearing a Boston Red Sox tee shirt, blue shorts, and blue aerobic shoes. Rose stared at him for a few seconds. He looked familiar, but she was unable to remember his name or where she had seen him before. Most of his steps were in time to the music, which meant he had some kind of experience with dancing or aerobic dance classes. However, he was having problems following the Zumba instructor's steps. He probably had not attended too many Zumba classes.

The women in the class ranged from teenagers to a lady who was at least eighty years old. Rose recognized most of the faces. The women standing near the front of the room were better at following the instructor's steps; these were the more experienced Zumba dancers. At the back of the room were the women who were a little shy; they often had less experience.

Rose looked around the room until she saw Kate and Lisa. Her friends were in the back right corner of the room. When Rose started to walk toward them, they both turned to look at her at the same time. With smiles on their faces, they moved slightly apart and gestured for Rose to come stand in the space between them. She moved across the room and joined her friends.

Kate yelled out, "You didn't miss much of anything. We were only warming up."

Rose focused on the instructor's footwork, trying to follow the steps as well as she could. Even though Rose was already familiar with many of the dance moves, there were a few new steps. When Nancy, the instructor at the front of the room, moved to the right, everyone in the room followed her. Most of the dancers then followed her as she stepped to her left and turned around. There were a few new people who were having problems following all of the steps, but because the same steps were repeated over and over again within the same song, the new people soon were able to follow along with the other people in the class. Arms rhythmically swirled; most of the arm motions copied the movements of the instructor's; some of the dancers, though, were happily using their own motions.

Another song started to play. Rose was more than twenty feet from the front of the room, and four rows of dancers were partially blocking her view of the instructor's movements. Even so, Rose was able to follow Nancy's motions without too many mistakes because she had danced the steps to this song many times in the past. Rose was used to watching not just the instructor, but also the reflection of the instructor in the mirrors covering two of the walls. Halfway through the song, Rose looked to her right to see her friend Kate. Everyone was supposed to be turning around, but Kate was walking in place for a couple of the steps. Kate then turned around after most of the other people in the room were finished with their turns. She looked at Rose and waved. Even though it was obvious that Kate didn't know all of the steps or the routine, she was still having fun. Rose raised her arms over her head and began to move them in circles; Kate and Lisa watched her and then started to do the same arm movements.

From the front of the room, Nancy's voice was heard: "I love those circular arm movements." She then began to do the same arm motions herself, and most of the other people in the room followed along. After another minute, the music stopped, and everyone went to the side of the room to get some toning sticks. As they were waiting in line to pick up their plastic sticks, Nancy walked over to Rose and said, "I'm so happy to see you again."

Rose hugged Nancy and then said, "I'm so happy to be here. My knee was bothering me for awhile."

"That's too bad. Are you okay now?"

Rose raised her left knee and pointed to it. She was wearing long workout pants so that no one could see the scar. "Yeah, it feels perfect."

Nancy asked, "Are these two new people friends of yours?"

Rose introduced Kate and Lisa to Nancy, as well as to several of her other friends. Rose then turned toward the noises coming from the two baskets of toning sticks. Every time someone picked up one of the sticks, it made noises. The toning sticks in the left basket were yellow; each stick only weighed a pound and a half. The purple sticks in the right basket weighed two and a half pounds. By the time it was Rose's turn to choose her toning sticks, all of the purple weights had already been taken. She picked up a pair of the lighter weights and carried one in each hand as she walked back to the right rear corner of the room. Kate and Lisa followed her lead: they chose the same one and a half pound weights and then walked quickly back to join Rose. As noises from the toning sticks sounded throughout the room, the music started. The noises immediately began to follow the same rhythm of the song that was playing: Kelly Clarkson's "What Doesn't Kill You (Stronger)."

Lisa moved over closer to Rose and said, "Like the song says, 'I dream in colour.'[15] And I really do dream in color. What about you?"

Rose said, "Yeah, I dream in color, too." She paused for a few seconds before adding, "Last night, I dreamed again about the Pilgrims. I'll have to tell you about it at work later."

"Okay."

Rose, Kate, and Lisa continued to follow the steps and arm motions of Nancy, who was in her usual position at the front of the room. Before the song was even half finished, though, Rose, Kate, and Lisa were doing only about half of the arm movements. It was obvious from their fast breathing and sweat that all three of them were tired. Suddenly, Lisa dropped one of her toning sticks. It bounced on the floor a couple of times before she picked it up. She sighed deeply and then commented to Rose, "More exercise like this should help us all to be 'stronger' and 'stand a little taller.[16]'"

Rose shook her head in agreement before raising her toning sticks high above her head and saying, "So, do I look taller?"

Lisa laughed as they both moved with longer steps across the wooden floor. After the song was over, everyone put their toning sticks back into the baskets at the front of the room. Rose drank from her bottle of water as Kate said, "I think I need to exercise more."

Rose agreed: "So do I."

Lisa placed one of her hands on Rose's shoulder and her other hand on Kate's shoulder. "We're having so much fun together. We'll have to come again on another Saturday morning."

Rose said, "That'll be so nice."

They continued to do more Zumba dances together. Near the end of the class, the theme song from the movie *Footloose* began to play. After a minute of following the instructor's steps, most of the people in the class knew the routine. When the instructor waved her arms and started happily turning around, Rose realized that it was time to dance around the room. People turned, waved at each other, and smiled as they danced into different places around the room. After Rose had arrived on the other side of the room, she found herself near the one man who was taking the class. He was standing near the purses and had stopped dancing. His crooked eyes shifted among the different purses; he appeared to be looking for something. Rose stopped moving and asked him, "Did you drop your keys or something?"

"No."

"Well, what are you looking for?"

"I just need my water bottle. Oh, here it is." He picked up a water bottle with green and tan designs on it. The designs looked like dollar signs, but they also could have been vines twirling around some branches.

Rose hesitated for a moment before asking, "Have we met before?"

As the music stopped playing, the man said, "You work at First National Consumer Bank, right?"

"Yeah, I do." Rose thought for a moment before adding, "You're the guy who likes antiques."

"I do."

"What's your name?"

"Smith. Greg Smith." Even though he had tried to introduce himself in the same fashion as James Bond always did, his crooked eyes took away from the positive impression. After looking over Rose's shoulder, he said, "You're Rose, the drive-through teller."

"Yeah, I am." Rose took a drink from her water bottle and then asked, "So, do you work in a museum?"

"No, but I do know some things about buying and selling antiques."

Kate, who was suddenly standing nearby, asked, "Speaking of antiques, Rose, did you bring the sampler with you this morning?"

"Yeah, I did." Rose walked over to the spot where she had placed her purse. She quickly removed the sampler and waved it at Kate. Another song started to play. Most of the women in the class began to put on shimmy hip scarves. These were thin scarves that were covered in coins, sequins, and other metallic items. Sort of like an apron, the scarf was tied around a woman's waist and hips. As a woman's hips moved, the metallic items on her hip scarf made noises. As long as the woman was dancing in time to the music, she would be adding to a song's sounds with her body's motions.

Rose didn't have her shimmy scarf with her that day, but she still moved back to her spot on the wooden floor and danced some more with her friends. Finally, the instructor put on some cool-down music, and everyone followed the instructor's motions and performed a variety of stretches.

Kate nudged Rose's shoulder. "Do you know that man?"

"Which man?"

"The one over there. He's the only man in the class."

Rose looked at where Greg had been dancing. He was no longer standing there. "So, where is he?"

Kate pointed off to the side of the room. Rose looked at where Kate was pointing. Greg had stopped stretching and was staring at the purses again. This time, though, his eyes seemed to be focused mostly on Rose's purse. The sampler was lying partially inside of an exterior pocket of the purse.

Rose walked over to stand next to Greg. In a hesitant voice, she asked, "Are you looking for something again?"

He turned to face her before saying, "Yeah. I was curious about your sampler. It looks like it's partially in your purse."

The music had stopped, and the instructor waved happily as everyone got ready to leave.

"What would you like to know about the sampler?"

"I was wondering when it was made. If it's old enough and you want to sell it, I can tell you where the best places are."

Rose's face showed her relief. "It's so nice that you're trying to be helpful."

His face looked slightly upset as he asked, "What did you think I was doing?"

"Oh, nothing." Rose sighed. "I was just wondering because you seemed interested in my purse."

Greg laughed. "I'm not a thief."

"I know that now. And I think you're trying to be helpful."

"Can I look at the sampler?"

"Normally, I wouldn't mind, but I have to go right now. I don't want to be late for work." Rose looked briefly at his face; his eyes still appeared crooked in their expression, but they also looked happy and bright as they stared back at her own eyes. Sighing, Rose reached into her purse, pulled out a paper, and wrote on it. "Here's some information about me. Go to my *Facebook* page, and I'll 'friend' you. You'll be able to see a picture of the sampler on my page."

"Thanks. After I see the picture of your sampler, I'll tell you if I notice anything that might be helpful."

"Okay." Rose, Kate, and Lisa left the gym together and got into their cars. They then drove to their homes and got ready for work.

PERMISSION TO LEAVE

Rose was energized from her workout and quickly got ready for work. After she had pulled into the First National Consumer Bank's parking lot, she looked down at her watch. She was only four minutes late for work, but it would be another two minutes before she could park her car and get inside of the bank. As she walked toward the front door of the bank, she blinked her eyes in surprise to see Kate's perfect timing: her friend had pushed open the door at just the right moment. Rose did not even have to slow down; she kept walking straight through the open doorway. "Thanks, Kate."

"You're welcome." Kate closed and locked the door. "That Zumba class this morning was so much fun."

"Yeah, it's always a fun class, and I love the music."

"After all that exercise, is your knee okay?"

"It's fine." Rose raised her left knee slightly and then straightened it out. "I think the exercise helped it a little bit."

"I'm so glad to hear that." Kate placed her hand on Rose's shoulder. "We're going again next Saturday, right?"

"Maybe I can go, but maybe not." Rose looked at the calendar on the wall before adding, "I might not be able to go next Saturday."

"Why not?"

"I might be in New York visiting my grandmother."

"Is she sick?"

"No, I just need to look at this old watch case of hers and compare it to the sampler."

"That sounds like fun."

"Yeah, it should be."

"Did you check with Harry yet about going on vacation for a few days or longer?"

"I was planning on speaking with Harry today. I'm actually hoping I can leave right away, like maybe tomorrow."

"Knowing Harry, I'm sure he'll be okay with that."

"Yeah, Harry's such a great boss. Anyway, I might be able to go to Zumba next Saturday, or I might have to wait and visit my grandmother then. Either way, you can always go to the class without me."

"Lisa and I just might do that." Kate smiled, walked over to her teller window, and began to work with the night deposits and loan payments.

Rose left the bank lobby to put her purse in the break room. Then she set up her teller drawer and started to help drive-through customers.

By nine thirty, no more customers were at the drive-through windows. Rose went to the break room, drank some water, and then came back. Only one customer was in the lobby. As she walked close to the customer, she realized that he was Greg, the guy who liked history and antiques. She said, "So, we meet again."

Greg turned around, looked at Rose, and smiled. "Yeah, we do keep on running into each other."

"So we do." Rose looked closely at Greg's crooked eyes. The slanted appearance of his eyes was not due to their physical form, but rather was due to how he was looking at her: his eyes looked straight into her eyes and then moved so that they were focused slightly beyond her face. He appeared to be looking over her shoulder at someone or something behind her.

After Rose watched Greg's face for another few seconds, his smile changed. He moved a step closer to her, and she realized that he was attracted to her, possibly because she had been staring at him.

Rose looked down at the floor and said, "I have to get busy."

"Okay." Greg was still looking beyond her face, rather than at her face. "I don't want you to get into trouble because you're talking to me."

"Thanks for understanding." Rose turned to walk toward Harry's office, but Greg reached out and placed his hand gently on her elbow.

"Once we're 'friends' with each other on *Facebook*, we'll get to know each other better."

"That sounds like a plan. Good-bye."

Greg took his hand off of Rose's elbow and waved to her.

She walked over to see Harry, who was standing outside of his office.

"Hi, Harry."

"Hi to you, also, Rose. How is your knee feeling today?"

"Really good. I'm exercising it."

"Are you going to a gym or exercising at home?"

"I went to a gym for my Zumba class this morning, and I'm planning on going dancing at The Dancin' Feelin' tonight."

"That's great, Rose."

"How are you, Harry?"

"I'm fine, too. This beautiful weather helps, especially on the weekend."

"Yeah, it does." Rose paused, inhaled, and slowly exhaled. "I have a favor to ask."

"Go right ahead and ask." Harry smiled. "I'm thinking of going to the beach this afternoon, so I'm in a really good mood this morning."

"The beach sounds wonderful, and I hope you have a lot of fun."

"Yeah, I will. I love spending time with my wife and kids." Harry turned his head toward his desk, looked at the picture of his family, and then said, "What kind of a favor do you need?"

"I need to visit my grandmother in New York."

"Is she okay?"

"She's fine. I just haven't visited her for a while. She's in Albany, and I need to compare a sampler to an old watch case of hers."

"What's a sampler?"

"It's a piece of cloth with different examples of stitches and decorations on it. One of my ancestors made a sampler."

"Is the sampler connected in some way to the watch case?"

"Possibly. The sampler might have parts of a map on it; these map designs could show us where a watch for the watch case might be."

"Is the map about some place in New York?"

"No, it looks sort of like Cape Cod Bay and Plymouth." "Really?"

"Yeah, it does. Also on the sampler is some kind of code that might be referring to the *Mayflower*. My grandmother might be able to help with the code section of the sampler. So I really need to go and visit her."

"Well, when would you like to go?"

"If it's okay with you, I was thinking of leaving tomorrow and possibly trying to return to Rhode Island on Monday, but I wouldn't be able to come back to work until Tuesday at the earliest."

"If you came back to work on Tuesday, you'd probably be a little tired from the trip."

"Yeah, but I might be okay at work on Tuesday, especially if I plan on coming in a few hours late."

Rose and Harry both laughed. Then Harry said, "No one else is taking any vacation time now, so I'm okay with you taking a few days off. We'll be fine here."

"Thanks so much, Harry."

"You're welcome."

"If I need to spend more time with my grandmother and cannot come back to work until Wednesday, I'll send you an e-mail and let you know what's happening."

"If you need the whole week, Rose, go ahead and take it. You still have quite a bit of accrued vacation time that you need to use anyway."

"I know some auditors are coming on Wednesday, so I'll try to be back to work either Tuesday or Wednesday."

As Rose headed back to her teller window, she noticed that Greg was still in the bank. Right next to Harry's office, he was leaning on a table and writing something on a piece of paper.

A drive-through teller waved at Rose, so she went back to her own drive-through window. Several customers were in line. When she had finished helping all of them, she looked around the bank's lobby to see if Greg was still there. He was nowhere to be seen. Rose sighed, and Kate noticed. Since no more customers were in the bank, Kate pulled up a chair next to Rose's window, sat down, and said, "You seem unhappy about something."

"Do I really, Kate?"

"Yeah, you do."

"I was just looking for that historian/antique guy. His name is Greg."

"Oh, he left a little while ago. Do you like him, Rose?"

"I don't think so. He might be the counterfeiter."

"Well, we don't know anything yet. Greg is probably completely innocent."

"Do you really think so, Kate?"

"Yeah, I do. If he were guilty, why would he come back again to the same bank?"

"That's a good point."

"Anyway, when he was here, it looked like the two of you were staring at each other."

Rose blushed. "I didn't really mean to stare at him. I was just watching the way his eyes were looking past me into strange places."

"Maybe you like him."

"I don't know." Rose paused and then raised her voice slightly. "Besides, I don't even know if I want to divorce Travis."

"Your husband came into the bank a day or two ago with a lady."

"Yeah, I noticed them both."

"Do you know who the lady was?"

"No, I never met her before." Rose sighed and then looked out her drive-through window. There were no customers waiting for help.

Kate glanced around the lobby. Only one customer was there, and Lisa was helping him. "Travis and the lady could just be friends."

"Possibly, but they were standing sort of close together."

Kate reached over and lightly touched Rose's hand. "If they're dating, you might find out tonight. You're going to the dance with me and Lisa, right?"

"Yeah. I might have to leave a little bit early, though. I'll probably have to get up early tomorrow morning to get ready to see my grandmother."

"Are you leaving sometime tomorrow?"

"Probably. Harry said I could take a few days off."

"Harry's always so generous about everything."

Without any hesitation, Rose said, "Yeah, he is. It's so easy for us to get permission for vacation time."

"Many people these days have to ask for vacation time months ahead of time."

Rose laughed. "Not just people today, but people in previous centuries sometimes had problems getting permission to leave."

"Really?"

"Yeah. Early in the seventeenth century, the Separatists couldn't get official permission to leave England."

Kate's eyebrows moved, showing her confusion. "Back then, couldn't people just jump on a boat and go sailing somewhere?"

"No, they couldn't. They needed the correct paperwork to leave England and go to a different country. Some of the Separatists tried to leave England secretly."

"Is that when they went to America?"

"No. In 1607, Separatists from Scrooby tried leaving England with the intent of going to Holland. They were caught while trying to leave the country and put in jail."

"That's too bad. Did they eventually get out?"

"Yeah, they did, Kate. They tried leaving England a second time, and the men Separatists were separated from their women and children."

"That must have been horrible."

"The men were carried away into a storm. Even though they were okay, their wives and kids wouldn't have known that."

"Back then, there were no telephones."

Rose laughed and then said, "There especially was no texting on cell phones."

Sarcastically, Kate replied, "Really?"

Rose tried to explain her laughter: "On Thursday night, in one of my dreams, I was acting like I was texting on my cell phone."

"So, why is that funny?"

"I was dreaming that I was in England in the beginning of the seventeenth century. Two British women acted in a negative way to my texting."

"Oh, so there was a cultural misunderstanding."

"Yeah, there was." Rose paused for a moment before saying, "Anyway, after a while, the seventeenth century Separatists were split up."

"So the separatists were separated into groups?

"Yeah. Some of them were separated from their wives and children; eventually, they were joined back together again in Amsterdam."

"That must have been a happy reunion."

"They would have sung psalms and given 'thanks' to God for safely bringing them back together again."

Rose and Kate were silent for a moment as they imagined groups of joyful Puritans being re-united with their loved ones. Then Kate asked, "Are you driving to see your grandmother in New York?"

"No, it's a little far for me to drive, especially if my knee starts acting up again."

"Are you thinking of flying or taking a train or a bus?

"I'm planning on taking the train, but I don't have any train tickets yet. I'll call my parents when I get home this afternoon. They're going to buy the tickets for me."

"That's really nice of them."

"Yeah, it is. My parents are always like that."

Kate pointed to the window in front of Rose. A customer had pulled up and was rolling down his car window. Kate went back to her teller station; Rose turned around and watched as the customer in the blue car signed the back of his check. He then pulled out a deposit slip and started to slowly fill it out. After a minute, he paused in order to speak with Rose: "I know today's Saturday, but what's the date?"

"July 7."

There was at least one other car that was waiting behind his blue one. The customer in the second car, a lady with a baseball cap on her head, was getting upset. She looked at her watch, pulled off her baseball cap, and looked at her watch again. Then she opened up her car's window and waved a bank deposit envelope in the air. She seemed to be indicating that she was all ready for immediate help.

The customer in the first car was now looking through his billfold; he was probably trying to find his driver's license. After another minute, he found it. Finally, he put his license, deposit ticket, and check into the pneumatic canister, which he then sent through the tube carrier to Rose.

"The deposit ticket says a five hundred dollar deposit, but your check is larger than that. Do you want the difference in cash?"

"Yes, please."

Rose checked the customer's account balance, but there was not enough to cover the cash he was requesting. She started to explain this to him, but before she could finish her explanation, the baseball-cap lady behind him psyched out. She jumped out of her car and yelled, "You're making me late for work! And you're stealing time from me—just like in that movie *In Time.*" She then opened up the envelope, took out the paperwork inside of the envelope, tore up the envelope, and threw the pieces in the air. After yelling some more, she got back into her car, backed up, swerved around the blue car, and exited the bank's parking lot. Her car was not fast enough to lay down a strip of rubber, but the lady still tried it. Her car's tires only skidded on some gravel, which slowed her down even more. She then had to wait for at least twenty cars on the main road to go past her before she could pull out into the traffic.

The customer in the blue car had been watching the lady in his rear view mirror. After she left, he said in a depressed voice, "Everyone always says I'm late. And that I drive too slowly. In fact, I'm often late because I drive too slowly."

Rose's face showed her own sadness. "You're not the only one who's late all the time."

"Really? Who else is late?"

"I am."

"So then what happens? Do people get mad at someone as pretty as you?"

Rose laughed. "Thanks for the compliment, but yes, people sometimes get mad at me, too."

Another car had pulled up behind the blue-car customer. Rose finished explaining to the blue-car customer why she couldn't give him any cash back.

He said, "But I have a savings account here, too." He reached into his glove compartment, pulled out a bank statement, and sent it through the tube to Rose.

After Rose had put a hold on his savings account, she sent his money and deposit receipt back to him through the tube carrier. She then said, "Many people get upset at slow drivers, but it's better to be too slow than to be too fast. You don't want to injure yourself and other people in a car accident."

"I know. I just sometimes want to be faster. I hate it when I'm late. And I hate wasting—or stealing—other people's time." He smiled at Rose as he very slowly pulled away from the drive-through window. By the time Rose had finished waiting on another car at her drive-through window, the blue car was still waiting at the end of the parking lot; the slow customer needed a long enough pause in the steady stream of traffic so that he could pull out slowly onto the main road.

Rose waited on several more customers. When there were no other customers in line at her window, she walked over to Kate's teller station and asked, "When I come to work late and you cover my teller window for me, am I stealing your time—like the time thieves in that movie *In Time?*"

Kate laughed. "You're kidding, right?"

"No, I'm really worried about it. I don't want to take your time away from you."

Kate looked intently at Rose's face before saying, "Whether I stand in front of your teller window or mine, I'm still getting paid the same amount of money for being at work. Also, you only get paid for the time you're actually here in the bank, so you get less money when you're late."

"You're so kind, Kate."

"I'm not just being 'kind.' I'm telling you the truth."

"Thanks."

"Also, you were the one who was kidnapped and injured in the bank robbery. After what happened, the fact that you can even come back to work at all is wonderful. You have far more courage than I do."

"You're the best friend I've ever had. Thanks again, Kate."

A couple of customers came in through the front door of the bank; Rose went back to her own window and looked out into the parking lot to see if she had any customers. A car was just pulling up to her window. It was the lady in the baseball cap. The lady quickly stuffed her checks and other pieces of paper into the canister. After she sent the canister through the tube carrier, she said, "I'm sorry about being such a pain earlier. I just didn't want to be late for work."

"So, did you get to work on time?"

"Yeah, I did. And then my boss wanted me to run a few errands for her, including going to the bank." The customer laughed. "So, here I am again."

Rose took the customer's stack of papers out of the canister. There were two deposit tickets and a stack of checks to go with each deposit ticket. She quickly finished both transactions and sent two deposit receipts back to the baseball-cap lady.

The lady smiled as she said, "You're really fast. Time must be important to you."

"Yeah, it is. I love clocks."

"Well, there's no way you would ever be late for work or anything else in your life."

Rose's smile became frozen on her face.

"You look a little cold," the baseball-cap lady said.

Rose stared at the lady. "I actually feel cold. Since it's July, I should be warmer."

"Maybe the bank's air conditioning has been set too low."

"I'll check it in a minute." There was another customer behind the baseball-cap lady who was getting impatient. "Are you all set for today?"

"Yeah, I guess I am." The lady did not move her car. Instead, her right hand went to the air conditioning controls in her car's dashboard. After she had turned down the air conditioning, she paused for a few seconds and then turned up the volume on her DVD player. The song "Time in a Bottle" by Jim Croce was playing.

"I love this song," she said as she slowly closed her car's window. She began to hum, and then her cell phone rang. She was speaking into her phone as she slowly moved her car forward toward the main road in front of the bank. She was moving even more slowly than the man in the blue car had done.

The next customer pulled up in front of Rose's window. Angrily, she said to Rose, "That lady was so slow. Now I'll be late for work."

Rose tried not to smile. After she was finished helping the customer, she sighed and sat backwards in her chair.

Lisa came up to her and said, "I loved going to your Zumba class today."

"Yeah, I had a lot of fun, too. It was even more fun than usual because you and Kate were there."

"Is your knee okay after all that exercise?"

"Oh, I'm fine. How about you? Do you have any muscle aches or pains?"

Lisa laughed. "Not yet, but I sometimes feel muscle aches the day after an exercise class."

After a pause, Rose asked, "So, have you had any good dreams lately?"

"Yeah, a few nights ago, I dreamed about dancing in the bank vault again with my husband Mike."

"Can you tell me about what happened in the vault, or is it too…personal?"

"It must have been exciting and personal, but I only remember some different colored lights."

"So you dream in colors?"

"Yeah, I do. How about you, Rose?"

"I do, too. Sometimes the colors are really bright."

"Have you had any interesting dreams lately?"

Rose smiled. "I started something really different. I'm doing a dream story."

"What's a dream story?"

"I plan out a story ahead of time about what I want to dream about. Then I try to have a lucid dream about the beginning part of the story. After I have a dream about the beginning of the story, I plan out the next part of the story. Every night, I try to continue the story until I get to an ending."

"Do your actual dreams change from your plans?"

"Yeah, they usually change—at least a little bit."

"What is your dream story about?"

"The Pilgrims."

"Did you begin your dream story yet?"

"I did. Last night, I dreamed about the Separatists."

"Are the Separatists the same as the Pilgrims?"

"Some of them are. The Separatists left England to find a new home in Amsterdam and then moved again to Leiden.

Then some of the Separatists came over to New England on the *Mayflower*. These were the Pilgrims. Some of the Separatists, though, remained in Leiden."

"Were you in the dream?"

"Yeah, I became one of the separatists."

"Well, that makes a lot of sense."

"Do you really think so?"

"Yes, I do. After all, you are separated from your husband."

"Some of my dream actually was about my separation and divorce."

"Was your husband Travis in your dream?"

"No, he wasn't. At least, not that I can remember."

"Interesting." After pausing for a few seconds, Lisa asked, "Was Greg—that antique/historian person—in your dream?"

"No, he wasn't. Anyway, tonight I was planning on trying to dream about the next part of the story: the Pilgrims will decide to leave Leiden and go to the New World."

"Does that mean you might want to go to a new world, too? Maybe you're more interested in Greg than you realize."

"Oh, I don't know about that. We'll have to wait and see what happens."

"Have you thought about connecting your dream story to your sampler?"

"The sampler could connect to my dreams, but I don't remember dreaming about it yet."

A customer walked into the bank, and Lisa went back to her teller window. For the next half hour, everyone in the bank was busy. At noon, the front door of the bank was locked. Within a half an hour, the remaining customers had been helped, and all of the teller drawers were locked up.

Lisa, Kate, and Rose briefly discussed what time they would be meeting each other at the ballroom dance hall later. They then said good-bye and got into their cars. Lisa was the first one to leave the parking lot; Kate was the second, and Rose was the third.

After Rose got home, she had a sandwich for lunch and called her mother.

"Hi, mom."

"Hi, Rose. How was work this morning?"

"The usual mixture of customers. Some were nice, and some were mean. Nearly all of them were in a hurry."

"No one ever has enough time. That's a part of our modern lifestyle."

"So it is. Anyway, my boss said that I can take some vacation time. I can go visit Granny tomorrow."

"Good. I'll have your dad buy the tickets."

"Thanks so much, mom."

After she had said good-bye to her mother, Rose began to pack a suitcase for her trip. Ten minutes later, her mom called her back. "There's a train leaving Providence for New York Penn Station tomorrow morning at 7:20. You'll arrive in New York at 10:50, get on a different train at 11:45, and arrive in Rensselaer about 2:15."

"That sounds great."

"When do you want to come back to Rhode Island?"

"As long as a train is leaving New York in the afternoon, I'd prefer to come back on Monday."

"You don't want to stay longer?"

"In the middle of the week, some auditors are coming to the bank. Even though my boss said I could stay for as long as I liked, I know he wants me back to work as soon as possible."

"Okay." Rose heard her mom saying to her dad, "If possible, Monday afternoon is when Rose wants to leave New York."

After what seemed like only a few seconds, Rose's mother said, "It's all set. Your dad just booked your tickets online."

Rose wrote down the information that her mother told her about the trains and then said, "Tomorrow morning, I'll plan on taking a taxi to the train station."

"No, your dad and I will pick you up at your place. How does six o'clock in the morning sound?"

Rose sighed. "That time sounds great, especially since I know I can't talk you into letting me take a taxi."

"No, you can't."

Rose laughed. "You're such a great mom!"

"Thanks, Rose. You're a great daughter!"

"Thanks, mom. And thanks for helping me so much with this trip."

"You're welcome. I'm so happy you're able to visit my mom. She loves to see you."

"I love seeing her, too."

"So, we'll see you tomorrow morning at 6:00. And we'll bring your tickets with us."

"Okay. Thanks again, mom."

After Rose had said good-bye, she called her grandmother and told her about the train times. She then spent the rest of the afternoon doing housework, packing for the trip, choosing clothes to wear on the train trip, and getting ready for ballroom dancing. About 7:30, she ran out to her car and drove to the ballroom dance hall. As usual when she was running late, a large number of slow drivers were out on the road in front of her, and most of the traffic lights were red. Every time the traffic stopped, she looked at the clock in the dashboard of her car and then at the watch on her wrist. She had found out from her past driving experience how to relax in traffic situations: she would check the number of minutes that she was losing. Most often, she thought she was losing ten or fifteen minutes when, in reality, she was only losing a minute or two. Finally, she pulled into the dance hall's parking lot. She had to park at the back of the lot, but she was glad the weather was nice. As she walked up to the front door of the dance hall, two other cars pulled into the parking lot. Rose smiled—at least she was not as late as these people were. Besides, arriving "fashionably late" at a dance hall was better than being late for other things.

BALLROOM DANCING

Rose walked casually up the stairs and through the door into the dance hall. After paying her fifteen dollars, she went over to the table with Kate's and Lisa's purses on it. Sitting down, she put on her dance shoes. Even though she was too late for the dance lesson, she would still learn more about ballroom dancing tonight. Often when she danced with some of the more-advanced dancers, they would lead her through new steps.

When Rose stood up and looked around the room, she saw Kate, who was dancing with a man in a green suit. After the song ended, the man went to get a drink at the bar. Kate walked over to where Rose was standing, and they both sat down.

"Is Lisa here?" Rose asked.

Kate pointed over to the far left corner of the dance floor, where Lisa and her husband Mike were dancing.

Kate took a sip of her bottled water and then moved another bottle of water over to Rose.

Rose opened up the water and then said, "Thanks. How much do I owe you?"

"Nothing but your smile."

Rose smiled. "So, I really wanted to be here for the 7:15 dance lesson, but I had to finish packing for my trip to see my grandmother."

"When are you leaving?"

"Tomorrow morning."

"Do you need a ride to the airport?"

"No, thanks. I'm taking a train instead of a plane."

"How about if I give you a ride to the train station, then?"

"Thanks so much for offering, but my parents really want to drop me off at the train station."

"When are you returning?"

"I'll be back home late Monday night. I might go to work on Tuesday."

The song "Dance with Me" started to play; a man walked up to Rose and smiled. When she looked into his crooked eyes, she realized that he was Greg—the man who had been at The Fitness Studio earlier that day. As the lyrics of the song said, "I want to be your partner,"[17] Greg asked her, "Rose, would you like to dance with me?"

"I'd love to, Greg." She stood up and was led off onto the dance floor. Once they had started dancing, Rose said, "So, you know how to dance in a ballroom, as well as in a gym."

"Yes, I do. And it's a really nice surprise to see you here tonight."

Rose smiled. "I like to dance, but I'm not yet a very good ballroom dancer."

"You're better than I am."

"No, you're just saying that to be nice."

"Why would I lie about something like that?" Greg stumbled slightly, and Rose wondered if he had done it on purpose in order to prove that he was someone who could be trusted.

"So, Greg, you told me once before that you're really good at history, right?"

"Yes, I really am."

He led Rose through a turn; she stopped talking because she had to concentrate on her dancing.

When the song was over, Greg walked Rose over to her table. He then asked, "Can I sit with you over here?"

"Of course you can."

"Excuse me a minute." He hurried across the room to a different table, where he had left his street shoes and a jacket. His street shoes were a pair of blue sneakers, which didn't match the formality of his other clothing. He brought his possessions over to Rose's table.

She commented, "Your sneakers look comfortable."

"Yeah, they are. That's why I like to wear them almost everywhere—at least until I change into my ballroom dance shoes." Greg pointed to the formal pair of dance shoes that he was wearing.

"Those shoes look nice, too."

"They are, especially for dancing. Would you like to dance this waltz with me?"

"I'd love to."

Rose stood up and followed Greg out onto the dance floor. Because she wasn't as experienced as some of the other dancers, she and Greg didn't move too fast. When they were on the opposite side of the dance floor, another couple almost bumped into them. As Rose followed Greg's lead into a turn, she came face to face with the man in the other pair of dancers; he was her husband Travis. Before she had a chance to say anything to her husband, Greg led her through a series of progressive quarter turns. They then did a hesitation turn, and Rose was happy that she could follow Greg and correctly do all of the turns. They continued moving down the dance floor.

After another minute of dancing, Rose briefly glanced around the dance floor. At first, she could not spot her husband Travis. Then, as they spun around one of the corners of the room, she saw him again. He was leading his dance partner off of the dance floor and over to the bar. Rose looked at Greg and asked him, "Is it okay if I get us some drinks?"

"I'll get them. What would you like?"

"I'm uncertain. Let's see what they have." Rose walked toward the bar, and Greg followed her.

Rose's husband Travis was ordering a beer and a soda. When Rose was about three feet away from him, he turned around, saw Rose, and said "hi" to her.

Rose shook her head in a greeting. "So, how are you doing these days?"

"Okay. How's your knee? Can you dance okay?"

"It's fine. I even went to my Zumba class this morning."

"That's so wonderful. I'm so glad you're feeling better."

"Thanks." Rose and Travis stared at each other. Then Greg took a step closer to Rose, touched her elbow, and said, "Hey, Rose. Do you know this guy?"

Rose, Greg, and Travis all introduced themselves.

Travis then said, "Rose, this here is Ellen." His hand moved up to rest lightly on Ellen's shoulder. "You might remember her from the other day when she came into the bank with me."

Rose blinked her eyes as she looked at Ellen, who had pretty long blonde hair and gorgeous blue eyes. Rose quickly turned her head to look at Travis, who picked up the two drinks he had ordered; he and Ellen then walked over to their table. He glanced briefly at Rose. She was closely watching him and his interactions with Ellen. After he had turned back to focus on Ellen, she and Travis smiled at each other. Rose frowned.

Greg cleared his throat. Rose looked away from Travis and glanced at Greg. He was holding onto their drinks. He set them down on their table. The song "No Time" by the Guess Who began to play. Greg pulled Rose up onto the dance floor, and they began to dance the Cha Cha. She noticed that her husband was dancing with Ellen again. As Travis and Ellen turned around, Travis was facing in Rose's direction, and their eyes met. After exchanging a quick glance with Rose, Travis turned around again so that his back was facing her. The line "On my way to better things"[18] was heard. As Rose continued to watch Travis's back, she heard, "There's no time left for you."[19] For the rest of the song, she did not see Travis's face, but only his back.

When the song stopped, Greg and Rose walked around the room to get to their table; they found themselves to be the only ones there. Greg took a sip from his beer. "Are you having fun tonight?"

"Yeah, I am. I just wish I could dance better."

"If you're really having fun, you could take ballroom dance lessons in a dance studio."

"Are you taking any lessons?"

"No, not right now."

"Well, you know a lot more about the dance steps than I do."

Greg smiled at her. "Thanks. It's taken me a while to learn the basic steps, but I enjoy dancing. Plus, I like meeting people at the dances."

"Yeah, I like meeting people, too."

Lisa and her husband Mike came over to the table. After everyone was introduced and seated, Lisa said to Rose, "Kate told me that you're going to see your grandmother tomorrow morning."

"Yeah, I am. I'm taking the train."

"Are you leaving from the Providence Station?"

"Yeah. Then I'm switching to a different train in New York."

"Oh, I thought your grandmother was in New York."

"She lives in Albany, so I'm first taking a 7:20 train to the New York Penn Station. Then I'm switching to an 11:45 train to Rensselaer. My grandmother is picking me up and driving me to her house."

Greg took out a piece of paper and started writing on it. Rose looked at what he was writing; while his hand covered a part of the paper, she could see "11:45" in the right hand corner. He put the paper into his billfold. Before Rose could ask him what he was doing, Lisa asked her, "Can I give you a ride to the Providence Train Station?"

"No, thanks. My parents really want to drop me off. They always enjoy every possible chance to visit with me."

"Will you be staying here tonight until the dance is over, or are you leaving early?"

"I think I'll stay until eleven. I can take a nap on one of the trains tomorrow."

An announcement was made that the Foxtrot mixer was about to start. Rose and Kate got up and stood in line on the right side of the room with most of the other women. The men formed a line on the left side of the room. As the foxtrot music started, the first man and the first woman stepped forward and began dancing with each other. Then the second man and woman danced together; the third man and woman danced, etc. The couples all danced down the center of the room, between the two lines of people, until they got to the end of the room. Each man danced with his partner over to the end of the woman's line, said good-bye, left her at the end of the line of women, and walked across the room to wait at the end of the line of men.

The Foxtrot stroll was interesting because people had the chance to dance with and meet new people. Sometimes the dancers who were paired together would have similar dancing abilities, and sometimes they would be at different levels. Friends often danced with each other, and strangers also often danced with each other. Being surprised by new and old dance partners was a part of the excitement of the Foxtrot stroll.

As Rose waited in line, she talked with Kate, who was standing in front of her. They discussed different kinds of ballroom dance shoes. When they got near the front of the line, Kate looked over at the men, made a strange sound, and said, "Rose, are you okay with dancing with your husband Travis, or do you want to switch places with me?"

Rose looked at the line of men. Travis was watching her with a strangely distant expression on his face. Rose then said, "If we switch now, he'll notice."

"You're right. He's seen us already. He'll notice if we switch positions."

Rose sighed. "So, I guess I'll have to be nice and polite; I'll have to dance with him."

"You're always nice and polite."

"I don't know about that," Rose said. "And I don't know if I can be nice and polite tonight. Travis is so cold and distant."

Kate stepped forward and began dancing with the man in front of Travis.

Rose inhaled deeply, looked across at Travis, and took a couple of steps forward. Travis's face was still cold-looking. He held out his hand politely, and Rose put her hand into his. They slowly moved into correct dance positions. They used to dance very close together. Tonight, however, more space than normal was separating them. As they started to dance down the center of the room, the song "It Had to Be You" by Harry Connick was playing. Rose kept her eyes to her left. She knew that she was supposed to look over Travis's left shoulder, rather than watching his face, but she purposefully kept her eyes far to the left of his left shoulder. When they were about halfway down the room, Rose stumbled slightly. Travis asked her, "Are you okay?"

"I'm fine, thanks. How about you?" Rose still kept her eyes to her left. As they moved into a turn, she noticed that her arms and Travis's were very stiff. It felt like she was dancing with a wooden or a plastic model, rather than with a person.

"I'm fine, too."

For the rest of the dance, both of them were silent. Finally, Rose found herself left at the end of the women's line, and Travis was nowhere to be seen.

After a few seconds, another lady was added to the end of the line. She said to Rose, "You don't look too happy. Was he a bad dancer?"

"Oh, no, he was a great dancer. I'm just a little tired tonight."

The lady behind Rose began talking about the names of several of the Foxtrot steps. Rose just nodded her head in agreement as her eyes turned back to look at the line of men. She couldn't see Travis anywhere. However, she did notice Greg, who was tapping his right foot in time to the music as he waited for his turn to dance.

Rose's next two trips down the center of the dance floor were with strangers. One of them taught her how to do a better quarter turn, and her mind became focused on dancing, rather than on trying to decide if she wanted to dance with Travis again or not.

After the Foxtrot stroll was over, Rose went back to her table.

Greg was already seated. He said, "We didn't dance the Foxtrot together yet."

"Oh, we'll have to do that the next time they put on Foxtrot music."

"Okay, it's a date." He smiled at Rose, and she awkwardly smiled back.

Greg took a sip of his beer and then waved at Rose's purse. "Are the pansies on your purse like the flowers on your sampler? Or are they different kinds of flowers?"

Rose looked down at her purse. It had several pansies sewn into the top front section of its leather. She then glanced over at Greg's face. "How do you know so much about the sampler? I didn't have a chance to 'friend' you yet, so you couldn't have seen the picture of it on my *Facebook* page."

"I saw it briefly in the studio this morning. Also, you talked about it in the bank. I think it was a day or two ago."

"Oh." Rose furrowed her brows and then continued, "Yeah, you're right. I think I did say something about a flower or flowers on the sampler."

"I heard you say something about the Pilgrims and your sampler. Do you think the sampler was made by one of the Pilgrims?"

"Probably not. I don't think it's that old."

Greg frowned slightly before commenting, "Well, even if it wasn't made in the seventeenth century, it could still be worth a lot of money." His eyes looked at Rose's face. For once, his eyes were not crooked; they stared directly at her face with a hopeful expression in them.

Rose looked back at Greg. "Are you an antique dealer?"

"No, not exactly, but I do know a lot about history. I have two of my favorite history books in my car. I'll go and get them."

While Greg was getting his books, Rose watched the dancers. In less than five minutes, Greg was back again. As he sat down next to Rose, he said, "This is Nick Bunker's *Making Haste from Babylon.*"

"I like the cover. One of the Pilgrims has a dog."

Greg laughed. "A lot of people would first notice the ships and the log cabins on the cover. You must like animals."

"Yeah, I do. I have two cats." Rose looked at the map on the back cover of the book and then asked, "Does Nick Bunker explain why the Pilgrims left for the New World?"

Greg smiled. "I was just reading about that a day or two ago." He opened up the book, flipped through some of the pages, and then stopped to silently read a few lines. "Bunker is explaining right here about the reasons for leaving. He discusses what William Bradford said about leaving Europe in his book *Of Plymouth Plantation.*"

"I have a copy of that Bradford book. I borrowed it from my mom."

"That's a great book. It was written by the person who was the Governor of Plymouth for many years."

"Yeah, you're right. I haven't had a chance to read the whole Bradford book yet, but I know the Pilgrims left England to avoid persecution and to be able to practice their religion as Separatists."

"That's right. They went to Amsterdam in 1608. After about a year, they moved to Leiden, where they stayed for twelve years. In 1620, they left on the Mayflower for the New World."

"So what does your book say about the reasons for leaving Leiden?"

"According to Nick Bunker's explanation of Williams Bradford's ideas, there were four reasons why the Pilgrims left Leiden. One reason was the 'poor conditions, endless work, and a harsh diet.' Another reason was the 'gradual weakening of morale,' which was related to the 'hardships of manual labor.' Bunker explains that people working with linen could get a lung problem called byssinosis. A third reason was 'the burdens inflicted on children.' The last reason was 'the hopes the Pilgrims had of conveying the Gospel to the New World.'"[20]

"I think many of the Pilgrims just wanted more freedom generally: freedom of religion, freedom of the press, and freedom to have their own homes and land."

"Yeah, you're right. There was also the freedom of not being put into prison. Can you imagine being put into prison for saying things that a king doesn't like?"

"No, I can't imagine that, or at least I can't imagine it when I'm awake. Possibly, I might be able to dream about seventeenth-century prisons, but I don't think I really want to."

"Back then, prison must have been so much worse than it is today."

"You sound like you know about prison." As Rose stared at Greg's face, he looked away at the dance floor. After a few seconds, Greg waved at his two books that were lying on the table. He picked up the second book.

"People today often think that the Pilgrims just got passage on the *Mayflower* for free." Greg opened the book and started to explain. "Thomas Weston was the leader of the Adventurers. Cushman, Carver, and over sixty other people were also members of this group of people."

"What did the Adventurers have to do with the Pilgrims?"

"These were the ones who gave the Pilgrims some money in exchange for an investment contract. The Pilgrims obviously had to pay them back for their investment. Godfrey Hodgson, the author of *A Great and Godly Adventure*, said:

> *Mayflower's* voyage was, on the part of the Adventurers, a hard-headed commercial investment, and one which they, and in particular Weston, took advantage of to bilk the religious Pilgrims of large amounts of money....Weston, having raised seven thousand pounds from his investors, laid out not much more than fifteen hundred pounds in equipping the settlers.[21]"

"So the Pilgrims were liable for a debt worth at least 7,000 pounds, but they only got 1,500 pounds of goods?"

"Yeah. Some historian said that the 'merchant adventurers who financed the *Mayflower's* voyage...treated the Pilgrims much as a loan shark treats a man in financial difficulties.'[22]"

"We all know what loan sharks are like." Rose paused before adding, "I know money has been a big part of history."

"Everyone knows how important money is."

"There have been thieves throughout history. Even the Bible mentions them."

"Really?" Greg asked with a surprised look on his face.

"Yeah. One of the ten commandments is 'You shall not steal.'" (Exod. 20:15 RSV).

"No one follows all of those commandments anymore."

Rose stared at Greg for a few seconds before saying, "People should be following all of the commandments. They're from God."

Greg laughed before saying, "I was just kidding."

Rose smiled hesitantly, unsure about whether she could believe him or not. She then said, "Anyway, I never realized before that things like high interest rates and loan sharks existed in the seventeenth century."

"How about pirates? They've been sailing on the oceans for centuries."

Rose said, "You're right. I guess as long as there's any money around, there will be loan sharks, thieves, and pirates."

"Definitely."

"Hard-working people should be able to spend their own hard-earned money in whatever way they want to, without worrying about it being stolen away by a lazy thief."

"I don't think thieves are lazy." Greg's facial expression showed that he meant what he had just said. "Many people think that being a thief is an easy way to earn a living, but taking someone else's hard-earned cash still means that the thief will be doing some work. Sometimes, being a thief is even dangerous. So, in a way, being a thief is a tough job, not an easy one."

Rose frowned and then looked down at her knee. "Thieves often hurt innocent people."

"I'm sure they do, but most thieves probably don't mean to hurt anyone."

Rose was still frowning. She looked out at the dancers; they were all happily dancing to East Coast swing music.

She turned back to Greg and asked, "Do you know if the Pilgrims helped the investors to finance their own trip?"

"Yeah, they did. The ones who were going on the *Mayflower* had to sell off their homes and belongings. Some of the other Pilgrims contributed fairly large financial amounts, like William Brewster, Thomas Brewer, George Morton, John Carver and his wife, William Bradford, John Turner, William White, Edward Winslow, and Isaac Allerton."[23]

"You seem to know a lot about history."

"I do. When I was younger, I even thought about becoming a history teacher."

Rose laughed. "You should meet my mom."

"Does she also like history?"

"She's a high school history teacher."

Greg's eyes widened. "Oh, that's really neat! As her daughter, you probably know a lot about history, too."

"I know a little bit more than most people, but until lately, I wasn't really that interested in history. My mom would say things, and like most kids, I just wouldn't listen to her."

"How about now? Did she tell you anything about the sampler?"

"Oh, she thinks it's at least a hundred years old."

"What kinds of designs are on it?"

"Do the designs really matter?" Rose asked. She turned her head toward the dance floor, waved her right hand at one of the dancing couples, and then tried to change the subject: "Oh, look at Randy and Kathy dancing together! Aren't they great?"

Greg looked at the couple. They were dancing the Viennese Waltz; at the moment, they were doing a series of turns without any indication of slowing down or becoming dizzy. Greg said, "They're great. Are they professional dancers?"

"Yeah, they are the co-owners of The Dancin' Feelin.' That's a dance studio where a couple of my friends go for lessons."

Kate came up to the table, sat down next to Rose, pointed at the dancers, and said: "Now they're doing a promenade run-around."

Greg briefly watched the couple before looking at Kate. "I think it's great that you know the names of the steps they're doing."

"Thanks."

Rose said to Kate, "You not only know the names of the steps, but you can also do them."

"If you take lessons for just a few months, you'll learn a lot more steps."

Jim Davenport, one of Kate's friends, came up to their table. Kate smiled at him and said, "This is a merengue. Rose and Greg should be able to dance it with us."

Rose stood up. "I only took one dance lesson for the merengue, but I think I can still follow someone okay."

Jim held out his hand to Rose, and Kate coaxed Greg out onto the floor. The two couples danced near each other on the dance floor. Whenever Jim held up his hand for Rose to turn around, Greg also held up his hand for Kate to turn. When the music stopped, the two couples split up. Jim and Kate stayed on the dance floor together while Rose and Greg walked back to their table.

Greg pulled out a chair for Rose, and she thanked him. He sat down next to her and asked, "Are there any dancers on your sampler?"

"No, I don't think so." Rose looked away from him and took a sip of her soda.

"Did you know the shape and designs on a sampler sometimes indicate its age?"

"No, I didn't know that." Rose still was not looking at him. She sighed and then drank more of her soda.

"The earlier samplers were long rectangles, and the later ones usually were square."

"That's interesting."

"The designs also can indicate a sampler's age. What are sometimes called 'map samplers' were probably done in the nineteenth century or later."

Rose looked with surprise at Greg. "Really?"

"Yeah. Map samplers have geographical designs on them. Sometimes these designs can help to ascertain an age for the artifact. For example, a sampler with pictures of forty-eight states probably will be more recent than a sampler containing images of only forty-two states."

Rose was uncertain about what to say; she turned her head so that she could look at the dancers.

"Does your sampler have a map on it?"

Rose glanced at Greg, frowned, and then looked away from him again. After watching the dancers for a minute, she said, "There were flowers and months of the year on it."

"Months?"

"Yeah, January, February, March, April." Rose's voice abruptly stopped after saying the word "April."

"So, there are only four months on your sampler? Was it left unfinished?"

"I don't remember exactly." Rose was still watching the dancers. Suddenly, she stood up and said, "Oh, I have to say 'hi' to someone. I'll be back in a minute." Rather than walking through the middle of the dancers, she walked around the edge of the room until she reached the other side. She then moved over to one of the tables and said, "Hi, I'm Rose. Can I sit here for a minute?"

"Of course. You can stay for as long as you want to." The lady smiled before adding, "I'm Joan."

Rose sat down next to Joan and then looked back across the room. Because there were so many dancers on the floor, she was unable to see Greg anywhere. She did spot Kate, though, dancing with Jim. They were only about six feet away and were near the edge of the dancers.

Rose said good-bye to Joan and then walked over to see Kate and Jim. She tapped Kate's arm, and Kate stopped dancing and turned to face her. "Hi, Rose. Are you okay?"

"I'm fine. I just don't like that guy Greg. He's asking too many questions about my sampler."

"Oh, okay. Is there anything I can do to help?"

"Yeah, there is. I have to get up early in the morning anyway. If you could ask Greg to dance, I can grab my purse and leave while you're dancing with him."

"That sounds like a plan. Since this song might be almost over, though, I'll wait until the next song before asking him to dance."

"Thanks, Kate. I'll just wait here until the next song starts."

"Okay. I'll say good-bye to everyone for you."

"Thanks again. You are the greatest friend!"

"No, you are the greatest friend!"

Jim laughed. "If the two of you are both the greatest, where do I stand?"

Rose said, "You also are the greatest. With all of the people in the dance hall tonight, I'm sure it's okay if there are three great people."

The song stopped playing, and another one began. Kate said good-bye and quickly walked around the room until she was back at the table where Greg was seated. When she asked him to dance, he immediately accepted. A minute after they were on the dance floor, Rose came back to the table, changed her shoes, picked up her purse, and left the dance hall. By the time she had arrived back home, it was after ten o'clock. As she got ready for bed, she kept her thoughts focused on what she wanted to lucid dream about that night: the Pilgrims and the reasons why they wanted to come to America.

When Rose lay down, her eyes blinked at the brightness of the lamp next to her bed. As she closed her eyes, she saw some light streaming across the blackness in front of her. It looked almost like a comet's tail.

A Comet

As Rose fell asleep, the streaming light made her think about the comet on the sampler. Within the dark background of her closed eyes, a light began to shine. The light became brighter and more circular. It then assumed the shape of a comet in the sky. Just like on the sampler, its front part turned greenish-blue, and its tail was a white light.

Different people in colonial clothing appeared beneath the comet. They were all looking up at the sky with anxious faces. One of the people was Sir Dudley Carleton, the English ambassador to the Dutch. A voice said, "That star doth move!"

The comet's white tail of light began to look like moving stars and then like bullets from a gun, shooting across the sky. The light's rays acted as if they were small, fast suns, rising up and then moving quickly across the horizon. When the comet was no longer visible, Rose realized that she was moving ahead in time. She saw a group of people dressed in seventeenth-century clothing. Several of them looked sick and then fainted.

In the middle of the group of people, someone said, "So many are ill."

Another voice said, "There will be war."

"'Tis all because of the shooting star."

Rose said out loud, "This dream might be a nightmare. I need to wake up." She scrunched her eyebrows as she tried to open her eyes, but she was unable to wake herself up.

Within her dream world, Rose looked up at the sky. The comet was not there, but the clouds had the words "Leiden" and "July 1620" written across their white puffiness. Rose had no watch on, so she didn't know what time it was. The sun was low in the sky, so it was either early in the morning or late in the afternoon.

A lady walked up to her and said, "Good morrow."

"Good morning," Rose said.

The lady stood still, staring silently at her.

Rose asked, "Is it the morning or the afternoon?" The lady was still silent. Rose pointed to the sun. "Did the sun just rise?"

"Ay, the sun hath risen," the lady said in a voice that sounded distant. Her distant voice made her mouth fly off of her face and go flying up the street. The lady turned around to look at her mouth, which was already more than thirty feet away. She began to run up the street and chase after her mouth. When she caught her mouth, she placed it back onto her face. The lady turned back to briefly look at Rose before she disappeared around the corner.

Rose took a few steps and then peered inside a house. Both the door and the window were open. Seated around a table was a family: a father, a mother, and three children. The father was reading a prayer, and Rose heard a section of the "Morning Prayer." The Pilgrims prayed that all of their "thoughts, words, and deeds, may redound to the glory of thy name and good ensample of all men, who seeing our good works, may glorify thee our heavenly Father."[24]

Rose continued to walk down the street. After a few minutes, the sound of a bell ringing in a tower made some of the people leave their homes and go into other buildings. Rose saw a group of four children run into an old cement building. She went over to the open window and looked inside. The children were all seated on the dirt floor. On a bench in front of them were some knitting needles, yarn, and scissors. A cat was standing at the edge of the bench, watching the yarn, and waiting for the children to start moving it around.

One of the older children said, "It was much too early for that bell to ring. We nearly had no time for our morning prayers with our parents."

"Our family is very merry during prayer time."

"I had time to eat just one piece of bread."

"We must begin. Canst thou please hand me the yarn and the scissors?"

The youngest child passed the yarn and scissors to the older child.

"Thanks. I am so happy that thou art handing the scissors to me in a correct manner."

"I thank thee. Yesterday, thou showedst me how to pass the scissors. I was pointing the sharp blades at thee, like we were at war. Now I know how to point the handles at thee, like we will join our hands in peace."

"Ay, it is safest to point the handles, instead of the sharp blades, at the person which is receiving them. Thou art quick to learn things."

"That is because thou art a good teacher."

The two children smiled at each other. The oldest child showed the youngest one a finished pair of woven socks; he then explained how to do the first stitch.

"I cannot do that stitch," the Youngest Leiden Child said.

"Thou needest to watch my hands, which are moving the needles, instead of watching the needles."

"The wool maketh my hands itch."

"Thou canst learn how to make this stitch," the Oldest Leiden Child replied.

"I will not never be a good weaver."

"Ay, thou surely wilt be a good weaver. Weaving is a job that thou canst most easily learn."

The Second Oldest Leiden Child said, "Didst thou know that half of us Pilgrims in Leiden have become 'textile workers'[25]?"

"Ay. Many of my friends are weavers."

"Here in Leiden, when we get older, we will do good work in the textile trade. When we lived in Amsterdam, many of the laws were made for the trade guilds. The laws did not allow people like us to be hired."

The Youngest Leiden Child watched his older brother's hands and then tried to do the first stitch again. He was successful, and the other three children—all at the same time—yelled out, "Huzzah!" The Youngest Leiden Child knew his siblings were congratulating him. His face broke out into a giant smile. He then looked at his older brother and said in a soft voice, "I thank thee for helping me."

"Thou art working very hard, so all of us will have more food."

As Rose watched the children knit woolen socks, a piece of yarn fell to the floor. The cat immediately pounced on it and pulled it away. As the cat shook its head, the yarn started to move back and forth, like the pendulum on a clock. The sunlight soon disappeared, and shadows began to appear. It was evening. Rose looked for the children, but they were no longer in the building. She said out loud, "They must have gone home," but no one was near enough to hear her words.

Rose walked down the street until she came to a small house. She looked inside the open window. The only light in the ten by twenty foot room was a single candle. Two adults and four children were crowded around a small table. The parents were teaching the children how to read the Bible. The father said, "Geneva" and showed the youngest child a study note at the bottom of one of the pages. Rose realized that they were reading the *Geneva Bible,* which "was the first Bible to qualify as a study Bible, providing readers with copious notes, annotations, and commentary about the original manuscripts, clarification of ambiguous meanings, and cross references."[26]

Rose walked away from the window and carefully moved down the side of the street. There were pebbles, broken branches, and other items that she was unable to see too well in the darkness. The main source of light was the moon; sometimes, though, a little bit of light seeped out of a window from one of the houses.

After passing a group of five houses, Rose stopped walking. She heard a lady say, "We do not have no more." Rose thought the lady's voice sounded familiar. Was this lady someone she had heard before in her real life? Perhaps she was a customer in her bank or a sales lady in a store. Rose looked closely at the lady, who was dressed like a Pilgrim; her hat had a feather in it.

A Hammer-voiced Man said, "Thou hadst sold to me only a house that is very small and ten pieces of clothing and four shoes and some old dishes and two shovels."

The Feather-hat Lady's husband said, "Can you buy from us the tables and beds that are on the inside of our house?"

Rose realized that the Feather-hat Lady's husband was using "you" to show respect to the other man. The Hammer-voiced Man, though, was using "thou" to refer to the Feather-hat Lady's husband, possibly to say that he thought his customer was of an inferior status.

The Hammer-voiced Man stamped his foot as he said, "Ay, I also will buy those things from thee. And with more things of value, I can sell tickets to both of you."

Rose wondered about the word "you" that she had just heard. Was the man now trying to show respect, or was he using "you" because he needed a plural pronoun?

The Feather-hat Lady's husband said, "You now have everything that belongeth to us."

The Hammer-voiced Man asked, "Why do you wish to go on this voyage?"

"We wish to convert savages in the New World. And we need more freedom to worship God."

The Hammer-voiced Man turned aside and muttered half to himself, "Puritans!" He then made a sour face before turning back to look at the lady.

The Feather-Hat Lady frowned slightly before saying in a polite voice, "It pleaseth our most glorious Lord when we do His will."

Her husband said a quote from 2 Corinthians 5:9 in the Bible: "Wherefore also we covet, that both dwelling at home, and removing from home, we may be acceptable to him" (2 Cor. 5:9 GNV). Rose smiled as she realized that the bible verse was talking about doing God's will, whether someone stayed at home or left home.

The darkness of the street disappeared. The cobblestones in the road's surface were now reflecting bright lights, looking as if streetlights were shining down upon them. Rose glanced up into the sky; there were no streetlights there, but the moon and the stars were unusually bright. She looked back down at the road. She could now see some of the items that the Feather-hat Lady and her husband had brought: books, a big iron kettle, pottery, shovels, an ax, a saw, blankets, a tablecloth, and kitchen utensils.

The Hammer-voice Man said, "Good. Thou art almost ready to leave Leiden and sail across the ocean. Thou wilt not need none of these things in thy new home."

"We will need books and tools and kitchen items," the Feather-hat Lady said. "We have been praying that other Pilgrims will share their items with us."

The husband raised his right hand, which was holding onto a book. He opened up the book and said, "We are doing what the study note in the bible saith about leaving home: "[B]oth in this our pilgrimage here [on Earth] we may please him, and that at length we may be received home to him [in heaven]."[27] Rose understood that the note for the bible verse was talking about two different homes: one on Earth and one in Heaven. People could please God on this Earth and then travel to be with him in Heaven.

The Feather-hat Lady said, "Thou also, as a merchant man who is staying here in Leiden, may travel on a pilgrimage while doing the work of our Lord."

"Perhaps what thou sayest is true." The Hammer-voice Man's face seemed thoughtful for a few seconds, and then he looked at the stack of items near the Puritans' feet. "These goods are not everything that thou ownest. What about thine ostrich feather?"

"What ostrich feather?" the husband asked.

"The feather that standeth in the hat of thy wife."

The Feather-hat Lady reached up to her hat and ran her hand over the full length of the feather. A breeze started up, and the feather started to move around, looking almost like it was trying to escape. The lady's voice fluttered more than the feather as she said, "Please ask me not for that feather. 'Twas a wedding present given to me by my mother."

Her husband took off his own hat and handed it to the Hammer-voiced Man. "Thou wilt take my hat."

"Nay. I want the feather which quivereth in the hat of thy wife. 'Tis the most prettiest feather that ever I have seen. My wife needeth such a feather for her hat."

The husband took a step forward and clenched his fists; then his shoulders tensed up. His wife touched his elbow, and immediately, the man's shoulders became less tense while still looking strong. The husband did not swear, but when he spoke, the tone of his voice hammered out the words more strongly than the Hammer-voiced Man had ever done: "Thou knowest that women are weak. How dare thee do this to one of our women!"

The Hammer-voiced man looked down at the ground, and his eyes surveyed all of the possessions that were piled in front of his feet. With his eyes still turned toward the ground, he said in a slurky tone, "I need the feather of thy wife for my own wife."

The Feather-hat Lady looked at her husband. "Thou knowest that I am strong, which is why thou saidst I can go with thee on this first trip across the ocean, instead of staying behind with the wives that are weak."

Her husband said, "My love, I know thou art strong, but thou art still a woman."

She said in a tender voice, "I beseech thee, please let me do my part in our pilgrimage."

He looked into her eyes, which showed him her strength and her love. His facial expression changed. He said in a tender voice, "With all of my heart, I thank thee."

Slowly, she took her hat off and carefully took the feather out. Extending the quivering ostrich feather to the Hammer-voiced Man, she whispered, "Will this be enough?"

He grabbed onto the feather, which tried to fly away from him. It twisted and turned, making noises against the man's fingernails. Then the man squished the feather's edges so tightly that it was unable to turn around, fly off, or escape. "The feather and other possessions of thine have paid for thy passage. First, you will take the *Speedwell* to England, and then you will be sailing to the New World."

The Feather-hat Lady's husband said, "We thank thee."

The Hammer-voiced Man said, "Farewell."

The Feather-Hat Lady and her husband walked down the next street. After about ten steps, they stopped and looked at her hat. He then helped her to place the hat on top of her head. Their hands briefly touched before gripping tightly onto each other. As they looked into each other's eyes, they began to talk softly about their upcoming trip. Rose only heard some of their words: "Thanks be to our Lord."

"With only a few possessions, we are still blessed."

"When is our time to depart?"

"Soon, we will make haste for the *Speedwell*."

"And the *Speedwell* will be a fast ship."

"And we shall speed well to get onto the *Speedwell*." Their laughter was loud as they began to run down the street and away from Rose. Within a minute, they had reached the corner of the street, turned right, and were no longer visible.

Rose found herself standing by herself. A box slowly grew up out of one of the cobblestones in the street. She opened up the old wooden box, and her husband Travis climbed out of it. His left hand, though, was still inside of the box. He looked at Rose, frowned, and pulled his left hand out of the box. His hand had no wedding ring on it. However, a woman's hand was now attached to his hand. When he pulled his hand up higher, the entire woman climbed out of the box. Travis and the other woman stood there in the street, holding hands and staring at each other. Travis then gave her a kiss. The sun set and rose several times before Travis and the lady were finished with their kiss.

Rose then asked Travis, "Who is this woman?"

Travis turned toward Rose, but he seemed to be looking right through her as if she were invisible. He then looked back at the other woman, who was rubbing her knee as if she had hurt it. Travis asked her, "Can I help you with anything?"

Rose started to yell: "This isn't fair! You can't help this strange woman when you didn't even help me!"

Travis and the other woman went back into the box. Rose walked up to the box and looked inside, but Travis was no longer there. The box only contained pictures of him. Rose picked up a stack of the pictures. They were ones that Rose had taken. Some of the pictures had Travis with other people, but none of them contained Rose and Travis together.

A breeze started to blow, and the pictures flew away into the wind. Rose followed the pictures, flew into the air near them, and then turned onto a different street; she soon came to a church: the PIeterskerk. Across the street from this church was the Reverend

John Robinson's house, which was "called 'DeGroene Poort' ('The Green Close,' sometimes romantically misnamed 'The Green Gate')….in whose garden a dozen small houses were built for other members of the congregation."[28]

From her position above the street, Rose could see the small houses in the garden area. The windows were open, and groups of happy faces peered out at Rose. After a few moments, the people left the small houses and walked over to the Reverend Robinson's house. Rose followed them and landed on the street in front of the Robinson house. Looking into a window, she saw some people talking and some people humming music. A voice said, "Psalm 8."

Rose listened as different voices joined together in a joyful song. When the singing stopped, someone said, "Here are two of my favorite lines from that Psalm."

"Are you reading from the psalter or the bible?"

"I am reading Psalm 8, verses 8 and 9, from the bible." The room became quiet, and then the voice continued: "The fowls of the air, and the fish of the sea, and that which passeth through the paths of the seas. / O Lord our Lord, how excellent is thy Name in all the world!" (Ps. 8:8-9 GNV).

Various voices began to talk about the verse. Rose could hear some of the words: "Our path…the Atlantic…fowls and fish…*Speedwell.*" The voices next compared the words of the psalms in the *Geneva Bible* with the sometimes rephrased psalm wordings in Ainsworth's *Book of Psalms.* She heard the words "Atlantic Ocean," followed by discussion of the Fall and Winter weather in Northern Virginia and elsewhere. Several people began to cry. The crying noises were intermingled with words of comfort: "Peace…fare thee well…God is always with thee."

Several more psalms were sung. After the singers had stopped, two Puritans left the house, and Rose followed them. The first Puritan was a boy; he turned to the second one—an adult—and asked, "Do you know, Mister Edward Winslow, about the history of the book of psalms?"

"Ay, young lad. It was 'specially prepared for the fugitive congregations of 'Separatists' in Holland by Henry Ainsworth and published in Amsterdam in 1612.'"[29]

"Will a book of psalms be taken by the Pilgrims on the *Mayflower?*"

"Ay. The book of psalms will be taken to the new world, but I do not have knowledge of whose books will traverse the ocean and whose will remain behind. The copy of the book that thou wast holding in the house of our pastor may remain here with our pastor."

"Some of the songs were joyful, and some were sad."

"The singing of the psalms showeth the feelings of God's people."

"Mister Winslow, there were so many tears today."

"Ay, our congregation will be separated into those who will voyage to the new world and those who must remain behind."

Rose walked up to the Puritans and tried to interrupt their conversation by saying, "The Separatists will be separated into two groups when they really want to be united." Neither Edward Winslow nor the younger Puritan heard Rose's words.

Edward Winslow said, "With the very many sad tears today, there was also much joy about the voyage that soon will begin. All of us were 'making joyful melody in our hearts as well as with the voice, there being many of our congregation very expert in music; and indeed it was the sweetest melody that ever mine ears heard."[30]

The young Puritan shook his head in agreement as he and Edward Winslow began walking down the road together. As if they were moving in a different time frame from Rose's, they began to walk very quickly down the road and off into the distance. Within a few seconds, Rose could no longer see them.

She started to walk down the same road, hoping to be able to find the Puritans again. She said, "This is a lucid dream. I should be able to make them come back here."

Immediately, she found herself in a crowd of Puritans who were standing near a boat. One of the Puritans asked, "Doth our boat have a name?"

A different voice said, "Ay. 'Tis called the *Speedwell.*"

The crowd of Puritans was composed of multiple small groups of people; the smaller groups were all talking among themselves. Rose kept hearing three phrases over and over again: "Bless thee," "Pray remember me," and "Fare thee well." Some of the people were crying; some were hugging one another, and some were shaking each other's hands.

Next to Rose was a Puritan who pointed to a man in the middle of the crowd and said, "There is in front of us our John Carver."

John Carver looked at the Puritan who had said his name, smiled, and waved. He then raised a piece of paper up high above his head, and all of the Pilgrims immediately stopped talking. They looked at him, waiting expectantly for him to speak.

After a few seconds of silence, John Carver said, "Here is 'John Robinson's Farewell Letter.' He asked me to kindly read it to you." John began to read the letter. Rose was too far away to hear all of the words; however, she still realized that some of the words and ideas were similar to what would later be written into the *Mayflower Compact:*

Loving and Christian Friends,

I do heartily, and in the Lord, salute you all…after this heavenly peace with God and our own consciences, we are carefully to provide for peace with all men…with common employments, you join common affections truly bent upon the general good…[Y]ou are to become a

Body Politic, using amongst yourselves Civil Government, and are not furnished with any persons of special eminency above the rest to be chosen by you into Office of Government, let your wisdom and godliness appear, not only in choosing such persons as do entirely love, and will diligently promote, the common good; but also in yielding unto them all due honour and obedience in their lawful administrations....These few things, therefore, and the same in few words, I do earnestly commend unto you care and conscience, joining therewith my daily incessant prayers until the Lord, that he (who hath made the heavens and the earth, the sea and all rivers of water, and whose Providence is over all his works, especially over all his dear children for good) would so guide and guard you in your ways (as inwardly by his Spirit, so outwardly by the hand of his power) as that both you, and we also for and with you, may have after matter of praising his name, all the days of your, and our, lives.

Fare you well in him in whom you trust, and in whom I rest!...[31]

After John Carver had finished reading John Robinson's letter, several of the people who had listened intently to the letter began crying. Rose noticed that the Feather-hat Lady, with tears running down her face, was standing off by herself. Then one of the other Separatist women walked up to her and said, "It pleaseth God that thou wilt accompany your husband to the New World."

The Feather-hat Lady blinked her eyes multiple times, which made her tears stop falling; then she said, "I thank thee for thy words of comfort."

The Separatist Lady replied, "Thou art blessed."

"I thank thee, but thou art blessed also."

"Thou art more so. For on this voyage of God's people from Leiden to England and then to New England, not all of our men are bringing their wives," the Separatist Lady said. She then frowned while thinking about men being separated from their wives.

"We all know that women are weaker than men. After this first voyage, the Pilgrims will build a village. Then more women will sail to the new colony."

"And while our men build our village, they also may be at war with the Indians," the Separatist Lady said.

The Feather-hat Lady grabbed onto a pair of scissors that was hanging on a string attached to the waist of her apron. "We need to be of good courage."

"Many will be praying for thy safety."

"I have been praying that we will not never have a war with the Indians."

"I also have been praying for peace with the Indians."

"We are going to the New World to convert the Indians, so they will believe in our Lord and Savior, Jesus Christ. How can we convert an enemy that we are shooting?"

"Our Lord will determine if it will be a time for war or a time for peace with the Indians."

"Ay, thou art right." The Feather-hat Lady let go of her scissors, which paused in the air for a few seconds before dropping down to rest peacefully against her apron.

"Our most glorious Gospel says, 'To all things there is an appointed time, and a time to every purpose under the heaven'" (Eccles. 3:1 GNV).

"We must all be of good courage."

"Ay. Those of us that wait in Leiden for a later voyage also will have many problems."

"Leiden is now almost as bad as is London." The Feather-hat Lady reached up to the top of her hat. The feather was no longer there, but she kept moving her hand over the tiny hole where the feather used to be. As her hand moved, her facial expression seemed reflective; she looked like she was remembering past activities she had done with her feather. The memories were soothing to her anxious hand.

"Thou art right. The laws have changed."

"People that are not members of the Dutch Reformed Church are having many problems."

"The law now states that we can no more collect alms for ministers and orphans and old people."

Rose said, "So the government is trying to eliminate your welfare system for your church community." Both ladies shook their heads in angry agreement with each other; they looked almost as if they had heard Rose's comment.

"People have more poverty." The Feather-hat Lady was still touching the small hole in her hat where the feather used to be. The hole suddenly became larger until its emptiness nearly covered the whole top of the hat.

"War is coming with Spain and Austria." The Separatist Lady looked up into the sky and then focused on the horizon. "War will arrive too soon."

"Ay. I pray for the mercy of God on the people that live in Leiden."

"Many of the Dutch people have changed. They now are very mean to those of us who have a different religion."

"At least in the New World, we will have more freedom to worship our Lord and to help our people in need." The Feather-hat Lady placed her hands together, looking as if she were praying.

"Dost thou remember when stones were thrown at James Chilton? He was walking to his home from his church. He was nearly killed because the stone-throwers thought of him as someone that was different."

"Ay. That happened in April of last year."

"In times like these, we all need the help of God."

The Feather-hat Lady squeezed her hands together, blinked her eyes to hold back her tears, and then said, "Amen."

The ladies hugged each other. Then the Separatist Lady said, "Next year, we may have enough money to pay for our passage across the Atlantic. If it pleaseth our Lord, I will join thee in the New World."

"I will be the first one on the shore to welcome thee."

"And I will be so very happy to see thee again."

"Perhaps our Reverend John Robinson will sail with thee next year."

The two ladies hugged one last time. Then a bell started to ring. Rose wondered if it was the bell in the tower, which rang to tell people in the Yarn Market when it was time to go to work and when it was time to return home. She looked up at the tower, which said "July 1620," but she felt as if she were temporarily in a later time period. She heard some words being spoken by Bradford about the Pilgrims leaving Leiden: "So they left that goodly and pleasant city which had been their resting place near twelve years; but they knew they were pilgrims, and looked not much on those things, but lift up their eyes to the heavens, their dearest country, and quieted their spirits."[32] Rose remembered that these words about the Pilgrims were from Bradford's *Of Plymouth Plantation;* Bradford had used the word "pilgrims" while he was describing the people leaving Leiden on the *Speedwell.* From her readings about the Pilgrims' history, Rose knew: "It was owing to this passage, first printed in 1669, that the *Mayflower's* company came eventually to be called the Pilgrim Fathers."[33]

The bell from the tower was still ringing. Rose looked at the bell and concentrated on making it stop; she moved one of her hands above her head and twirled her hand around. After a couple of turns, she was able to make the ringing stop.

When Rose's eyes left the tower and turned back to look at the Separatists, she instead saw two ships: the *Mayflower* and the *Speedwell.* Both of the ships now were in Southampton, England. She knew that the *Mayflower* had been leased by the Pilgrims to carry some of them and their supplies to the New World. The *Speedwell* had been bought so that the Pilgrims would have more than one boat for the trip across the Atlantic Ocean; also, the *Speedwell* was supposed to be kept by the Pilgrims in the New World so that it could be used as their fishing vessel. It was hoped that selling fish and other goods would help the Pilgrims to get out of their debt with the Merchant Adventurers of London, the group of investors who were financing many of the costs of the Pilgrims' trip.

The main sails of the two ships were tall and strong; rather than being pushed around by the wind, they seemed to be controlling the wind. As Rose watched, clouds appeared and surrounded the sails. One of the clouds had a dollar sign on it. Within the cloud and next to the dollar sign were pictures of Thomas Weston and other Merchant Adventurers. Thomas Weston moved over to the dollar sign and began to pull on its top half. He stole a part of the dollar sign and then tried to hide from other people by putting on a blacksmith's outfit. Some of the other Merchant Adventurers also attacked the dollar sign, pulled off the parts that had been their investment money, put the dollar sign pieces into their pockets, and then snuck away from the cloud. The dollar sign became smaller and smaller until it disappeared. Some Pilgrims appeared within the cloud; after they had sold off some of the butter that they needed for their food on the ocean voyage, the dollar sign became partially visible again.

Another cloud had a contract in it, but its terms kept on changing. Finally, a finished version stood still; the cloud had turned gray, and the contract looked as if it were being held captive inside of a stone fortress—no one could change it again. Even though most of the Pilgrims were frowning in unhappiness over the changed terms, they still all walked up to the contract and signed it with a quill pen. The quill looked strangely like the feather from the Feather-hat Lady's hat.

After the Pilgrims were finished with the quill pen, they set it down, but it was still trapped with the contract inside of the gray cloud. The cloud moved until it landed just above the deck of the *Speedwell*. A disguised person, who might have been the master of the *Speedwell*, walked out of the cloud, stepped softly onto the deck of the ship, looked around to make certain no one was looking, and then put on additional sails that would make the ship leak water. He then said to one of the seagulls, "My friend, do not worry thyself. Those Puritans will not make us sail on this voyage with them. There is too little food, and 'tis too late in the year to begin a trip across the rough seas of the Atlantic."

Rose looked at her watch. In the center of the watch's face was a Pilgrim, who was pointing to a date: "August 5." Rose asked her watch, "Is this the old calendar date system that was used by the Pilgrims?"

The Pilgrim in her watch said, "Ay."

Suddenly, the watch's face changed so that it contained a picture of her husband, Travis. He was holding onto a different date: August 15th, which was the new calendar date system that is used in the 21st century.

Rose said to him, "No wonder I am late so much; I must be using the old date and time system of our Puritan ancestors."

The Travis inside of the watch said, "No, you're not using their system. If you were, you would be early all of the time, rather than late."

"Maybe I'm just trying not to follow a corrected time system, which is what our ancestors initially did."

"How can people correct a time system? Did they rewind their watches?"

Rose explained the history of time to the face on her watch: "In 1582, Pope Gregory XIII changed the calendar system because the real time was ahead of the old Julian calendars. In 1582, Catholic countries went to the new calendar system. The

Puritans, as well as England, did not change to the new system until 1752."

"Perhaps you're just confused about time."

Before Rose could respond, Travis's face disappeared from the face of her watch. She then asked, "Watch, are you just going to show me some dates, or can you show me what happened on August 15th?"

In a rhythmic voice, Rose's watch said, "Yes, I'll show you—yes, you'll see—exactly what happened when they crossed the sea." The hour and minute hands on the face of her watch began to move; the straight lines became wider and wider until they took on the form of ships. They were soon recognizable as small versions of the *Mayflower* and the *Speedwell*. Aboard the two ships were crewmen, passengers, and supplies. Both of the ships began to move around the circular watch face; they looked as if they were moving around a circular globe. Before they had navigated across the face of the watch, water began to flow out of the *Speedwell*. Both ships turned around and went backwards, returning to their starting point in England. The *Speedwell* was sold and disappeared from the face of the watch. Some of the passengers and crew members decided not to leave England again. Many of them looked scared as they also disappeared from the face of the watch. Remaining on the watch's face were the most courageous of the passengers and crew members; they all boarded onto the *Mayflower*, which was paused on the watch's face, waiting for enough passengers and a correct time to leave. More passengers were needed. Additional ones eventually appeared; they used the watch's second hand to swing themselves onto the watch's face. These "strangers" joined the Separatists ("saints") for the historic voyage of the *Mayflower*. According to the new calendar system dates that were now appearing on Rose's watch, the voyage would begin on September 16, 1620 and end on December 21, 1620.

MAKING CONNECTIONS

Rose suddenly realized that she was thinking about the Pilgrims, rather than lucid dreaming about them. She turned to look at her alarm clock. It had already gone off. About five minutes ago, she must have automatically hit the snooze button to stop the sounds from her alarm clock, which would have been the ringing tower in her dream.

Rose turned off all three of her alarm clocks and jumped out of bed. By the time she was dressed, it was just before six o'clock. When the doorbell rang, she opened the front door for her parents. Her mom said, "I know we're a little early, but we can help with any last-minute packing."

Rose hugged her mom. "I only have to put on my make-up and eat something."

Her mom laughed. "You can do those things in my car."

Her dad said, "As usual, we already stopped at Dunkin' Donuts. There's some breakfast in the car."

Her mom asked, "Are you all set to leave?"

"Yeah, I just need my suitcase." Her father followed her into her bedroom, gave her an envelope with her train tickets in it, and picked up the suitcase.

"I can carry that, dad."

"I know you can. However, I'm your father, so I should carry it for you."

Rose and her father exchanged smiles. She then picked up her purse, turned off the lights, and said, "Thanks. And thanks for these train tickets, too." She put the tickets into her purse.

Rose followed her parents outside and got into her mother's car. On the way to the train station, they ate bagels and drank coffee. Rose had enough time to put on some make-up. Once at the train station, her father helped her again by carrying her suitcase from the car into the station.

After they were all inside the train station, Rose's mom pulled a stack of papers out of her purse and handed them to Rose. "Here are some printouts with information about the Pilgrims. Reading these should keep you busy while you're on the train."

"Thanks, mom. I already packed a couple of your books, but these papers look interesting." Rose put them inside of her large purse. Then she and her parents said "good-bye" and hugged each other. Before she knew it, she was on the train, and it was moving out of the station.

For the first part her trip, Rose fell asleep. When the train reached Penn Station, one of the Amtrak car attendants woke her up. After switching to another train for the trip into northern New York State, Rose stayed awake and read some of the papers that her mother had given her. Before she had finished reading even half of the pages, the train pulled into the Albany-Rensselaer Station. She left her railroad car, walked into the train station, and spotted her grandmother right away.

"I love that tall red hat of yours, Granny. I can always easily see you in a crowd of people."

"That's why I always wear it whenever I'm picking you up."

Rose followed Granny out to her car. For much of the trip to Granny's house, they discussed each other's health and the activities of some of their cousins. Then Granny said, "Your mom told me that you're learning about our family's history."

"Well, I've been reading a little bit about John Robinson, but mostly, I'm reading about the Puritans and the Pilgrims. So I'm learning about our country's history, too."

"Have you found out anything interesting?"

Rose pulled some papers out of her purse. "Here are some printouts from an Internet Website. Mom gave them to me so that I'd have something to look at on the train. I have some books, too."

"I can't really look at those while I'm driving, but you can tell me all about them."

"This printout has a list of the *Mayflower* passengers. There were two groups of passengers: the Leiden group and the London group."

"I knew there were two groups, but how many were in each group?"

"The Leiden group had twenty-nine men and women; they were called 'Saints.'[34] These Saints were only a small percent of the total number of Separatists."

"How many Separatists were there?"

"I read in other sources that there were over three hundred Separatists in Leiden. Anyway, the Separatists, as you know, were the Puritans who left England to go live in Holland. Only twenty-nine of these Separatists were able to come over on the first *Mayflower*."

Rose's grandmother sounded sad as she said, "I know the Separatists were upset to be separated into two different groups— one group went to the new world and the other group had to stay behind in Leiden."

"Yeah, I know. I've read about the people in the two groups. They prayed and cried a lot when they parted."

"I can't even imagine what it was like for them. Would you be able to say good-bye to some of your relatives as they left for a whole new world?"

"I don't think I could do that." Rose was silent for a moment as she thought about leaving her loved ones. Then she said softly, "It would be like going through a divorce when you were madly in love with someone."

Her grandmother slowed down and pulled over to the side of the road. As soon as she was safely parked inside of the emergency lane, she looked at Rose, who was wiping her eyes with a tissue. A tear fell onto the pile of papers in her lap. It landed under the word *"Mayflower,"* giving the ship some water for its trip.

"Are you still in love with Travis?"

"I don't know. But I do know that I really miss him." Rose cleared her throat and looked at her grandmother. "I wish there was an easy answer."

Her grandmother reached out and touched Rose's hand. "Have you spoken with Travis about how you feel?"

"No, I haven't."

"You probably should. You might be surprised by his response."

"But what if only one of us is still in love? How can I talk to him about love if he doesn't love me anymore?"

"Did you and Travis talk to the minister at your church? He might be able to help you, or he might be able to suggest a marriage counselor."

"For about ten minutes, we did speak to our minister, but we haven't had a chance to go back again."

"Well, now you know one thing for sure: you need to find the time to see the minister again."

Rose blew her nose, smiled at her grandmother, and said, "Okay. As soon as I get back home again, I'll see the minister, either by myself or with Travis."

Granny started the car up and pulled out into traffic. After a few minutes of listening to the radio, she asked, "What happened to the twenty-nine Separatists?"

"Actually, a larger group of Separatists left Leiden, stopped in England to pick up more people and supplies, and then left for America on two ships: the *Mayflower* and the *Speedwell*. The smaller ship, the *Speedwell*, was taking on too much water, so it had to go back to England."

"That's too bad."

"Other groups of Separatists came over to the new world in later crossings, though."

"Isaac Robinson, our ancestor, was in one of those later groups, right?"

"He was. In 1631, Isaac—one of the Reverend John Robinson's children—came over to Plymouth."

"Do you have any more information about the 1620 Pilgrims on the *Mayflower?*"

"Yeah. There were twenty-two people who boarded the ship in London. These twenty-two people were called 'Strangers.' The London 'strangers' included relatives of the Leiden group, investors who were hoping to make money in America, and people who just wanted "to start a new life with new opportunities.'[35]"

"So these strangers joined the Puritans from Leiden."

"Yeah. There were also thirty-three children and twenty staff members. The staff members were sailors and servants.[36]"

"Are you sure those numbers are accurate? I thought there were 102 people on the *Mayflower;* those numbers you read total up to 104."

"Actually, I think the numbers are correct. They include two children who were born during the trip to Plymouth. One of them, Oceanus Hopkins, was born while they were sailing on the Atlantic Ocean, and the other child listed here is Peregrine White; she was born right after their arrival in Provincetown Harbor, but before they officially had settled in Plymouth."

"She could be thought of as the first baby born to the Pilgrims in the New World."

"Yeah, she was."

"Peregrine's name sounds interesting."

"The word 'Peregrine' means 'Pilgrim.' Here's a picture of Peregrine White's cradle." Rose held the picture up so that her grandmother could see it out of the corner of her eye.

"That's a cute-looking cradle."

"Yeah, it is. According to the Pilgrim Hall Museum's Website, the hooded wicker cradle was brought over on the *Mayflower* from Holland.[37] Now people can see the actual cradle at the Pilgrim Hall Museum."

"I took your mom to that museum when she was in kindergarten. We probably saw that actual cradle."

"My mom took me to that museum, too. I just don't remember too many of the details. I'd love to visit it again someday."

"The next time I come out to visit you and your mom, we'll have to go there together."

"I'd love that."

"Do you have anything else interesting there?"

Rose shuffled the stack of papers around. "Yeah. There's a listing of names, including those who lived, died, and had descendants."

"Does it say how many descendants there are?"

"Yeah, I think so." Rose read silently for a minute from the first page of the printout. "Here it is: Gibson claims that over half of the Pilgrims had descendants and there are 'more than fifty million living today.'[38]"

"We probably walk past distant relatives of ours every day and don't even realize it."

"Yeah, I'm sure we do."

Rose's grandmother slammed on the brakes to avoid hitting a car that went through a red light. Rose's purse went flying forward and landed upside down on the floor. As she picked up her purse and some of the contents that had spilled out of it, she said, "Hopefully, that driver isn't one of our relatives."

Her grandmother laughed before saying, "You never can tell."

"Because he went through a red light, he probably is related to me. He was late for something and driving in too much of a hurry to notice anything."

"Now that's not true. I know you're a good driver."

"You haven't seen me drive when I'm late."

"There's no way you'd ever be that bad."

Rose sighed before saying, "You're so sweet, Granny."

For the rest of the trip, Rose silently read from her papers while her grandmother focused on driving. When they pulled into Granny's garage, Rose got out of the car first. She removed her suitcase from the car's back seat while her grandmother closed the garage door, unlocked the house's front door, and held it open for Rose.

"Thanks, Granny." Rose went into the kitchen and over to the refrigerator. "Do you have any soda in here?"

"Yeah. Please help yourself."

Rose took out a Coke for herself and a root beer for her grandmother. They went into the living room, turned on the TV, and watched the news for a few minutes. Then Rose picked up her suitcase, and her grandmother said, "You can have your usual room."

Rose went to the spare bedroom. The room's walls were sponge-painted in blue, and on the bedside table was a lamp with an iron base that looked like the *Mayflower*. From her previous visits, Rose remembered how nice the ship would look when she lay down on the bed: the blue swirls of the wall as a background would make the *Mayflower* appear to be sailing on a series of beautiful blue waves.

Rose only had to unpack clothing for a couple of days, so she was finished quickly. She then pulled out two alarm clocks from her suitcase. As usual, there were no clocks in the room because her grandmother always wanted visitors to relax while they were in her home. Rose set up one of the clocks on the bedside table and placed the other one back in the suitcase. She then pushed the suitcase under the bed. Even if her grandmother came into the room, noticed the clock on the table, and took it away, there would still be the other clock that was hidden in her suitcase.

Rose took a little more time to fix her hair and to put on some fresh lipstick. She finally went into the kitchen. Her grandmother had started to cook a meatloaf for supper. Rose asked, "Can I help with anything?"

"Oh, no. You need to relax."

Rose laughed. "You need to relax, too, Granny."

"I will. I'm going to read the paper in a minute. Do you want to read a section of the paper right now while I finish up in here?"

"No, thanks. I have a couple of books from my mom that I'd rather read."

Rose went back to her suitcase in the spare bedroom; she found Godfrey Hodgson's book, *A Great and Godly Adventure The Pilgrims and the Myth of the First Thanksgiving,* and brought it back with her into the living room. She sat down on the couch and began reading.

About twenty minutes later, her grandmother came into the living room with the *New York Times.* "Is that book about the Pilgrims?"

"Yeah, it is. This section explains about the Pilgrims separating from some of the other Puritans. Here's a quote about the parting of the two groups of Separatists: 'It is a great mistake to think of seventeenth-century Puritans as cold, undemonstrative people. The parting was emotional, with sighs and sobs and prayers and tears.'[39]

"We both know they must have been sad to leave each other."

"Yeah. Other sources have said the same thing. I even had a dream in which the Puritans were sad about their separation."

"Really?"

"Yeah. I've been creating a dream story about the Pilgrims. Over the past three nights, I've been dreaming about their time in England, Amsterdam, and Leiden. Tonight, I plan on dreaming about their historic voyage on the *Mayflower.*"

"Tomorrow morning, you'll have to tell me about what happens."

"Well, I think you already know that the *Mayflower* landed in Plymouth, but the details about the voyage are really interesting."

A ringing noise from the oven's timer was heard. Rose's grandmother went out into the kitchen to finish preparing supper. Rose followed her, commenting multiple times on the wonderful food.

The table had already been set, so Rose could only help by getting out some more sodas. Within a few minutes, the meatloaf, potatoes, and green beans were out on plates. Rose and Granny sat down together at the kitchen table. While they were eating, they talked about Rose's dreams and several of the newspaper stories. After dinner, they both put the dishes into the dishwasher. Granny then sat down in the living room while Rose went to get the sampler and the paper that went with it.

After Granny had looked at the sampler, Rose asked, "Do you think that circle on the sampler is a comet?"

"It could be an image of a comet. Or it could be a direct or indirect reference to a comet. On November 28, 1618, there actually was a comet."

"You're so good at remembering dates, granny."

"Thanks, Rose. Back in the seventeenth century, many people would have considered a comet to be some kind of a sign, possibly showing God's anger."

"I can understand why. Even in our time, if the sky is clear, a comet can make some people nervous."

"I think some information about comets and the seventeenth century is included in the book *Making Haste from Babylon.*"

Granny got up from her chair, walked over to the bookcase, and took out a book. After a minute, she started reading from one of the pages: "Even an envoy as shrewd as Carleton had little doubt that the comet conveyed a message in code from another dimension. For Carleton, it foretold the outbreak of a great European conflict. 'We shall have … warres,' he wrote home, and he was right."[40]

Rose asked, "Who was Carleton?"

"When the Pilgrims were in Holland, he was the English ambassador to the Dutch."

Rose paused briefly before saying, "So, people back in the seventeenth century thought a comet conveyed a code from a different dimension."

"Then the picture of a comet on the sampler might be a reference to some kind of a code."

"Well, you already talked to my mom about the word 'May' and the flower that's next to it, right?"

"Yeah. I think the sampler is using 'May' with the flower to refer to the *Mayflower.*"

Rose traced her hand along the vines. "My dad thinks these vines look like a map of Cape Cod and Plymouth."

"I agree. I'm just wondering if there is some other code in the sampler."

"Granny, do you think the word 'treasure' in the sampler and the note means that there's a family treasure somewhere?"

Rose's grandmother thought for a few seconds before answering. "I guess anything's possible. Your great, great grandfather worked in a bank."

"My mom told me about that." Rose paused and then asked, "Did you know I work in a bank, too, Granny?"

"Of course, everyone knows you're a bank teller. It's an important position that's only for completely honest people." Rose's grandmother smiled, showing her happiness over her granddaughter's job.

"So, do you think we have a family treasure?"

"It's possible. My mom told me that your great, great grandfather was madly in love with the 1918 $10,000 bills."

"I've seen pictures of those bills. The back of the bill has the Pilgrims and the Reverend John Robinson on it."

"Do you have any $10,000 bills at your bank?"

"No, the Federal Reserve Bank doesn't even make such large bills anymore. I've never been able to touch a bill larger than a hundred dollar bill."

"Oh, that's too bad." Granny got up and walked over to her bookcase. She brought an album over to Rose, flipped through some of the pages, and then showed Rose a drawing that looked like it had been done by a child. "This is a picture of your great, great grandfather."

"Who was the artist?"

"My mother."

Rose looked closely at the right hand of the man in the picture. "Is this supposed to be money?"

"Yeah. When my mom was older, she told me that it was one of those $10,000. bills that your great, great grandfather loved."

"I wonder if your mom ever really saw any of those bills."

"She probably did. Otherwise, why would she draw one?"

"She even put the $10,000. bill in the hand of the one person who might have worked near some of those bills."

Rose looked at the picture for another moment and then said, "Back then, there weren't any credit cards. People and banks needed a lot of cash. Most people these days don't need large amounts of cash, unless they're drug dealers or criminals."

"Well, I know your great, great grandfather wasn't a criminal. He was highly trusted and respected."

Rose said, "Okay. Do you have the watch case? We can try to see if the case and the sampler make some kind of a code together."

Granny got up, went into her bedroom, and came back a minute later. In her hand was a box. She opened it up and showed Rose the gold watch case. There were lines, waves, and small dots engraved on the middle and bottom parts of the case. At the top of the case were more vines that were surrounding the word "May" and a small design that could be a flower.

"These lines look sort of like vines. What do you think, Granny?"

"I always thought they were vines. The waves must be the ocean or a river."

"Do you think the dots are flowers or plants?"

"The case would have been made for a guy. So those dots would probably be some kind of plants, rather than flowers."

"Do you think the round design near the word 'May' is a flower?"

Granny looked closely at the design. "I think it could be a flower, or it might just be the vine twisting a little bit near the word 'May.'"

Rose took the case out of the box and looked at the back. It was smooth with no designs. Rose opened up the case and looked inside. There were still no designs, but some numbers were near the hinge. "Do you know what these numbers mean?"

"I don't know. I always thought they were some kind of product number. Can I see them?"

Rose passed the case back to her grandmother, who moved the case forward and backward as she tried to see the numbers. "Can you read them to me, Rose?"

"One is 42, and the other one is 71. Actually, the second number has a hyphen or a minus sign in front of it. There also are some fractions that I can't read."

"I was hoping the numbers would be someone's birthday or phone number, but the numbers aren't familiar to me."

"Well, I'll write them down for right now. We can e-mail these numbers with some pictures of the case to my mom. I think she also wanted pictures of us together."

"I'd love to have pictures of us, too."

"Okay, I'll get my camera."

"Let's wait until tomorrow. I'm sure my next-door neighbor would love to take pictures of us, but she won't be back until after nine o'clock tonight."

"All right."

"I'll text her right now; we can take the pictures and e-mail them to your mom tomorrow morning."

Granny sent a text on her cell phone. Within a minute, she received a positive response from her neighbor. "Tomorrow morning at nine o'clock, she'll come over and take our pictures."

"Okay. I'll be ready, but you'll have to wake me up in time so that I can put on my make-up."

"You don't need make-up. You're young and beautiful."

"Thanks, Granny."

Rose's grandmother took the watch case and put it up against the middle of the sampler. "I wonder if anything else is coded."

Rose and Granny both looked at the two objects together. Rose lay them down on the coffee table and tried different positions. She even tried flipping both the case and the sampler over to see if the backs of the objects added anything different to each other's designs.

Finally, Rose said, "I don't see anything. How about you, Granny?"

"No. I only see the vines, waves, and dots. When the case is on top of the sampler, though, the vines on the sampler and the case seem to be connected. They also appear slightly square-shaped."

"They do seem a little bit too square, almost like they're forming some kind of a grid."

"Well, your dad is good with maps. He might be able to figure something out."

"While we have the case, sampler, and camera all together, I might as well take a few pictures now. We can then just do the pictures of us in the morning."

"Okay."

Rose took pictures of the objects from different angles. Granny helped her by moving the two objects into different positions on the coffee table.

"So, Granny, it's obvious that the watch case and the sampler are connected to each other. One of our ancestors must have made the sampler to connect to the watch case."

"Well, the sampler was probably made by the grandmother of your great, great grandfather—the one who worked in the bank. I know this lady was into making samplers. My mother had a few of her samplers, but she had to sell them when she needed money."

"Oh, that's too bad. I would have loved to have seen more samplers like this one."

"Me, too. Anyway, in order to match the sampler, the watch case would have been seen by your great, great, great grandmother—do I have enough 'greats'?"

"So the watch case was probably made in the nineteenth century, sometime after 1850."

"Yeah."

Rose picked up the photo album on the coffee table, walked over to the bookcase, and put it back on one of the shelves. As she stood there, she looked at some of the DVD's on two of the other shelves. After silently reading some of the titles, she said, "I never saw this movie before."

"Which one?"

Rose took one of the DVD's off the shelf. "This one. It's called 'Desperate Crossing The Untold Story of the Mayflower.'"

Granny walked over to Rose, took the DVD out of her hand, and put it into the DVD player. "It's a great movie. I'll get us something to munch on while you're watching the first few minutes."

Rose sat down on the couch, picked up the remote control, and started to run the DVD. As soon as the actual film began, she paused it and waited until Granny came back from the kitchen.

"You didn't have to pause the movie for me. I already saw it before."

Rose said, "I knew by the way you looked at the DVD that you wanted to see the whole movie again."

Granny smiled. "You know me too well."

Rose hit the "play" button, and they both opened up their sodas and started to eat the chips and carrot sticks.

Halfway through the movie, Rose paused the DVD. "Do we need a break for a few minutes?"

"Yeah, I'll put a bag of popcorn into the microwave."

"Okay." While waiting for her grandmother to make some popcorn, Rose read a part of a study guide by Duane A. Cline titled "The Pilgrims and Plymouth Colony: 1620." When her grandmother came back into the living room, Rose said, "This printed study guide has some interesting information about the *Mayflower*."

"Really?"

"Yeah. Because the hold of the *Mayflower* had been used to carry barrels of wine around to different places, it was known as a 'sweet ship.'[41]"

"Why was the ship called "sweet"?"

"I'm sure the wine helped the hold to be a lot better in many ways, especially in comparison to some of the other ships back then. This study guide explains that the wine casks would sometimes leak; the spilled wine 'neutralized the garbage and other filth which sailors in those days threw into the hold instead of bothering to drop it overboard. That explains why the Pilgrims lost only one' person on their sixty-six day voyage.[42]"

"The alcohol in the spilled wine would have made the hold cleaner and safer."

"Also, the *Mayflower* probably smelled a lot nicer than many of the other ships."

Granny handed a bowl of popcorn to Rose before saying, "Even though there's no wine in this popcorn, it still smells really good."

"Yeah, it does. Thanks for making it."

"You're welcome."

"I love this kind."

"It's even low-fat. Let's watch the rest of the movie."

Rose put her study guide papers on the coffee table and hit the "play" button on the remote control. As she watched the movie, her eyes focused intently on the appearance of the ship and the Pilgrims; her expression showed her intent to participate in the Pilgrims' journey. Later that night, when she would be trying to have a lucid dream about the Pilgrims, she wanted to accurately envision their voyage to America.

When the movie was over, Rose helped Granny to clear away the bowls. They then got ready for bed.

VOYAGE OF THE MAYFLOWER

As Rose fell asleep, she focused on the *Mayflower* lamp that was next to her bed; the lamp's base soon grew into the actual ship. No seagulls or other birds were flying around its masts, so Rose knew that the ship was not very close to shore. It was already sailing across the Atlantic Ocean.

Rose said out loud, "I'm even later than the *Mayflower* was." She looked at her watch. Its hands jumped backwards to September 16, 1620, which was the date when the *Mayflower* left England on its famous voyage that ended in New England. The hands on Rose's watch twirled forward in time, jumping into the month of October.

Rose flew into the air, across the water, and onto the *Mayflower's* top deck. She then found herself going straight down a ladder onto the middle deck—the one between the upper deck and the cargo hold. The middle deck was only about five and a half feet tall. While she was able to stand up straight, she still found herself stooping over because she was worried about hitting her head on the low ceiling. She knew that the deck was also called the "Tween Deck" or the gun deck; on some ships, the middle deck was where cannons and cargo were stored.

Rose looked around and saw a gun room in the stern—the back section—of the ship. She walked over and looked inside. There were cutlasses, short swords, knives, muskets, gunpowder, and even cannons. "It looks like the Pilgrims have enough weapons."

None of the Pilgrims heard her speak, but one of the cannons did. It rolled forward, moved out of the gun room, sped across the middle deck, and stopped in front of one of the *Mayflower's* windows. Red paint appeared on its wheels and frame.

Rose said to the cannon, "I don't think the cannons in the seventeenth century had red paint on them."

Words shot out of the cannon: "This lucid dream is thine. If thou really wantest me to, I will take off my red paint."

"Oh, I don't want you to be naked."

"I thank thee. I really want to keep on wearing this paint."

Thick ropes with hooks on them came down from the ceiling and tried to grab onto the cannon, but the cannon was able to stay far enough away from the hooks to remain free. Standing tall on its stone wheels, the cannon looked ready to fight for its freedom. It then rolled forward and backward as it tried to grind its own road into the wooden deck of the *Mayflower*.

Two dogs—a mastiff and a spaniel—went up to the cannon and started to bark. One of the Pilgrims walked up to the dogs, looked toward the window, and then said, "Peace." The dogs stopped barking, wagged their tails, and lay down next to the cannon. The Pilgrim man walked over closer to the window. With the sun's light falling onto his head, his hair now looked red. Rose's heart beat faster. She wondered if the Pilgrim was her husband. She asked, "Is that you, Travis?"

The Pilgrim man did not hear her question. He turned around right in front of the window. Rose could now see his face and realized that he wasn't Travis. She looked into the window and saw her own reflection in the glass. Her eyes looked droopy, her mouth was frowning, and her skin became pale. She saw the sadness in her own face and felt like crying.

The red-haired Pilgrim was still facing the window, but he did not see Rose or her reflection. He said, "Where the waves of the ocean hit the sky, the weather for the future is sometimes visible."

One of the other Pilgrim men walked up to the red-haired Pilgrim and asked, "What didst thou say about the weather, Myles?"

Rose realized that the red-haired Pilgrim man was Captain Myles Standish, who was hired by the Pilgrims to be their military commander. Now that he was standing near another Pilgrim man, Rose saw that Myles was really short. Her husband Travis was quite a bit taller. Both men, though, had strong muscles; their movements were always energetic. As if he was trying to show off his muscles to Rose, Myles raised his arms sideways, up to the same level as his shoulders, and then stretched his fingers outwards even more. Even with his jacket on, he looked very sexy. Rose could see the muscles of his upper arms and shoulders pushing up against the cloth of his jacket.

Myles turned away from the window and looked at the other Pilgrim. Rose liked how the different angle of the sun's rays affected the shades of red in his hair. The shape of his neck was strong, but the skin looked soft. The white collar of the shirt underneath his jacket was too large; it was covering up most of his neck. Rose reached out one of her hands, trying to move his collar so that she could see more of his neck. She wasn't able to reach him.

Rose couldn't remember if the Myles on the *Mayflower* was married. She looked at his ring finger; there was no wedding ring, but the Pilgrims didn't believe in wearing a lot of jewelry. He could still be married. If this was her lucid dream, though, maybe she could make him be single, whether he was married or not.

Myles told the other Pilgrim, "The weather stayeth the same, John."

"Good."

Myles asked John how he was feeling: "How dost thou?"

"Good. I and my wife Katherine are blessed to be on this ship." Rose realized that this second Pilgrim was John Carver, who was married to Katherine. He was a church deacon and the first governor of the Plymouth colony.

"Thou already knowest that I love this ship. My wife Rose also liketh the *Mayflower*. Especially, she loveth the name of this ship because it is named for a pretty flower."

John and Myles kept talking, but Rose didn't hear them. She was busy looking around the deck, trying to find the woman who might be Rose Standish. Since Myles Standish's wife and she both had the same first name, perhaps Rose Standish would look like herself, especially since this was a lucid dream. She saw several women who were all alone; none of them looked like she did. Even so, Rose Standish could still be one of them.

Rose Hopkins sighed and looked back at Myles. He moved one of his hands and put it on top of the cannon.

The other male Pilgrim asked, "Is that cannon the best one that we have with us?"

"Ay." Myles brushed at the side of the cannon. "Dost thou see this scrape?"

The other Pilgrim walked up closer to the cannon, looked at the scrape, and shook his head. "It looketh like it was made by a sword."

"Ay, 'twas made by a sword. I remember the day when it happened."

"Was the cannon scraped during a war?"

"Nay, it happened during training." Myles slid his arm down the length of the cannon. The muscles in his arm looked hard as he moved it down and even harder as he moved his arm upwards again along the cannon's length. "A new man tried to show how good he was by twirling a sword in a circle, but the sword slipped from his hand and scraped against the cannon."

Rose asked Myles, "Did that really happen, or am I creating a story within a dream story?"

Myles and John didn't hear her; they moved away from the cannon, walked over to one of the compartments on the deck, and sat down together on the wooden floor. The cannon turned itself toward Rose and said, "You are creating a story within your story." It then turned back to the window and stood guard over that section of the ship.

In the center of the middle deck, Rose saw a cradle for a baby, boxes, a wooden chest, clothes, blankets, and wooden platforms being used for beds. There were wooden dividers so that privacy was possible for some of the passengers. Rose, though, could see over the dividers. She started to count the Pilgrims. She first counted a hundred and two passengers. Then she heard a baby crying. She counted the passengers a second time; there were now a hundred and three of them. One of the passengers said the name: "Oceanus." Rose realized that the crying baby was Oceanus Hopkins, who was born on the *Mayflower* during its voyage across the Atlantic Ocean. Oceanus and the Pilgrims near him seemed even more crowded together than they did in the *Desperate Crossing* film.

Rose yelled out: "Can any of you Pilgrims see me or hear me?"

Everyone ignored Rose, which meant that she was invisible. Perhaps her subconscious mind was telling her that she was a descendant of the Reverend John Robinson, who didn't physically come over on the *Mayflower*.

A wave of water suddenly went across the upper deck of the ship. One of the Pilgrims stared at the water. After a few seconds, he opened up a bible and read the following verse: "Wash me thoroughly from mine iniquity, and cleanse me from mine sin" (Ps. 51:2 GNV).

Rose asked, "Are you trying to tell me that I'm guilty of sin?"

The Pilgrim did not respond to her question; he was now silently reading the bible.

Rose asked in a softer voice, "Am I not good enough to join the Pilgrims?"

The Pilgrim lifted up his head before saying, "Ay." Even though Rose knew that he could have been responding to something he had just read in the bible, she thought that he was instead trying to answer her question.

Rose's thoughts moved into the conscious part of her mind, like a wave was sweeping them forward. For a while now, she had been trying to avoid her present by living in the past. She was late for everything. Her friends at work kept on having to "cover" for her. During the bank robbery, she had been unable to scream at the right moment, so even being shot in the knee was her own fault. She had screamed too late. Then both her knee pain and her anti-pain drugs had made her grouchy. She had screamed at Travis too much. Their fights had broken up their marriage, so her separation from her husband was mostly her own fault. She had done many other things wrong in her life. Even though she kept on trying to be good and often went to church, she was still a sinner.

A tear fell from Rose's face. Like a tiny wave, it flew down onto the wooden floor of the ship's middle deck. It then tried to climb back up again onto Rose's face, but the tear was too slippery. It went right past her face and hit one of the crossbeams in the ceiling of the ship. As it was absorbed by the wooden crossbeam, the damp section of the wood looked like a large version of the wooden cross that her parents had given to her at her baptism.

Rose sat down on a bench and looked out at the Pilgrims. They were talking quietly to each other, playing games with their children, sewing, and reading. Candles were set up in different sections of the middle deck.

Rose said, "You all look so much better behaved than I am."

One of the passengers walked over to a wooden chest, opened it up, and removed a copy of the *1599 Geneva Bible*. The passenger took the bible over to a wooden bench, sat down, and began reading out loud: "For there is no difference: for all have sinned, and are deprived of the glory of God, / And are justified freely by his grace, through the redemption that is in Christ Jesus" (Rom. 3:23-24 GNV).

Rose was shocked. Surely, she was completely different from these Pilgrims. She could not be as good as they were, could she? She knew that the Pilgrims wanted a new life and more religious freedom; they were also very courageous and trusting in God. They were going into a New World, where all of them could easily be killed. She knew they were afraid of illness, starvation, and the Native people in the New World, but they were still going on their dangerous voyage.

She thought again about the bible verse. It was one of her favorite ones, and she was happy to be reminded of it. She did not have to pay any money for her sins to be forgiven; she only had to ask for redemption through Jesus Christ, her Savior. She knew that he had given his life on the cross so that her sins would be forgiven, but she still did not think that she was as good as the Pilgrims were.

Rose walked over to the chest where the Pilgrim had found the Bible; she opened up the top of the chest. Inside were papers, bibles, a copy of Henry Ainsworth's Psalm book, and other books. William Brewster's name was on several of the letters, so Rose guessed that the wooden chest belonged to him. Rose reached over toward the back of the chest and picked up one of the papers; it was the farewell letter from John Robinson. She read the beginning:

> Loving and Christian friends, I do heartily, and in the Lord, salute you all: as being they with whom I am present

in my best affection, and most earnest longings after you, though I be constrained, for a while, to be bodily absent from you. I say, constrained: God knowing how willingly much rather than otherwise, I would have borne my part with you in this first brunt, were I not, by strong necessity, held back for the present. Make account of me in the mean while, as of a man divided in myself, with great pain, and as, natural bonds set aside, having my better part with you.[43]

Rose looked out at the Pilgrims and said, "So, the best part of John Robinson—his 'affection'—is here on the *Mayflower.*" None of the passengers heard her. She turned to the end of the letter and read the closing: "An unfeigned well-willer of your happy success in this hopeful voyage, I[OHN] R[OBINSON]."[44]

She stared at the shapes of the letters in the closing. Was this letter and possibly other letters by John Robinson actually on the *Mayflower,* or was she just dreaming that they were? Either way, she knew that both his ideas and his affection were a part of the Pilgrim's voyage to the new world. She realized that she was connecting emotionally and intellectually with one of her ancestors within a dream voyage of the *Mayflower.* As a descendent of John Robinson, there must have been at least a small part of herself that was as good as some of these Pilgrims were. Also, like many of the Pilgrims, she had accepted Jesus Christ as her Lord and Savior. He had saved her from her sins by giving up his own life for her salvation. She said, "Thank you, my Lord, for all that you've done for me."

Rose looked around; the passengers now were reacting in different ways to being on the ship. Some of them seemed okay; others looked very pale and sickly. A few were throwing up. Rose thought of turning her head away and not watching the sick people until she realized that they were being helped and cared for by their friends and family members.

"Here, thou canst lie on top of my blanket. Having more softness will help thee to feel better."

"I will empty that pot for thee."

"This evening, thou wilt not help to distribute the food for our meal. That is a task for myself, thy friend, to do."

Rose looked to the middle section of the group of passengers, noting that more of the healthier ones were there. One of these passengers suddenly stood up; his motions seemed to be saying to Rose, "Look at me." He was wearing a black hat, a brown jacket, some light tan pants, a wide collar, and an off-white shirt. He was silently reading the words of different psalms from Ainsworth's *Book of Psalms.*

Another passenger stood up and asked the Brown-jacket Pilgrim, "Canst thou choose a psalm for us to sing? Thou canst read the words out loud a few times. Then all of the children will know the words and can sing along with us."

"I can choose one, but which psalm will please thee the most?"

"The one that will teach about our Lord to our children."

For a few minutes, the two passengers discussed which psalm would be the best one. Other passengers also began to talk about which psalm to sing first.

The Feather-hat Lady said to another female Puritan who was seated next to her, "Every day, we have been singing the music of the psalms in the same order."

"Ay, normally we do follow that order so that we will finish singing all of the psalms every month."

Another voice said, "It seemeth onto me that we can make a new order."

"What sayeth thou?"

"We can some days use the old order and some days use a new order."

"If we sing out of order, we will not remember if no psalms were not sung."

"We can sing more than one music; we can sing two or three musics."

"We have enough time to sing all of our psalms in the old order and in a new order."

"Ay, we have much freedom and time to sing many psalms, as long as we do not awaken the crew members whilst they are sleeping during the night."

The Pilgrims continued to discuss which psalms to sing. They finally decided that they liked two Psalms: Psalm 100 and Psalm 114. Psalm 100 was about shouting praise to the Lord and about His presence for people of all ages. Psalm 114 was about the miracles that helped the Israelites to leave Egypt, and it had water references in it.

As Rose continued to listen to the discussion, she realized that singing psalms was an important part of their culture. During this time, there must have been "a widespread 'psalm culture,' in which poets, theologians, and devoted dilettantes produced hundreds of translations, paraphrases, and adaptations of the psalms, as well as meditations, sermons, and commentaries. Countless others turned to the psalms for inspiration, consolation, entertainment, and edification."[45] On the *Mayflower,* as well as in other settings, the Puritans would have discussed the words of the psalms in both the Ainsworth's *Book of Psalms* and the *1599 Geneva Bible.* They might even have compared the words in the 1599 bible from Geneva with those in the 1611 King James version of the bible. While the Puritans used the bible from Geneva, John Alden, one of the crew members, brought the 1611 King James version on the *Mayflower's* 1620 voyage.

The Pilgrims finally decided on an order for their music: they would sing Psalm 100 first and Psalm 114 second; then, they would revert back to their usual order for singing some more psalms. The Brown-jacket Pilgrim started to read the words of "Psalm 100" from Ainsworth's *Book of Psalms.* Most of the children already knew all of the words, so some of them began to sing the first stanza of the psalm while the words were being read: "Showt to Jehovah al the earth. / Serv ye Jehovah with gladnes; / before him come with singing merth, / Know that Jehovah he God is."[46]

They sang as if they were wonderfully in love with singing together within a group. The notes from the music rose up from the psalter and joined the music flowing from their energetic voices. An ocean of sound waves flowed sweetly within the air, enhancing their spirits. They were joyously singing together, and each one was a part of the community. They were happy to hear each other's voices—it didn't seem to matter to any of them if one person's voice was better than someone else's.

After the Pilgrims finished singing several psalms, one of the crew members from the upper deck climbed down a tiny wooden ladder. When he reached the floor of the middle deck, he clasped his hands together in happiness and said, "Your psalms are making so many of us happy." Several of the Pilgrims thanked him. The crew member then slowly climbed back up the ladder, waving good-bye as he stepped out onto the upper deck.

About ten minutes later, another crew member came down the tiny ladder into the group of Pilgrims. As he reached the middle deck, the Pilgrims who were singing psalms stopped. Some of the passengers stared at the crew member. Others looked down at the floor; they appeared to be trying to avoid eye contact with this person. He was obviously disliked. When Rose looked closely at him, she realized that he had the same physical appearance as the mean crew member in the *Desperate Crossing* film. He was healthy, but he liked to swear and often made fun of any of the Pilgrims who were sick. Standing at the bottom of the ladder, he surveyed the passengers who were lying down because they were not feeling well. Then he said that he wanted to help throw "half of them overboard before they came to their journey's end and to make merry with what they had."[47]

The deck became dark and then light, indicating the passage of a day. Then the moon and the sun went up and down, lighting up the *Mayflower* in different ways with the passage of time. More than a week elapsed.

The trip across the Atlantic Ocean was less than half finished when the swearing crew member became sick. Even though none of the ill Pilgrims had died during their voyage, this crew member did. His body lay on the deck until a giant hand reached out of the sky and threw his body overboard. Rose asked, "Am I dreaming about a giant hand or did that really happen?"

Possibly in answer to her question, one of the Pilgrims said, "'Twas the giant hand of our God that did throw him into the ocean."

"Really?" Rose asked.

From the sky came a book: William Bradford's *Of Plymouth Plantation*. The book opened itself up and then explained to Rose what had happened: the swearing crew member was the first and only person to be thrown overboard on the *Mayflower's* voyage, and his death "was an astonishment to all his fellows for they noted it to be the just hand of God upon him."[48]

The ocean voyage continued with multiple storms happening; the *Mayflower* began to leak. Then one of the main cross beams of the boat cracked. The captain of the ship, the carpenter, the crew, and the passengers discussed what should be done about the beam.

"That broken part of the ship is one of the most important beams."

"We should return to England."

"What will happen to our wages?"

"Our lives are more important than our money."

"We are less than halfway across the ocean."

"But the *Mayflower* is 'strong and firm under water.'"[49]

"The Puritans from Holland brought a giant iron screw with them."

"The screw is large enough to help structure homes. If it can raise up a roof, it can move the cracked beam upward."

"Then we will place this wooden post under the cracked beam. The post will support the beam."

"We can caulk the decks to fix the leaks."

"We will be very careful with the sails."

Rose watched as the ship was repaired. Then "they committed themselves to the will of God and resolved to proceed."[50]

The *Mayflower* continued on its journey. Before long, another storm arrived, making the ship pitch back and forth on the rough seas. Heavy rain was splashing into the water from the ocean; both the rain and the ocean's waves were washing over the *Mayflower's* deck. One of the passengers, John Howland, walked carefully on the rolling surface of the upper deck. Suddenly, he was caught up in a crashing wave. Even though he tried to grab onto the wooden edge of the upper deck, he was still washed over the side of the boat, landing more than six feet under water. He waved his arms, trying frantically to push himself up to the surface of the water. One of his hands found a thick rope that was attached to the *Mayflower*. He was able to hold onto the slippery rope until he was pulled in close to the ship. One of the crewmen yelled out, "Is John fallen over the 'larboard' or the 'starboard' side?"

Even though no one responded to the question, some of the crew members still moved to the correct side of the boat. They used a boat hook and other devices to pull John back onto the upper deck of the *Mayflower*.

After John Howland was rescued, some of the crew members congratulated him by yelling out: "Huzzah!"

Another voice asked John how he was doing: "How do you fare?"

Rose couldn't hear John's response, but she saw that he was alive and happily talking to other people.

A third voice said, "Heaven sent thee good fortune!"

Then William Bradford, who would be the second governor of Plymouth, said, "It pleased God that he caught hold of the topsail halyards which hung overboard and ran out at length."[51]

Rose found herself saying, "Thanks be to God!"

One of the Puritans said a prayer of thanksgiving.

The storm stopped, the sun came out, and a rainbow filled the sky. The sun became the moon, and the lights kept changing their brightness. Days were passing by. With each new day, the weather changed, but the scenery remained the same: the waves of the Atlantic Ocean moved toward a far-off horizon, where the different shades of blue from the waves and the sky flowed into each other.

Later in the journey, one of the children started to complain about sleeping near the chickens. "They are making many noises. Every night, they scratch the bottoms of their cages."

Another child said, "They make noise because they are like us. They want to escape from the cages that are too small for them."

A different voice said, "Ay, they are just like us; they are cooped up in a very tiny space."

"Please, can the chickens be let out?"

"The poor things do not know what is going on."

"They are used to running around outside."

"They cannot climb up the ladder to the upper deck, so they will not escape from the ship."

"They will be safe outside of their cages."

"Nay, they should not be let out. There is no space, and they will make the floor smell bad."

"Ay, the chickens will ruin the sweet smell of the wine in the wood of the floor."

The first child said in a wimpy voice, "It smelleth not too bad near the chickens; the smell is very much worse near the goats and the sheep."

"The chickens are not making scratching noises because they are bad."

"Ay, the chickens are good animals. They are scratching so much only because they are hungry. They are trying to find some grain or some bugs to eat."

When the children stopped talking, one of the chickens started to make scratching sounds, which quickly became louder and turned into clucking noises. The noises became even louder until they began to sound like words being yelled out by a person.

STOLEN DREAMS

Rose was awakened by a voice calling her name. After a few seconds, she realized that her grandmother was knocking on the door while yelling out her name.

"Thanks, Granny. I'll get up right away."

"It's already after eight o-clock, and this is the third time I've tried to wake you up. If you don't open the door to show me that you're awake, I'll have to come in."

"I'm coming." Rose sighed, grabbed the clock from the bedside table, and put it under her pillow. Then she walked over to the door and opened it up for Granny, who was already dressed in a beautiful light blue dress. "Oh, Granny, you're going to look so much nicer than I will for our pictures this morning."

"No, that's not true. You know you're beautiful. Don't you remember? You won third place in a beauty contest."

Rose laughed. "That's when I was a teenager. I'm a lot older now."

"No, you're not."

"Anyway, I'd better have a shower and get dressed."

"I'll be making breakfast."

"Thanks."

Half an hour later, Rose went into the kitchen. Her grandmother was just putting some eggs, bacon, and English muffins on plates. Two coffee mugs were already filled with coffee.

"Granny, how were you able to have such perfect timing?"

"By listening to the sounds you were making, I figured out when you would be walking into the kitchen."

Rose and her grandmother sat down at the kitchen table and began to eat. "I know you're good at scheduling things, Granny, but you outdid yourself this morning."

"After working all those years as a receptionist in a dentist's office, I should be able to schedule things."

"So, can you teach me how to be on time?"

"Your only problem is your knee injury."

"My knee is feeling better now, but I'm still often late for things."

"What things are you late for?"

"Work."

"Well, maybe because of the bank robbery, you're subconsciously scared of going to work again."

"You're right about that. I still have dreams about the bank robbery."

"Have you spoken to your doctor?"

"Oh, I can sleep okay, and I think the dreams are helping me. In a dream I had on the Fourth of July, I used lucid dreaming techniques and tried to change the ending of the bank robbery."

"Did it work? Were you able to fix anything?"

"I changed a few of the details. Then I added on a different ending."

"What was the new ending?"

"I was still shot, but afterwards, I met our ancestors on a clock and went backwards in time."

"By going into the past, you were trying to change something. Probably the bank robbery."

"I'm not just late for work. These days, I'm usually late for everything."

"You used to be on time for everything."

"Yeah, I know."

Rose's grandmother thought for a few seconds and then said, "Practice will help."

"Really?"

"Yeah. For example, you could practice cleaning up a room by always following the same steps in the same order. Logically, the length of time that the process takes should stay the same or decrease."

"I never thought of doing housework that way."

"You probably don't take extra time when you're putting on make-up."

"No, I don't think I do."

"Have you ever timed yourself when you put on your make-up?"

"No, I haven't tried timing myself, except when I'm doing exercises."

"You should try it while you're putting on make-up. You'll probably find out that putting on make-up always takes you exactly the same amount of time because you follow the same series of steps. For example, I'm sure you put on a moisturizer before your foundation."

"You're right. When I put on make-up, I do follow the same process. However, when I do other things, like getting dressed, I follow different processes. Sometimes I change my outfit more than once, and sometimes I don't."

The front doorbell rang. Granny got up and returned a minute later with her next-door neighbor. Rose stood up, and Granny introduced them to each other. Her neighbor was given a cup of coffee and a bagel. After they all had finished breakfast, the neighbor took pictures of Rose and Granny; Rose then took pictures of Granny with her neighbor.

After the neighbor left, Rose copied all of the pictures onto her grandmother's computer and e-mailed some of them to her mother and father. Then she packed up her suitcase before helping

Granny make lunch. While she and Granny ate, Rose told her about the most recent part of her Pilgrim dream: "Voyage of the *Mayflower.*" Then, they talked about their ancestors.

By one o'clock, Granny and Rose were on their way to the train station. When they arrived, they hugged each other, and Granny hugged Rose an extra two times. "These extra hugs are for your mom and dad."

"Okay. I'll be sure to tell them. Are you going to visit us on Thanksgiving again?"

"Of course. I'm also planning on visiting you some time before Thanksgiving."

"The beaches in Rhode Island are beautiful in August."

"I know they are. I'll speak with your parents about a good time for me to visit."

"You might want to check out the weather forecast, too."

"I will."

Granny hugged Rose again and said, "Luv you."

Rose responded, "Luv you more."

"Luv you the most-est—and there's nothing greater than 'most-est.'"

"Yes, there is, Granny. The Pilgrims used to say two or more comparison words to show extra meaning."

"Really?"

"Yeah, the Pilgrim kind of comparison is: I have very much more than the most greatest love for you."

"Actually, the very most greatest love comes from our Lord Jesus Christ."

"Granny, as usual, you are so right."

They hugged again and said good-bye. Then Granny left the train station to drive back home.

Rose went through the usual lines, showed her tickets, got on the train, and sat down. She pulled out a book and several articles; she then started to read about the Pilgrims' arrival in

America. She was planning on lucid dreaming that night about the actual landing of the Pilgrims, and she wanted to know more details about what had happened.

When the train began moving, Rose kept on reading. After about a half an hour, she noticed someone standing in the aisle next to her. She looked up and said "Hi" to the train's car attendant.

He bowed slightly, touched his hat, and asked Rose, "Do you need anything?"

"No thanks. I'm fine."

"I couldn't help but notice you're reading about the *Mayflower.*"

"Yeah, I am. I'm trying to learn about my ancestors. I'm descended from the Reverend John Robinson."

"The pastor to the Pilgrims?"

"Yeah, you know your history."

"I just know a little bit about the Pilgrims, but I'd like to learn some more."

"Really?"

"Yeah. I've been told that my ancestry is connected to William Brewster, who was one of the Pilgrims."

"That's wonderful!"

"I think it's so neat that you're reading about the voyage of the Pilgrims while you're on a voyage yourself."

"Yeah, well, I'm on a train. The Pilgrims were on a ship."

"Your trip should be shorter and more comfortable than theirs."

"I hope so."

They both laughed. Then the car attendant asked, "What part of their trip are you reading about?"

"I'm actually reading about the end of their trip—when they were landing in America."

"When exactly was that?"

"November 19, 1620." Rose hesitated and then added, "That's according to our modern calendar. The Pilgrims actually were using a calendar that was ten days earlier."

"They landed on November 19?"

"No, after crossing the Atlantic Ocean, they first spotted land on November 19."

"Was it Plymouth?"

"Actually, they first spotted Cape Cod. They did not try to land, though."

"Really?"

"Yeah, they were supposed to go to a place that was then called 'Northern Virginia.' The modern location of their intended landing spot was near the Hudson River; this place is where their contract stated that they could legally land and establish their colony."

"Did they go to the Hudson River?"

"No, they tried to, but it was far too dangerous for their ship to travel to the south, so they turned back. I'll read you a sentence from this book." Rose turned to the page that she had just been reading and said, "[T]he seas on the Atlantic side of Cape Cod are treacherous in the extreme."[52]

"I guess the Pilgrims didn't have the same navigation equipment that we have today."

"No, they didn't. They also didn't have any buoys and markers like we have now."

"So what happened next to the Pilgrims?"

"They spent only two days trying to get to the Hudson River; then they gave up and wrote the *Mayflower Compact*. Some people even think that the Pilgrims settled in Massachusetts on purpose so that they could make their initial contract void."

The train attendant waved his hand back and forth as he said, "Whether they settled in Plymouth on purpose or not, the *Mayflower Compact* still is one of our country's important documents, right?"

"Yeah, it was signed by two groups of passengers on the *Mayflower:* the Leiden Separatists and the 'Strangers' from

England. That type of political agreement is important in democracies. According to the *mayflowerfamilies.com* Website, these people were even 'creating their own government.'[53]"

"That's an interesting idea."

"It is, and other experts who have studied the history of democracy also say that the *Mayflower Compact* was a very important document. A different source—a study guide by Duane Cline on the *rootsweb.ancestry.com* Website—says something similar." Rose pulled out a paper from her purse and read, "This Compact became the constitution of the Plymouth Colony. It was the first document of American democracy to establish 'government of the people, by the people, for the people.'"[54]

One of the other passengers in Rose's car walked up to the attendant and asked, "Where's the snack car?"

The train attendant waved good-bye to Rose and walked forward with the other passenger. He helped her to open the door and go into the next car, which was the snack car.

In the next ten minutes, several other people walked past Rose's seat, but she didn't look at any of them. She was reading her book again. Then she noticed a pair of blue sneakers that looked familiar. She glanced up at the person, but his back suddenly was turned toward her, and he was walking quickly away from her and into the next car.

Rose read another sentence before deciding to find out who the person with the blue sneakers was. She placed her book and papers into her large purse; then she stood up and went toward the door at the end of her car. She opened up the door, stepped through, closed the door behind her, and then paused. She was still standing on a metal floor, but it wasn't firm: it was shuffling beneath her feet. Was it encouraging her to move forward or telling her to go backwards? She felt faint and grabbed one of the metal vertical handles that were attached to the side walls of the railroad car. The handle felt a little too cold for the month of July, and she didn't feel any steadier. She still felt like she was being shuffled around. Narrow drafts of wind entered the slits between the side, bottom, and top sections of the loosely connected cars. Even though the air was warm, she shivered.

Rose looked down at the shuffling metal floor. The open space between the cars was large enough so that she could see the railroad track, dirt, stones, and clumps of crabgrass flying past beneath her feet. To get to the next car, she would have to carefully step over that open space between the cars, as well as walking from one shuffling floor to the next shuffling floor. The movements of the floors were not the same. When one floor was up, the other one was slanted down.

The door behind her opened up. Rose turned around and saw another passenger standing in the doorway. He was waiting patiently for her to move out of his way. He had earphones on and was listening to a song from his cell. It sounded like Grand Funk Railroad's "Locomotion." The passenger noticed that Rose was staring at him; he began to stare back at her. He then started to sing along with the song on his cell: "[D]o the Loco-motion with me"; he hummed a couple of lines and then sang: "Jump up / Jump back."[55]

Rose didn't want to carry on a conversation with the stranger. She turned away from him and looked back at the open space between the two cars. Her left knee began to ache. There was no way that she was going to jump across that space. After another few more seconds, she inhaled, took a giant step, and landed on the shuffling floor of the next car. Without looking back at the other train passenger, she opened the door and quickly walked into the snack car. As she moved slightly to her left, the passenger who had been behind her closed the door, waved at her, walked briskly to an empty table, and sat down.

Rose stood still as she looked around the snack car. Small tables with benches were on both sides. Her eyes moved along the full length of the car's metal floor, trying to find the pair of blue sneakers. Everyone was seated on benches in front of tables, but she could only see some of the people's shoes. When she looked up at the passengers' faces, none of them—except for the singing passenger—looked familiar. The blue-sneakered person must have already gone forward into another car. Rose looked toward the door at the far end of the snack car. She could see the middle aisle section of at least the next two cars, but there were no people in her line of vision.

Rose sighed, sat down at the closest table, and ordered a coffee and a bagel with cream cheese. After her food was brought by the waiter, she took out an article from her purse. She began to read about the Pilgrims and their search for a landing site in the New World.

Before Rose had finished her coffee and bagel, the train's alarm sounded. From one of the cars in front of the snack car, a loud yell was heard. Then the brakes were suddenly applied, but the train did not seem to slow down. Rose and several other passengers stood up and walked forward, trying to see what was happening by looking through the doors and into the cars in front of them. Nothing could be seen, except for a bunch of other passengers who were also looking through their car's doors and windows. Rose walked over to one of the windows on the left side of the train, but she still couldn't see anything.

Suddenly, the steel floor of the train rose up slightly; Rose slid backwards and started to fall down. As her feet slid, she tried to grab onto one of the benches. Her grabbing hand only made the bench fall over onto her knee. Then something hit her in the head, and she sprawled down on the ground. She looked upwards, but didn't see anything. She turned her head toward the back of the snack car and saw benches and tables that had toppled over. Some of them were lying on top of each other. There were broken dishes all over the car, but most of the people appeared okay.

Some of the passengers were standing up. When Rose reached up to see if her head was okay, she saw the blue sneakers again. Then she heard a voice, "I'll help this one."

Immediately, Rose recognized the voice as Greg's. She tried to scream, but no noise came out of her mouth. As she opened her mouth to try again, she saw Greg take a step and grab onto her purse. He opened up her purse, tossed out all of the papers, and found the sampler. As he dropped the purse and began to walk away, Rose saw his clenched-up fist squishing and squeezing the life out of her sampler. Scared about the safety of the cloth treasure made by one of her ancestors, she finally was able to scream. Sirens from outside of the train drowned out her voice; no one seemed to be hearing her yells. Finally, her screams weakened and then stopped as she lost consciousness.

Several hours later, Rose woke up in a hospital. When she rang the bell, a nurse came in right away. "How are you feeling?"

"I think I'm okay." Rose frowned and then said, "I think I have a few bruises."

"Where does it hurt?"

"On my head, elbows, and knees, especially my left knee." Rose sat up and looked at her left knee. A bruise and a scrape were visible.

"We've already taken several x-rays, and the good news is you don't have any broken bones."

"What's the bad news?"

"The doctor thinks you have a concussion, so you'll have to stay here for a day or two."

"Where am I?"

"In a hospital."

"What city?"

"You're in the Northern part of New York City."

"Okay. Can I have my purse and cell phone so that I can call my parents?"

"We already called your family."

"Can you let them know that I'm awake now?"

The nurse smiled broadly. "Yeah, I'd love to make that phone call for you."

"Thanks." Rose lay back down and then suddenly sat up again. "Can I still have my purse? I think a thief stole my sampler out of it."

"What's a sampler?"

"It's a piece of cloth with designs and words sewn into it."

"Okay. We locked up your purse for you; I'll go and get it right now."

The nurse left and then returned in a few minutes with the purse. Rose looked inside. The sampler was missing, but everything else was there, including the papers that Greg had thrown around the car. Rose sighed. "The sampler's missing."

"Okay. I'll let the police know."

After the nurse left, Rose looked at the listing of TV shows before deciding to read some of the Internet articles from her mom. She pulled out some of the papers from her purse. About fifteen minutes later, with the papers still in her hand and pictures of the *Mayflower* in her mind, she drifted off to sleep.

NEW WORLD POLITICS

As soon as Rose fell asleep, she found herself on the middle deck of the *Mayflower*. It was daytime, and many of the Pilgrims were taking turns climbing up the ladder to the top deck. Rose asked one of Pilgrims, "What's happening up there?"

The Pilgrim didn't hear her; he just continued walking in a line with other Pilgrims toward the ladder; then when it was his turn, he climbed up to the higher deck.

After a few minutes, there was a break in the train of passengers who were climbing up the ladder. Rose walked up to it and carefully climbed to the top deck. When she finally was standing on the upper deck, she noticed that only men were there with her. They were all looking over the side of the boat in the same direction.

One of the Puritan passengers said the word "land" as he pointed toward the land on the horizon. He asked a crew member, "Canst thou tell us what is the name of that land?"

The crew member shook his head sideways and went back to his task of resetting one of the sails.

The ship jumped over a series of overlapping waves with changing amounts of sunlight; the *Mayflower* was moving ahead into a later time. Now it was noticeably closer to land. One of the crew members said, "We're too far to the north."

Another crew member said, "Northern Virginia is to the north, which is why 'tis called 'Northern' Virginia."

"We are too far to the north."

Several of the male passengers left the upper deck and went back down to the middle deck. Rose followed them. When she stepped off of the ladder, she first saw the Feather-hat Lady, who was talking to another female Puritan: "From the window over there, I saw a bird flying across the water to the sand on the shoreline."

"Was it a seagull?"

"Perhaps. It was too far away to see its markings."

"I know thou lovest birds."

"Ay, that is why on our voyage I have been sleeping nearest the chickens."

"Doth thy husband like birds, too?"

"Ay, he doth. When he discovered how much I loved birds, he studied them. Now he loveth them, too."

Rose looked around at some of the other Pilgrims. She could see the joy on their faces as they began to praise God for bringing them safely across the Atlantic Ocean.

One Pilgrim started to sing "Psalm 8," and other Pilgrims began to sing along with him. Rose was able to hear some of the words of the psalm: "...our Lord, how excellent-great is thy name in all the earth..."[56]

Perhaps because of the singing, some of the male passengers who had stayed up on the upper deck now came down to the middle deck. More psalms were sung; then the passengers discussed going further to the south in order to find North Virginia.

"If we stay here, our patent will not be any good." The Pilgrim waved at a stack of papers, and Rose realized that he was referring to their legal paperwork for starting a North Virginia colony.

"Must we follow every law that King James dictateth? We are in a different place with no legal papers."

"I think the king is glad that we moved away from Leiden and back to an 'English' land."

"We are not in a land belonging to England."

"Wherever we live, we will become a new English colony."

One of the Puritans began to read a bible. The Feather-hat Lady's husband walked up to him and said, "William, pray pardon me."

Rose realized that the man with the bible was William Brewster. He had been an assistant and elder under the Reverend John Robinson; now he was an elder and the spiritual leader of the Pilgrims.

"How dost thou?"

"Good."

William Brewster asked, "How may I help thee?"

"I am so thankful that we will be stepping onto land again."

"Ay, as am I."

"Walking on a boat that is sailing on an ocean doth not feel too good in my stomach."

"I know how thou feelest."

"What art thou reading in the bible, William?"

"Psalm 138." William Brewster looked down at his bible and then said, "Much of the psalm is about praising and worshipping our Lord. It even mentions singing: 'And they shall sing of the ways of the Lord, because the glory of the Lord is great'" (Ps. 138:5 GNV).

"Doth a different verse in that psalm saith something about being strong?"

William said, "Ah, verse three saith, 'When I called, then thou heardest me, and hast increased strength in my soul'" (Ps. 138:3 GNV).

"Thanksgiving and strength from God are connected in that psalm."

For a few minutes, the two men continued to discuss Bible verses. Then William Brewster closed his bible and walked over to a table. He placed his bible on top of a different-looking bible.

Rose walked up to the pair of bibles. The one that Brewster had just been reading was the 1599 Geneva study bible. The other bible was the 1611 edition of the King James Authorized Version. Rose said out loud, "The 1611 bible looks like the one that belonged to John Alden."

No one responded to Rose's statement. The Feather-hat Lady's husband said "farewell" to William Brewster, walked back to the ladder, and climbed up onto the top deck. Rose followed him.

A crew member was moving one of the sails. The Feather-hat Lady's husband asked him, "Are we heading south?"

"Ay."

Rose looked toward the ocean. She could see a rock sticking out of the water to their left, and a swirling circle of water to their right. One of the crew members said, "There have been many shipwrecks in the waters before us."

The Puritan asked, "Dost thou know how many shipwrecks?"

Rose responded, "I heard that, between 1843 and 1859, about five hundred ships were wrecked in this area."[57]

The crew member ignored Rose's information and said, "I know not the actual number of wrecks, but I know there have been many."

"Should we be sailing south at this time of year?"

"Nay, that is where all of the problems are. I think we should stay up here in the north."

Crashing waves started to hit the *Mayflower*. Rose's stomach felt funny. Within her dream, she closed her eyes, hoping that the waves would calm down. They didn't; she still felt the waves slamming into the ship's deck while she was trying to stand up on it. She sat down. When the waves became calmer, she opened up her eyes. Only a couple of days had elapsed, but the Pilgrims were back in the Cape Cod area. They had given up trying to sail to the south; the passengers were now talking about finding a home to the west of Cape Cod. Some of the voices started to argue about where they would be landing and about who would be in charge.

"Our patent saith that we must go to Northern Virginia."

"Why must we live in the wrong place?" the Feather-hat Lady asked. "Can we try again to sail to our land in Northern Virginia?"

"There is no choice for us. The waters to our south are too rough."

"How can we rightly be living here?"

"Our papers are for Northern Virginia. It will not be lawful for us to land in the north."

"Our land must be rightly ours."

"Then we can give our land to our children."

"Who will be in charge? Whose laws will we follow?"

"We must follow the laws of our Sovereign Lord King James," a Red-coated Gentleman said.

There was quiet for a moment while some of the passengers turned and stared at the non-Puritan Pilgrim in the red coat. They kept staring at the gentleman as if he were crazy or doing something wrong.

The gentleman's face showed his embarrassment. "I think that I said my thoughts the wrong way. King James will understand that we are in the New World. This is where many new and strange things are happening."

Several small groups of passengers began murmuring among themselves. Then one of the passengers said some words that Rose had heard while watching the History Channel's *Desperate Crossing The Untold Story of the Mayflower* DVD with her grandmother: "Only common law rules now." [58]

The facial gestures and words from the passengers showed that they were discussing common law and written law.

Another one of the passengers said more words that Rose had heard while watching the History Channel's DVD: "We can make our own laws." [59]

As the passengers kept speaking to one other, some of their dialogue became visible words that began to fly through the atmosphere of the *Mayflower*. Rose reached out and touched one of the word groupings; it said, "Mayflower Compact." Some of the flying words were coming from the farewell letter written by the Reverend John Robinson. The flying words from the letter joined with other flying words until a completed document was created. Rose read the *Mayflower Compact* out loud:

> In the name of God, Amen. We, whose names are underwritten, the loyal subjects of our dread Sovereign Lord King James, by the grace of God, of Great Britain, France, and Ireland King, defender of the Faith, etc.
>
> Having undertaken for the glory of God, and advancement of the Christian faith, and honour of our King and country a Voyage to plant the first Colony in the northern parts of Virginia do, by these presents, solemnly and mutually, in the presence of God and one of another, covenant and combine ourselves together in a CIVIL BODY POLITIC for our better ordering and preservation, and furtherance of the ends aforesaid, and by virtue hereof to enact, constitute, and frame such just and equal laws, ordinances, acts, constitutions, offices, from time to time, as shall be thought most meet and convenient for the general good of the COLONY, unto which we promise all due submission and obedience.
>
> In witness whereof, we have hereunder subscribed our names. Cape Cod, 11th of November in the year of the reign of our Sovereign Lord King James, of England, France, and Ireland, 18 and of Scotland 54. Anno Domini 1620.[60]

After Rose finished reading the *Mayflower Compact*, it floated through the air and landed on a wooden table next to a feather pen in an inkwell. As Rose watched, forty-one men took turns signing the historic document:

John Carver, William Bradford, Edward Winslow, William Brewster, Isaac Allerton, Myles Standish, John Alden, Samuel Fuller, Christopher Martin, William Mullins, William White, Richard Warren, John Howland, Stephen Hopkins, Edward Tilly, John Tilly, Francis Cooke, Thomas Rogers, Thomas Tinker, John Ridgdale, Edward Fuller, John Turner, Francis Eaton, James Chilton, John Craxton, John Billington, Moses Fletcher, John Goodman, Degory Priest, Thomas Williams, Gilbert Winslow, Edmund Margeson, Peter Brown, Richard Britteridge, George Soule, Richard Clarke, Richard Gardiner, John Allerton, Thomas English, Edward Dotey, and Edward Leister.[61]

After all of the men had signed the *Mayflower Compact*, Rose looked around the deck. Her eyes fell on Myles, who was standing near the ladder; he looked like he was going to climb up to the top deck at any moment.

Rose said to Myles, "The Separatists have found a home!" Even though he didn't hear her, she continued to speak to him: "The *Mayflower Compact* shows the Pilgrims' intent of forming a political entity, one that will be loyal to King James while formulating laws for a new colony in the New World." Myles took a step closer to the ladder, started to climb up, and gradually moved away from Rose. Speaking to Myles's back, she said, "Freedom means to follow laws, as well as to formulate them."

One of the Pilgrim ladies must have heard Rose's statement about freedom, for she said almost the same thing: "Freedom meaneth to make good laws and then to follow them in a goodly manner."

The voice of a child cheered: "Huzzah!"

Rose looked at the child and noticed that he was holding onto a chicken. The child said, "The chicken no longer sitteth in its cage. Now it runneth free!"

The Feather-hat Lady went up to the child. "Here, I will take care of the chicken."

"Thou only wilt put it back into the cage."

"The chicken will be very happy in its cage. That is where its home hath been for two months."

The child gave the chicken to the Feather-hat Lady, who put it back into its cage. The lady then said, "When we have a home on shore, then thou can let the chicken out of its cage."

"Ay, my lady. I thank you for helping me with the chicken."

"I thank thee for playing with the chickens and for being kind to them."

The chicken quietly had gone back into its cage, but it was now starting to cluck. After Rose opened her eyes, the clucks began to sound like someone's steps.

MEETINGS

Rose was awakened by the sounds of a nurse's steps. The nurse picked up Rose's chart and said, "Hi. I'm Mercy."

Rose laughed. "Is your name really Mercy?"

The nurse smiled. "I used to think my parents wanted me to be a nurse, so I asked them one day. They said that I was named after Mercy Bradford, one of the *Mayflower* passengers."

"Oh, I wonder if we're related."

The nurse frowned and looked down at Rose's chart. "I thought your last name was Hopkins."

"Yeah, it is. My maiden name is Rose Bradford."

"Oh, then I suppose we could be related. Anything is possible."

"My father's family has told him that he's descended from William Bradford, but we don't have the actual lineage written down anywhere."

"Oh, with *ancestry.com* and U.S. census data, you might be able to trace your lineage. There are a lot of other Websites, too, where you could do research." Mercy reached over to Rose's wrist and checked her pulse before asking, "How are you feeling today?"

"I'm okay." Rose paused before adding, "I think my headache might be gone."

"You don't sound too certain about your headache." Mercy raised her chin slightly and smiled at Rose. "Are you just saying that because you want to go home today, or do you really feel better?"

Rose looked down at the floor and then back up at Mercy. "Okay, I still have a headache. When can I have some more Ibuprofen?"

Joanne took Rose's blood pressure.

"How's my blood pressure?"

"It's not too high: 130 over 87."

"Do you know if the doctor will let me go home today?"

"Doctor Sam Fuller will let you know in a little while. He's supposed to be in at ten o'clock."

"I have to be feeling good enough to go home today."

"Why is that, Rose?"

"Last night, I dreamed about going on a voyage, so to make my dream come true, I should go on a real trip today."

"Where did you go last night in your dream?"

"I don't remember everything, but I was with the Pilgrims. They arrived in the New World and signed *The Mayflower Compact.*"

Mercy picked up Rose's chart and wrote down the blood pressure numbers. "That must have been a great dream. Winston Churchill is often quoted as saying *The Mayflower Compact* is 'One of the remarkable documents in history, a spontaneous covenant for political organization.'"[62]

Rose reached over to the book lying on the table next to her bed. "I know it was a political and historical document, but I don't remember the exact words of the 'Compact.' I'm curious now, so I'll have to read the actual wording while I wait for breakfast. I do get some breakfast, right?"

Mercy laughed. "Yeah, it should be here any minute."

The door to Rose's room opened, and another nurse wheeled in a cart with different trays of food on it. She passed one over to Mercy, who placed the tray on Rose's bedside table and then twisted the top of the table over Rose's bed.

Both of the nurses waved as they left. As Rose ate her oatmeal, she first watched the news on TV. There was some information about the train crash, but a reason for the crash was not mentioned. More than thirty people were injured in the train crash, but no one had been killed. After watching the pictures of the train crash for just a minute, Rose turned the TV off and read *The Mayflower Compact* several times. She then continued reading about the Pilgrims in one of her books.

Mercy came back into Rose's room and asked, "Are you done reading *The Mayflower Compact?*"

Rose looked up at the nurse and smiled. "Yeah, I finished reading it. I like the whole idea of everyone signing a document about obeying all of the laws. We should have everyone today sign a document about agreeing to obey all of our laws."

"I think we have too many laws today for something like that to work."

"Yeah, you're right, Mercy."

"The laws that the Pilgrims agreed to obey are the ones that they themselves created, so in a sense, the 'Compact' is a document that ties everyone together into a cohesive and democratic group."

Rose smiled. "They are agreeing to follow their own laws, but the 'Compact' also mentions the 'reign of our Sovereign Lord King James.'"[63]

"That's right. They aren't agreeing to only follow their own laws. They're also acknowledging that King James is their king."

Rose sighed. "It's nice, though, that the two different groups of Pilgrims—the Puritans and the other *Mayflower* passengers—vowed to follow the same set of laws."

A voice from the open doorway of Rose's room said, "So, what do you think of vows made by people who are alive today?"

Rose immediately recognized her husband Travis's voice. Her eyes widened, showing her surprise. She quickly turned her head in his direction, but then stopped herself from looking at his face. Her voice sounded slightly upset as she asked, "You're not talking about wedding vows, are you?"

"Well, you're not wearing your wedding ring or even your engagement ring."

Rose glanced at her left hand, which had no rings on it. She then looked across the room at Travis's hand. He was wearing his wedding ring. When she gazed at his face, she realized from his expression that he had noticed her looking at his ring. She nervously glanced out the window to her left and then said, "Travis, it's nice that you came here to visit me, but it's a long drive for you."

"It's only a little over four hours."

"You must have gotten up early to get here at ten o'clock in the morning."

"I needed to see you, and I couldn't sleep anyway."

Rose looked back at Travis. He had dark circles under his blue eyes and was watching her intently. She moved the table away from her bed and sat up with her legs over the side of her bed. "Did my mom call you?"

Travis hesitated before saying, "Yeah, she did. She was worried about you." He paused for a few seconds before quickly adding, "I was worried about you, too." The tone of his voice showed his feelings for her, but he was still standing near the door of her room. His body posture looked almost like he wanted to leave, and he was standing closer to the door than he was to her. Rose sighed and glanced down at her knee. The scar was showing. She pulled one of the sheets over so that it covered both of her legs before saying, "I think it's nice that you stopped by."

"I didn't just stop by. I'm staying." The strength of Travis's voice showed that he meant what he was saying.

"I don't think they'll just let you stay in my room." Rose looked over at where Mercy had been standing. She was no longer there or anywhere else in the room. Mercy had probably left her alone with Travis on purpose.

"I have a hotel room within walking distance, and my boss knows that I might need to take more than a day or two off."

"What?" Rose asked. "I thought I could go home today or tomorrow."

Travis's face lit up with joy. "That would be so great!"

Rose looked at how happy Travis was and smiled. "They just want to keep me here for a day or so because I bumped my head and have a headache. Otherwise, I'm okay."

"Good! As soon as they release you, I'm driving you home. You can stay with me."

Rose frowned. "I don't know about that."

"Why not? We're married. It's about time we got back together again."

"We still have problems. I don't think my being sick right now will make things any better."

Travis's chin looked frozen in place as he said, "You have to come back home with me."

"No, I don't. And you can't tell me what to do!"

"I'm not telling you what to do." Travis took a step forward so that he was closer to Rose. "I'm just trying to help."

Rose sighed. "Thanks for trying to help me, Travis, but I want to make my own decisions."

Travis said with a sarcastic tone in his voice, "Okay, so what do you want to do? Walk from New York to Rhode Island with a headache and a bad knee?"

"It's not really any of your business!" Rose stared at Travis until he turned his face away and looked out toward the window on the other side of her bed.

After a few minutes of cold silence, Travis said, "I told your parents that I'd get you back home safely. You really should come back to Rhode Island with me."

"No, I don't think so. Look at us! Even now, we're fighting."

"What are you going to do? You don't want to stay in New York, do you?"

"I was going to take a train back home again. Under the circumstances, I don't think the train company will charge me for another ticket. In fact, they're likely to even give me a free taxi ride from the hospital to the train station."

Before Travis had a chance to say anything else, Mercy appeared at the door. She waved at Travis and then walked past him while pushing a cart. She removed Rose's food tray before giving her a piece of paper and a pencil. "Rose, just in case the doctor wants you to stay here for another day, you should fill out this meal paper. You just need to check off the items you like."

"Thanks, Mercy." Rose looked down at the paper and then started checking off a few of the boxes. "It's a good thing I love turkey."

Travis took a step forward into the room as he said, "If the doctor keeps you today, Rose, I can bring you some lunch and supper."

"You know that I really do like turkey."

"Yeah, but you also like salad, pasta, hamburgers, pizza, chicken, and anything chocolate."

"The menu has salad, chicken, and other things on it."

"Are there any chocolate items?"

Rose looked down at the menu and then back up at Travis. "No. How about if I call you after the doctor sees me? Then I'll know if I'll be staying here for another day or not."

"Okay, but if you haven't called me by eleven o'clock, I'll call you before I bring you some lunch."

"All right. I'd love a cheeseburger for lunch."

Travis smiled as he turned to leave. After taking a step toward the door, he stopped. "I almost forget. Your mom gave me a couple of books to give to you."

"What kinds of books?"

"They're all history books. Your mom said you were reading about the Pilgrims."

"Yeah, I am. Do you have the books with you?"

"They're out in my car. I can bring them in right now, if you want."

"No, that's okay. If I have to stay until tomorrow, though, it would be nice to have another book to read. I've almost finished the two books that I brought with me."

"Okay. If the doctor keeps you here for another day, I'll bring you the other books at lunchtime."

"And a cheeseburger and fries?"

"Yes, definitely. Is twelve noon okay?"

"Noontime sounds great. Thanks, Travis. I'll see you later."

Rose watched Travis as he walked over to the door of her room, where he turned around quickly. He was obviously trying to see if Rose was still watching him. She was. They both smiled at each other, and then he left.

Mercy said, "The doctor should be here any minute."

Immediately, a man in a white uniform walked into the room. His nametag said, "Dr. Samuel Fuller."

He picked up Rose's chart and asked, "How are you feeling today, Rose?"

"Okay. Just a slight headache. And my knee is a little sore." Rose showed her knee to the doctor.

"Well, we already took some x-rays. If your knee doesn't feel better by tomorrow morning, we'll run some more tests."

"So you want to keep me here for another day?"

"Well, hopefully, you can go home tomorrow, but we'll see how you're doing."

"Okay. So how about my headache?"

Dr. Fuller looked at Rose's eyes with a small light. "You seem to be better today. However, you were unconscious. I think a neurologist should come in and check you out. He might want to run one or two tests."

Mercy asked, "Which doctor will it be?"

"Dr. William Brewster."

Rose said, "That's really interesting. You and Doctor Brewster both have the same names as passengers who were on the *Mayflower.*"

"I don't know about Dr. Brewster, but I know I'm descended from Samuel Fuller. He was a *Mayflower* passenger. He also was a doctor and a church deacon. Since the seventeenth century, many of my relatives have been doctors."

"That's so neat. I'm descended from John Robinson, the pastor of the Pilgrims before they left Leiden."

Dr. Fuller looked at Mercy and said, "Mercy, you're descended from William Bradford, the second governor of Plymouth, right?"

"Yeah, I am. A lot of the people in our country are descended from the Pilgrims. It's too bad that many of them don't even know who their ancestors are."

Dr. Fuller looked back at Rose and said, "Okay. I'll check back with you later."

After the doctor had left the room, Mercy said, "Dr. Brewster is only at the hospital between twelve and two. Maybe you should have your husband bring you a cheeseburger for supper, rather than at twelve noon."

"Oh, so I can't have any lunch?"

"Yeah, I'll bring you a turkey sandwich earlier, maybe around eleven thirty."

"Okay."

"You can use the line phone to call your husband."

"Okay. Can I call my parents, too?"

"Of course. I'll be back in a little while."

Rose called her parents first. She told them about how she was feeling. They tried to convince her into letting Travis drive her back home again. Rose finally said, "I'll think about it. Whether we stay separated or go back together again, we'll still have to talk about things."

When Rose called Travis, she told him about having to stay in the hospital for at least one more day. He said, "That's probably the best way. They might have to do more tests."

"Yeah. Also, I have to see another doctor, and he won't be here until twelve or later."

"Should I bring you some lunch at a later time, or just wait until supper?"

"Supper should be fine. I'm a little tired anyway, so I should take a nap this afternoon. How about bringing supper about six o'clock?"

"Six o'clock sounds great. If you need anything earlier, please call me."

"Okay, I will."

After saying good-bye, Rose lay back down in her bed and immediately fell asleep. The nurse woke her up for an early lunch, and Dr. Brewster came in about noon. After he checked her records, he did a few other tests.

"You have a minor concussion, Rose. By tomorrow, you should be feeling better."

"If my headache goes away, will it be okay for me to go home?"

"Probably, but we'll see later."

"Thanks," Rose said. Before she could ask Dr. Brewster if he was descended from the Pilgrim William Brewster, he disappeared into the hallway. She said to Mercy, "Dr. Brewster must be a descendant of one of the Pilgrims."

"Why do you say that?"

"He disappeared very quickly. He's good at hiding himself. The William Brewster who was a Pilgrim had to hide on the *Mayflower*."

"Really?"

"Yeah, he was trying to avoid being arrested."

"What did he do?"

"In Leiden, he was a publisher. King James, the British king, didn't like some of the things he published."

"I guess freedom of the press wasn't possible back then."

"Not in England. There was more freedom in Holland."

After saying good-bye, Mercy left. Rose went back to sleep again. She had a short dream about Travis, but it wasn't a lucid dream. When she woke up about five o'clock, she didn't remember her dream, but she was thinking in a positive way about seeing her husband that evening. She turned on the TV and watched a *Law and Order* show.

About an hour later, someone knocked on the door. Rose yelled out "Come in."

Travis entered; he was carrying two books, as well as a bag of food. He smiled at his wife before taking cheeseburgers, fries, and sodas out of the bag. After placing all of the food on the bedside table next to Rose, he asked, "Is there a reason why you're reading about the Pilgrims?"

Rose slid some of the food over closer to Travis before saying, "I'm curious about my ancestry."

"I know you're a descendent of John Robinson, the Puritan pastor, but I've never seen you read history books before." Travis started to eat one of the cheeseburgers while Rose began eating some French fries.

After a minute of silence, Rose said, "I'm just interested in my heritage. Haven't you ever been curious about yours?"

"Yeah, but I've never really had the time to do any research."

"There are references to a 'Travis Hopkins' in Bradford's book. Wouldn't it be interesting if you were descended from that Hopkins, the one who was on the *Mayflower?*"

"Really? Where is my name listed?"

Rose picked up *Of Plymouth Plantation,* looked in the index, and then turned to page 68 of the book. "It says here that you're one of the 'principal men' who went with Standish in a shallop on December 6th, 1620, to try and find a good place to set up their home."[64]

"I've never been called 'a principal man' before."

Rose looked at his face. She could tell that he was being completely serious.

"You know you were the principle man at our wedding."

Travis smiled. "Just at the wedding?"

Rose laughed. "Okay, you've always been my principal man."

"Really?"

"Yeah." Her eyes lit up as she added, "Oops! I forgot about my dad."

"Well, I guess it's okay if you also care about your father." Travis took a bite of his cheeseburger while Rose looked at the color of his hair. It was reddish-brown, and it looked a lot neater than Myles Standish's hair did. When Travis picked up his can of soda and took a drink, Rose watched his bicep muscles. He was wearing a sleeveless tee shirt, so his arm muscles looked much nicer than Myles Standish's did. When Travis put the soda can down on the table, Rose realized that she had been looking at his bare arms; she hadn't even noticed that he was wearing the tee shirt she had given to him on his last birthday. An eagle and an American flag were flying in the wind on his shirt. She had bought that shirt for him because he loved birds and was patriotic.

"So, I love that shirt of yours, Travis." She watched his facial expressions intently to see how he reacted to her use of the word "love."

"You already know that I'm madly in love with this shirt. I'm also still madly in love with you, Rose."

"I love you, too, Travis. I always have."

"Then why are we separated?"

"Because of our fights."

They were both quiet for a moment. Travis then asked, "How are you feeling tonight?"

"Okay. The doctor said I might be able to go home tomorrow."

"That sounds great. I'll give you a ride home."

Rose's face showed her anger. "You can't just tell me what to do."

Travis asked in a sarcastic tone: "Do you want to drive yourself home?"

"I'm over eighteen. I can do what I want to. I can drive, take a train, or even fly back home." Rose turned on the TV and turned up the sound so that she wouldn't have to listen to Travis.

A nurse came into the room and asked, "Can you please turn down the TV? It might bother the other patients."

Rose said, "Oh, I'm really sorry." She turned the sound down, and the nurse left.

Travis and Rose didn't speak to each other for the next few minutes. They both quietly ate their food and didn't look at each other's faces. Finally, Travis was done eating. As he was leaving the room, he said, "Good night, Rose. I'll call you in the morning."

Rose watched the news, did some reading about the Pilgrims' arrival in the New World, and fell asleep before nine o'clock.

LOOKING FOR A HOME

Rose realized that she was lucid dreaming again when she found herself on the upper deck of the *Mayflower*. She looked at the sun, which had the following date and time written in blazing yellow rays across its face: "Saturday, 11/11/1620, at 11:11 p.m." Rose wondered if the elevens in the date and time were real or fake. It was also strange that an eleven o'clock time at night would be blazing across a sun.

Rose shielded her tired eyes from the sun's bright rays and then looked down slightly. The shore was close enough so that she could see numerous trees, including pine, oak, and juniper. The beach was very sandy, rather than rock-covered.

Next to Rose on the *Mayflower* were some wooden pieces of a small boat. There were some tools—an axe, a saw, and a hammer—near the pieces of wood. Some of the Pilgrims began to talk about the wooden pieces of the small single-sail boat, which they referred to as a "shallop."

"Someone might have cut out pieces of the wood from the shallop."

"Maybe 'twas needed for a fire to keep someone warm."

"What sayest thou?"

"Perhaps the shallop was not broken by accident."

"Nay, I think the shallop was broken when too many people were sleeping in it."

"Ay, there was too much weight."

"I saw the people who were sleeping in it."

"I saw them, too."

"It must have been an accident."

"The shallop needeth to be repaired."

"Sir John Alden will repair it."

"While John repaireth the shallop, we can use the longboat and explore the coastline."

Some of the men readied themselves to go ashore. A tall young man turned to a shorter, more experienced-looking Pilgrim. The shorter man was muscular and had red hair. Rose immediately realized that he was Myles Standish, the soldier who had been giving military training to the Pilgrims. She knew he was married, but he still kept reminding her of Travis because they both had red hair. Maybe this was how her subconscious was trying to help her to connect with her husband.

The tall young man asked, "Myles, what if we are ambushed by the Indians? There are too many of them for us to win."

Rose glanced briefly at the tall young man and then looked back at Myles. He was scratching his chin in the same way that her husband did. Rose realized that she was controlling Myles' actions within her lucid dreaming; she was making Myles act like her husband Travis. She closed her eyes and tried to picture her husband in a Pilgrim outfit, hoping that he himself—rather than Myles—would appear within her dream.

Rose opened her eyes, but Travis wasn't there. She still saw Myles with the tall young man and another Pilgrim. The second Pilgrim asked Myles, "What should we do? If too many Indians shoot at us with their arrows, should we run away to the boat, or should we stay and fight?"

The tall young man asked, "If we run away, should all of us follow thee to the boat, or should we run down different paths?"

Myles turned to the tall Pilgrim. "What dost thou think?"

"If they are not shooting at us with their arrows, we should try to be friends. We can share some of our food with them."

The second Pilgrim said, "Nay, we should not share no food with them. We have not enough food for our own women and children."

Myles nodded his head in agreement. "Ay, we are low on food. But we can still offer them a small amount. And we can give them some other things, like clothing and shoes and dishes and tools."

"What will happen if the Indians attack us?"

Myles looked at the nervous expression on the Pilgrim's face before replying, "If they immediately attack us, then we shall stay together. There are not enough of us to divide up into groups. We can fight together or run for the longboat together."

"How will I know what to do?"

"I will make signs with my hands to show thee in what direction to fight or to run." Myles moved his hands, showing the Pilgrim some examples of signs to stay and fight, as well as signs to run and hide.

Rose said, "Those hand gestures look like the ones my husband Travis makes. Are you really making those hand gestures, Myles, or am I creating them so that you'll look like my husband?"

The tall Pilgrim ignored Rose and said to Myles, "Ay, when the Indians attack, we will watch for the motions of thy hands."

The other Pilgrim asked Myles, "Thou hast taught us many positions for our swords. Canst thou show me which is the one that is thy favorite?"

Myles said with a smile, "I will show thee when we have reached the beach."

Myles and fifteen other Pilgrims got into the longboat and rowed to the Cape Cod coastline. When they reached the shoreline, the Pilgrims got out of the longboat, waded through the water, and walked out onto the sand. Myles said, "I will now show my favorite position for my sword to all of you." He quickly pulled his sword up out of its case and curved it upwards, where he stopped the sword's motions. "From here, I have a choice of doing many different moves, so this is my favorite positioning."

After watching Myles's sword, the Pilgrims tried the same sword position. They then stood quietly on the beach for a few minutes, carefully surveying their surroundings. When a pair of birds noisily flew off of a tree's branches, all of the Pilgrims' faces seemed anxious as they turned to watch the birds' movements. The Pilgrims were obviously listening and watching for signs of Native people, so any noise at all immediately grabbed their attention. After they had finished exploring the shore, they then cut off some juniper branches.

One of the Pilgrims said, "These are the best branches. They smell so sweet."

"Ay, and they will keep us warm." He shivered and then curved his arms around his chest, showing a posture that craved more warmth.

"It will be a blessing to taste food that is hot."

The Pilgrims stood quietly for a minute. They seemed to be thinking about being warm. One of the Pilgrims licked his cracked lips; he was probably thinking about drinking warm soup. Another one bent forward, rubbed his gloved hands together over a make-believe fire, and then quickly moved his hands backwards, away from the heat; he was acting as if he had just rubbed his cold hands together too close to the top of a very warm fire.

One of the older Pilgrims said, "Juniper makes a most lively fire. With juniper, we need to be watchful of the sparks."

"Ay. Even my children have had training, so they can do that correctly."

Later that day, they brought the juniper branches back to the *Mayflower*, where they were still sleeping every night.

Rose looked up at the sun. With its rays circulating out from its center, the sun looked like a clock. It soon changed into the moon and then back to being a sun again. The date would now be Sunday, November 12. The sunshine fell upon the Pilgrims, who were on the *Mayflower*. They listened to a sermon, prayed, and sang psalms together. They then spent the rest of the day with their families and friends.

On the next day, Monday, many of the *Mayflower* passengers and crew members came ashore. The women did laundry while the men cut wood, looked for water, and explored the coastline. The children showed their joy at being on land again by running, waving their hands, and playing with branches, stones, and shells.

Rose's sampler suddenly appeared in the middle of the beach. On the sampler was a picture of the sun that changed into a moon. The sun and moon pictures kept on switching places. Rose realized that multiple days and nights were passing. As more time passed, the sampler began to grow. It kept on growing until it covered the whole shoreline.

Some Pilgrim men began to explore different sections of the giant sampler. As they walked down a path in a forest, one of the Pilgrims said, "We must be very careful of the Indians."

A second Pilgrim said, "Indians in Virginia have killed many of the settlers."

"And the Indians in the colonies that belong to Spain have also killed many of the explorers from Europe."

The Pilgrims walked up to a mound of dirt and stopped. The mound looked like something was buried there. The Pilgrims dug into the mound until they found some corn. One of them said, "This corn belongeth to the Indians."

"Ay. They are hiding themselves deep inside the forest."

"Dost thou wish to go looking for them?"

"We cannot speak their language."

"There are too many Indians for us to fight with them."

"Why did they bury their corn?"

"The Indians wanted to keep their corn safe."

"There are other things here that were buried with the corn."

"Treasure is sometimes buried in the ground."

"The corn is treasure. It was buried because it will be used for seed. The Indians will use it in the Spring."

"Nay, I think not. The corn was put into the ground because it was discarded."

All of the ears of corn were collected. Then one of the Pilgrims asked, "Should we leave payment for the corn?"

"If we leave items of value in the ground, they only will be stolen."

"Or the items will be ruined by the animals in the forest."

Finally, the Pilgrims decided to take the corn away without leaving any kind of payment. After they had brought the corn back to their boat, they were very thankful to have found some food. They discussed with their fellow Pilgrims what had happened on their trip ashore. One of them wrote down some notes in his journal: "And sure it was God's good providence that we found this corn, for else we know not how we should have done, for we knew not how we should find or meet with any of the Indians, except it be to do us a mischief."[65]

Rose realized that, even though many of the Pilgrims might have wanted to give the Natives something in return for taking their corn, they were unable to do so. They had not yet established any kind of a relationship with the Native people, so it was impossible to communicate with them about purchasing their corn.

On another trip across one of the paths on the sampler, the Pilgrims found corn and beans in a different mound of dirt. They brought it back to their boat. Then they found skeletons in some other mounds. They helped themselves to some household items in one of the Native people's homes. On another trip, the

Pilgrims had no shovels, and the ground was frozen. They used their swords to dig into the mounds of dirt and retrieve some ears of corn. Rose was surprised to see the number of items taken by the Pilgrims from the Native people's homes and burial sites.

Another day began. Rose was on a path in the forest, and the words "The First Encounter" appeared on her sampler. She knew this phrase meant the first meeting between the Pilgrims and the Native people. She looked around, but only saw some of the Pilgrims. One of them said, "I will read a prayer in the bible. It is called 'A Godly Prayer to be Said at All Times.'" He began to read the prayer out loud; Rose heard some of the words that were near the end of the prayer: "Let thy mighty hand and outstretched arm (O Lord) be still our defense, thy mercy and loving-kindness in Jesus Christ thy dear Son our salvation...."[66]

After the Pilgrims were finished praying, they carried some items down to their boat and then went back up the path into the forest to have breakfast. Suddenly, arrows began to fly. Brass tops, deer horns, and eagles' claws were attached to some of the arrows. Most of the Pilgrims ran down to the shore, where they had left their muskets. After they recovered their muskets, they joined Captain Myles Standish, who was already shooting at the Native people. Rose looked around, trying to see if Travis would also show up, but he didn't. Only Native men and Pilgrim men were present in the forest. Their arrows and bullets flew into the trees, bushes, and undergrowth of the forest.

Some of the Native people were crying words that Rose could not understand. From the group of Pilgrims came the words "Well! Well!"[67] Then Rose heard the words "Be of good courage!"[68]

The Native people began to scream: "Woach woach ha ha hach woach."[69] Then one of the Natives strode forward and stood behind a tree. He was close enough to the Pilgrims for their bullets to easily reach him. This Courageous Native grabbed an arrow, slid it into his bow, and let it fly. One of the Pilgrims stooped down low, and the arrow made a whizzing sound as it flew inches above his head and torso.

The Courageous Native shot two more arrows; neither one hit any of the Pilgrims. Then three bullets from muskets went past the Courageous Native; he didn't run, but rather stayed where he was. Finally, one of the Pilgrims took aim at him directly. The Courageous Native gave an "extraordinary cry and away they all went."[70] The Pilgrims followed the Native people for about a quarter of a mile. The Pilgrims then shouted and shot bullets from their muskets. Finally, they decided to return to their boat. In their first armed encounter with the Indians, no one was hurt. One of the Pilgrims said, "Thus it pleased God to vanquish our enemies and give us deliverance."[71]

After this initial encounter between the Pilgrims and the Native people, eighteen arrows were picked up by the Pilgrims. Master Christopher Jones, the captain of the *Mayflower,* said that he would be sending them back to England.

When she returned to the *Mayflower,* Rose saw one of the Pilgrim men writing down the following note in his journal: "[B]y the especial providence of God, none of them either hit or hurt us though many came close by us and on every side of us, and some coats which hung up in our barricade were shot through and through."[72]

On another day, Rose saw some of the Pilgrims try to kill some deer. Even though they were unsuccessful, William Bradford was caught by one of the Native people's deer traps. After his fellow Pilgrims laughed at the rope trap that was curled around his leg, they helped him to escape. Even though the rope from the trap must have scraped his leg, Bradford seemed to be walking normally as he and his fellow Pilgrims continued on their hunting excursion.

Days and nights went past as the Pilgrims kept on exploring the Plymouth Bay area; they were looking for a good home site. Near the end of December, 1620, they decided to settle in Plymouth; they began to make plans for the colony and started to build the first house.

On a different day, Myles Standish and at least four men went on an expedition to look for Native people. After some empty Native homes were found, a musket was fired into the forest. One of the Pilgrims, possibly Myles, had just shot an eagle. Rose watched as the limp body of the eagle was carried off by the Pilgrims. She knew they needed the bird's meat for food, but she also knew that her husband Travis would never have shot an eagle. He loved to watch birds fly.

This scene made Rose certain that the Myles in her dream was not the Travis in her reality. Would she remember this difference when she woke up? Would she want the real Travis when she woke up? She prayed that she would.

More time went past. Some sailors were walking along the shoreline. One of them—a Sharp-eyed Sailor—was looking at the ground, possibly trying to find crabs. He suddenly stopped and pointed to some movement several feet ahead of him. Within the sand was a small puddle with moving water. The Sharp-eyed Sailor went up to the edge of the puddle, bent over, and pulled out a herring. It was still alive; the sailor put it in a sack and then said, "The master of our ship, Captain Christopher Jones, will want this fish."

"Dost thou think that he will share it?"

"Nay, I think not. The fish is too small."

"It seemeth to me that too many of us are looking at this one small fish with hunger in our eyes."

"Our master should have it." The other sailors soon shook their heads in agreement, but they still focused their eyes for a long time on the one tiny fish.

Two Pilgrims were standing about thirty feet away from the soldiers. One of the Pilgrims said, "So far, we only have found one cod."

"We pray to find more fish."

"Ay, we need hooks that are small to catch them."

Rose looked out at the ocean; she saw many fish and a few whales. Seagulls were flying over the ocean and sometimes landing on the shore. She turned to look at the trees behind her. Even though it was winter, other birds were flying in the forest. They began to make swishing noises; they sounded as if they were moving the branches with their feet as they flew from one tree to another. The swishing noises became louder and closer together. When the noises were almost continuous, Rose opened her eyes.

Plymouth Rock Canopy Building

Plymouth Rock

Pilgrim Hall Museum

Mayflower Cow Statue in the Plimoth Plantation Visitor Center
Photo Usage Courtesy of Plimoth Plantation

The *Mayflower II*
Photo Usage Courtesy of Plimoth Plantation

Mayflower II Sail and Rigging Museum Display
Photo Usage Courtesy of Plimoth Plantation

The Captain's Cabin on the *Mayflower II*
Photo Usage Courtesy of Plimoth Plantation

Inside the Captain's Cabin on the *Mayflower II*
Photo Usage Courtesy of Plimoth Plantation

A Fireplace on the *Mayflower II*
Photo Usage Courtesy of Plimoth Plantation

A Cannon on the *Mayflower II*
Photo Usage Courtesy of Plimoth Plantation

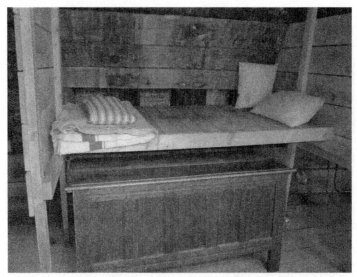

A Bed and Chest on the *Mayflower II*
Photo Usage Courtesy of Plimoth Plantation

A Sleeping Area on the *Mayflower II*
Photo Usage Courtesy of Plimoth Plantation

A Wampanoag Home at Plimoth Plantation
Photo Usage Courtesy of Plimoth Plantation

Interior of a Wampanoag Home at Plimoth Plantation
Photo Usage Courtesy of Plimoth Plantation

The Meetinghouse in the English Village at Plimoth Plantation
Photo Usage Courtesy of Plimoth Plantation

On the *Mayflower II's* "Tween" Deck
Photo Usage Courtesy of Plimoth Plantation

Cannons in the English Village Meetinghouse at Plimoth Plantation
Photo Usage Courtesy of Plimoth Plantation

Home Construction in the English Village at Plimoth Plantation
Photo Usage Courtesy of Plimoth Plantation

An English Village Building at Plimoth Plantation
Photo Usage Courtesy of Plimoth Plantation

A Fenced-in Yard in the English Village at Plimoth Plantation
Photo Usage Courtesy of Plimoth Plantation

Inside an English Village Home at Plimoth Plantation
Photo Usage Courtesy of Plimoth Plantation

An Outdoor Oven in the English Village at Plimoth Plantation
Photo Usage Courtesy of Plimoth Plantation

Dancing Role-playing Actors at Plimoth Plantation
Photo Usage Courtesy of Plimoth Plantation

Praying at a Re-enactment of a Pilgrim Wedding at Plimoth Plantation
Photo Usage Courtesy of Plimoth Plantation

A Role-playing Actor at a Wedding Feast Table at Plimoth Plantation
Photo Usage Courtesy of Plimoth Plantation

Living with the Past

As Rose was waking up, she heard a nurse rolling a cart into her room. The cart's wheels were making swishing noises. The nurse said in a cheerful voice, "You just love oatmeal, right?"

"Actually, I do. My mom used to make me oatmeal all the time when I was a kid."

"So you had oatmeal every day?" The nurse placed a tray with oatmeal, coffee, juice, and yogurt on the table in front of Rose.

Rose laughed. "Actually, I had cold cereal more often than oatmeal. But when my mom cooked breakfast, it was usually oatmeal with raisins and a little bit of brown sugar." Rose put a spoon in her oatmeal and stirred it around. "I know this is a hospital, but this oatmeal still looks really plain."

"You're very observant." The nurse smiled. "It's just plain oatmeal with some milk, but I might be able to get you some raisins."

"No thanks. I know you're really busy after that train wreck on Monday. I'll be okay with this blueberry yogurt for something sweet."

After the nurse wheeled the breakfast cart out of the room, Rose turned on the TV and began eating. Another nurse came into the room. Rose looked over at her and recognized Mercy, who asked, "Is your headache better today?"

"Actually, it is. I feel completely normal again."

"That's great! After you finish eating, you may want to have a shower and get dressed. Your clothes are in the closet."

"Thanks, I will." Rose began to eat her yogurt as Mercy left the room. On the TV, a reporter was talking about Monday's train wreck. It had happened because an SUV had hit the back of a larger truck, forcing both of the vehicles onto the railroad tracks. The train's locomotive had driven through the vehicles without going off of the track, but broken metal from the SUV and the truck had done damage to the locomotive and other cars. The driver of the SUV was probably drunk; the news reporter claimed that the driver had refused to take a breathalyzer test.

The reporter explained more details about the sequence of events. Right before the train knocked the two vehicles off of the railroad track, the truck driver had saved the SUV driver by pulling him out of his vehicle. According to the reporter, both men were lucky to be alive. Even though the SUV's drunk driver was seriously injured from his initial crash into the truck, he was likely to live. Minor injuries had happened to the truck driver, several railroad employees, and at least twenty passengers.

Rose watched the pictures on the TV screen; she was surprised at the level of destruction from the train accident. It looked like many of the windows were either broken or popped outwards from their frames. Five cars were disconnected from each other. Three of the cars were on their sides. The snack car that Rose had been riding in appeared to be in the worst shape. The front of the car was crushed. The door that had been at the front of the car was now nowhere to be seen. The back half of the car looked like it was lying on a hill of scrap metal. There were dishes, broken tables, and pieces of chairs from the snack car scattered all over the tracks. Mixed in with these items were pieces of lounge chairs, shredded pillows, ripped blankets, and torn mattresses from at least one other railroad car.

Rose continued to watch pictures from the train wreck on the TV as she ate her breakfast. Multiple people were investigating the accident scene. After Rose was finished with her breakfast, she had a shower, found her clothes in the closet, and put them on. When she walked back out to watch the TV again, there were more scenes from the train wreck, and the railroad tracks were being cleared of debris.

A reporter said, "It'll be at least a week before any trains can use this section of the tracks."

On the television screen, a chart showing delays for several train routes appeared. The same reporter's voice explained that the listed trains would still run, but they would be using detours for a section of their routes, resulting in added rail time before the passengers arrived at their destinations.

Rose reached over to the small table on the side of her bed, but before she could find her return train ticket that was in her purse, she heard a knock on the door and yelled "Come in."

Dr. Fuller walked into the room, leaving the door open. "How are you feeling today?"

"Wonderful! Even my headache's gone."

The doctor picked up Rose's chart and looked at some of the writing on the top page. "Well, it looks like all of your vital signs are normal again."

"Can I go home today?"

Before Dr. Fuller could answer, Travis walked into the room. "Am I interrupting anything? Should I come back?"

Dr. Fuller turned toward Travis's voice before asking, "Who are you?"

"Travis. I'm Rose's husband."

In a loud voice, Rose said, "We're separated."

Travis took another couple of steps into the room so that he was near Rose's bed. "I'm hoping we'll get back together again."

The doctor smiled and then turned back to look at Rose's chart.

"So can I go home today?"

The doctor wrote a few words on the chart before putting it down. "You should be okay if you go home today, but you live in Rhode Island, right?"

"Yeah, I do."

"If you go home this morning, I'd rather you not take a train ride home by yourself. It would be better if someone else drove you home." His eyes moved to his right, resting on Travis.

Travis's smile lit up his face. "I'd love to take her home, doctor. It'll give us a chance to talk."

Rose's eyebrows were raised as she asked Travis, "Did you and the doctor plan this whole thing out ahead of time?"

Travis laughed. "No, but if I hadn't been so upset yesterday about how you were feeling, Rose, I probably would have considered something like that."

"Okay, Travis, I believe you." She sighed before continuing. "And thanks for offering to take me home. It's really a good idea. We'll be able to talk about things."

The doctor said, "Okay, you can go home this morning, Rose. I'll let Mercy know." He waved, turned around, and walked out of the room.

The telephone next to Rose's bed rang. She picked it up and began talking to her father. "I'm okay. I just have a few scrapes and bruises."

"When your mom and I got the phone call from the hospital, we were so upset." He paused for a second and then asked, "Is Travis there?"

"Yeah, he is."

"Good, I wanted to go out to see you right away, but your mom convinced me to wait and let Travis see you instead."

Rose looked over at Travis and asked him, "Did you call my parents, or did they call you?"

"Someone at the hospital called me, and then I called your parents."

Rose started talking to her father again. "Travis is going to take me home later today."

"Are you okay with that, or should I come and give you a ride home?"

"I think it's a good idea for Travis and me to talk with each other. Riding back to Rhode Island together will give us a chance to do that."

"Okay."

"So, can I call you in a little while, dad? My oatmeal and coffee are getting cold."

"Oh, I'm sorry. Can you call me or your mom once you're in Travis's car and on your way home?"

"Yeah, I will." Rose hung up the phone, and Travis sat down in the chair next to her bed. He watched her as she took a sip of her coffee. "Do you want some of my coffee, Travis?"

"No, thanks. It's probably decaf."

"Yeah, I think it is." Rose took another sip. "It's also lukewarm."

Travis reached over and touched the side of the coffee cup. "It feels more like cold."

Rose laughed. "You're right, it is. That's what I hate about hospital food. By the time it's brought up to the room, it's usually lukewarm or cold."

"About a block from the hospital is a doughnut shop. When we leave, I'll pick up some hot coffee for us."

"A bagel would be nice, too."

"Two bagels—one for each of us—would be even better."

Mercy walked into the room and brought some papers and a pen over to Rose. "Your paperwork will be all set once you sign these forms."

"Okay." Rose made believe she was reading the top form, and then she just signed several papers without bothering to read anything else.

Mercy shook Rose's hand. "I'm so happy that you're feeling better. Take care."

Rose said, "Thanks. You're a really great nurse. You take care, too,—of yourself—not just of all your patients."

As Mercy turned around to leave, Travis asked her, "Do you know where Rose's luggage is?"

"Oh, I'm sorry for not showing you." Mercy walked over to the closet and opened up the door. "Everything in here is Rose's."

Rose put her book into her suitcase. She and Travis then left the room with Travis carrying everything, including her purse.

While they walked through several corridors in the hospital, Rose was limping slightly. As soon as they stepped outside into the parking lot, her limp disappeared.

Travis led the way over to a bright red Mustang. "Oh, you have a new car."

"Yeah, I bought it right before driving up here."

"So, can I drive it?"

Travis opened the trunk, slid his suitcase backwards, and put Rose's suitcase into the front part of the trunk. "I promised the doctor that I'd drive you back to Rhode Island, but as soon as we get back to our home state, I'll give you the keys." He smiled as he closed the trunk and held open the front door for Rose.

Rose sighed; then she stepped closer to Travis and leaned against the side of the car. "I know you're good at keeping your promises."

Their eyes met. Travis took a step closer to Rose and then slowly reached his left hand forward, brushing his fingertips lightly across her chin. Rose inched closer as his lips slowly moved toward her face. Beneath the warmth of the summer sun, Rose's blue eyes glanced up at Travis's blue eyes with the blue of the sky forming a soft frame for his head. The blues gradually faded as they both closed their eyes for their first kiss since their separation.

After just a few seconds, Travis pulled back. "Oh, I'm really sorry. I didn't mean to do anything that might get you mad."

Rose laughed. "I'm not mad, and the kiss was something that I wanted, too."

"Really?" His face lit up so that his eyes were sparkling more than the bright rays from the sun.

"Yeah, I did." With difficulty, Rose moved her eyes away from Travis's face and looked down at the cold gray of the asphalt beneath her feet. "However, if we're only happy together for a minute or two once every few days, I don't know if that's what we really want."

Travis sighed and took a step backwards. "We can talk about things on our trip back home."

Rose looked up at Travis and smiled. "Okay, that sounds like a plan."

After they both got into the car and put on their seatbelts, Travis drove to a doughnut shop and then out onto the highway. He turned on the radio, and "Fly Like an Eagle" by the Steve Miller Band began to play: "Time keeps on slippin', slippin', slippin' / Into the future."[73]

"Oh, I love that song. Can you turn it up?"

Travis turned the volume up. After the song was over, he turned the sound back down again. "It's strange that you still love that song."

"Why?"

"Because ever since your accident, you've been late for everything."

"That's because my knee hurts me sometimes."

"Even so, you're living in the past, rather than slipping into the future."

"No, I'm not living in the past."

"You're having dreams about history and your ancestors."

"I'm learning about my family. That doesn't mean I'm living in the past."

"Don't you think being late all the time is living in the past? It's like you're always trying to go backwards."

Rose's loud voice showed her anger when she asked, "Why are you picking on me now? I just got out of the hospital."

Travis glanced over at Rose's face and then turned back to watch the road again. "I'm sorry, Rose. I didn't mean to pick on you. I was just trying to help."

"That's why we're separated—because you're trying to help me too much."

"No, I think we're separated because we've been fighting too much."

Rose reached forward and turned the volume up on the radio.

Travis turned it back down again; Rose immediately turned it up. Travis sighed and left the volume up high.

After a few minutes of boring songs on the radio, Foreigner's song "Cold as Ice" began to play. Rose turned the air conditioner up higher and then glared at Travis. He turned the air conditioning down, but she turned it back up again. He turned the vents on his side of the car toward the ceiling. Rose turned her vents toward Travis's side of the car and then glared at him. Finally, Travis sighed, pulled over to the side of the road, turned the car off, and said, "Okay, let's talk."

For a moment, they both stared angrily at each other; neither one spoke a single word. Then Travis asked, "Do you really think I'm as cold as ice?"

"Sometimes."

Travis silently watched the cars speeding past them on the highway. "Okay, I know I'm not perfect." He turned back to look at Rose. "How about you? Are you perfect?"

"Of course not. Only God is perfect."

Travis smiled. "So we do agree on something: only God is perfect."

Before Rose had a chance to reply, Travis began to stare into the rearview mirror. He then said, "Oh, no. We're in trouble for something."

Rose pulled down her sun visor and looked in the mirror. There was a police car behind them. One police officer stayed in the car while the other one walked up to the driver's side of Travis's car. Rose could see the officer's name tag through Travis's window; it said, 'Joseph Billington.' The officer asked Travis, "Is everything okay?"

"Yeah, we're fine."

The officer frowned and then asked, "Can I see your license?"

"Yes, sir, Officer Billington." Travis took his license out of his billfold and gave it to the officer, who walked back to the police cruiser and spoke with his partner.

Rose asked Travis, "Do you know what we did wrong?"

"Well, we weren't speeding; that's for sure."

Rose laughed before saying, "Possibly one of the brake lights isn't working on your car."

"It's a new car; everything should be okay."

A minute later, Officer Joseph Billington walked over to Travis's window. After giving Travis back his license, the officer asked him, "What's the emergency?"

"There isn't any emergency."

"Then why are you stopped in the emergency lane on the highway?"

Travis opened his mouth to say something and then changed his mind. He instead looked blankly at the officer.

Rose leaned forward slightly so that she could see the officer's face and then said, "It was an emergency. I was yelling, and Travis didn't want to get into an accident or anything. He was trying to keep us safe."

"Well, this is not the safest place to park. There's an exit less than a mile from here."

"Thanks, officer." Rose paused and then said, "Please don't give Travis a ticket. This whole thing is all my fault. I just got out of the hospital, and I was upset."

"Are you okay? Do you need to go back to the hospital?"

"No, thanks, officer. I'm okay physically. I was just grouchy, and we were fighting."

The officer asked her, "Are you two married?"

"We're separated."

Officer Billington smiled. "Well, it looks like you two are together, at least for the moment."

Rose glanced over at Travis before saying, "I guess we are together. At least for right now."

Officer Billington walked over to stand beside Rose's window and then asked her, "Did this man do anything to you?"

"No, Travis would never hurt me."

Travis said, "Officer Billington, none of this is Rose's fault. It's all my fault. I was picking on her for being late."

Rose added, "Lately, I've always been late, so you had a good reason to be upset at me."

"That doesn't really matter, Rose. It was just a bad time to bother you because you weren't feeling well."

Rose looked at Travis. Even though there was a distance of a couple of feet between them, she felt like they were much closer together. She reached out and touched his hand. He looked at her happy face, squeezed her hand, and said to the police officer, "Thanks so much for trying to help us, officer."

The police officer stood outside of the passenger's side window and carefully watched Rose and Travis communicate with each other through their eye contact. After a minute, the officer asked them, "Where are you going?"

Travis turned to face Officer Billington. "I'm driving Rose home to Rhode Island."

Rose looked at the officer's name tag again and said, "So, your name is Joseph Billington. Are you descended from Francis Billington, the one who was on the *Mayflower?*"

"I don't know much about my ancestors." He turned toward the police cruiser. His partner started to wave at him. Officer Billington told Travis and Rose, "You need to move your car somewhere else."

Travis smiled at the officer and said, "Yes, sir. We weren't thinking too clearly, but now we are."

Officer Billington walked back to his cruiser. His partner was already in the driver's seat, and the engine was running. The siren was turned on, and then the police cruiser pulled out onto the highway.

Rose said, "Thanks, Travis, for trying to take the blame for something that was my fault."

"It was all my fault."

"No, it was my fault."

"Are we fighting again?"

Rose laughed. "Yeah, I think we are. Let's try to not fight anymore, okay?"

Travis started up the car as he said, "Okay." He turned the radio and the air conditioning down before pulling out into the traffic on the highway.

Rose said, "Having a last name like Billington is interesting for a police officer."

"Why is that?"

"Well, Francis Billington was called a 'troublemaker' in several of the books that I've read. To have the same last name as a troublemaker might be embarrassing for a police officer."

"Possibly, but most people don't know who Francis Billington was."

"I know who he was."

"What kind of trouble did he get into?"

"If you want to stop the car for a minute, I'll get one of the books my mom gave me to read."

"Okay. I just hope the same police officers don't notice us in the emergency lane again."

"They were driving really fast, and I don't see them anymore. They have to be miles ahead of us."

Travis pulled over into the emergency lane and then helped Rose to find Nathaniel Philbrick's book *Mayflower A Story of Courage, Community and War*. After just a minute, they were back on the highway again.

Rose looked in the book's index and quickly found a section about Billington.

"Was Billington one of the Pilgrims or a crew member?"

"He was one of the Pilgrim passengers. He was only fourteen years old."

Rose read silently for a few minutes and then said to Travis: "The author Philbrick says, 'Like his father, the Billington boy had already developed a reputation as a troublemaker.'[74]"

"What did he do?"

"While on the *Mayflower*, he shot off a gun near some gunpowder. He almost started a fire that would have blown up the whole boat."

"I can see why he'd be called a 'troublemaker.'"

"Francis Billington also did something good: he found a five-mile wide lake that helped to supply the Pilgrims with fish and fowl."

"That was nice of him, especially considering the fact that many of the Pilgrims probably didn't like troublemakers like him."

"It says here in the Philbrick book that Bradford 'had no great love of the Billington family.'[75]"

"Bradford was William Bradford, the second governor of the Pilgrims, right?"

"Yeah, he was."

"So, Rose, what did other members of the Billington family do to make Bradford not like them?"

"His father got into a fight with Miles Standish and was almost punished in public."

"Were there any other Billington troublemakers?"

"Yeah, Travis, there were. Francis's older brother John got lost and wound up with the Nausets—Native people on Cape Cod; this was the Indian tribe that the Pilgrims had stolen corn from."

"Really?"

"Yeah, the Pilgrims dug up their gravesites, too."

"I always thought of the Pilgrims as heroes. It's nice to know that they messed up sometimes, too."

"Before I started to read about the Pilgrims, I also thought of them as heroes. And now, Travis, I still think of most of their actions as heroic. I don't know if I could have boarded the *Mayflower* with the courage that they had."

"I feel the same way, Rose."

"Anyway, even though Bradford didn't like the Billington family, he still ordered more than half of the adult males in Plymouth to go rescue John Billington from the Nausets."

"That's really interesting, Rose."

"When Bradford ordered half of the men to go and rescue the Billington teenager, he must have forgiven the family for being troublemakers. This reminds us that we too should forgive each other for our sins."

"The Bible says, 'For if you forgive others their trespasses, your heavenly Father will also forgive you'" (Matt. 6:14 RSV).

"Yeah, we need to forgive each other. We also need to love each other."

Travis glanced over at Rose and smiled. "We already do love each other, don't we?"

Rose shook her head in agreement. "We just need to figure out how to live with each other without fighting all of the time."

For a few minutes, Travis and Rose were silent. Rose read a few more pages from her book again. "This is interesting."

"What?"

"The Pilgrims eventually apologized to the Nausets and paid them back for stealing their corn."

Travis said, "They didn't just sin and ask for forgiveness. They repaid their victims."

"They also became friends with their victims."

"Really?"

"Yeah. The author of this book makes an interesting comparison."

"What?"

"He compares Winslow and Hopkins to John Billington."

"Who were Winslow and Hopkins?"

"They were two really good Pilgrims."

"How were they good?"

"According to Philbrick, they were successful 'in strengthening their settlement's ties with Massasoit and the Indians to the west. It would be left to a boy—and a Billington at that—to do the same for the Indians to the east.'[76]"

Travis smiled. "I don't know if it was John Billington who helped the Pilgrims' relationship with the Nausets or the men who went to rescue Billington."

"Billington must have connected in a positive way to the Nausets; otherwise, they would have killed him."

"You're right, Rose. So the Billingtons messed up sometimes, but they also did some wonderful things."

Rose briefly glanced over at Travis. "In our time, being a police officer with a name like Billington is definitely interesting."

"The Pilgrim teenager, Francis Billington, must have liked guns and gunpowder, but he didn't know how to use them correctly. The current-day police officer, Joseph Billington, has to be more of an expert when it comes to the proper use of guns."

Rose shook her head in agreement. "I'm sure the officer who stopped us knew how to use his gun. He was very professional and seemed really nice, too."

"I'm glad he stopped to help us."

"Yeah, so am I. He really did help us, too."

"That he did. We're not fighting right now."

"It's so nice being with you, Travis, except when we're fighting."

"I love being with you, too, Rose."

They were both silent for a few moments. Then Rose turned off the radio, took out her phone, and said, "I'd better call my mom."

"Say 'Hi' to her for me."

"I will." Rose hit a couple of the keys on her cell; within a few seconds, she said into her phone, "Hi, mom. Travis and I just started our ride back to Rhode Island."

"Are you feeling okay?"

"I'm fine. How are you and dad doing?"

"We're okay, too."

"Did you get that e-mail I sent to you from Granny's computer?"

"Yeah, I did. Your dad looked at the pictures of the watch case and then read the numbers that you e-mailed. He figured out what the numbers meant."

"Really? What do they mean?

"They're the longitude and latitude for Plymouth, Massachusetts."

"Interesting."

Rose talked to her mom for another few minutes and then put her phone away. After Rose told Travis about the meaning of the numbers, they talked about their jobs for a while. Then he asked her, "Have you learned any more interesting things about your ancestors lately?"

"Yeah, I did some reading in the hospital."

"What did you read?"

"I'll show you. You'll have to stop again, though, so I can get a different book out of the luggage."

Travis pulled over into the emergency lane and helped Rose to get the book.

Once they had gotten back into the car and were driving on the highway again, Rose said, "So, I've been travelling with the Pilgrims by having lucid dreams about their voyage."

"Are the dreams all the same?"

"No, they're all about different parts of the Pilgrim voyage. Every night, I've been trying to lucid dream about the next segment of the voyage to the New World." Rose explained about her dreams over the past week. "Tonight, I'm hoping to dream about them building homes in Plymouth, Massachusetts."

"This is really interesting timing."

"In what way?"

"I'm hoping we'll be able to see Plymouth together."

"Oh, that would be nice to do some day."

Travis smiled slightly and then asked, "How do you plan what you'll be dreaming?"

"Well, each day, I've been reading about another segment of the Pilgrims' voyage. As I'm going to sleep, I think about the details of that part of the voyage. So far, it's been working really well."

They were both quiet for a few minutes. Rose started to read silently from her book. Once every ten or fifteen minutes, she told Travis some of the information. She also looked up answers to a few of his questions. Before they had a chance to fight again, they arrived in Rhode Island. Travis immediately pulled over into the emergency lane. He got out, walked around to the other side of the car, opened up Rose's door, and handed her the car keys. Rose said, "Thanks, Travis, but I'm a little tired. I can wait until tomorrow to drive."

"Are you okay?"

"Yeah, I'm just a little tired." Rose got out for a minute to stretch and then sat back down again in her seat.

"All right." Travis got back into the car and drove the rest of the way to Rose's apartment. He carried her luggage into her living room and then said, "I have a surprise for you."

"Oh, really?" Rose's face showed her interest.

Travis took out his billfold and pulled out two pieces of paper that he had printed from his computer. "Here's one part of the surprise."

Rose looked at the first piece of paper, which had information about a Plymouth, Massachusetts hotel reservation. "Oh, is this for tonight?"

"Yeah, it is. I can change it, though, if you're too tired to follow the map on this picture of the sampler." He handed the second piece of paper to Rose.

"How did you get this picture?"

"After I talked with your mom about the stolen sampler, she e-mailed me this picture. It's the same one that she e-mailed to your grandmother last week."

"Oh, this is so neat. The picture came out really well. If I didn't have to go to work as soon as possible, we could try to follow the arrows on the map."

"I already spoke with your boss in the bank. He told me that you could have the rest of the week off."

"The only problem is that some auditors are supposed to be in the bank. They might even be there today."

Travis smiled. "No, not anymore, they're not. I spoke with your boss yesterday."

"You called my boss?"

"No, actually, he called me. He wanted to know how you were doing."

"So, what did Harry say about the auditors?"

"He said they're coming next week, instead of this week."

"In that case, I do have some vacation time left. This week would be a good time to use some of it." Rose smiled.

"And all of your relatives want you to look for the sampler's treasure."

"So I do have an important job to do."

"Yeah. And I'd love to help you, Rose, if you'll let me."

"Can you also get time off from work?"

"Yes, my boss said that I don't have to be back at work again until next Monday."

"That's so neat. We can have a little vacation together."

"I already have a suitcase packed in the Mustang, but do you need to repack a suitcase before we drive to the hotel?"

"Does the hotel have a pool?"

"Of course it does. I know how much you love indoor heated pools."

"Then I definitely need to repack some items. I don't have a bathing suit in my suitcase."

Travis moved Rose's suitcase into her bedroom. "While you repack, can I help myself to a soda?"

"Yeah, I need one, too." Rose turned to go out into the kitchen, but Travis stopped her.

He said, "I'll get sodas for both of us."

"I think I have some protein bars and chips, too, that we can munch on."

"I'll find them." Travis left the room and came back a minute later with sodas and snack items.

Rose quickly packed some different clothes into her two suitcases. She added some suntan lotion into the smaller bag. Travis picked up the suitcases, and they left Rose's apartment.

Travis asked, "Is it okay if we wait on eating until we get to Plymouth?"

"Yeah, I think we should wait until we've checked into the hotel. That way, we can avoid most of the worst rush-hour traffic."

Travis put Rose's suitcases into the trunk of his new car, held open the door for her, and then got into the driver's seat. After they were out on route 95, Travis said, "Tell me more about your dreams of the Pilgrims."

"I'm actually creating a dream story. It's like each of my dreams is one chapter in the story."

"What have the chapters been about?"

"On the first night, I dreamt about the beginning of the Pilgrims—about their life in England. Then on the next night, I tried to lucid dream about the second step in their journey—when they left England."

"What are you planning for tonight?"

"I'm going to try to dream about what happened in January 1621."

"What will you do if the lucid dream you're planning for tonight doesn't happen?"

"Then I'll just keep trying to dream about that part until it does happen. So I might have to dream for two or more nights until a planned lucid dream actually happens."

"You could keep dreaming for months about things that happened to the Pilgrims in the New World. When will your dream story reach its conclusion?"

"I haven't decided yet." Rose looked out the window for a minute and then asked, "Have you had any interesting dreams lately?"

"Yeah. I had one last night."

"What was it about?"

"I went into the basement to put laundry into the washer."

"Does your current apartment have a washer and a dryer in the basement?"

"No, it doesn't. I was in a house that looked sort of like our house did."

"So how was it different?"

"It had twelve washers and dryers, five dishwashers, ten different sinks, and lots of soap."

Rose started to laugh.

"What's so funny?"

"It sounds like your dream house was really clean."

"Actually, the house was clean, but I was dirty."

Rose looked sad. After a moment of silence, she asked, "So what happened?"

"I tried covering myself with soap and jumping into the washing machines, but it didn't work."

"You were probably too big to fit into the washers."

"Actually, I wasn't too big. The problem was that I was too dirty. None of the washers would work correctly with me inside."

"Then I tried the dishwashers and sinks, but they didn't get me clean, either. The water kept on foaming like crazy, and it would look dirty, but it didn't get me clean. I still was dirty."

"So, what do you think the dream means?"

"I think of myself as someone who is dirty."

"Well, I know you like to work on cars, but even so, you're usually very clean."

"Thanks."

"And you never wear cologne, but you still smell good."

"I think my dream just means that I'm feeling guilty about not helping you enough with the housework."

Rose was silent for a moment before responding. "Well, you never did like to do the laundry. Even with my knee injury, I had to walk up and down the stairs to do all of our laundry."

"I'm sorry for that. I had never done the laundry before, so I didn't know how to run the washer and dryer."

"I know you told me that, but I thought you were just making up an excuse."

"Well, I wasn't. And I've learned how to do laundry now, so if we get back together again, I promise to help out more."

"The laundry doesn't take that much time anyway."

"I'll help with other housework tasks. We can make up some lists and split everything up evenly."

Rose was silent for a moment before saying, "I know you mean well, Travis. I'll think about it."

"I know you like to mow the lawn. If you want to, we can take turns doing the things we both like and the things we both hate."

Rose took out some bottled water from the cooler and offered one to Travis.

He smiled at her before saying, "Thanks. You read my mind."

"Well, after sharing our dreams, we're both reading each other's minds."

Travis said, "You're right."

Rose opened Travis's water for him, and then he said, "Look in the glove compartment."

"Okay." Rose opened it up and asked, "What am I looking for?"

"A map."

"Doesn't your car have a GPS?"

"Yeah, it does. But we'll still need a map."

Rose pulled out a folded-up paper from the glove compartment. "Oh, it's a map of Plymouth."

"Once we get to our hotel tonight, we might want to look at the map and decide where we'll go tomorrow."

"Okay." Rose put the map next to the picture of the sampler that was already in her purse. The two papers fit perfectly next to each other.

Rose and Travis arrived at their hotel before five o'clock, checked in, and then went to a nearby restaurant. After they were seated at a table, a waitress gave them menus and took their drink orders.

Travis looked at his menu. "I would love either shrimp or lobster."

Rose started to read her menu, but then stopped in order to stare at a man who was seated two tables behind Travis. She said softly to Travis, "I know the man over there at that table."

After turning around to see the man, Travis looked back at Rose and asked, "Is he the one you were dancing with last weekend?"

"Yeah, he is."

"Were you on a date with him?"

"No, of course not." Rose blushed. "I met him first in the bank where I work, and then he went to the dance hall. His name is Greg Smith."

"It's strange that he's just shown up here—at another place where you just happen to be."

"I know. He probably was with me on the train to Albany. He might be the thief who stole my sampler."

Travis turned around to look at Greg Smith again. "He looks guilty."

"With those eyes of his, he always looks guilty."

"He'd better not be following you."

"If he actually is the thief who stole my sampler, he should run away from me, rather than follow me."

"He saw you first in the bank, right?"

"Yeah, I don't think I met him before that."

"If Greg knows you work in a bank, maybe he wants to break into the vault or something."

"I guess that's possible. There are a lot of bank robbers around these days."

Travis looked thoughtful for a moment. "I'll go over and talk with him."

"I'm the one who knows him. I should go over and speak with him."

"No, if he's following you, then I'm more likely to get some kind of information out of him. I can act like we're strangers."

Rose hesitated and then said, "Okay."

Travis went over to the table where Greg was seated and said, "Hi. You look familiar."

Greg looked at Travis and frowned. "No, I don't think I know you."

Travis was about to go back to his seat when his eyes widened. Rose saw his facial expression and walked over to see what was happening.

When she reached the table, she saw what had caused Travis's reaction. On the table, lying on top of a newspaper, was a sampler that looked just like hers. As she watched, Greg slid the sampler beneath the newspaper so that it was no longer visible.

Rose said, "That's my sampler! You have to give it back to me."

Greg looked up at Rose and immediately recognized her. "Hi, Rose. What are you doing here in Plymouth?"

"I want my sampler back."

"It's not yours," Greg said as he stood up. He reached into his billfold, raised up a twenty dollar bill for the waitress to see, left the bill on his table, and then started to walk out of the restaurant.

Rose took out her cell phone and dialed "911." As she was talking to the operator about sending police over to the restaurant, Travis followed Greg outside. Rose heard some yelling, and then a minute later, Travis came back inside the restaurant.

"Greg left in his car, but I wrote down his license plate number."

"That's good. The cops will be here soon."

"I would have tried to keep Greg here by physical means, but I didn't want anyone to get hurt. He pulled a gun out of his jacket pocket."

"Did he try to shoot you or anyone else?"

"No, he just waved it at me and then got into his car."

"I'm glad you're okay. It's more important to be alive than to have the sampler. Besides, the picture we have of the sampler may help us just as much as the actual sampler."

Travis and Rose sat down at their table again. The waitress took their order. Five minutes later, two police officers walked into the restaurant. The waitress sent them over to Travis and Rose's table.

After the officers were told about what had happened, someone at the police station was called; Greg's license plate number was checked. A minute later, the officer who had contacted the station received a text reply on his cell phone. After looking at his cell, he said, "The license plate was stolen. Is there anything else you can remember about the car or this 'Greg' person?"

Travis said, "No. I wish I could."

Rose also could not remember anything, but she said, "Because he was at my bank, he should be in at least one picture taken by the security cameras."

"It would be great if you could fax us a picture of him. Here's a card with the fax number on it."

The other police officer, who so far had remained silent, said, "We'll still need proof that the sampler he has is yours."

Rose said, "How about if we e-mail you a picture that we took of the sampler?"

"Depending on the quality of the picture and the kind of sampler, a picture might help. My e-mail is right there on the card."

Rose said, "Okay, we'll send you a picture of the sampler from our hotel room tonight. The picture of Greg from the bank will probably take a few days."

Travis shook hands with both of the officers and then said, "Thanks for helping us. You were really fast at getting here, too, especially with the rush-hour traffic."

One of the officers handed Travis a form. "If you can, please fill in this form and send it to us with the pictures."

As the officers were leaving, the waitress brought some shrimp and lobster over to Travis and Rose. After they were done eating, they went back to the hotel, found the e-mail from Rose's grandmother with the attachment of the sampler picture, sent a copy of the picture to the police officer, used the pool together, and then went to their separate hotel rooms. Rose watched TV for an hour, read about the Pilgrims for about twenty minutes, focused on Pilgrims landing on a beach, and then fell asleep.

Building Homes

Rose looked around for a beach, but she didn't see one. She wondered briefly if she was lucid dreaming or not. When she saw some Pilgrims, she realized that she was dreaming another part of her dream story. She asked, "What date is it?"

The Pilgrims had been standing up, but they were now lying down inside of a "common house," which stored items for all of the Pilgrims to use. One of the Pilgrims said, "Today is January 14, 1621."

Another voice said, "Even for a day in January, 'tis cold."

The walls of the common house were made of wooden boards, and the roof looked like thatched straw. On one side of the building was a chimney that also looked like it was made out of straw. A thin trail of smoke was coming from the chimney, but there was no smell of any food being cooked. The fire must have been lit for warmth.

Rose took a few steps closer to the house. The front door opened, and one of the Pilgrims stepped outside. He was wearing a brown coat and a hat. In his right hand was an axe; he began walking on the path toward Rose. Before he bumped into her, she moved off of the path. She smiled at him and said, "Hi," but he did not hear her. He kept on walking, went past Rose, exited the Pilgrim village, and stepped between two trees in the forest. After another couple of steps, he was no longer visible.

Rose smelled something burning and turned back to look at the common house. There was smoke coming out of the straw roof and chimney. One of the Pilgrims inside of the house ran out. Only a few feet from the door were two sick-looking Pilgrims; they were lying down on blankets.

"Fire! We must get outside," a voice deep inside the common house yelled.

The feather-hat lady, whose eyes were watering, walked toward the door. She was carrying her hat, which had a lot of black streaks on it from being burned in the fire. As she approached the door, she stopped to help the two sick Pilgrims near the door to stand up and walk out the door with her.

From inside the common house came a voice: "William, thou needest to come with us."

Deep inside the common house, Bradford was coughing and wheezing. His face was as gray as the smoke from the fire. To steady his weak body, one of his hands was pressed against the wall while he also tried to roll a large barrel of gunpowder toward the door. Pieces of smoldering straw fell down from the roof, landing upon him and the barrel.

A voice said, "Thou art too sick to move that barrel. Let us help thee."

William Bradford, with help from other Pilgrims, brushed off the smoldering straw pieces and rolled the barrel of gunpowder toward the door. They kept on moving until the barrel was safely outside and away from the house.

By this time, the entire straw roof was on fire. Rose was getting really warm, but she still wanted to help. "This is a lucid dream," she said out loud. "I should be able to do something."

She tried to go through the front door, but several Pilgrims were rolling more barrels toward the door. Despite the cold weather, the Pilgrims were sweating. One of them said, "With the help of our Lord, we can move these barrels and save our house."

Soon, all of the barrels were moved outside and away from the house. The entire straw roof burned off of the building, but the Pilgrims managed to put out the fire before any other major damage was done. The wooden frame and logs were blackened near the top, but otherwise, the house appeared okay.

The Pilgrims walked back into the building. Bradford went inside first. He looked ill, but he was not as bad as some of the other Pilgrims. Several of them were barely able to move. Many of them had been carrying snow and water to help put out the fire; now they had wet clothing. Multiple wet blankets were removed from the building and hung up to dry on nearby bushes and trees. Eventually, all of the Pilgrims went back inside the now-roofless building. Smoke from a small fire began to rise up from inside the building's walls. The Pilgrims said a prayer about how thankful they were that no one was seriously injured in the fire.

On another day in January, Rose watched as Francis Billington, a fourteen-year old Pilgrim, climbed into a tree on Fort Hill and saw a big lake. He then climbed down, went back to the Pilgrims, and told them about the lake he had found. Even though Francis Billington had a past history of being a troublemaker, some of the Pilgrims believed him. They went to look at the big lake; they then named it after the fourteen-year old who had found it: Billington Sea. The faces of the Pilgrims showed their happiness that a troublemaker could become someone who was helpful to his community.

Another sun appeared in the Eastern sky; a new day was starting. Rose watched a couple of the Pilgrims praying together. They had not yet had breakfast or started work. One of the Pilgrims said, "I will read to us 'A Prayer to Be Said before a Man Begin His Work.'" He started to read the prayer, and Rose heard some of the words: "...we may faithfully travail in our estate and vocation, without fraud or deceit,...grant that we may humble ourselves to our neighbors..."[77]

After the Pilgrims had finished their prayers, they had breakfast and then began their work. Some men began to cut wood, and several were building a house. Some pieces of wood were taken to the site for the home. Then a frame was put together by using logs with no nails; instead, chunks of each log's edges were cut out so that the ends of the logs would fit into each other. Once the frame was set, the sides of the home were completed, and a straw roof was woven onto the top of the house. This single home was completely built in less than a minute. One of the Pilgrims said, "That was the fastest house that we have ever built."

Another Pilgrim put down his axe before saying, "Ay. This could not never have happened this fast."

"We must be dreaming."

"Or we may be a part of a dream in the mind of someone else."

Rose said, "This really is a dream. There's no way things could happen this fast in real time, especially for someone like me."

None of the Pilgrims heard her, but one of them looked up at the sky. "The sun hath moved halfway across the sky."

"Ay, six hours have gone by."

"The daytime hours of the winter are always faster than the daytime hours of the summer."

Rose said, "Oh, I know what you mean. You're talking about how time was figured out in your century. The day and the night were split up into twelve parts. In the summer, because the sun was out for a longer time, each hour in the day was longer than each hour in the night. For the winter, the days were shorter than for the summer, so the twelve 'hours'—the parts of the days— would be shorter in the winter than the hours in the summer."

The Pilgrim men were still ignoring Rose. She looked at the women, who were busy washing clothes, cooking, and cleaning. The Feather-hat Lady was in one of the houses. She had her hat on. Even with its black streaks from being burned in the fire, the hat still looked pretty. As the lady poured a gravy-looking liquid into a large pot, she spilled some of the liquid on the floor of her house. She picked up a shovel, scooped up the part of the dirt floor that was wet, and brought it outside of her home. Her face had a broad smile on it as she emptied out the messed-up dirt.

Another Pilgrim lady was outside. She and the Feather-hat Lady bowed their heads to greet each other; then the Pilgrim lady asked the Feather-hat Lady why she was so happy: "What cheer?"

"I like the dirt floors that we have here in new Plymouth. They are so very easy to clean."

"One of the women in our colony wanteth a floor made of wood, but I think dirt floors are so much better."

"Ay, to scoop up and throw out messes is easier than to sweep and wash a wooden floor."

The two ladies said "Farewell" to each other. Then the Feather-hat Lady stood in the doorway of her house and watched some of the children. Most of the kids were happily doing a variety of chores; different adults would often stop what they were doing to answer questions or to otherwise help one of the children. The positive and helpful environment made Rose wonder if—within her reality—she would want to be a part of such a setting. It was cold outside, and there were no cars, planes, computers, electricity, or running water. However, on all of the days when she had worked at the bank, she had never seen so many smiles as the ones she was witnessing in her dream world with the Pilgrims.

One of the Pilgrims went up to Myles Standish and said, "This winter, with so many of God's people being sick, thou hast been most helpful. I thank thee."

"I have been blessed to be healthy while so many have been ill."

"Ah, but thou hast been doing the most tasks of anyone that I know."

"Many good thanks."

A new sun rose up from the horizon and then descended into darkness. Myles Standish was standing in the same spot. He now looked extremely sad. John Alden, another Pilgrim, came up to him and said, "We know that thou miss Rose. She is now in heaven with our Lord."

"I thank thee for thy comforting words."

Rose Hopkins said, "It's so sad that your wife was one of the many sick people who died. However, you will find love again. In a couple of years, you will marry a second wife: Barbara. Also, in 1858, Henry Wadsworth Longfellow will write a romantic love poem about you, John Alden, and Priscilla Mullens. The name of the poem will be 'The Courtship of Miles Standish,' and it will tell about a romantic love triangle connecting you three Pilgrims together."

Rose's watch opened up and then began to talk to her: "Longfellow was very interested in the Pilgrims. Five of his ancestors were *Mayflower* passengers: John Alden, Priscilla Mullins, William Brewster, Richard Warren, and Henry Samson."[78]

Myles shook his head, acting almost as if he had heard Rose and her watch. Myles Standish and John Alden then walked over to a house and stepped inside. They were obviously close friends and probably roommates.

After the sun had risen and set multiple times, Myles Standish and John Alden walked out of the house. Rose asked Myles, "Is it still winter?"

He did not respond, but Rose's watch said, "Yes, it's February 17, 1621."

John Alden turned to Myles Standish and said, "Thou hath been voted to be the first commander of the Plymouth Colony militia."

"I thank thee for telling me about this."

More suns rose and fell across the sky, showing that time was passing. Then one day, the Pilgrims and some native Wampanoag people had a meeting. Squanto, one of the natives, came to help the Pilgrims. He showed them how to survive by growing corn, fishing, avoiding poisonous plants, and catching beavers.

Some more time passed. The word "Thursday" appeared in the sky beneath the rays of the morning's sun. A beaver was swimming near the edge of the Billington Sea. Two Pilgrims and Squanto soon spotted the beaver. One of the Pilgrims said, "The fur of a beaver is worth much money in England."

The other Pilgrim said, "And we need wealth to pay off our debt to the Merchant Adventurers."

"The Indians have been helping us to pay off our debt."

"Ay, they are most helpful. They give us fur and pelts when we trade with them."

"And Squanto has taught us how to catch beavers."

"We thank thee, Squanto, for helping us."

The Pilgrims and Squanto silently watched the beaver for a moment and then began to move closer. Rose made some noises, trying to scare the beaver away so that it wouldn't be caught, but the beaver didn't hear her. She tried to make louder and faster noises, but the beaver still didn't hear her. Suddenly, right before the two Pilgrims and Squanto closed in on the beaver, Rose sat up. She was wide awake, and her lucid dream was over. She turned off her alarm clock and then smiled as she realized that the noises she had been making at the end of her dream had been her attempts to mimic her own alarm clocks.

Fighting over Treasure

On Thursday morning, Rose got ready quickly. She was only five minutes late to meet her husband in the hotel's dining room. After she walked over to his table at the far end of the room, he stood up, pulled out a chair for her, and helped her to sit down. Their small wooden table had placemats covered in pictures of the *Mayflower,* ocean waves, a beach, and Pilgrims.

"Look at the maps I got from the front desk." Travis showed Rose two maps; both of them identified key tourist attractions in Plymouth, Massachusetts.

While Rose looked at the maps, Travis got up and walked over to the table with continental breakfast items on it. He brought back two coffees and put one of them in front of Rose.

"Thanks," she said while still looking at the larger map.

"Where do you think we should go first?"

After a few more seconds of staring at the map, Rose said, "I don't know. We could compare the picture of the sampler with the maps and then decide."

"Okay. Do you have the picture in your purse, or is it upstairs?"

Rose pulled the picture out of her purse. She held it half-way between herself and Travis. For a few minutes, they compared the picture with the maps of Plymouth. Then Travis asked, "Are you hungry?"

After Rose shook her head, they both got up, helped themselves to bagels with cream cheese, and then sat back down again. A minute later, Travis asked, "Does anything on the sampler resemble Town Brook or Jenney Pond?"

"I don't know. The map on the sampler is a little small to compare with these other maps."

"Maybe we should start by asking experts—people working in the Pilgrim tourist attractions."

"That's a great idea." Rose turned the larger map around in order to look at its listing of tourist attractions. "The Pilgrim Hall Museum might be a good place to start."

"Okay. Before going to the museum, though, we'll have to park somewhere." Travis paused and then pointed to a spot on the map. "Right here off of Memorial Drive is some parking."

"There's a Visitor Information Center right next to the parking."

"Okay, so we'll park, stop at the Visitor Information Center, and then walk to the museum."

After they had finished their breakfast, they went out to Travis's car. A few minutes later, they pulled into the parking lot and walked toward the Visitor Information Center. Three flags were flying beside the front doors, and a short stone wall encircled the sides and back of the building. Inside, the lady at the front counter asked, "Can I help you?"

Rose pulled the picture of the sampler out of her purse. Turning it around so that the lady could see the map at the bottom, she asked, "Does this look familiar to you?"

"I've never seen a sampler like that one."

"How about the map on the sampler? Have you ever seen a shoreline that looks like this one?"

The lady took out a large map from a drawer in her desk. After putting it on the top of the counter, she slid Rose's paper over several sections of the map's shoreline, trying to find a match. "I think it most closely resembles this part of the shore next to Plimoth Plantation. What do you think?"

Rose and Travis both looked at the two maps. Travis said, "It's not an exact match, but the shoreline may have changed some after the sampler was made." Travis looked at the maps for another minute and then said, "I think you're right. Plimoth Plantation is the closest."

Rose shook her head, agreeing with him.

"How accurate is your map?" Travis asked the Visitor Information Center lady.

"It's very accurate. It was just printed this year."

Travis frowned. "Then why does your map spell 'Plymouth' as 'Plimoth'?"

"That's a common question. At Plimoth Plantation, the people are trying to present a realistic representation of the Pilgrim settlement. The Pilgrims spelled 'Plymouth' with an 'i' instead of a 'y.'"

Rose looked at Travis. "It's only three miles to the Plimoth Plantation. Should we change our plans for today and go there first?"

"Whatever you want to do is okay with me."

The lady said, "You may want to wait until Saturday to go to Plimoth Plantation."

"Why?"

"There's a Pilgrim wedding ceremony at 2 p.m."

"That's interesting." Rose smiled at Travis, and he smiled back at her.

"We weren't invited, Rose, but would you like to crash a stranger's wedding?"

"I'd love to!"

The lady explained, "It's not a real wedding—just a fictional re-enactment of a 17th century Pilgrim wedding. Actors will play Robert Bartlett, Mary Warren, and Governor William Bradford."

Travis asked, "Is the governor getting married to Mary?"

"No, he will be running the ceremony and reading the vows to Robert and Mary."

Travis asked, "Why will a governor, instead of a minister, do the vows?"

The Visitor Information Center lady explained, "The Puritans believed that a wedding was a civil ceremony. Before they came to America, their weddings in Holland also were done by civil authorities, rather than by church authorities."

Rose asked, "Will the ceremony be outside?"

"Yeah, in the English village."

Rose looked out the window and said, "Hopefully, it won't rain like it's supposed to today."

The lady glanced at the darkening sky. "I think it's supposed to start raining later on—after lunch."

Travis said, "For today, as long as the rain holds off for a while, we can try to see both Plymouth Rock and the *Mayflower II*. Then we won't have to move our car. Tomorrow and Saturday, we can plan on seeing Plimoth Plantation."

Rose nodded her head in agreement. "That sounds like a good plan."

The lady handed Rose and Travis a map and some pamphlets with information about several of the local tourist attractions.

Travis said, "You have a lot of nice pamphlets here."

The lady smiled. "Nearly a million people a year visit Plymouth, Massachusetts.[79] We need to have a lot of readily available information about all of the attractions."

After Rose and Travis thanked her, they went outside. Travis started to walk toward his car, but Rose said, "I'd rather walk. It's only a few blocks to the rock."

"I think it's five blocks."

"I'm really okay, Travis. Thanks for worrying about me, but I'm back to normal again."

"Okay. We'd probably have problems finding a parking space near Plymouth Rock, anyway."

They started to walk toward Plymouth Rock. When they were in front of a store with a sale on all of its *Mayflower* tee-shirts, Rose said, "There's one thing we forgot to plan for."

"What's that?"

"Shopping."

Travis had taken a step ahead of Rose. He stopped, turned around, and said, "You aren't serious, are you? We already have a lot of places to go to."

"We have all day today for this part of Plymouth."

"You do remember that you were just released from the hospital yesterday?"

"Yes, but I'm feeling fine."

Travis sighed. "Why do you always have to go shopping?"

Rose frowned slightly. "What's wrong with shopping, especially if I'm paying for all of my own things?"

"On just your salary, you can't afford to go shopping."

In a loud voice, Rose said, "You can't tell me how to spend my own money." Several people had walked onto the nearby grass, trying to go past Rose and Travis, who were standing still on the sidewalk. Other people stopped walking in order to watch the fight.

"Yes, I can tell you how to spend money. We're still legally married." Travis's jaw was set in a position of strength.

"No, we're separated—we're not married anymore!" Rose's voice had risen even higher. A larger crowd was forming on the grass surrounding them, but neither Rose nor Travis seemed to notice.

"We're not legally separated. If you keep on charging everything on our joint cards, I'll be liable for the payments."

"Okay! Fine! I'll use my own card!"

Travis laughed sarcastically. "You don't have one."

"Yes, I do." Rose reached into her purse and pulled out one of her credit cards. "This one I got just last month, and it's all mine."

"I don't believe you. Can I see it?"

Rose handed the card to Travis, who looked at it, pulled out his keychain, and opened up a small pair of scissors attached to the chain.

Rose took a step closer to Travis and tried to grab her card, but he took a step backwards. With a wild expression on her face, she said, "You can't do that!"

Travis stopped moving and looked closely at the card. It had Rose's picture on it. The card was in his left hand, and the tiny pair of scissors was in his right hand. Both of his hands shook slightly, but he did not put the scissors away. He instead looked up at Rose and asked, "Why not?"

"I gave you that pair of scissors. If you use it to cut up my credit card, our marriage is over."

Travis looked down again at the credit card in the palm of his left hand. It was partially covering up his wedding ring. Sighing, he shifted the card further down toward his wrist. His wedding ring was now completely visible. Even with the clouds in the sky, enough sunlight was reflecting off of his gold ring to make it look brighter than it had just a few seconds earlier. "You charged the scissors on a credit card with both of our names on it, which means I probably paid more than you did for the scissors."

"No, you're wrong. I paid cash for the scissors."

"No, you charged them. I know you charged them. I always check the monthly statements."

Rose frowned. "Why do you always check the monthly statements? Are you spying on me or something?"

"Of course not. I'm just making certain no one is stealing and using our information."

Rose looked at Travis's face and sighed. "Let's not argue over how I bought a tiny pair of scissors. It doesn't really matter."

"Okay. How about if we stop using our joint credit cards until we're either divorced or married?"

"Even when we were married, you kept on telling me how to spend my own money."

"No, I'm not that mean."

"Yes, you are."

"You're calling me names again. And you're screaming at me."

"No, I'm not!" Rose screamed out so loudly that Travis took a step backwards.

He then said, "Ever since the bank robbery, whenever we have a fight, you scream. It's like you're trying to prove to me that you can scream."

"No, I don't have to prove anything. I can scream: aaaaahhhhhh! See, I can scream really well!"

"Look at yourself! You're screaming like a crazy person while you're standing near Plymouth Rock. This is where the Pilgrims, hoping for freedom, came to a new world. How can you scream to show your anger about a bank robbery while you're visiting a place like this?"

Rose glared at Travis's hands. "And what are you doing? You're threatening to cut up my freedom. That's the first credit card that I've ever gotten all by myself."

"Rose, I helped you to get a high credit score so that you could get your own credit card." Travis looked down at his hands. One was still firmly holding onto Rose's card, and the other one was holding onto the scissors. The sharp blades were now open and only inches away from her card.

Rose was still glaring at Travis's hands. "If you really need to cut something up, you can cut up the scissors. They belong to you, but you can't cut up the credit card. The credit card is mine."

"The way you spend money, you'd be better off with no credit cards at all."

Rose's voice was very loud as she asked, "Do I have to call the cops?" Two cars on the road heard her and pulled over; the people in the cars seemed uncertain about what to do, and then one of them started to dial a number on a cell phone.

Rose and Travis stared angrily at each other. Then a police officer suddenly walked up to them. "Is everything okay here?" Rose and Travis both turned to face the officer. Her nameplate said, "Mary Standish."

Travis looked around at several small groups of people who were standing nearby. "I guess everyone in Plymouth has been listening to us."

Officer Standish said, "Yeah, for some reason, a few people dialed '911' on their cell phones."

Travis tried to explain: "We were just having a fight. It's as if we're married again."

"Are you two divorced?" Mary Standish's eyes went from Travis's face to Rose's.

Rose quickly spoke up. "We're not divorced." She looked at Travis's scissors before adding, "At least, not yet."

Officer Mary Standish said, "I know that's a small pair of scissors, but it still could be a weapon. Can you please put it down on the ground?"

Travis partially stooped over to put the scissors down and then stopped. "Can I take the scissors off of my key chain first?"

The officer's voice was sharp as she said, "No, put them down on the ground."

Travis's hand trembled as he slowly dropped the key chain. The officer took a couple of steps forward and picked it up.

Rose asked, "Can you make Travis give me my credit card?"

Officer Mary Standish looked at Travis, who quickly passed the card over to Rose.

Travis sighed. "Am I in trouble?"

The officer said, "It depends. What have you done?"

"I didn't really do anything. We were just fighting." He looked over at Rose; the expression on his face was hopeful, showing his desire that she would support him.

Rose said, "Travis didn't do anything wrong. He was just trying to help. I think he's a little more anxious than usual because I was in the hospital for a couple of days."

"What happened? Did he hurt you?" the officer asked.

"Oh, no! I was injured in a robbery on a train. Travis would never hurt anybody." Rose's shocked face showed the officer that she was telling the truth.

"Okay." Mary Standish took the tiny pair of scissors off of the key chain, gave the scissors to Rose, and returned the key chain to Travis. "Do you two need to talk to someone?"

"No, thanks. We're okay," Travis said.

Rose shook her head in agreement. "If we can't work things out within the next few days, we'll talk to our minister some more. He has already given us a few ideas."

Travis stared at Rose's face until she looked up into his eyes. Neither one of them turned away, but they both looked intently at each other, sharing their desire to be together again. Travis said, "Once we're back together again, we'll want to stay together."

Rose and Travis were still looking at each other as the officer turned around and walked back to her car. For the next few minutes, Mary Standish sat in her car, filled in some paperwork, and occasionally glanced over at Rose and Travis.

Rose was still holding onto the small pair of scissors and her credit card; she put the card into her purse. She then raised up the scissors over her head. Even though the sun was not shining, the silver metallic scissors still sparkled. Travis moved his keychain up until one of the keys touched the scissors so softly that no noise was heard. He smiled at Rose, and she returned his smile as she moved the scissors downwards. Pointing the two handles, rather than the sharp blades, toward Travis, she slid them into his hand.

He asked, "So you trust me with these?"

"Of course I do, but a bigger question is: can you trust me now with credit cards?"

Travis laughed. "Have I ever really trusted you with credit cards?"

Rose sighed. "No, but I am usually the one who does all of the shopping, including buying all of your clothes for you."

Travis's face looked thoughtful as they began to walk toward Pilgrim Rock. "Okay, how about if we discuss money and credit card issues more directly?"

"We could make lists of expenses, like our minister already suggested."

"Okay. How about if we try that tonight?"

They began walking more quickly toward Plymouth Rock until Rose stopped in front of one of the stores. "Look at those glow-in-the-dark *Mayflower* tee-shirts."

Travis turned around and looked at the tee-shirts in the window. "Okay, I really do like those shirts. Even the price of sixteen dollars and twenty cents is neat."

"Yeah, 1620 is when the Pilgrims landed in Plymouth."

They went into the store and found matching *Mayflower* shirts. At the check-out counter, Rose searched in her purse for her new credit card. By the time she had found it, Travis had already swiped one of his credit cards into the card station on the counter.

Rose thanked Travis as the clerk put the shirts into one shopping bag. After they had left the store, Rose said, "Now I know how to get you to pay for things—I just have to make someone call the cops."

They both laughed; then Travis said, "I wish we could solve all of our problems that easily."

"I know." They continued their walk along Water Street toward Plymouth Rock. They were walking on "Pilgrim Path," which had various "Audio Stop's." At these points, people could stop, use headphones, and listen to information about the different historic statues, buildings, and other spots along the path.

Rose said, "I wish we had enough time to check out these audio stops."

"Me, too."

"So, have I really been screaming every time we have an argument?"

"Yes, you have been. But it's only been happening since the bank robbery."

"I didn't realize what I was doing. I'm sorry."

"I'm sorry, too."

"For what? You're always very logical when we fight. You don't scream."

"Well, I should have realized before now why you kept on screaming at me. Then I would have been more understanding of your problems."

Rose and Travis paused for a moment and smiled at each other. When they started walking again, they were walking more slowly, as if they were waltzing their way along the sidewalk.

Rose said, "We're missing a lot of landmarks. We'll have to come back another time and stay for a few more days."

"You said 'we,' instead of 'I.'"

"I guess I did."

A short distance before reaching Plymouth Rock, they came to the *Mayflower II*. Travis took a few pictures of the boat before saying, "I'm tempted to go on board the *Mayflower* right now."

"So am I." Rose looked at the *Mayflower* and then up at the sky. Even though the clouds did not look too bad, she said, "Just in case it starts raining early, we should stick to our plan and see the rock first." They continued moving toward Plymouth Rock.

The rock was covered with a cement canopy made of columns, a roof, and a floor. People could walk on the floor and see the actual rock through a hole in the floor. A metal cage surrounded the rock, though, so no one could touch it. The beach's sand led up to the rock, and stone piles were on both sides of the small beach. While taking pictures, Travis asked, "Do you know, Rose, if this is really where the Pilgrims first landed?"

"Possibly. The Pilgrims spent about a month exploring Provincetown and other places before deciding to live in Plymouth."

A lady wearing a plaid shirt, who was standing near Rose, said, "They explored Cape Cod, Clark Island, Corn Hill, Cold Harbor, and the First Encounter Beach." When Rose and Travis looked at the Plaid-shirt Lady, she continued, "I have some Internet printouts about Plymouth Rock."

Rose looked at the papers in the lady's hands and asked, "So, is Plymouth Rock really the stone where William Bradford first placed his feet? I don't remember reading anything in Bradford's book about a giant rock."

The lady read from one of the printouts: "Plymouth Rock...is reputed to be the very spot where William Bradford, an early governor of Plymouth colony, and other Pilgrims first set foot on land in 1620."[80]

"So people think the rock is where Bradford first stepped ashore?" Travis asked.

Rose said, "Bradford might have been the first of the Pilgrims to step on the rock, but I read in a different place that John Alden—the ship's carpenter—was the first of the people on the *Mayflower* to step ashore."[81]

The lady said, "It actually makes more sense that John Alden—a crew member—stepped ashore before William Bradford—a passenger."

"That does make sense," Rose said.

"Thanks. Anyway, it says on this page that the rock was 'unidentified for 121 years.' Then Thomas Faunce, the son of one of the 1623 Pilgrims, told people about the rock so that they would not build a wharf over it."[82]

Rose said, "Well, it's nice that we have Plymouth Rock as the possible landing spot for the Pilgrims."

The Plaid-shirt Lady shook her head in agreement and then walked over to the right side of the canopy building, where she continued to read her printouts.

Rose and Travis walked away from the rock and over to the railing. Travis snapped a few pictures of the items in front of him, as well as the ones to his left; there were boats, a wharf, stone walls, a beach, some buildings, and the *Mayflower II*. After he had finished taking pictures, he kept the camera in front of his face. Looking through the lens, he zoomed in so that he could see different items in more detail. While watching some pigeons on the beach, he suddenly stopped moving the camera and gestured to Rose. "Look at that man on the beach below us."

When Rose looked through the lens, her eyes widened in disbelief. "It's Greg Smith, the guy who stole my sampler."

"Can you tell if what he's holding is the sampler? When I looked at him, I could only see some kind of a cloth item; he was comparing it to the shape of the coastline."

"I can't tell from this distance, but it could be the sampler. It's the right size and shape."

Travis took his cell phone out of his pocket and dialed "911." After a few seconds, he explained to an operator what was happening.

Rose said, "Greg's walking away. Should we chase him?"

"After what happened yesterday, he's likely to have a gun again." Travis paused before adding, "You should wait right here for when the cops arrive. I'll follow him."

"Getting the sampler back is not worth either one of us getting hurt, Travis. You should stay here, too."

"I'll stay back far enough so that he won't realize anyone is following him. Tell the cops when they get here that it looks like he's headed toward the *Mayflower II*. If so, it might be fairly easy for them to corner him in one section of the boat." Travis jumped over the left side of the canopy building. "I'll call you and let you know where he's going. Just stay there, and tell everything to the cops."

Rose sighed, realizing that Travis was being logical, as well as protective of her. She put her camera up to her face, zooming in on Travis as he walked quickly along the beach and moved toward the *Mayflower II*. When she heard the siren of a police car on the street in front of Plymouth Rock, she turned toward it. Out of the passenger side of the car stepped Mary Standish, the same police officer whom she and Travis had spoken with just a half an hour ago. Another officer stepped out of the driver's side of the patrol car.

As the officers started to walk up to Plymouth Rock, Rose ran from the concrete building toward them. She stopped and explained to them, "The man who stole my sampler is headed toward the *Mayflower II*."

Officer Mary Standish asked, "Where's your husband—or is he now your boyfriend?"

"He's following the thief."

"Do you have the pair of scissors?"

"No, Travis does. I don't think the scissors will be much of a weapon against a gun, though."

"Are you sure the thief has a gun?" the second officer asked. His name tag said, "John Carver."

"He had a gun yesterday, so he probably still has one."

"Okay," Mary Standish said. "You need to stay here. We'll go over to the *Mayflower II* and find him."

As the officers started to walk quickly back to their car, Rose said, "Wait a minute. I should come with you. Travis said he would call me and let me know where he is." As her cell phone rang, the officers watched her answer it.

"The officers are here with me." Rose stopped talking to listen to Travis and then asked him, "Are you still following Greg?" After another few seconds, Rose hung up and explained to the officers, "Travis has followed the thief onto the *Mayflower II.*"

"Thanks," Mary said as she and her partner moved toward their car again.

Rose asked, "Can I come with you if I promise to sit in the car?"

The officers looked at each other, shook their heads affirmatively, and let Rose get into the back seat of the patrol car. After a very short drive, they pulled up to the building that was in front of the *Mayflower II.* While Rose waited inside of the car, the officers got out and went up to the entrance of the building. They paused for a minute to speak with a lady who was selling entry tickets for the *Mayflower II.* The lady waved them through without collecting any money.

Rose got out of the car and walked up to the entrance. She asked the lady, "How much for a ticket?"

"There are already too many people on board the *Mayflower.* You'll have to come back in an hour or so."

Rose started to explain that her husband was on board, but the lady still would not let her go through the doorway. Rose walked away from the door and moved to her left, trying to see if Travis was near the exit area.

Suddenly, a gunshot was heard. While everyone turned to look in the direction of the shot, Rose walked quickly through the exit door. After she was about ten steps inside of the exit, she had to move to the side of the walkway so that several groups of people could pass by her. One of them said, "You have to leave. Someone has a gun."

Rose thanked the stranger, but a moment later, the walkway was clear. She again began to walk quickly toward the boat. Her steps appeared purposeful, and her knee did not seem to be bothering her. Before she realized it, the walkway turned into a bridge that connected the walkway on the shore to the *Mayflower's* deck. Rose stepped aboard the *Mayflower*. Pausing, she looked around. No one was visible aboard the upper deck, which is where she was standing. She walked forward to a small cabin area with a door on its left and a ladder on its right. The ladder had a piece of cloth draped along its length. Obviously, the intent was to keep people from going up to the small section in the front of the boat where a cannon was standing. The door leading into the small cabin had a rope across it, but the rope was fairly low. People could easily step over it; even so, Rose just stood outside of the cabin and looked inside. She could see a bed, as well as an old map, an ink well, and a feather pen on top of a table. Atop one section of the map was a long piece of thin wood with a rectangular sliding block in its center. Rose reached across the rope and grabbed the piece of wood.

She jumped backwards when a stranger's voice spoke angrily to her: "Why art thou stealing the cross-staff?"

Rose turned around and looked at a man who was dressed up as a Pilgrim. He was one of the staff members who were trained to dress, act, and speak like the Pilgrims. Rose said, "Thanks for telling me what this item is. I thought maybe it was used in navigation, but I didn't know its name."

"Ay, the navigator needeth the cross-staff to figure out the latitude of the boat. Dost thou see the degrees and the minutes, which are marked on it?"

"Yes. I think they're the same numbers as the ones inside my grandmother's watch case."

"Well, I know not about a case for a watch. But I do know about the cross-staff. The navigator slideth the transom to help him figure out the latitude of the ship."

"So the transom is this rectangular sliding thing."

"Thou must not take that transom. 'Tis against the commandments of God to be a thief."

"I'm just borrowing it for a few minutes, in case I need a weapon. I'll be very careful, though, and return it back here after I'm done with it."

"If thou dost use it as a weapon, thou wilt break it."

"If that happens, I promise to pay for it."

Before the role-playing Pilgrim could say anything else, another gunshot was heard. The Pilgrim man turned around to look in the direction of the gunshot. Then a child in a group of tourists started to cry. As soon as the role-playing Pilgrim went over to calm down the child, Rose quietly moved toward an opening in the deck. Her steps were steady, and her left knee moved normally. Once she reached the opening, she slowly began to climb down the stairs to the next lowest level. When she heard Travis's voice, she stopped moving and looked to her left. In the dim light, she saw a gun pointing at Travis. The two police officers were nowhere to be seen.

Greg Smith, the man holding the gun, said to Travis, "Okay, it's your turn. I'll hold the cargo hatch open while you join the others down below." Greg bent over and moved his left hand to the floor while keeping a firm grip on his gun with his right hand. His left hand moved one side of the cargo hatch up from the floor.

Travis took a step toward the hole and then looked at Greg. Because Rose was on the stairs behind Greg, Travis could see her. His breathing became faster, and Rose moved her mouth, trying to indicate to Travis that he should talk in order to cover up any noise that she was about to make.

Travis asked Greg, "How can I be sure you won't shoot me when I'm down there?" While he was talking, Rose carefully moved down two more steps of the stairway.

Greg said, "I'm just trying to earn some money for the essentials in life—food, clothing, a European vacation, a bigger house, a new car..."

"Really?"

"Yeah. Now get moving into that cargo hold! I'm not planning on hurting anyone, but I will if I have to."

"Okay. I'm moving," Travis said as he started to take a step forward, but his foot hesitated. The cold darkness of the cargo hold was worse than a basement with no lights, and his foot looked like it was sliding on ice toward ice, rather than stepping forward.

As she watched Travis's hesitation, Rose slowly moved down the final two steps of the stairway; she was now standing on the middle deck of the ship. She raised the cross-staff and moved one of her feet forward—she was about to run at Greg with the intent of knocking the gun out of his hand.

Suddenly, a voice coming from the stairway said, "Put it down." Rose looked upwards and saw Officer Mary Standish at the top of the stairs. Mary had a gun in her hand and was pointing it at Greg, who immediately dropped the cargo hatch. His crooked eyes moved back and forth between Rose and Mary.

With Greg no longer looking at him, Travis took his car keys out of his pocket. He grabbed onto the attached small pair of scissors and opened them up. Before he was able to attack Greg, though, the thief placed his gun on the wooden deck and raised his hands; he was surrendering.

Rose walked over to Travis and helped him to open up the door covering the cargo hold. Several people, including a police officer, climbed up out of the cargo hold. With the small pair of scissors still in his hand, Travis walked up to Greg, "Where's the sampler?"

"I don't know what you're talking about."

Travis walked forward another step, raised the scissors, and pointed them at the left side of Greg's shirt, where there was a bulge. "What are you hiding there?"

"Where?"

"Inside your shirt?"

Greg touched the bulging side of his shirt and then took a step backwards. Mary Standish grabbed onto one of his arms so that he wouldn't move further away.

Travis stepped forward again, extended his scissors, opened them up, and made a slit in Greg's shirt.

Greg yelled, "You can't do that! Even when I'm in jail, the police always take good care of my clothes!"

Mary Standish laughed. "Thanks for saying something nice about police officers." She looked over at Ed Winslow, her partner, and asked, "Should we guess how many times Greg has been in jail?"

Ed said, "At least five or six."

Mary said, "No, it's got to be more than that, especially if we count the initial arrest, not to mention the actual prison time after a conviction."

Greg looked at Mary. "You're really good at guessing, but I'm not going to tell you anything."

"Well, you must be an expert by now about prison life. Perhaps when you're in jail tonight, you can mentor some of the other prisoners."

Greg said, "I'm still not saying anything. You can just talk to my lawyer."

While Greg was speaking to Mary, Travis put his hand inside of the tear in Greg's shirt, pulled out the sampler, and tried to hand it to Rose. However, Greg's right hand grabbed onto one side of the sampler. He and Travis both pulled on it.

Rose said, "You're going to tear the sampler in half."

Travis said, "Let go of it."

Greg gripped harder onto the sampler as he said, "You're the one who needs to let it go."

With Mary's help, Travis finally pried the sampler away from Greg, who yelled out, "Hey, you can't just steal that away from me. It's mine."

Rose laughed. "No, the sampler's not yours. I have a picture sent to me by my grandmother. The picture proves that it belongs to me."

Greg stared at the sampler and then said, "I was wrong. That sampler is not mine. I've never seen it before. I thought something fell out of my wallet and down into the inside of my shirt." He reached into his shirt pocket and showed his wallet. "Here's my wallet. I always keep it in my shirt pocket so that it's safe from pickpockets." He scratched his head and then said, "I wonder how your sampler got inside of my shirt."

Rose said, "We all know that you put it there."

"Did you see me putting your sampler inside of my shirt?"

Rose shook her head before saying "Of course not."

Greg said, "It must have happened when I was doing my laundry. Someone left the sampler behind in the dryer, and it wound up inside of my shirt."

Everyone but Greg laughed. Then Mary Standish said to Greg, "How about if we get going?"

He asked, "Where are we going?"

Mary replied, "Where do you think?"

He sighed, turned around, and started to walk toward the stairway. Before he reached the first step, though, someone else began to climb down the narrow stairs. Everyone watched as a pair of old boots were followed by a gray skirt covered with an orange apron. The person walking down the stairs was one of the Pilgrim actors.

Greg said, "Sorry about this" as he pulled the Pilgrim lady off of the stairway, shoving her to the floor. Mary Standish checked to make certain the Pilgrim lady was okay. The lady said, "I am fine. Perhaps thou canst make that wicked man stop. 'Tis wrong to hurt people by pushing them off of stairs."

Mary looked at the stairway. Her partner, Edward Winslow, had already climbed halfway up the stairs in pursuit of Greg.

Mary said to Rose and Travis, "We'll need both of you to make statements. I'll have someone check with you in a few minutes." Mary then went running up the stairs and disappeared.

Rose said, "I only hear Mary's footprints above us. Greg and the other police officer must have left the boat."

Travis shook his head in agreement and then waved his hand at the sampler that he was holding. "Well, at least we have the sampler now."

"Yeah, we do. And it's not even torn."

Rose and Travis closely examined the sampler. They then smiled at each other before Travis asked, "Are you okay, Rose? Does your knee hurt?"

"Oh, I'm fine. How about you, Travis?"

"I'm okay, too."

"Just thinking about going down into that hold must have been scary."

"It was a little scary looking down into the darkness, but I was more worried about you."

Rose sighed. "I was worried about you, too. I don't know what I'd do without you."

With happiness in their eyes, Rose and Travis stared at each other. Rose immediately noticed when his eyes moved from her eyes and focused on her lips. She parted her lips slightly, slowly inhaled the warm summer air, and then exhaled a warmer breath. Travis moved his mouth closer to hers. Rose shifted her chin slightly upwards so that her lips were only inches away from

Travis's. When they kissed, they grabbed onto each other's hands. Neither one of them noticed that the sampler fell fluttering to the wooden deck of the *Mayflower II*.

A voice interrupted their kiss: "Dost thou know whose sampler this is?"

At first, neither Rose nor Travis listened to the voice. When the same person asked the same question a second time, they slowly pulled away from each other. Rose looked over at the person who had been talking to them. It was the Pilgrim lady who had been pushed down the stairs by Greg. Rose asked her, "Are you sure you're okay? You really were shoved down a lot of stairs."

"I am in great health. How dost thou fare?"

"I and Travis are both okay, right Travis?" He smiled and shook his head, indicating that he was fine, too.

Rose asked the Pilgrim lady, "Were you asking us about something?"

"Ay. Doth this sampler belong to thee?"

"Yes, it does. Thank you." Rose reached out her hand, and the Pilgrim lady gave her the sampler.

"Is this cross-staff also an item which belongeth to thee?"

Rose looked around for the cross-staff. It was lying on the floor next to her foot, right where she had dropped it. She said, "Oh, no. It's not mine. Thanks for reminding me. It belongs here on the *Mayflower*."

"I will put it into its proper place." The Pilgrim lady picked up the cross-staff and climbed up the stairs.

Travis said, "Let's go up to the top deck. If there are any police officers around, we can try to do our statements right away, rather than having to go to a police station."

"Okay." Rose paused before going up the stairs. "It's nice that we have stairs to use. The Pilgrims only had a ladder."

"That must be the ladder over there."

"It's tiny."

"If the Pilgrims were carrying things, I don't know how they could go up and down that ladder."

Rose took a step up on the stairs. "They would have helped each other."

"True."

Rose continued to go up the stairs. "Once the Pilgrims climbed up to the top of the ladder, they had to climb through that small opening to get onto the upper deck."

Rose climbed out onto the upper deck and moved aside so that Travis could finish climbing up the stairs; he soon was standing next to her. Rose and Travis both surveyed the surrounding area. Greg and the police officers were nowhere to be seen. Travis pointed above their heads to one of the crow's nests. "I didn't realize how small the crow's nests were back then."

"The *Mayflower II* has two nests, so the original *Mayflower* must have had two of them, also."

"Can you imagine climbing up those ropes to get into one of the crow's nests?"

"I don't want to imagine something like that. My knee's almost normal again, but just thinking about climbing up there makes it ache."

Rose took a few steps toward the front of the boat, where the Master's Cabin was. The door to the cabin was open, so they could see inside. "This was probably the best place in the whole ship."

"While it's really small, the Master of the ship had more room and privacy than any of the other crew members or passengers." The cabin had a table, a bench, a bed, pillows, a hammer, curtains in front of the bed, and other items. On the table were some navigation instruments and a map.

Rose and Travis turned away from the Master's Cabin and started to walk toward the ship's exit. They walked slowly, paused often, and looked at the different displays. There were pictures, explanations, and various items that illustrated how the Pilgrims lived. Rose paused in front of a display about a traverse board. "So, this is the kind of compass that was used back then."

Travis silently read the explanation and then said out loud, "Yeah, the crewmen recorded the direction and speed of the ship by placing pegs in the holes of the board."

"I wonder what would happen if the pegs were placed at the wrong times or in the wrong places."

"I don't know for sure, but my guess is there would be problems. The Captain of the ship would need correct information on this board to figure out the boat's position."

"I can see how one or two small mistakes could easily make a ship get lost."

Once Rose and Travis left the *Mayflower II* Visitor Center, they went to one of the nearby restaurants. After sitting down at a table, they ordered some cheeseburgers and fries. Then Travis suggested, "While we're waiting for our food, we could look at the sampler."

Rose pulled out several items from her purse. She handed Travis a map of Plimoth Plantation and the sampler; she held onto a picture of her grandmother's watch case. They spent a few minutes silently looking at the three objects.

Rose said, "The latitude and longitude numbers on the watch case are the same as the ones for Plymouth."

"The map on the sampler is very similar to this one section of the Plimoth Plantation map. What do you think, Rose?"

After comparing the maps some more, she said, "You're right. The sampler map may be slightly different only because of its use of stitches."

"The differences in the maps also could be due to the minor changes in the coastline that we talked about this morning."

"I think your idea of the minor coastline changes over time makes the most sense." Rose compared one of the maps to the sampler again. "The difference is minor, and a later time might mean that there will be a smaller coastline due to erosion, right?"

"I think so, but we can check out the real coastline when we go to Plimoth Plantation."

"So, Travis, do you think we should just go straight to Plimoth Plantation, or should we still go to the museum first?"

"Because it might rain, we would be better off going to the museum this afternoon. The museum might have some information that will help us to figure out the sampler."

"Okay. We should also go to the police station."

"You're right, Rose."

"We can find out if the police have Greg in custody or if he escaped."

"If he's in prison, we don't want the police to let him go because they don't have enough to hold him."

"We'll need to write a report and probably sign some forms."

"The police station will be open all night. Maybe we should go to the museum first."

"Okay. That sounds like a great plan."

After their lunch was served, Rose and Travis ate their cheeseburgers while they looked at some of the pamphlets for Plymouth visitors. They also compared different versions of Plymouth maps.

By two o'clock, Rose and Travis had finished eating, left the restaurant, and walked up to the Pilgrim Hall Museum. The building was made of stone, except for the glass section in the middle where the two front doors were surrounded by large windows. The right section of the lawn had flowers that led up to some stone stairs. Six columns were on the right front part of the museum, and a small fountain was to the left of the flowers.

Rose and Travis went up the stairs and through the glass front doors in the center of the building. They paused to admire the stained glass window in the front lobby. The center section of this window had the *Mayflower* in it. Travis paid their entrance fee. They looked at 17th century exhibits, Pilgrim artifacts, and historic paintings. They also watched a fifteen-minute orientation film about the Pilgrims.

As they were leaving the museum, Rose said, "I loved the paintings and the clothing exhibits."

"I liked the paintings, too, as well as the tools. The film was also very informative."

"Even though I've been reading a lot about the Pilgrims, I still enjoyed watching the film. Just seeing people dressed like Pilgrims was interesting."

"The actors we met on the *Mayflower II* also had great Pilgrim costumes."

"Their language, too, was really neat."

It was already after three o'clock. Rose rested on a bench while Travis retrieved his car and picked her up. They then went to the police station. An officer explained to them that Greg Smith had escaped, but police reports were still needed. After filling in all of the paperwork, Travis and Rose went back to their hotel, ate supper, and used the pool together. As they were leaving the pool and walking to their hotel rooms, they discussed their plans for seeing Plimoth Plantation the next day. "Rose, what time would you like to meet me for breakfast?"

"Any time you like would be great for me."

"How about three o'clock in the morning?"

Rose could tell by the expression on his face that he was kidding. "No, that might be too late. I think we should get up earlier. How about one o'clock?"

"That sounds like a good time to me, but since it's almost ten, maybe we should just stay awake until one. We could watch TV together."

Rose stopped walking and turned to face Travis. His expression was serious as he said, "We're married. We could stay with each other tonight."

Rose dropped her eyes to the ground. She then reached out and grabbed onto his left hand. She touched his wedding ring before looking up at his face. "Yes, we are married."

Travis knelt down on the ground and said, "I really want to apologize for not helping you enough after the bank robbery."

Rose looked intently at Travis. "You've been so nice while we've been out here in Plymouth." After a few seconds, she added, "Except for trying to cut up my credit card."

"I'm sorry for that, too." Travis stood up and lightly touched Rose's wrist.

"Well, both of us weren't very nice after the bank robbery."

"No, you were wonderful," Travis said. "I know you were in pain. The medication wasn't helping enough."

Rose started walking down the hallway toward their hotel rooms. "The pain medication partially helped to hide my pain, but it made me feel so tired."

Travis was walking next to Rose, but they were not holding onto each other's hands. "I should have just asked you right away how to work the washer and dryer, rather than having you walk up and down those stairs to do all of our laundry."

"The doctor wanted me to take it easy, but anyway, that's not what our problem is right now."

"What do you think our problem is?"

"Like our minister said, we need to talk more."

"We're talking right now."

Rose laughed. "Yeah, we are, but we should still speak with the minister some more. He's likely to have some suggestions that'll help us."

"Okay." The tone of Travis's voice showed that he had only said "okay" to make Rose happy.

"We don't want to get together again and then start fighting all of the time, like we did before."

Travis sighed. "All right. Tomorrow, I'll call and make us an appointment. We could also make a list of our expenses tonight."

"We could, but it's getting late."

"How about if we just relax while we're on this trip? We can plan on discussing our expenses next weekend."

"Okay." Rose stopped walking. She stood in front of the door to her hotel room and looked inside of her purse for her key. Travis put his left hand on her shoulder and his right hand under her chin. Rose looked up into his eyes as he was saying, "I love you."

"I love you, too, Travis."

"Really?" Travis's eyes lit up.

"Yeah. I just think we need to figure out how to deal with our fighting before we get back together again." Rose started shivering.

"Are you okay?"

"Yeah, I'm just getting cold out here in the air conditioned hallway in my wet bathing suit."

"That's a relief. I thought you were shivering because you were upset at me."

"No, Travis. I'm not mad at you—at least not at the moment."

"That makes me so happy, Rose."

Rose and Travis smiled at each other before Rose asked, "So what time are we really meeting tomorrow morning?"

"Plimoth Plantation is open at nine."

"Should we have breakfast around eight?"

"That sounds great, Rose. I'll see you then." Travis touched her chin. When she smiled at him, he softly kissed the top of her mouth and then the bottom of her mouth. She touched his shoulder and lightly kissed both of his lips at the same time. Travis then helped her to find her keys, opened her door, and waved good-bye.

Rose said, "Good night" and then watched Travis as he walked to his room, which was the one next to hers. He opened his door and looked back at his wife. They both waved at each other and closed their doors.

Rose showered, put on some warm flannel pajamas, and did some reading. Right before falling asleep, she read about memory holes that were dug by the Native people:

> All along this narrow, hard-packed trail were circular foot-deep holes in the ground that had been dug where 'any remarkable act' had occurred. It was each person's responsibility to maintain the holes and to inform fellow travelers of what had once happened at that particular place.[83]

Rose fell asleep without remembering to set her alarm clocks.

MEMORY HOLES

The forest was really dark. After following a turn in the path, Rose nearly tripped on a broken branch. It was lying across the pathway and looked limp, tired, and sad. She wished the branch were living and attached to a tree; the branch immediately moved up off of the ground and flew up into a nearby tree. Rose realized that she was lucid dreaming, and one of her thoughts had already changed something. Perhaps this dream was one that would allow her to change other things.

Rose continued walking down the pathway. After moving past another ten trees, she stopped to look at a hole on the right side of the path. When she wondered if the hole was a memory hole, a Native man walked out of the forest and onto the pathway in front of her. He was dressed in a small deerskin loincloth; the upper part of his body was naked. He smiled joyfully at Rose and said, "Welcome, English lady!"

A look of surprise appeared on Rose's face. During her recent lucid dreams, the Pilgrims had not been able to see her. She asked, "Can you see me?"

"Ay."

"Why can you see me?"

"Because I am here to tell thee about memories from the past."

Rose thought for a few seconds before responding. "I can see you, and I can see the Pilgrims, but the Pilgrims can't see me. I don't understand why you can see me."

"I know not why. Maybe thine idea of time is confused."

Rose smiled. "You're right about that. I'm always late."

"Sometimes, 'tis good to be late. If thou art looking at memories, thou hast to be late."

"Why?"

"Because thou art living in a time later than when an event happened."

Rose still looked confused, but she said, "Okay. So what is your name?"

"Samoset. What is thine?"

"Rose." When Samoset looked like he wanted more explanation, Rose added, "I'm a descendant of John Robinson."

"John Robinson?"

"He was the pastor to the Pilgrims."

Samoset said, "I remember him not."

"He had to stay in Leiden, so he didn't come over on the *Mayflower*. In 1631, his son Isaac came over to Plymouth Colony on a different ship called the *Lion*."

Samoset laughed before saying, "Thou really art confused about time. The year is only 1621."

Rose blushed. "Yes, I am confused about time. But at least now, I'm too early."

"Too early?"

"Yeah. I'm from the future, and maybe you can help me."

"How?"

"Next to the pathway is a hole. Is this a memory hole?"

"Ay."

"So, are you going to tell me about a wonderful event that happened here?"

"Nay, I am not."

"Why not?"

"Because thou art too much in the future."

"That might be true. But even so, if this is a memory hole, you're supposed to tell me about an event that you remember."

"I am not going to tell thee about a memory; instead, I will show thee by using a modern tool from the future."

"How can you use a tool from the future?"

"This dream is thy lucid dream, Rose, so I will use a tool that thou wantest me to use."

"Okay. Which tool?"

"Pictures from a TV."

"So you'll tell me a story, but it'll look like I'm watching the news on TV."

"Ay, my story will be like a TV story." Samoset waved a hand toward the memory hole. The date "March 16, 1621" crawled out of the hole and then disappeared down the pathway and into the forest. Next, a 2-D version of Samoset emerged from the hole. The 2-D Samoset walked up onto the path, into the forest, down a hill, across a brook, and continued walking until he came to the Pilgrims' colony in Plymouth, Massachusetts. With no hesitation at all, he kept on walking right into the village itself.

2-D Samoset's strong, purposeful stride was immediately noticed by some 2-D versions of Pilgrim men. They yelled at him to stop, but he didn't even slow down; he continued walking toward what the Pilgrims called the "rendezvous," which was where the women and children were supposed to stay if there was anything dangerous happening.

In the rendezvous were some fifteen 2-D women and children. At first, they did not move; they appeared to be a part of a picture that was up against a fence. When Samoset looked like he was going to walk into the rendezvous, the 2-D women and children moved off of the picture and ran around inside the rendezvous.

Some of the 2-D Pilgrim men ran onto the pathway leading into the rendezvous and stood in front of the 2-D Samoset. Instead of shooting him, the men stood still with steady feet, folded arms, and strong jaws. They were blocking the path so that Samoset couldn't advance forward into the rendezvous.

The 2-D Samoset stopped walking. He saluted the 2-D Pilgrim men and then "with great enthusiasm spoke the now famous words, 'Welcome, Englishmen!'"[84]

The 2-D Pilgrims stared at the 2-D Samoset; they were surprised that he had spoken to them in English. One of the 2-D Pilgrims asked, "Who art thou?"

"Samoset. Who art thou?"

Several of the 2-D Pilgrims introduced themselves to Samoset. When Myles Standish introduced himself, Rose looked closely at him. He still was almost as cute as her husband. Today, though, he looked two-dimensional, as if he were in a TV show.

A Pilgrim man with a green felt hat asked Samoset, "Where did you learn English?"

"Pemaquid Point in Maine." For the next few minutes, Samoset talked to the Green-hat Pilgrim man about learning English from fishermen who often came to fish near his home in Maine. As he talked about the fishermen, he even said many of their names.

The Green-hat Pilgrim man walked up closer to Samoset and put a coat on him, covering his naked arms, shoulders, and chest.

One of the rendezvous women was also wearing a green felt hat; she walked up to the edge of the rendezvous and began to wave her hands at the Green-hat Pilgrim man. He took off his hat and waved it at the matching-hat woman, who was still waving her hands at him. After another minute of them both waving at each other, the man walked over to the woman at the edge of the rendezvous. Because they were standing so close together, Rose decided that they had to be married to each other.

The Green-hat woman said, "Thou only hast two coats."

"Ay," her husband said.

"Thou gavedst one of thy coats to the Indian."

"Ay. Samoset, the Indian, was cold."

"Dost thou think that he hath no coat?"

"Ay. 'Tis very cold outside. If he had a coat, he would be wearing it."

A Pilgrim lady with a white linen cap on her head walked up to the green-hat married couple and said, "The Holy Gospel of Jesus Christ, according to Luke, saith that we must share our clothing and food with those who have none. I think the word in the bible is 'part,' which meaneth to share. I remember some of the verse: '...He that hath two coats, let him part with him that hath none: and he that hath meat, let him do likewise'" (Lk 3:11 GNV).

The Green-hat Husband and Wife smiled joyfully at the White-cap Lady's use of the bible verse. The husband then said, "I thank thee for remembering that verse."

The White-cap Lady said, "This is a memory hole, so we should remember many things."

The wife said, "Ay. Many good thanks."

Rose said to the wife: "I'm sure if your husband's only remaining coat is lost or ruined, one of the Pilgrim men will give him another one."

The wife didn't hear her, but the husband acted as if he had heard Rose's voice; he said, "If my only remaining coat is lost, it might be a blessing."

"How so?"

"Many men in our colony would be very pleased to give me one of theirs."

Because the Pilgrim man emphasized the word "give," Rose knew that he meant someone would "give" him a coat, rather than just loaning one to him.

The husband and wife gazed with love into each other's eyes. Then a boy and a girl ran up to the couple. When the children grabbed onto the wife's hands, Rose realized that they were the offspring of the Green-hat Couple. The children showed their parents a section of the bible—Matthew 18—that they had been reading and studying together. The mother said, "Like that lost sheep, if thou art ever lost, we will look for thee forever."

The father said, "Ay, we would not permit thee to stay lost."

When the mother said, "We are blest to have each other," her husband and children shook their heads in agreement before exchanging hugs with one another.

The loving, joyful movements of this family seemed different from the motions of the other Pilgrims. Rose looked closely at the Green-hat Couple and their children. After a moment, she realized that the family really was different. They had changed. They were no longer a group of 2-D figures, but were now multi-dimensional. Their movements became faster. Rose saw them moving backwards and forwards in time: They walked backwards and looked like they were living in Leiden; then they walked forwards onto the *Mayflower*, landed in Plymouth, and kept running forward into the future with generations of their children, grandchildren, and great grandchildren.

Within the minds of the multi-dimensional family, many happy memories began to form. Soon, the memories were so many that they filled up the single memory hole. More memory holes were needed, and more of them were created. Rose began to walk down the forest path again, looking at the multiplying memory holes. Some of them even went into the forest. One of the memory holes began to cut down trees and build houses, which became more and more modern-looking as time went on.

After a few more minutes of walking on the path, Rose noticed a memory hole that looked older than the newly created ones. She stopped and looked into it. This memory hole seemed to be glowing, so she knew that it was an important one.

Instead of Samoset, Squanto—another Native person—appeared next to Rose. He also looked into the memory hole.

He spoke English even better than Samoset did. Squanto said to Rose, "'Tis March of 1621." He then waved at the memory hole and explained what he remembered about a peace treaty: "Edward Winslow was a Pilgrim. He was an ambassador who was sent to talk to Massasoit about a peace treaty."

"Could Massasoit speak English?"

"Nay, he could not. Some others were interpreters of his words."

"Were they as good at English as you are?"

"Nay, they were not. They explained the speech of Winslow, but they 'did not well express it.'[85]"

"How did you learn to speak English so well?"

"I was stolen from my home and taken to England as a slave."

"That's horrible!"

"When I escaped, I came back to my home in Pawtuxet. Most of my people had died from sickness."

"That's really sad. A lot of people were sick back then. I read in a book that about half of the Pilgrims died during the first winter."

"Ay, much sickness happened in the winter of 1620, as well as before 1620."

"So did Massasoit say 'no' to a peace treaty?"

"Nay, Massasoit said, 'Ay.' He was very happy. He wanted peace, so he wanted the Pilgrims to sign a treaty."

"Really? He wanted a peace treaty?"

"Ay, during that time, there were many wars. Massasoit wanted to save his people. And the Pilgrims had the best weapons. They had guns and cannons."

"So did anything else happen when Winslow talked to Massasoit?"

"Ay, Massasoit liked the sword and body armor that was worn by Winslow. Massasoit wanted to buy them. But Winslow did not sell any weapons to him."

Rose laughed before saying, "That's sort of funny. While discussing a peace treaty, Winslow and Massasoit talked about buying and selling weapons of war."

Squanto pointed to the memory hole. It looked wet, but the weather was nice. There had been no rain. Rose looked more closely into the memory hole and saw a tiny river flowing inside of it. As she continued to watch the water, Massasoit appeared beside it. Around his neck were a bag of tobacco and a chain of white bone beads. He had red paint on his face. Some Native people were with him. Their faces were painted black, red, yellow, and white.

Suddenly, Myles Standish walked up to Massasoit. He and Massasoit saluted each other. Rose stared at Myles and sighed. Even though she knew he was short, his posture made him appear taller than those who were standing near him. As Rose continued to stare at him, he seemed to grow even taller.

Myles Standish began to walk again. He, Edward Winslow, and some other Pilgrims escorted Massasoit to a house that was only partially built. Inside of the house were some cushions and a green rug. Governor John Carver then appeared and went inside the partial structure. Following the governor into the house were a couple of Pilgrims; they were playing musical instruments. Rose heard the sounds of at least one drum and one trumpet.

The Native people who had come with Massasoit were now also inside the house. They were interested in the trumpet noises. After a few minutes, the Pilgrims gave a trumpet to one of the Native people. He stared at the different parts of the seventeenth century trumpet, which had no valves and no finger holes. The trumpet looked like an s-shaped continuous tube with a large mouthpiece. The Native person tried to play the instrument.

After hearing a few of the loud sounds, Rose covered up her ears and gazed down at the floor. However, she could still hear the non-rhythmic noises coming from the inexperienced trumpet player. Then there was a brief pause in the sounds as the trumpet was passed to a different Native person. This second player was even worse than the first one. Rose was glad that she wasn't too close to this memory, and she felt sympathy for the Pilgrims who were in the same room with the bad trumpet noises.

A moment later, the trumpet was passed to a third inexperienced player.

"Ay, 'tis thy turn to make some joyful sounds."

Rose stopped looking down at the floor. Her eyes moved up higher and higher until she saw the joyful faces of the Pilgrims and Natives. They were having fun, and the noises from the inexperienced players were a part of that fun. Rose smiled as she removed her hands from her ears. The noises became louder, but they also seemed to be more pleasant. She clapped her hands, adding her own excitement into the musical moment.

Amid all of the noise, Carver and Massasoit kissed each other; they then ate some meat and water. Finally, they created a peace treaty, which included statements about not hurting each other, not stealing tools, and not carrying weapons while visiting one another. Rose read one part of the peace treaty out loud: "If any did unjustly war against him, we would aid him. If any did war against us, he should aid us."[86] The treaty also said that Massasoit would tell his neighbors about the peace treaty, and King James would be Massasoit's "friend and ally."[87]

The trumpet noises were still loud and joyful as Rose moved away from the memory hole. She no longer saw Squanto anywhere, but she heard some different noises. She looked to the right side of the path and saw what first appeared to be another memory hole. As she watched, its shape changed from circular to rectangular. Wooden stairs appeared; they led down into a basement.

Rose moved closer to the stairs and looked down into the basement. She waited patiently for something to happen, but nothing did. The basement noises seemed to be slightly louder, but nothing could be seen from where Rose was standing. She finally walked through the rectangular opening and moved slowly down the stairs, pausing after every step. Finally, she arrived in the basement, which now looked familiar to her.

The basement's walls and floor were made of cement. Even though it was July, the room felt cold. Noises came from the water pipes near the ceiling. Rose looked upwards. The hot and cold water pipes were in their usual positions. She looked over to her right. There were boxes containing winter clothing, a Christmas tree, and some ornaments. Near the boxes was a table with some tools on it; next to the table were shovels and a rake.

Rose knew this basement. It was the one in the home where she and Travis had lived when they were together. After several years of marriage, they had separated.

They had then sold their house and moved into separate apartments. Rose sighed as she remembered what had happened right before they had separated. She looked over to the left side of the basement, where the washer and the dryer were. They were still there.

A noise was heard on the stairs leading into the basement. Rose saw herself at the top of the stairs. She was holding onto a big laundry basket full of dirty clothes. Travis's voice could be heard. "If you want me to do any housework, you'll have to wait a few minutes."

The memory version of Rose shouted at Travis, "It can't wait. The clothes should be done now."

"I need to change the oil in my car before it gets too dark outside."

"Why can't you change the oil tomorrow?"

"I'll probably have to work overtime again."

The memory version of Rose screamed in an even louder voice: "The oil change can wait until the weekend. The clothes have to be done right now."

"Why do the clothes need to be done right now? I can do them after supper."

"Yesterday, you said you'd do the clothes."

"You know I had to work overtime."

"Well, I'm running out of clothes."

"You have a closet full of clothes."

"You know that I can't wear most of them right now. I only have five pairs of slacks that will fit over my knee brace, and they're all dirty."

"I'll do the laundry after we eat." Rose heard Travis's footsteps above the basement as he walked across the hallway and into the living room. When he went outside to change the oil in his car, he slammed the front door.

The memory version of Rose limped over to the front door, opened it up, and screamed out, "You know I'm supposed to rest my knee. I shouldn't be carrying things while going up and down the stairs."

The real Rose in the basement realized that her screams really were too loud. She was scaring Travis away. Even though she was on pain medication and not feeling well, she was still really loud. Travis's voice didn't sound too happy, but at least he hadn't been yelling like she was.

Rose heard noises and looked up toward the top of the stairs. The memory version of herself was walking down the stairs while holding onto the laundry basket. Rose sighed as she remembered how she had to walk down the stairs: she had moved her left knee with the knee brace to the lower stair, shifted her weight over onto her left knee, felt the pain get worse because of the added weight, bent her right knee, and moved her right foot down onto the same step where her left foot was positioned. She then would begin the process over again. When she was halfway down the stairs, her left knee was in much more pain. She paused to rest for a moment, but it didn't seem to help.

Rose knew what was going to happen next. She said, "Oh, no" as she saw the memory version of herself shifting her weight again; her left knee buckled. To avoid falling down the stairs, she had grabbed onto the stairway railing with both of her hands. The laundry basket fell down the stairs. The memory version of Rose did not fall, but her knee really hurt as she slowly walked down the rest of the stairs, picked up the basket, moved the clothes into the washer, and started the machine. When she turned around to begin the painful journey back up the stairs, she paused for a moment and looked directly at the spot where the real Rose from the future was standing. The real Rose was invisible to the memory Rose, but the real Rose knew that the memory version of herself was thinking about the future and about possibly never getting better. In the past, she had asked herself, "What will happen if I have to spend the rest of my life with this pain?" She had not yet found an answer to her question.

The memory version of Rose then slowly went back up the stairs. With every step, her tired feet seemed to be making more and more noises. Finally, when she got back upstairs, Travis was there. The oil change must have taken less time than her task of starting the laundry, or perhaps Travis had changed his mind about changing the oil. He asked, "What's for supper?"

The memory version of Rose said, "Nothing. I didn't make it yet."

"That's fine. I can wait."

"Well, you're going to have to wait for a really long time!" The memory version of Rose stomped across the floor. She then slammed the front door; several moments later, the tires on her car squealed as she drove away. The real Rose knew that seeing Travis sitting there and asking for supper had been the final action—or was it inaction? She had no longer wanted to be married to him. Even though he had called her many times and tried to apologize, she had been too mad at him.

Rose heard some noises coming from her cell phone. She looked in her purse, but her cell phone wasn't there. After hearing another ring, Rose looked over at her bedside table. She finally realized that she was awake when her real cell phone, which was lying on the table, kept on ringing.

DECIPHERING FLOWERS

Rose picked up her cell phone and said, "Hello."

Travis's voice asked, "Did I wake you?"

"Not really. I was sort of awake. What time is it?"

"Eight fifteen."

Rose sighed. "I guess I'm going to be a few minutes late."

Travis laughed. "Don't worry about it. We're on vacation, remember?"

"I forgot to set the alarm clock."

"It's okay if you're a little late. You've been through a lot with the train robbery; you need some time to relax."

"Thanks, Travis. You're being really nice. I'll meet you for breakfast in about twenty minutes."

"Okay."

Thirty minutes later, Rose left her hotel room and joined Travis in the dining room. As she walked over to where he was sitting, he looked at her ring finger. Rose was wearing her engagement ring, but not her wedding ring. He stood up, smiled at her, softly clasped her left hand in his right hand, and then softly kissed the engagement ring.

Rose laughed as she looked at the ring on her hand. "So, you noticed?"

"How could I miss something like that?"

Rose and Travis got some coffee, bagels, and yogurt; then they sat down and began to eat their breakfast. While they were eating, Rose pulled out the sampler and its picture. "Look at this section of the sampler, Travis. There's a small extra stitch next to the May flower. It's not really visible in the picture."

Travis compared the sampler to the picture. "You're right. The picture is only two dimensional, which is why we didn't notice it."

"The stitch might have been pushed forward a little bit when you and Greg pulled on it yesterday."

Travis looked at the stitch again in the sampler before saying, "I don't know. It doesn't look like it was torn or pulled out."

"If the stitch was there when Greg had the sampler, Greg would have thought the extra stitch meant something."

"That might be why he was looking around yesterday on the *Mayflower II*."

From her purse, Rose pulled out a picture that she had taken of her grandmother's watch case. "I think the stitch might mean where the top of the watch case should be placed. In the picture of the watch, we can see the top of the watch case has a small indent that fits the extra stitch in the sampler."

"It looks almost like a keyhole."

"The watch case's indent is where the watch's key should be placed."

"The watch had a key?"

"Yeah, it's supposed to go into the top of the watch and wind it up, which is why there's a place in the top of the watch case for the key to enter."

"So, Rose, does your grandmother have the key?"

"I don't think so. She would have told me. The key must be with the clock."

While they finished breakfast, they talked about their families. Then Rose looked at the sampler and the pictures again. "I don't think the sampler's picture of the *Mayflower* has anything to do with the watch. The years are all wrong."

"Wasn't the *Mayflower II* built after World War II?"

"You're right, Travis. It was built between 1955 and 1957."

"How old is the watch?"

"It has to be at least a hundred years old. The sampler, too, is at least a hundred years old."

"So it makes no sense that someone would refer to the *Mayflower II* at least fifty years before it was built."

Rose shook her head in agreement. "The word 'May' and the flower on the sampler must be referring to the original *Mayflower*, the one that arrived in Plymouth in 1620."

"So, Rose, do you think we should just go directly to Plimoth Plantation today?"

"That sounds like a plan. We don't really need to go back to the *Mayflower II*, unless you want to do some more sightseeing on the ship."

"Right now, I'm more curious about Plimoth Plantation."

Rose pulled a map out of her purse. "We can try to find the section of the coastline near the Eel River, which is what the sampler shows."

Travis pointed at the map. "There are some other places, too, that we should check out."

"We have to see the 17th Century English Village and the Wampanoag Homesite."

"I know." Travis paused briefly. "The only problem is the wedding isn't until tomorrow. I really want to see the wedding."

"So do I." Rose looked at Travis; they both smiled.

Travis reached out and gently picked up Rose's left hand. "We could go to the English Village twice: once today and once tomorrow."

"That sounds great."

They briefly held hands and looked happily at each other's face. Then they went out to the car. Travis opened up Rose's door and showed her the lunch bag in the back seat. "I've brought some water and snacks for us."

"Oh, thanks, Travis."

"I'll even be carrying the bag."

"Okay. I'll carry my purse."

Travis started the car up. He pulled out of the parking lot and turned around two corners. "I love the names of the streets here in Plymouth."

"Yeah, so do I. This one's called 'Leyden Street.'"

"It's even spelled using the seventeenth century version of 'Leiden.'"

Rose pulled out a map of Plymouth. "Many of the streets here were named for Pilgrims, like Howland, Brewster, Winslow, and Allerton."

"What about Samoset Street?"

"That street was named after the first Native person who welcomed the Pilgrims."

"Really?"

"Yeah. In March 1621, Samoset just walked into Plymouth and welcomed the Pilgrims."

"With the past history of firing guns and arrows at each other, Samoset's entrance took courage."

"Yeah, it did. He also knew enough English to communicate with them."

Travis went past the field where the Farmer's Market was held every Thursday; he continued to follow Warren Avenue until he turned onto the Plimoth Plantation Access road. After he pulled into the parking lot, he parked the car, let Rose out, and removed the lunch bag from the back seat.

Rose asked, "So, we're going to the Visitor Center first, right?"

"That sounds like the best way to get some more information. They might have another map of just the Plimoth Plantation area."

"We'll have to save all of the maps we're getting to give to my dad. He loves maps."

"I think maps are neat, too. It's strange how there are so many different formats to depict the geography of a location."

Travis and Rose walked to the front of the parking lot and through a large wooden arch-shaped gate. There were posters on the front part of the arch and trees on both sides. Holding hands, Travis and Rose walked down some stairs and up a sidewalk toward the Henry Hornblower II Visitor Center.

As they walked up to a sign, Travis asked, "Who's Henry Hornblower?"

"He's the founder of Plimoth Plantation."

A group of tourists walked past them and went beneath a triangular-shaped archway. Rose and Travis followed them under the archway and then went through the front door of the Visitor Center.

At the first desk, Travis paid for his and Rose's admission tickets. The lady behind the desk gave them a map before pointing to a corridor to her left. "If you go through that door and down to the theater, you'll be able to see a short orientation film about the Plantation."

Travis thanked the lady; he and Rose walked down the corridor. As they reached the door of the theater, it opened up, and about twenty people came out. Rose followed her husband into the theater, and they sat down next to each other near the front of the room.

While they waited for the film to start, Rose took out a ballroom dance schedule of classes from her purse. "Are you still taking dance lessons, Travis?"

"No, not in over two months."

"Then who was that lady you were dancing with last week?"

Travis looked at Rose. "Are you jealous?"

"Maybe I am, especially since you first brought her into the bank."

Travis laughed. "You know I still love you."

"I know, but I'm still curious.

Travis looked at Rose, who was staring intently at his face while trying to read his facial expression. He sighed before saying, "She was someone from work, but we weren't really dating—at least not seriously. We were just hanging out together to have something to do."

"It looked like you were dating, especially when you came into the bank."

"Oh, her car had broken down, so I drove her around to a few places. Then she actually asked me out. Because I didn't want to make her feel bad, I said 'Okay.' That's when we went to the ballroom dance hall."

"So you only went out that one time?"

"Yeah. She asked me out again, but I wouldn't date her anymore."

"Really?"

"Yeah. She was too pushy, and I missed you too much." Travis looked at Rose's thoughtful face and then asked, "How about you? Have you been dating other people during the last few months?"

Rose took in a deep breath before saying, "No. I thought about it, and I dreamed about it. But I didn't. I was still in love with you."

"So who were you dreaming about?"

Rose laughed before saying, "You won't believe me."

"Try me."

"Okay. I was dreaming about Myles Standish."

"The Pilgrim?"

"Yeah." Rose looked at the dance-lesson schedule that was still in her hand. "We'll have to take dance lessons together again."

"I'd love to."

Rose and Travis discussed what evenings would fit best into their schedules. Then Rose put the dance schedule back into her purse and took out her sampler. She and Travis compared the Plimoth Plantation map with the sampler.

After a few minutes of carefully looking at both items, Rose said, "These maps are the same."

"Yeah, they are. I think we should start looking in this section of the Plantation." Travis pointed to a spot to the right of a small group of four trees.

"It's too bad there's no pathway in that section of the Plantation."

"As long as we walk near the river, we're likely to be able to get through the forest without too many problems."

Another tourist who was sitting behind them said, "Excuse me, but there is a pathway near the Eel River."

Rose and Travis turned around and looked at the tourist who had spoken to them. He was seated next to a woman who was shaking her head in agreement with him.

Rose showed her map to the man in the row of seats behind her. "Is there a path that's not on this map?"

"Yeah, there's a really nice one. It even has some wooden platforms and stairs."

"Thanks," Rose said. She turned to Travis. "I guess we should go to the Wampanoag Homesite first. It's near the Eel River, so we can look for that pathway."

Before Travis had a chance to respond, the film started to play on the big screen in front of them. They silently watched the film *Two Peoples / One Story*, which was produced in 2006 by the History Channel. It contained some information about Plymouth and the role-playing actors at Plimoth Plantation.

After the film was over, Travis held open one of the theater's doors for Rose. Other tourists followed Rose through the open door. One of them was shading his eyes from the bright lights; he put a hand in front of his face as he moved his dark cap slightly forward. The last tourists to leave were the man and woman who had told Rose and Travis about the secret pathway. Travis thanked them again and then closed the theater's door.

Before Rose and Travis left the Visitor Center, they stopped in front of a statue that partially resembled a cow. The left part of the statue had a cow's head, and the upper half of the animal's body was a model of the *Mayflower*. The animal's four legs looked like Pilgrims' legs; black shoes with golden buckles were on the bottoms of the legs.

Rose said, "This *Mayflower* cow is different from all of the other ones I've ever seen."

Travis laughed. "I've never seen a real cow. Have you?"

"I've never been this close to one."

"So, Rose, did the *Mayflower* have a cow like this one on it?"

"I don't think the 1620 *Mayflower* voyage had any cows on it. There were pigs, goats, and dogs. And probably cats."

"Even if the 1620 *Mayflower* had no cows, later Pilgrims would have brought them over."

"You're right. They did." Rose reached out and touched the top part of the statue, which was a large model of the *Mayflower*.

She took a picture of the *Mayflower* cow statue and then followed Travis as he walked toward the Museum Shop, which was one of the sections of the Visitor Center.

Before they entered the shop, Rose touched Travis's arm. "I would love to go shopping here, but don't you think we should wait until later to do our shopping?"

Travis laughed. "I can't believe you don't want to go shopping."

"I do, but I think finding the spot indicated on the sampler is more important to do first." Rose looked into the window of the Museum Shop, and she inhaled quickly because of what she saw inside. "On second thought, those Pilgrim dolls are really cute."

When they walked into the shop, Rose immediately picked up one of the dolls. "This one has to be Myles Standish."

"Does he look like the Myles from your dreams?"

"Sort of."

"Are you sure this doll is Myles Standish?"

"Yeah."

"How can you tell?"

"The red hair and the sword." Rose looked at Travis's puzzled face and added, "Myles had red hair, and he was the professional soldier who taught the Pilgrims how to fight."

As Rose continued to look at the doll, she felt her purse move slightly and turned around. The tourist with the dark cap was standing there. His hand was no longer hiding his face, but was rather holding tightly onto a gun. She gasped as she saw his crooked eyes and recognized Greg Smith. He said, "Give me the sampler."

Rose stood still, and Travis took a step forward. Greg then turned the gun toward Travis and said, "Don't move. I'm good with guns."

Rose asked, "Why do you want the sampler, anyway? It isn't worth that much."

Greg turned the gun toward Rose before saying, "I know there's a map on it."

"The map won't lead to anything expensive. None of my ancestors had any money."

"Just hand over the sampler."

"Okay, I will. But can you answer one question for me, first?"

"Maybe. What's the question?"

"Are you a counterfeiter?"

Greg frowned and then rubbed his left arm across his forehead. His eyes looked around the shop. There were at least five other people in the store, but no other person was close enough to them to notice what was happening. "Why are you asking me about that? Are you trying to cause trouble?"

"No, I was just wondering."

"Why are you asking me if I'm a counterfeiter?"

"Because you were in my bank about the same time as a counterfeiter was."

Before Greg could respond, Travis grabbed onto Rose's left hand. He started to pull it slightly, as if he were trying to tell her something. He then said, "Your name's Greg, right?"

"Yeah." Greg looked at Travis.

"Well, Rose told me that you came into the bank immediately after the counterfeiter."

Greg looked back at Rose. "Is that right? You think I came in right after the counterfeiter?"

Rose's eyes went down to the ground as she tried to make her facial expression blank and unreadable. She then said, "Yeah, I think so. I was just wondering if you knew who the counterfeiter was." She looked back up at Greg's face, which now had a relieved look on it.

Greg moved his gun forward slightly as he said, "Okay. No more talk. Just give me the sampler."

Rose tried to open up her purse, but she was still holding onto the Myles Standish doll. Her right hand started to shake.

Greg said, "Rose, give your husband your purse."

"Why?"

"His hands aren't shaking, so he should be able to find that sampler."

Travis said, "Okay. I'll get the sampler for you, Greg." Rose gave Travis her purse. Travis opened it up and took out the sampler. As he extended the sampler toward Greg, Rose raised her right hand, which was holding onto the doll. When Greg grabbed onto the sampler, Rose's hand came down. The Myles Standish doll hit Greg's gun, knocking it out of his hand. Before Greg could react, Travis tackled him, pushing him to the ground. Rose picked up the gun and stepped back a few steps.

A familiar voice from the front of the store said, "Please bring the gun over here and put it on this table." Rose looked toward the voice; it belonged to Mary Standish, the Plymouth police officer.

"I'm so happy to see you, Mary," Rose said as she put the gun on the table near the front door. Mary immediately picked up the gun; she walked over to where Travis and Greg were fighting on the ground. Travis was hitting Greg's nose. Greg's right hand was hitting Travis's shoulder.

Edward Standish, another Plymouth police officer, came through the front door and then walked directly over to where the fight was happening. Kneeling on the ground, he grabbed onto Greg's right arm. Travis stopped hitting Greg's nose and stood up.

Rose asked, "Are you okay, Travis?"

"I'm fine, Rose. How about you?"

"I'm great, but I wasn't the one who was being hit." Rose gently touched Greg's chin and then his shoulder.

Officer Mary Standish asked, "Where were you hit, Travis?"

"On my shoulder, but I'm fine. See?" Travis raised his arm up and down. "It doesn't even hurt."

Officer Mary Standish looked down at Greg, who was still on the floor, and said, "Okay, Mister. It's all over."

Greg slowly stood up. Now that he had a red nose, his eyes looked even more crooked than they usually did.

Rose said to Officer Mary Standish: "Greg tried to steal my sampler again. Also, he's a counterfeiter."

Greg said, "No, I'm not."

"Yes, you are. The bank's camera stamps the time on the pictures. Once the police have looked at all of the evidence, they'll be arresting you also for being a counterfeiter."

"You just said a few minutes ago that I came into your bank after the counterfeiter."

"I was lying. I only said that because I didn't want you to shoot me for being a witness to another crime of yours."

The counterfeiter sighed. "So what? One picture isn't enough evidence."

"It will be if the time stamp is the same as the counterfeit bill transaction at Lisa's window."

Greg made an angry face at Rose as the police officers put handcuffs on his wrists.

Officer Mary Standish asked Travis, "How did you manage to get Greg onto the ground?"

Travis laughed. "One of your ancestors—Captain Myles Standish—helped us."

"Really? How can that be?"

Rose's eyes moved around the room. When she saw the Myles Standish doll on top of a model of the *Mayflower*, she ran over, picked up the doll, and brought it back to Mary Standish.

"Here he is. I threw him at Greg, and this Myles Standish doll knocked the gun right out of his hand."

Mary laughed. "So, are you going to buy that tough little doll, or can I?"

The store clerk, who had followed Rose back from the model of the *Mayflower*, said, "I have more than one of those Myles Standish dolls."

Rose said, "I want this one." She softly stroked the doll's hair.

Mary smiled. "Okay. I won't try and outbid you for the doll. I don't think either one of us wants to pay more than what is listed on the price tag."

"Thanks, Mary."

"You're welcome, Rose. I'll just buy a different one. This other one's really nice, too." Mary Standish took one of the other Myles Standish dolls off of the shelf, followed the clerk over to the cash register, and paid for it. Then Mary and her partner escorted Greg Smith out to their police cruiser and drove away.

Rose was still stroking the doll's hair. "The hair's even more messed up now than it was before."

Travis laughed. "Do you want a different doll?"

"No, I really want this one. The messed-up hair is cuter."

"If I had known before how much you love messed-up red hair, I would've changed my hair years ago." Travis started to move his hair around in an attempt to make it look messed up. "See? I can dye it, too."

Rose turned to Travis, reached up, and patted Travis's messed-up hair, so it was neater. "Your hair is perfect, Travis."

"No, it isn't. It's more brown than red."

Rose smiled at him. "Are you jealous of this doll?"

"Yes, I am. Myles is getting a lot of attention from you."

"Well, you shouldn't be jealous. You're better looking than Myles."

"Including my hair?"

"Especially your hair. It's smoother than Myles's."

"Yeah, his hair is a little bushy-looking."

"I also love your hair's light brown color with a slight tint of red in it." When Rose saw Travis's expression of uncertainty, she added, "Don't you dare do anything to your hair."

Travis sighed. "Okay. I don't really want to dye my hair, anyway."

Rose picked up a Pilgrim female doll that was carrying a baby.

Travis asked, "Is that supposed to be the baby who was born on the *Mayflower?*"

"I don't think so. Oceanus Hopkins—the baby born while the *Mayflower* was at sea—was a boy, and this one's obviously a girl."

"Weren't there other babies born after Oceanus?"

"Yeah, Travis; there were. Another boy, Peregrine White, was born when the *Mayflower* arrived in New England, but before the Pilgrims had settled in Plymouth."

"I like the Oceanus baby better."

"Really? Why?"

"His last name—Hopkins—is the same as ours."

Rose smiled. "You're making a lot of sense, Travis. You know how much I love the name of 'Hopkins.'"

Travis smiled back at Rose before saying, "Several of my ancestors also have the first name of 'Oceanus.' Is it possible that I could be descended from Oceanus Hopkins?"

"No, I don't think so. Oceanus wasn't alive in 1623, so he didn't live for too long." After pausing briefly, Rose added, "I think some of your relatives have the same names as the descendants of Stephen Hopkins, who was Oceanus's father."

"Oh, really? What names are you thinking of, Rose?"

"Your father's name is Stephen Hopkins, right?"

"Yeah. I already know Stephen was one of the *Mayflower* passengers."

"His wife was Elizabeth, and you have an aunt by that name, right?"

"Yeah, I do. We call her 'Aunt Betty.'"

"Constance and Giles are two of Stephen Hopkins's children."

"Constance is one of my grandparents, and Giles is the generation before Constance." Travis's voice was excited as he continued, "I'm curious now about whether or not I'm really descended from one of the Pilgrims. I'll have to do some research into my ancestors."

"I've been learning a lot about Pilgrim history, so I'll be able to help you."

"Thanks. I would love that." Travis smiled. He looked almost like he was going to kiss Rose, but he didn't. She sighed, knowing that he didn't like to kiss her in public.

Travis looked at several shelves with some books on them. He walked over to one of the shelves and asked Rose, "You've been doing research. Which one is your favorite?"

Immediately, without even thinking, Rose replied, "I love William Bradford's *Of Plymouth Plantation.*"

Travis picked up a copy of Bradford's book. "This should keep me busy while you're doing more research."

"Yeah, it will. You'll love the book. William Bradford was the second governor of Plymouth; he kept being re-elected for a total of thirty-three years."

"He must have been well-liked."

"Definitely."

Travis was looking at one of the appendixes in the book. "The *Mayflower* passengers are listed in here. Wouldn't it be interesting if we are both descended from the Pilgrims?"

Rose shook her head in agreement and then looked down at her hands. She was still holding onto the female Pilgrim with the baby. "This baby's so cute. She almost makes me want to have one of my own."

"So, can I talk you into having kids now?" Travis's expression was hopeful.

Rose smiled at him. "Perhaps. Lately, I've been thinking a lot about kids." She gripped the mother-with-a-baby doll tightly in her left hand as she picked up the Myles doll in her right hand. "I have to buy Myles, but the woman with the baby is also neat."

As Rose pushed the dolls together, Travis asked, "Would you like to buy more than one of the dolls?"

Rose laughed. "Okay, you talked me into it. I need a whole family of Pilgrim dolls." She walked over to the sales clerk and handed her the dolls.

Travis gave the clerk the Bradford book and then paid for everything. After the clerk put *Of Plymouth Plantation* and the Pilgrim dolls into a shopping bag, Travis picked it up.

Rose asked, "Are you sure your shoulder's okay for carrying that?"

"I'm fine. How's your knee doing?"

"Great, but I should still carry the bag, Travis."

"Why?"

"I made you go shopping again. I should have to carry that bag."

Travis laughed. "For a change, you were in a hurry to rush right past a store without even looking at it. I made you look in the window, so I was the one who made you go shopping."

"Okay, it's all your fault, but I still bought the dolls. We should take turns carrying the bag."

"All right, we'll take turns, and since I'm already holding the bag, I'll be first."

Travis carried both the shopping bag and the lunch bag in his right hand. Rose smiled as she followed him out of the shop, into the corridor, and finally through one of the doors of the round section of the Visitor Center. Once outside, they began to follow a dirt pathway through a forest. At a fork in the road, Travis and Rose veered to the right, following the pathway that led to the Wampanoag Homesite. A few minutes after they had turned, Rose tugged at the two bags that Travis was still carrying. "It's now my turn."

Travis gave her the shopping bag. "This bag's heavy because of the book, not because of the dolls, so I'll let you carry this one bag for a few minutes."

"Okay."

"Can I borrow your camera to take a few pictures, Rose?"

"Definitely."

Rose handed her purse to Travis; he took the camera out, took a picture of her, and then continued to hold onto the camera, her purse, and the lunch bag. When they approached the Wampanoag Homesite, he took some more pictures.

Rose said, "This bag does get heavy after a while."

"Here, let me carry it." Travis took the shopping bag while Rose took back her purse and the camera.

"There's one good thing, Travis, about carrying a bag all day."

"What's that?"

"It's much nicer to be carrying a bag than to have nothing to carry." Rose paused and then smiled. "I've been thinking a lot about families lately—about what it would be like to be carrying a baby around everywhere."

"Really?"

She stopped walking and turned to look at Travis. "All of the research I've been doing about the Puritans has helped me to think about things. I also have realized that my dreams are starting to include children in them."

"Really?"

"Yeah. Last night, I had a lucid dream about a Pilgrim family."

"What happened?"

"It was actually a dream about memories. I realized that having children would mean creating not just our own memories, but our ancestors' memories, too."

"Does this mean you really want to have kids?"

"Yeah, I think so. I understand a lot more about families, ancestors, and timelines. I don't want to see my family stop now, but I rather want it to continue into the future."

"It was only two months ago, Rose, when you were claiming that you didn't want kids. Have you really changed your mind, or are you just thinking about wanting kids?"

"I used to be worried about whether or not I could be a good mother. Having my knee injured in the robbery didn't help matters."

"Were you worried about getting better?"

"Partially. I also was worried about my abilities in general—not just my physical ability."

"You'll make a great mother, Rose."

"Thanks, Travis." She looked seriously at her husband as she added, "And you'll be a great dad one day."

Rose started to walk forward again and then said in a humorous tone, "Carrying the bag with your book and my dolls in it has helped me to be certain about having kids. I know that I'm physically capable of carrying a baby, my purse, and lots of baby items."

Travis laughed. "Here, would you like to carry one of these bags some more?"

"No, that's okay. You can hold them for a while." Rose paused briefly and then added, "I've been thinking a lot about my family lately. As I get older, I want to have more family members, instead of fewer."

Travis shook his head in agreement. They both continued to walk up the path deeper into the forest. When they arrived at a sign welcoming people to the Wampanoag Homesite, Travis reached out and touched it. He turned to face Rose, and she took a picture of him with his hand touching the cranberry-colored sign. The white and yellow words on the sign seemed very bright in the morning sunlight.

"I love cranberries," Rose said.

"I know you do. That's why I'm touching the sign."

As Travis's smile became larger, Rose took another picture.

He moved his hand down to his side, walked over next to Rose, and placed the bag on the ground near their feet. He then said, "Now it's your turn to have your picture taken."

Rose gave him the camera and walked over to the sign. "Should I smile?"

"If you want to. You always look beautiful, whether you're smiling or not." Travis began to take multiple pictures of Rose. He moved into different places, so he could take pictures of her from different angles. He zoomed in for some close ups and zoomed out for some whole-body pictures.

After the first few pictures, Rose smiled; then she started to laugh when she realized that Travis was doing a photo shoot. "I'm not a model."

"You look like one."

After Travis had taken at least fifty pictures, Rose put one of her hands in front of her face.

Travis paused for a few seconds before saying, "Even your hand is beautiful." He then took another ten pictures before putting the camera into his pocket and picking up the lunch bag and the shopping bag.

Travis and Rose continued walking along the dirt pathway; soon, they had entered the Wampanoag Homesite. There were three different kinds of homes, one of which had three fire pits inside. The homes were circular. The frames of the houses were made of curved cedar saplings that were tied together. Bark was attached to the outside of the sapling frames. Rose bent over to follow Travis through the door of one of the homes; she paused to look at the sleeping cots that lined the inside walls. They were made of wooden branches with deerskin blankets draped over them. The home contained woven bags, mats, fishing nets, fire utensils, a hatchet, baskets, tools, arrows, and bows. Reeds and pieces of wood were under some of the cots.

A Native man, who was one of the Plimoth Plantation employees, stood up. He was dressed in a deerskin outfit. He invited Travis and Rose to sit down, which they were happy to do. Rose asked, "Is your deerskin the kind of clothing worn in the seventeenth century?"

"Yes, it is. I am speaking modern English, though, so that you can understand me."

Rose asked, "How long have you lived here?"

"My people have been here for over 10,000 years."

"Really?"

"Yes."

"In 1620, were you mad or scared when the Pilgrims first landed?"

"They dug up some of our ancestors' graves and stole our corn seed, so we were mad at first."

Rose said, "I can understand why."

"Yes, we were also scared of the guns, but we still used our arrows in defense of ourselves and our land."

Rose said, "Massasoit signed a treaty with the Pilgrims, and the two groups of people lived peacefully with each other for decades."

"Yes, we traded beaver skins and fish for such things as tools and beer."

Travis stood up and said, "We have to leave in a few minutes, but we want to thank you for welcoming us into your home."

"You're always welcome here." The Native man went outside. He joined another Native person, who was planning on using fire to burn out a part of a tree in order to make a mishoon, which was a kind of a boat.

The second Native man said, "Do you want to see the mishoon being made?"

Travis smiled. "I'd love to, but we don't have enough time right now."

Rose said, "I think we have another minute or two." She looked over at Travis, who shook his head affirmatively.

Rose continued, "I heard that you can also show us how Native people dance."

The two Native persons danced for a few minutes. When they stopped, the first Native person asked, "What do you think?"

Rose smiled. "I've been learning how to do ballroom dances. Seeing you dance different steps is wonderful."

"If you want us to, we can show you how to play the game of 'hubbub.'"

Travis said, "That sounds like a loud game."

"Some people think it is."

Travis looked over at Rose, who looked at her watch before saying, "We really have to get going, but we might be able to stop back later today or tomorrow."

"Okay." The Native people went inside one of the houses; Travis and Rose began to walk to the other side of the Wampanoag Homesite. They passed by a cornfield in the middle of the Homesite and then walked toward the Eel River Pond. Before they reached the water, they turned onto a dirt path; there were no signs that indicated where the path was going.

Rose paused, pulled out one of her maps, and checked it. "Yeah, this looks like the unmarked path we need."

Travis and Rose started walking on the trail; they were moving slightly uphill. On the right side of the path was a wooden fence that stopped people from walking down to the Eel River Pond. On the left side was a forest with many trees, bushes, and small plants.

After a few minutes, Travis and Rose came to a section of the path that was made of wooden boards; there also was a wooden fence on both sides of the path. A section of the path had narrow trees growing through its wooden boards. Rose walked over to a wooden bench, sat down, and started to compare the sampler with one of the maps of Plimoth Plantation. Travis joined her. After a few minutes of looking at the maps with Rose, he stood up and walked over to the part of the fence that was overlooking Eel River Pond. "The treasure is near the shore of the Eel River, rather than the shoreline next to the Eel River Pond."

Rose walked over to stand next to Travis. "You're right. We need to move up further along the path, but we should keep comparing the real shoreline with the shorelines on the different maps."

"The treasure looks like it's about thirty feet from this curve on the Eel River."

Rose handed two maps and the sampler to Travis; she then took the bag with the book and the dolls in it. "It's my turn."

"Okay." They walked up the trail for another minute; they then heard some noises from some people who were further up on the path. One of the people said, "I'm so glad it's Friday. Tomorrow, I'm going to a birthday party for one of my nephews."

"That sounds like fun."

"Do you also have the weekend off, or are you working overtime?"

"I'd love to work overtime, but I don't think there's enough money for any of us to work overtime right now."

"Do you think we'll finish this fence today?"

"It's possible."

Rose and Travis were getting close to the workers, who were digging a hole near the fence. Next to the feet of the workers were some wooden poles and extra shovels.

Travis put his hand out for Rose to stop. He then whispered to her: "We can't do anything with the Plantation employees out here. I don't think they'll let us run around digging holes in the forest."

Rose shook her head in agreement. "There's one other problem."

"Really? What's that?"

"We don't have a shovel."

"You're right."

"Once the Pilgrims needed shovels and didn't have any. They used their swords to dig up corn from frozen mounds of dirt."

"We don't have any swords or knives, either." Travis took out his keychain and looked at the tiny pair of scissors. "I don't think these will work too well."

Rose laughed as she took out her own keychain. "I don't see anything here, either, that'll work."

Travis looked on the ground at the wooden poles. There were several shovels lying next to them. "I wonder if the employees are going to leave their tools here when they go home tonight."

"Probably not." Rose pulled the sampler out of her purse. "It's strange that the sampler might have a shovel on it, but we don't have one."

Travis looked at the sampler and laughed. "That little thing really does look like a shovel."

"It could be something else, too, like a bell."

Travis looked at the sampler again. "I think it's a shovel."

Rose put the sampler back into her purse and then asked, "Do you have a big light we could use? I only have that tiny flashlight you bought me for my keychain."

"I only have a little flashlight, too."

"Are you talking about the flashlight next to the scissors on your keychain?"

"Yeah." Travis laughed. "We'll have to buy each other some big flashlights."

"Even if we had a big flashlight, I don't think I want to be out here at night. There will probably be a lot of bugs."

"I know how you hate bugs, Rose. We'll have to come back tomorrow during the day. These two employees won't be working on a Saturday."

Rose walked toward the workers, and Travis followed her. When she was a few feet from the employees, they stopped digging and looked at her. She said to them, "It's really hot out here. Will you be finished soon?"

"No, we'll be repairing this fence until four o'clock tonight."

The second employee said, "We'll be taking a short lunch break in a little while, and then we'll be here the rest of the afternoon."

The closest employee said, "We'll probably be back here Monday morning, finishing up by doing a little bit of landscaping." Pointing toward a box of flowers, he added, "We have some perennials that need to be transplanted."

Rose asked, "How can you dig holes in this heat?"

The closest employee leaned on his shovel and smiled at Rose. Even though he was covered in sweat, he was wearing a shirt, a baseball cap, and long jeans. "I actually like working outside when it's hot."

The second worker shook his head in agreement. "I love working outside in the summer. It's much better than working outside in the winter."

The closest employee said, "Sometimes, I even like working outside in the winter. As long as I have my waterproof, fur-lined boots, I'm okay."

Rose said, "It must be really pretty out here when it's snowing."

"The trees do look nice when they're covered in snow. I think they look even nicer in leaves, though," the second employee said.

Everyone was quiet for a few minutes. The employees continued to dig.

"So, do you normally just do outside work?"

"We sometimes fix things indoors, too," the closest employee said.

"Have you ever done any of the role-playing acting?"

"Not yet, but I've been thinking about it. I like to help out with whatever tasks need to be done."

"Your positive attitude reminds me of something Captain John Smith once said."

"Was that his comment about the ant and the bee?"

Rose smiled at the closest employee and then said, "So, you've been reading about the Pilgrims and their culture."

"Yeah, I've been doing that for years now."

Travis asked, "What did Captain John Smith say about ants and bees?"

The closest employee stopped shoveling and looked at Travis. "In one of Captain Smith's letters, he said that 'If the little Ant, & the sillie Bee seek by their diligence the good of their Commonwealth; much more ought Man.'[88]"

Rose added, "Everyone thinks great things about Captain John Smith and his helping to establish the Jamestown, Virginia, colony."

Travis asked, "Was that before or after the Pilgrims went to New England?"

Rose looked at the closest employee, who said, "It was before the Pilgrims. In 1608-1609, Captain Smith was a leader of the Jamestown colony."

Rose added, "Captain Smith wrote about Virginia, but he also visited New England. In 1616, he wrote *A Description of New England,* which describes New England as a wonderful place with lots of resources for people who are willing to work hard."

The closest employee added, "He even gave New England the name 'New England.'"

Travis asked, "Really?"

Rose answered, "Yeah, Captain Smith wrote about New England having lots of harbors where ships could land. He also claimed there were lots of stones, metals, fur, food items, and land that anyone could own. Smith said there were so many fish that even a little boy could catch fish on the stern of a ship.[89]"

Travis asked, "Did the Pilgrims know about Captain Smith's description of New England?"

The closest employee said, "Some people in Europe did. I'm sure that's why some of the other people—the 'strangers'—came over with the Puritans on the *Mayflower.* Some people in Europe thought that going to the New World would be their only chance to get ahead in life. They thought they could get all kinds of things—like good land, a house, and better food."

Rose said, "Well, many of the Pilgrims did do very well in New England."

The closest employee said, "Except for the ones who died during that first winter."

They were all silent for a minute. The closest employee then looked at Travis, who seemed to have stepped backwards a few steps and was peering into the forest. The other employee also looked at Travis and then said, "It's been nice talking with you both, but you're not really supposed to be out here on this path."

"Okay. We were just curious about where the path goes. We didn't see any signs or anything," Travis said.

"There are no signs on this path, which means people should be taking the other paths."

"Okay. Thanks for telling us about Captain John Smith." Travis and Rose began to walk back down the pathway toward the Wampanoag Homesite. After they were far enough down the path so that the employees could not hear them, they stopped.

Rose looked at her watch and asked Travis, "So, what do you think we should do now?"

"Well, how about if we wait a few minutes and then walk back up the path? We could check to see if they left any of their tools behind."

"They probably didn't leave their tools behind."

"You're right. People normally keep their tools somewhere safe, even when they just leave for lunch." Travis looked guiltily down at the ground as he said, "However, while you were talking about Captain John Smith, I bent over slightly, moved my foot under the fence, and slid one of the shovels partially under some vines. The shovel might still be there."

"Okay. If the shovel is there and we 'borrow' it, we'll just have to make certain we get it back to them."

"I agree. We don't want to be thieves."

Rose laughed. "We're starting to act like the Pilgrims."

"How so?"

"They stole corn and other items from the Indians."

"Are you kidding me, Rose?"

"No, they really did take some corn that wasn't theirs. They needed the corn for food, so they had a better excuse than we do."

"Did they actually steal the corn on purpose?"

"Yeah, they did, but they were planning on giving the Indians some stuff in return."

"Did they ever pay them back for the stolen corn?"

"Yeah, they did, Travis, but it was after one of their teenagers was kidnapped."

"Okay. We'll make certain we return the shovel. I wouldn't want either one of us to be kidnapped."

"Perhaps we should also pay interest—or some kind of rental fee. We could give a donation to the Plimoth Plantation Organization."

Travis smiled. "Well, we are paying for our tickets to visit the tourist attractions."

"We should pay for more than that. We'll be digging up holes in the forest with their shovel."

"Okay. We won't really be stealing if we give them back the shovel with a donation to pay for its use."

"We'll also have to replace the dirt again, so we don't leave any holes in the ground."

"Yeah, we don't want anyone to get hurt."

"Maybe we should just buy our own shovel and bring it with us tomorrow."

"I don't think the employees here would be happy to see us carrying a shovel around."

"You're right. It's better if we 'borrow' the shovel, but let's see if it's still where you hid it."

They walked back up the pathway to the point where the fence was being repaired. The employees had left for lunch. Travis quickly found the shovel that he had partially hidden. He picked it up, showed it to Rose, and said, "I'm going to place this somewhere safe, so no one else will 'borrow' it."

Rose sighed. "Okay."

They walked up the path for another fifty feet. Travis then said, "Wait here." He jumped over the fence and ran into the forest with the shovel in his hand. He came back several minutes later. "The shovel's in a safe place."

Rose laughed. "I hate 'safe places.' I always lose anything that I put in a 'safe place.'"

"Well, this place should be easy enough to find."

"Are you sure you'll be able to find it okay tomorrow?"

"Yeah. It's under a bush next to a large oak. Tomorrow, once we walk up to this spot, we just have to go that way for about ten feet. There's a slight clearing, and we'll be able to see the large oak tree right away."

"Okay. Do you think we have time to look around a little bit right now?"

"I don't think so." Travis scratched his head. "We don't want those same employees to see us up here again."

"Tomorrow morning, we'll have to get down here fairly early."

"Yeah, we'll need enough time to find the treasure—if there is a treasure—and still see the Pilgrim wedding in the afternoon," Travis said.

"To avoid running into those employees on this path, we should probably go back the same way we came."

"Yeah. We could go to the Visitor Center and have some lunch, unless you'd rather just have some of the snacks we brought."

"After all of the walking around we've been doing, I'm really hungry. I want more than these snacks."

"So do I. Let's go to the Visitor Center."

Rose and Travis walked quickly back through the Wampanoag Homesite and then over to the Visitor Center. In the lunch room, they had turkey sandwiches and then decided to go to the Nye Barn.

There were not too many animals in the Nye Barn, but Rose and Travis had fun interacting with a few of the goats. They then went up the path on a hill toward the Craft Center. On the way to the center, they walked through the Colonial Education Site.

On the right side of the path were wooden rectangular boxes containing different kinds of plants and small signs explaining how the Pilgrims used the plants.

At the Craft Center, Rose and Travis admired the crafts that were being made and displayed by several artisans. One of the artisans was a Native lady. She was busy weaving a mat.

Rose watched her weave for a few minutes and then asked, "Do you know anything about samplers?"

"Just a little bit."

Rose pulled her sampler out of her purse before asking, "What do you think of this one?"

The Native lady stopped weaving in order to look at Rose's sampler. "I think it's well done."

"Do you think this little picture is a shovel?"

"I don't know. It could be a shovel or a bell." The lady looked more closely at the sampler and then said, "I think it's probably a bell because there's a musical note sewn into the nearby vines."

"Thanks." Rose took the sampler back and began to look at one of the circles on its edge. "This circle looks strange."

"In what way?" Travis asked.

"The color of its interior is slightly different from everything else on the sampler."

Travis looked at the circle on the left side of the sampler. "It looks sort of opaque, like it's empty."

"Can I see the sampler again?" the Native lady asked. Rose gave her back the sampler.

After looking at the circle for a moment, the lady said, "If the intent was to have nothing visible in a hole, it could be a memory hole."

Rose said, "I love memory holes. I had a dream about them last night."

"Really?" the Native lady asked.

"Yeah, it was one of my best dreams."

Travis asked the Native lady, "Can you tell us about memory holes?"

"Yes, I can. The Pilgrims were told about memory holes by the Native people they met."

"That's interesting. Memory holes were made by Native people?"

"Yeah, the holes were made where something important had happened. Whenever people walked near a memory hole, they would talk about the event."

"That would be a great way to remember not just events, but also important people and loved ones."

"You're right. A memory hole connects history to the geographic place where it happened. One of the books I have here describes the Pilgrims learning about memory holes from the Native people." The Native lady got up, went over to a desk, and pulled out several books. After looking in the index of one of the books, she brought it over to Travis and Rose. She then said, "This book's author explains that 'to walk across the land in Southern New England was to travel in time.'[90]"

Rose looked at the cover of the book, handed it back to the lady, and said, "Even now, to walk across a place like Plimoth Plantation is like travelling through time. I'm having so much fun."

"I'm so glad you're enjoying your visit with us."

Rose smiled. "Thanks. You've been really helpful."

The Native lady put the books back into the desk drawer. As Rose and Travis were leaving the Craft Center, they said good-bye to the lady. Once they were outside, Travis asked, "Is your knee okay?"

"It's fine."

Travis looked at the path leading to the English Village. "It's already after four o'clock. Do you want to go over to the village for a little while, or would you rather wait until tomorrow when we'll have more time to look around?"

"We're fairly close to the village. Maybe we could walk over and just check it out for a few minutes."

They followed the path up to the English Village, entered through a gate, and went into the meetinghouse. On the first floor, several tourists were seated on a couple of the wooden benches. One of them was praying silently. Rose and Travis went up to the second floor of the house. Two cannons were in the large room.

Rose explained to Travis, "The second floor of this building was the fort, and the first floor was the church."

They walked over to one of the windows and looked out at the rest of the village. A wooden fence enclosed all of the buildings. There was a dirt walkway that ran down from the meetinghouse and through the center of the village. Wooden fences separated most of the homes and yards from each other. The houses were made of wooden boards with thatched roofs. Some of the houses had chimneys, and some did not. Many of the yards had gardens in them, and one area had cows in it. There were goats, chickens, a few trees and bushes, stacks of branches, a hill of firewood, an enclosure for hay, and a big stone kiln that was inside of a small wooden building.

They took a few pictures, and then Rose pointed toward an open area of the village: "The wedding tomorrow will possibly be over there—where the wooden picnic tables are."

"That's probably where they're having the wedding feast afterwards. The actual wedding could be there or somewhere else."

"Well, we'll be surprised tomorrow."

"Do you want to look around some more? We could talk to some of the Pilgrim role-playing actors."

"That sounds like fun."

They walked down the stairs onto the first floor of the meetinghouse. A Pilgrim man was seated on one of the benches. Rose and Travis walked up to him. "Can we sit here, too?"

"Ay. I would love your company."

After they were seated on the bench, Rose stretched out her left leg and rubbed her knee.

Travis looked at her and asked, "Is your knee okay?"

"It's great. I just felt like stretching."

Travis asked the Pilgrim, "It's after five o'clock. Will you be closing soon?"

"Ah, we are within the last hour of daylight. Soon we will close up the gates, and visitors will go to their homes."

Rose sighed. "The end of the day always comes too fast."

"Ah, especially on a summer evening, the time runneth away."

Rose smiled. "Time always used to run away from me. It would run away in the mornings, afternoons, evenings, and nights."

"Didst thou scare Time so that it now runneth away from thee?"

"No, I don't think so."

Travis said, "That's not true. You've always liked clocks and watches, so possibly you did scare Time."

"So, how should I make Time more of my friend?"

The Pilgrim smiled. "Both of you can take a trip with Time. You can learn of your past history."

"Yes, we have been doing that."

"Then thou wilt know that this village be a place where the present Time hath connected to an historic Time."

Rose shook her head in agreement. "Yes, you are so right."

When the Pilgrim man stood up, Travis said, "Speaking of Time, we should get going, Rose. We don't want to make this kind Pilgrim work overtime—not unless he really wants to."

"I thank thee, Sir, for thy understanding. And may God bless you both."

Rose and Travis stood up. Rose said, "God has blessed me many times. May He bless you, also."

Travis said, "Thank you for being so helpful."

"Fare thee well."

Rose and Travis both said good-bye before walking out of the meetinghouse, along the pathway, and back to Travis's car.

Once they were out on the main road, they decided to buy some take-out food and bring it back to their hotel rooms. By seven o'clock, they had finished eating supper in Rose's room. They used the pool, watched some TV together, and finally kissed each other good night. Rose kept thinking about all of the things she was thankful for as she fell asleep.

A TIME OF THANKSGIVING

It was Thanksgiving. When Rose walked through the door into the dining room, everyone looked up and smiled. Seated around the dining room table were Travis, Rose's parents, Granny, and some other relatives. They were all patiently waiting for her to join them. She walked over to her chair and then realized that the smiles were all frozen; she was probably really late. As she continued to look at the faces, they kept exactly the same expressions.

Rose asked, "Is this a dream?"

Her mother said, "Yes, this is a dream. It's a lucid dream."

Rose replied, "Thanks for letting me know, mom."

In the middle of the table were a turkey, stuffing, ham, vegetables, rolls, mashed potatoes, and sweet potatoes. Rose's mother said a short prayer of thanksgiving. Then they began to move the bowls of food around. When Rose touched the bowl of green beans, she said, "This is really cold." The heads of Rose's relatives moved up and down, showing their agreement.

Rose's mother said, "We didn't mind waiting for you, Rose. We love you."

"But you waited too long for me. You should have started to eat before I got here."

Travis reached over, grabbed Rose's hand, and kissed it. "I love you, too. I will never again do anything without you."

Rose sighed. Even though she was happy that her family had waited for her, she still wished that she had been on time. She said, "If this is a lucid dream, then I should have been on time, rather than late."

Her mother said, "You can't change the past."

Travis cleared his throat and then said, "I disagree with you. Sometimes people can do things over again."

Rose's mother asked, "Have you ever really changed the past?"

Travis smiled broadly. "Yes, I have. Since Rose's train accident, I've been supporting her, rather than leaving her to do things on her own. She now knows that I love her."

Rose hugged Travis and gave him a big kiss. She then said, "Sometimes history repeats itself. Then we can do things differently the second time around. While we can't erase the first event that happened, we can add other things, so the first event is seen in a different way."

Travis said, "We can change how people think about our past actions."

Rose gave Travis another kiss. Everyone at the table clapped their hands, showing how happy they were about Travis and Rose being together again.

Rose said, "If this is a lucid dream, then I really should be able to change the past. I shouldn't have to wait for it to repeat itself."

She waved her left hand back and forth over the table; at the same time, she looked intently at her watch as it moved with her hand. The hour and minute hands on her watch began to move backwards and then stopped.

Suddenly, the food items started to steam; they were now really hot. She looked at Travis, who said, "You are definitely on time today. In fact, you are really early."

Rose smiled as she said, "Yes, we can change our reality, and maybe we can even change our past."

Rose picked up her glass of apple cider; it was cold. She said out loud, "I thought I was on time, and everything was hot." Her glass of cider became hot and then too hot. The glass slid slowly downwards through her partially-opened fist. She looked at the wooden floor and then back up at the glass. To stop the glass from sliding down to the floor and breaking, she tried to grab onto it again, but she was too late—the glass fell onto the floor and broke.

"I was late again, and I thought I was starting to be on time."

Travis asked, "When were you late?"

"I was late just now—when I was trying to catch my glass of cider. If I had been on time, I would have caught it before it fell down and broke." The glass pieces and cider were lying on the floor. Suddenly, in response to Rose's desire, they put themselves back together again, landing in one piece within Rose's hand.

Rose looked at the items sitting on the table. "We don't have a salad."

Her mom said, "If this is a lucid dream, then someone will bring one, right?"

Rose looked around. A lady from a couple of her dreams, the Feather-hat Lady, walked up to the table. She was carrying a ceramic bowl with a salad in it. Rose looked inside the salad bowl; it had some strange-looking leaves and other unusual plants. When Rose looked away from the salad, she realized that she wasn't in her own house anymore; she was now outside with the Pilgrims. As she sat on a stool in front of a wooden table, she looked at the two rows of houses that began on her left and right sides. The rows of houses climbed up a hill. On top of the hill was a cannon.

Rose stood up; she was now in the middle of a commons area. The wooden table had moved so that it was next to her. A bench and some stools were placed around it. The Feather-hat Lady suddenly appeared next to the table; she was holding a brown ceramic bowl containing salad.

A Pilgrim lady with an orange hat walked up to the Feather-hat Lady. Neither one of the ladies noticed that Rose was there with them. The two women greeted each other by bowing their heads. The Feather-hat Lady said, "Good morrow to thee."

The other lady asked, "How now?"

"I am well. Art thou also well?"

"Ay, I am very well."

When the Feather-hat Lady noticed that the other lady was looking at her bowl of salad, she raised the bowl up slightly and asked, "Dost thou enjoy eating the greens here in Plymouth?"

"Ay, the salad leaves here are better than the ones in Leiden."

"The meat also hath much greater taste."

"The food is better because it is fresher."

"'Tis very fresh. I picked these leaves early this morning—before the high tide came up onto the shore."

"Were the leaves covered in their early-morning moisture?"

"Ay. My hands became cold from the dampness, but I was so very happy to find these greens."

"I too am joyful about our fresh food. In Leiden, I did pray for just one taste of food like this."

"Heaven hath sent us good fortune in our new home."

Ruffling noises came from the bushes at the edge of the forest near the commons area. The two ladies turned toward the noises, which increased in loudness until gobbling was heard. Suddenly, a turkey walked out from behind a bush and then entered the commons area. It was only ten feet away from the two ladies, who both stared at it. The turkey stretched out its tail feathers in a gorgeous-looking fan shape. After waving its tail at the two ladies, the turkey turned around and headed back toward the edge of the forest. As the turkey walked between two bushes, it made the branches move. The turkey continued to walk forward, making other branches move. Finally, the moving bush branches stretched out and connected into some moving tree branches. As the branches on the trees moved with the same kind of waves, the tree trunks held the branches upwards, showing the strength of their wood. The waving branches and tree trunks began to grow taller as they stood together upon their ground and circled around the colony of Plymouth, Massachusetts.

From a different part of the forest, gunshots were heard. The rustling branches were joined by gobbling noises; these noises moved deeper into the forest, gradually becoming less noticeable. Finally, there were no moving branches and no gobbling noises.

The Feather-hat Lady said, "I think the turkey escaped."

The other Pilgrim lady said, "Ay. 'Tis now far away and safely hidden within the depths of the forest."

A few minutes later, a Pilgrim with a black hat and a large gun came running into the commons area. He paused in front of the two ladies, placed the barrel end of his musket on the ground, and leaned against its upper handle section. The gun looked to be about five feet tall, and its metal frame easily held the weight of the Pilgrim. He touched his hat in a greeting and then asked, "Hath thou seen a turkey?"

The Feather-hat Lady said, "Ay, we did see a turkey. It ran in among the trees." She pointed into the forest, but in a different direction from where the turkey had gone.

"I thank thee." The Pilgrim hoisted his gun up onto his shoulder, waved, and headed in the direction that the Feather-hat Lady had indicated. Both ladies watched him leave the commons area, walk past the bushes, and enter the forest.

When the Pilgrim was no longer visible, the Orange-hat Lady said, "He was in great haste."

"So he was, but I think that he will not never catch that turkey."

"Thou knowest we may need the meat of that turkey."

"Ay, but we do not need it today."

The Orange-hat Lady laughed. "I agree with thee. And that turkey was most pretty."

"We do need some turkeys to be alive for the next year."

"And for the years after next year."

"For our children."

"For the children of our children."

Rose took a step forward and said to the ladies, "My family always has turkey on Thanksgiving."

Neither lady heard Rose. They were both looking toward the forest, where the waving branches were now quiet.

A few minutes later, a slight breeze began to blow, and several green leaves floated onto the top of the table. One of the leaves changed its shape until it looked like a turkey feather.

The Orange-hat Lady asked, "Doth that feather belong to the pretty turkey?"

"I know not."

"Dost thou think he will return for it?"

The Feather-hat Lady touched the area of her hat where her feather used to be and then said, "Nay, I doubt he will come back here into an open area."

The Orange-hat Lady twirled the turkey feather between two of her fingers. "Doth this feather now belong to me or to thee?"

"To thee."

"Nay. The wind blew it closer to thee." She handed the feather to the Feather-hat Lady.

"I thank thee, but thou shouldst have this feather." The Feather-hat Lady handed the feather back to her friend.

Her friend accepted the feather with a smile. "'Tis interesting how we were talking about green salads and turkeys, and then the wind blew some green leaves and a turkey feather onto the table in front of us."

"Ay, that is most interesting, especially for harvest season. The trees do not have any more green leaves on them."

Both women turned to look at the forest; the only leaves now left on the trees were yellow, red, orange, and brown. When the women turned back to look at the table again, the leaves on the table had changed to a yellow color.

The Orange-hat Lady said, "I like the warmth of the summer."

The leaves changed back to a green color. Facing the forest, Rose said to the trees, "It's harvest season, which means it's probably early in October, but it might also be in the last part of September. Your leaves should be red, yellow, orange, and brown, rather than green." The leaves heard Rose and changed back to their autumn colors.

The two Pilgrim ladies were both looking at the trees. "The seasons change so quickly," the Feather-hat Lady said.

"Ay, it seemeth like only a moment ago when the leaves were green. Then they changed to red and yellow."

"The seasons are a part of the plan of our Lord for our world."

"Ay, they are."

The Feather-hat Lady touched her hat again.

Rose said to her, "Since you had to give up your feather, you've been touching that spot on your hat a lot."

The Feather-hat Lady asked the Orange-hat Lady, "Did God plan to have that feather of a turkey fly onto our table?"

"I think so. Our Lord doth make many goodly things happen."

The Orange-hat Lady was still holding onto the turkey feather. She extended it to the Feather-hat Lady. "Dost thou want this turkey feather? It will add more beauty to thy hat."

"The feather is of a most perfect size for my hat."

"The color and pattern of that feather will match thy hat nicely." The Orange-hat Lady put the feather into her friend's hand. "I know how thou didst give up thy first feather."

"Dost thou really know?"

"Ah, thou didst give thy feather as a part of thy payment for passage on the *Mayflower.*"

Both ladies were quiet for a minute. Then the Orange-hat Lady said, "The turkey feather is thine."

"I thank thee very much. Thou art most generous."

"Thou art welcome, but our Holy Father is the one which thou shouldst thank the most."

"Yes, I am most thankful to our Lord." The Feather-hat Lady pressed her hands together, said a short prayer, and removed her wide-brimmed hat. There was a linen cap still on her head; her hair was tucked neatly inside of the cap. Slowly, she tried to insert the end of the turkey feather into the wide brim of her hat, but there didn't seem to be a feather hole. "I know that a hole for a feather is in my hat. I used to have an ostrich feather right here." She pointed to a spot on the left side of her hat and then handed her hat over to the Orange-hat Lady.

"Perhaps the humidity hath made the hole to close up." The Orange-hat Lady looked closely at the spot where the hole was supposed to be. She then grabbed some scissors that were hanging from an orange ribbon attached to her belt. Carefully, she rubbed the end of the scissors' blades until a tiny hole opened up in the hat. She then handed the hat back to the Feather-Hat Lady, who inserted the end of the turkey feather into the new hole. With a big smile, she placed the hat on her head. Immediately, her posture improved. She looked taller. Even though nothing was keeping the feather inside the hole in her hat, the feather still stood up tall in its correct spot.

"Thou lookest more pretty than that turkey!"

"I thank thee. Thou art pretty, too. And thou art most kind."

"So art thou."

A slight breeze blew; the feather stood even taller atop the brim of the hat. The Feather-hat Lady reached her left hand up above her head until she touched and then softly stroked the turkey feather. "I do not wish to lose this new feather. I must stitch it very securely into my hat."

The Orange-hat Lady looked up at the sun as if she were looking at a clock. She then said, "Soon our fellow Pilgrims and the visiting Indians will be ready to dine, but thou hast a few moments to secure that feather in thy hat."

"I will stitch the feather in its place very quickly. I must excuse myself, but I will make haste."

"Good-bye to you."

"I will return soon. I promise not to be late."

"Fare thee well."

As the Feather-hat Lady walked quickly to her family's cabin, several Pilgrims moved toward one of the tables set up in the commons area. They stopped walking and started talking to each other. One of them asked, "Dost thou know if all of our men have returned from hunting for fowls?"

"Ah, they have."

"How many men were sent out to go hunting for our harvest festival?"

Someone named E.W. said, "...four men..."[91]

"This will be another great time to give thanks to our Lord."

"Ay, 'tis the first time for us to give thanks for a bountiful harvest in New England."

"Governor Bradford doth know how to lead us well. He hath chosen a great time for a celebration of Thanksgiving."

Rose said, "This celebration of yours in 1621 is what people in the future will call 'The First Thanksgiving.'" Rose paused for a few seconds, but none of the Pilgrims seemed to be listening to her. She then said, "Other times of Thanksgiving will be celebrated in the future. George Washington, for example, declared a Day of Thanksgiving on November 26, 1789. Abraham Lincoln, in an official 1863 proclamation, made Thanksgiving a national holiday that would be celebrated every year on the last Thursday in November; he said that American citizens should observe 'a day of thanksgiving and praise to our beneficent Father who dwelleth in the heavens.'[92] In 1941, President Franklin Roosevelt changed the date for Thanksgiving to the fourth Thursday in November."

Rose was fairly certain that the group of Pilgrims in the commons area had not heard her words about Thanksgiving; however, immediately after she had finished talking about the holiday, the Pilgrims started to pray together. Their prayer included four parts that Rose knew to be "ACTS": Adoration, Confession, Thanksgiving, and Supplication. The group of Pilgrims first told God how much they adored him. Second, they confessed their sins. Third, they expressed their thanks. Fourth, they asked for help with their own needs and with the needs of others.

When the Pilgrims had finished praying, they began talking to each other. The lighting changed, so Rose knew that some time had elapsed. Then Massasoit and ninety Native people came into the village. Some of the Natives were carrying five deer, which were presented to the Pilgrims. The reactions of the Pilgrims showed that deer meat was considered to be a special treat. Everyone was smiling. The Natives were happy to give this gift, and the Pilgrims were happy to accept it. As more people entered the commons area, Rose moved to one of its edges.

Some of the same greetings were said over and over again among different groups of people in the commons area: "Good morrow," "How now," "Peace," "Many good thanks," and "May God bless thee." Some spits had been set up and were cooking different meat items. Inside many of the homes, Pilgrim women were busy making soup. As preparations for a feast progressed, small groups of people continued to interact with each other. Then some of the Pilgrims began to sing the twenty-third Psalm from their Psalm-book. Rose heard some of the words: "Jehovah feedeth me, I shal not lack; ... He gently leads me quiet waters by."[93]

In what seemed like only a minute's time, many food items, including the deer, were prepared, cooked, and moved to some tables in different parts of the commons area. There were duck, geese, oysters, lobster, fish, eels, clams, corn, popcorn, carrots, onions, cucumbers, cabbages, beets, radishes, salad, nuts, and dried berries. Before beginning to eat with their guests, the Pilgrims said a prayer, thanking God for providing for their needs and for letting them be a part of his plans for New England. A bible verse about giving thanks was a part of the prayer: "And let the peace of God rule in your hearts to the which ye are called in one body, and be ye thankful" (Col. 3:15 GNV).

The Pilgrim women, all of whom were wearing aprons, served food to the men and the children before they began to eat anything. There were no forks, only spoons and knives, so most of the food was eaten by people who were using their fingers.

Rose saw a green leaf land on one of the tables. As she watched the leaf flutter in the breeze, it changed to a brown color and then broke up into pieces. One of the Pilgrim ladies noticed the leaf and said in a timid voice, "Another winter cometh."

Her husband said, "Ay. But let us not be fearful. We are much better prepared than we were last winter. And we are now of good cheer."

"Thou art correct. We can be thankful for our homes and our food."

"And we now have our allies: the Indians which are the closest to our colony."

The Pilgrim lady looked at several of the Native people who were talking to a family of Pilgrims. "Ay. We have our friends and our families."

Once everyone had finished eating, the children began to play together. Several Native children were racing; they ran in front of the Pilgrim lady and her husband before going back to the opposite edge of the commons area. After another few trips around the commons area, the racing children stopped running. They walked over to where two Pilgrim children were possibly playing a version of Knicker Box, which was a game with marbles and a box containing arches. There weren't any marbles or boxes, but the children still seemed to be playing Knicker Box by using round stones and a string of arches made from curving branches. The first Pilgrim child took a round stone and tried to roll it through an arch. The stone was supposed to get through the arch without hitting anything or bouncing backwards, but it hit one of the arches and knocked it over. The second child tried and was more successful; his stone rolled through two arches. After the second child stood up, the two groups of children stood staring at each other for a few seconds. Then the Pilgrim children offered some round stones to the Native children, and all of them began to play the game together.

Not only the children, but also the adults were having fun. Rose noticed two young men who were arm wrestling with each other. She walked over closer to their table. The shorter man was winning, but he probably wasn't as short as Myles Standish. Rose wondered if Myles was anywhere close by. She looked around, hoping that her lucid dreaming techniques would work. Suddenly, Myles walked up to the table where the two other men were seated. He asked, "How dost thou fare?"

One of the men said, "Well."

Myles then sat down and showed them how to improve their arm-wrestling technique. Rose knew that Myles had been hired to do the military training for the Pilgrims, and she was fascinated by his training techniques. He explained positioning as he showed the men how to do different arm positions; then he made the men mimic his motions. Finally, he arm wrestled with each of them and explained what they were doing wrong.

Rose sighed as she thought about what a great mentor and father figure Myles was. Travis would be an even better father figure. He would be less directive and more modern in his approach. She had already seen him being a perfect uncle with his niece and nephew, so she knew what kind of a father he would be.

Rose sighed again. Even more than seeing Myles, she really wanted to see Travis. It would be so nice if she could make him appear. She closed her eyes tightly and took a deep breath. She then tried to make him appear by thinking only about him. When she opened up her eyes, he was still nowhere to be seen.

This part of her lucid dream was about the seventeenth century. Was it impossible to have Travis appear in 1621? She promised herself that she wouldn't try to control his actions in any way. She only wanted to see him. She looked all around the commons area, but Travis still could not be found.

After another few minutes of watching for Travis, Rose walked over to a different section of the Pilgrim village. She saw a Pilgrim who was seated at a table and writing down something on a piece of paper. She read what was on the paper: "We have found the Indians very faithful in their covenant of peace with us, very loving and ready to pleasure us. We often go to them, and they come to us."[94] The Pilgrim man put his initials on the paper as "E.W." Rose assumed that the gentleman was Edward Winslow.

After watching what was happening during this festival of thanks, Rose knew that Edward Winslow's notes were accurate. The Pilgrims and Native people were getting along very well with each other. She wished that she and Travis were able to get along as well. She knew they were still in love with each other, but just yesterday, they had been fighting so much that police officers had been called. Perhaps she and Travis needed a "peace treaty" to help them resolve their differences. She tried to make a peace treaty appear, but nothing happened.

Rose looked back at Edward Winslow. He was still writing on his piece of paper. Another Pilgrim gentleman who looked like he was at least fifty years old walked up to Winslow and asked, "How dost thou?"

Winslow put his pen down, stood up, and said, "Good. And thou?"

"I am very blessed to be here."

"Ay, thou didst hide on the *Mayflower* and didst leave England safely with us." Rose realized that Edward Winslow was talking to William Brewster, who had been a professor and publisher in Leiden. He now was the Pilgrim's lay pastor.

William Brewster said, "I am so joyful that I was safely hidden and not arrested."

"Ay, we are all glad that thou art with us in New England. On the *Mayflower*, where didst thou hide?"

William Brewster smiled. "Thou didst not never see me? I was on the 'tween deck with thee."

"I saw thee after thou camedst out of thy place of hiding." Edward Winslow looked thoughtful as he tried to remember where he had first seen Brewster when the *Mayflower* had set sail. "Before then, I think thou wast hiding beneath a blanket."

"I was staying warm beneath a blanket that was made of wool, which did hide me. Every day, morning and evening, I have thanked our Lord for helping us to find this New World."

"He hath blessed us all. '[O]n our behalf give God thanks who hath dealt so favorably with us.'⁹⁵"

"I will pray right now." William Brewster said a prayer and then walked toward the commons area. Edward Winslow sat down and began to write some more notes.

The Feather-hat Lady and her husband walked up to Winslow's table. The husband asked, "How now?"

Edward Winslow greeted the couple by waving his pen happily in their direction.

"What art thou writing?"

"'Tis a letter to be sent with *Mourt's Relation*."

"What's *Mourt's Relation*?"

"'Tis a journal about our Plantation at New Plymouth."

Winslow read aloud one of the sentences that he had just written down: "Our harvest being gotten in, our governor sent four men on fowling, that so we might after a special manner rejoice together after we had gathered the fruit of our labors."⁹⁶

"Thou art writing about our joyful first harvest."

"Ay."

"'Tis been three whole days of making friends with the Native people."

"And 'tis been three days of giving thanks to our Lord."

"Wilt thou have William Brewster publish thy notes?"

"Maybe in the future—after he hath brought a printing press into New England."

"Wilt thou save thy notes for such a long time?"

"Nay. Soon, I will send my notes in a letter to a friend, telling him about the 'worth' of our 'plantation.'"[97]

"Plymouth is a great plantation."

"Ay, I am writing much about our colony."

"That's a goodly idea. What else art thou saying in thy paper?"

"I also am writing 'certain useful directions' for future Pilgrims which 'intend a voyage' to our colony."[98]

"Some of my Leiden friends are praying about another voyage; they wish to come over on the next ship."

"I know many of our people who are now in Leiden but desire to be here with us."

Rose said, "Yes, the Reverend John Robinson wanted to be here. But at least his son Isaac will come over on a later ship. It will be in 1631, and I'm sure—even then—Isaac will be happy to follow through with his father's dream."

None of the Pilgrims seemed to have heard Rose talking, but one of them said, "Sometimes, 'tis very difficult to be separated from our loved ones by the ocean."

Rose nodded her head in agreement as she thought about being separated from Travis. They were not separated by an ocean, but they were not together like happily married people should be. She closed her eyes and prayed that they would be together again, even if they sometimes still would have fights.

When Rose opened her eyes, she found herself in the forest. A line of men led by Myles Standish and a group of Native people were showing off their military weapons and skills. Several arrows flew through the air and landed on one of the trees. A thudding noise was heard every time an arrow hit the trunk of the tree. The tree waved its upper branches slightly, acting as if it wanted the arrows to stop. Then gunshots were heard. Rose watched as some Pilgrims fired at the same tree. With each bullet that hit the tree, a piece of bark broke off, flew away into the air, and eventually landed deep within the forest. When a second series of gunshots was heard, the tree's branches moved more quickly. Then one of the branches broke away. It twirled around, acting like it was trying to find a landing place on the ground. Some roots from its own tree were visible, but the branch did not seem interested in them. It finally dove to the ground, making a thudding noise as it landed on top of an arrow that was sticking out of the dirt. The broken branch bounced up and down on top of the arrow, hammering at it and forcing it to go more deeply into the ground. The back end of the arrow, which had a claw attached to it, bounced back up and hit the branch; the arrow's claw formed scratches in the bark of the branch.

One of the Pilgrims standing near the tree said, "That broken branch and the arrow look like they are at war with each other."

Another voice said, "Ay. They have their differences."

"They need a peace treaty—one like we have with the Indians."

Laughter was heard. Rose said, "You're so happy to be at peace." She waited a few seconds to see if anyone would respond before continuing, "Your peace treaty with Massasoit will last for seventy years."

One of the Pilgrims said, "That broken branch and arrow are still moving."

Rose asked, "Do you think the fighting branch and arrow are symbols of past or future wars?"

No one replied to Rose's question, so she answered it by herself, "They could be some kind of dream symbols about war in any timeline, whether the war is happening in the past, present, or future. The 'war' might also be fighting between two people, like the fights between me and Travis."

Two men, who were standing close to Rose, began talking to each other. One of them said: "'Tis better to practice with our weapons, instead of to fight with them."

"Ay, I am so thankful that we are at peace with the Indians."

"There is now great peace amongst the Indians themselves."[99]

"They are so happy to no longer be fighting with one other."

"Over the past three days of our feasting with Massasoit's ninety Indians, they have been so joyful."

"Everyone is very happy."

"And 'we, for our parts, walk as peaceably and safely in the wood as in the highways in England. We entertain them familiarly in our houses; and they, as friendly, bestowing their venison on us.'[100]"

As Rose thought about a war in Europe and compared it to the peace in Plymouth, she gave thanks for her new-found desire for peace within her own life. She prayed that her Lord and Savior Jesus Christ would help her to scream less at Travis and to be a better person. She thanked the Lord for helping her to acquire knowledge about her family, her ancestors, and her marital problems. She then quoted one of her favorite bible verses: "[G]ive thanks in all circumstances; for this is the will of God in Christ Jesus for you" (1 Thess. 5:18 RSV).

As Rose finished praying, her Thanksgiving dream slowly reached the end of its third day of festivities. The Pilgrims and Native people waved good-bye to each other as they parted to go home. Rose felt as if they were also waving good-bye to her and wishing her well in her own future endeavors.

LOST AND FOUND

On Saturday morning, Rose woke up even before any of her alarm clocks went off. She sat on the edge of her bed for a few minutes, thinking about the dream that she had just had. In order to remember as much as possible, she began to write down what had happened. As she was writing about the last part of her dream, her mind made connections to earlier sections of the dream. Her mind eventually moved backwards in time to the beginning of her dream when she was celebrating Thanksgiving with her family.

Rose realized that her dream story had ended with the happiness of the Pilgrims and Native people at their 1621 Thanksgiving festival. She was glad that she would be able to see more of the story—about the Pilgrims in 1627—by going to Plimoth Plantation today. She then said a short prayer out loud, "I thank you, my Lord, for your presence in the life of my ancestors and for showing me so many parts of this life. I also thank you for your continuing love and guidance."

Rose turned on the weather channel on the TV. The temperature for the day was again going to be over ninety degrees. She tried on a pair of blue shorts and a matching V-neck tee shirt. After looking at herself in the mirror for a minute, Rose went back to her suitcase and changed into a summer dress. Then she put on a pair of sandals, her watch, and her make-up. Finally, she packed up her suitcases. By seven forty-five, she was all ready to go and walked over to the hotel's dining room. As she sat down to wait for Travis, she looked at the clock on the wall and then at her watch. They both said the same time: nine minutes before eight o'clock. She was nine minutes early, so she pulled out an article from her purse and began to read it.

Five minutes before eight o'clock, Travis came into the dining room. When he walked over to Rose's table, she looked up at him. They were both silent for a moment, just watching each other's faces. Travis's eyes were bright, and his smile made Rose smile as she stood up to hug him.

Travis was the first one to speak: "You're even more beautiful today than you were yesterday."

"Thanks. You look really great, too. In fact, you look too nice to be running around a forest digging holes and trying to find buried treasure." He was wearing sneakers, a pair of green shorts, a tie, and a white short-sleeved shirt with buttons.

After they got coffee, bagels, and yogurt, Rose told Travis about her lucid dream from the previous evening.

"It must have been so nice to have a happy ending to your dream story."

"Yeah, it was."

"You aren't going to try to dream about what happened to the Pilgrims after Thanksgiving?"

"A lot of wonderful things happened after that famous harvest festival, but I think these events can be parts of other stories. Before the Pilgrims settled down and celebrated that first Thanksgiving, they were in other countries. When they left their old world behind, they wanted the freedom of a new world. They eventually achieved their dream, and their beliefs became a big part of the American dream."

"Your dream story included connecting to the American dream."

"Yeah, it did."

"That's so great. Lucid dreams are something that I keep trying to do, but I usually can't."

"Well, practice helps. I wasn't too good at lucid dreaming until I started trying to dream about the Pilgrims."

"Maybe I should try a dream story, too. If it's about something that's really important to me, the lucid dreaming techniques you've told me about might work better."

"I thought you were able to go to sleep focusing on one thing and then were able to dream about that one thing."

"Yeah, but I just can't control anything within the actual dream."

"Well, did you have any dreams last night, Travis?"

"I did."

"Is it something you can tell me about?"

Travis looked at Rose and laughed. "Since we're still married, I think it's okay for me to tell you about one of my sex dreams."

Rose looked around the dining room. At one of the nearby tables was a family with two children. "I'd love to hear about your sexual fantasies, but this might not be a good spot."

"I was only kidding. I wouldn't really do something like that here."

"I know you wouldn't." They smiled at each other and finished their breakfast in silence.

As they stood up, Travis asked, "Are your suitcases all packed up?"

"Yeah, they are."

"Is it okay if I put your suitcases in the car, so we can check out of the hotel right now?"

"We'll be driving back to Rhode Island tonight, right?"

"I think so, Rose, unless you want to stay longer."

"We should probably leave tonight; then we'll be able to visit our parents tomorrow."

"Okay. We live close enough so that we can come back here as often as we want to."

They went to their rooms to get their suitcases.

At the door to her hotel room, Rose looked at Travis, who was standing next to her, instead of walking away to his room. She asked, "Do you need to get your suitcases, too?"

"No, I already put them in my car."

Rose hesitated and then asked, "Would you like to come in with me?"

"I'd love to."

Rose opened the door and then stood back so that Travis could come inside. He remained outside in the hallway as he lifted his hand and brushed the left side of Rose's head, moving her hair slightly backwards. He looked into the room and still did not move to enter. "The only problem is, if I come inside, I won't want to leave."

Rose's breathing quickened, and her eyes fluttered. She walked silently into the room. Travis looked at her expectant face and took a step into the room. He lightly brushed her hair again. Before either one of them had a chance to think about it, their lips moved close together. Their breathing became synchronized even before their lips met. From the alarm clock, which Rose had apparently not turned off, Billy Ocean's "Caribbean Queen (No More Love on the Run)" was playing. "Now we're sharing the same dream / and our hearts they beat as one."[101] Neither Rose nor Travis seemed to notice the music. As their lips parted, their breathing began to follow the same rhythm as the song's.

After finishing the lengthy kiss, they looked into each other's eyes. Travis said softly, "I know you really want to see the Pilgrims get married today." His lips came close to Rose's, and they kissed again. Their lips embraced each other, looking like they didn't ever want to separate.

Rose stepped backwards and sighed, glancing down at the floor to avoid looking into Travis's eyes. "I really want to see the wedding, too. It's the only one they're going to have all year." She looked up, hesitated, and said, "If we plan on staying here for a little while, we'll probably be here all day long."

Travis looked sad. It was obvious that he wanted to stay longer in Rose's hotel room. He reached out and touched her hand. "Of course. Whatever you want is okay with me."

"We'll be able to talk to each other as we walk around the different tourist attractions."

"Can we kiss some more, too?" Travis asked in a light-hearted tone.

Rose laughed. "Of course we can. We just shouldn't kiss like we were a minute ago in front of any kids."

"Okay." Travis paused for a moment and then added, "Even though kids are always at the tourist attractions, we'll be running around the forest—all by ourselves—for a while this morning."

Rose walked over to the alarm clock and turned off the radio. Travis picked up her suitcases, and she closed and locked the door. He carried her suitcases out to his Mustang, placed them in the trunk, and then held open the passenger side door of his car; Rose sat down. After he had gotten into the driver's seat and started the engine, Travis asked, "Do you think we'll find the watch today?"

"I hope so."

"If you want to, as soon as we get to Plimoth Plantation, we can go straight into the forest to look for the watch." Travis had pulled out onto the main road. "Does the wedding start at two o'clock?"

"Yeah, it does."

"If we find the watch quickly enough, we may have a little extra time to do some more sightseeing."

"Then we can eat lunch at the Plantation and see the wedding."

"I brought a picnic lunch for us, just in case we want to eat while we're looking for the watch in the forest."

"So, you really do want to be alone with me in the forest."

Travis grinned broadly as he drove around a turn in the road. "Some quiet time with you would be really nice."

Rose laughed. "Would you prefer me or the treasure?"

"You know that you're more important to me than any treasure."

"Thanks, Travis." Rose looked out the window for a moment and then turned back to him. "I've been really lost without you."

"Me, too."

"So, we're going to talk some more with our minister about our fights?"

"Definitely. We just need to learn how to communicate better with each other."

Rose shook her head in agreement. "We're already communicating better. This trip was a great idea of yours."

"Thanks." Travis looked briefly over at Rose's happy face and then turned back to watch the road. "You're correct, though. We still should speak to our minister and get some suggestions."

When they arrived at the Plimoth Plantation Parking Lot, Rose looked at the car's clock and then at her watch. "This is perfect timing. In less than a minute, they'll be open." Travis picked up the bag with their picnic lunch in it. As they walked through the archway and started down the stairs, Travis held out his left hand to Rose; she smiled as she put her right hand into his. She could feel his strength as he held onto her hand. He was wearing his wedding ring again. The touch of his ring made his hand feel even stronger.

Travis bought their tickets, and they walked through the Visitor Center and over to the Wampanoag Homesite. Within half an hour, they were on the unmarked trail. They walked up to the area where the fence had been repaired.

"It looks like the fence is all fixed, except for needing the flowers."

Rose followed Travis up the trail for another thirty feet. They stopped, climbed over the wooden railing, and went into the forest. They soon came to a large bush with a bird's nest in it.

Travis stopped walking and said, "I don't remember this bush being here yesterday."

"Should we go back to the path? Maybe we climbed over the fence at the wrong spot."

"I think we came over the fence in the right place. Let's try walking this way for another minute. I might not have noticed that bush yesterday."

Rose followed Travis past the bush and through a small grove of pine trees. There was a clearing with a path running through it. Travis said, "We're definitely in the wrong section of the forest."

"Is this clearing the wrong one?"

"Yeah, it's too large. Also, I don't remember this path." Travis walked up to a path veering off to their left. "There's a hole next to the path here."

Rose walked up to the hole. "It's not very big, but it could be a memory hole."

"I wonder...."

"What?"

"If I step into the memory hole, will I remember where the shovel is?"

Rose laughed. "I don't know. How about if we go back to the fence?"

"Okay."

Travis and Rose went back to the fence, climbed over it, and began to slowly walk up the trail. After every few steps, they stopped walking and looked over the fence into the forest. At each stop, Travis said, "No, it's not here."

When they reached the place where the fence was being repaired, they stopped walking. Travis said, "I think we've gone too far."

"You're right." Rose pointed at the box of flowers. "While we're here, the plants look like they need some water."

Travis jumped over the fence and watered the flowers by using one of their bottled waters. When he came back to Rose, he said, "If we can't find that shovel, it'll stay lost. And we won't be able to return it."

"That means we'll really be thieves."

"We need to keep looking for that shovel."

"I think we should pray first."

"That's a good idea. With the Lord's help, it'll be much easier to find that shovel."

"The New Testament has some parables about being lost and found."

"In chapter 15 of Luke, there are three parables told by our Lord and Savior Jesus Christ about being lost and found."

"One of them is about the Prodigal Son."

"The two others are about a lost coin and a lost sheep."

"The meanings of all three stories have to do with the joy of being found and returned to our Lord."

"I remember one of the verses from the parable about the lost son: '["F]or this son of mine was dead and is alive again; he was lost and is found!" And they began to celebrate' (Luke 15:24 RSV)."

"I love that story about the lost son who comes back home again and is found."

"Yeah, so do I. The son apologized for his sins and was forgiven."

Rose and Travis bowed their heads. Travis began their prayer with adoration: "Dear Lord, we love everything about you."

Rose continued their prayer: "And we confess that we have sinned."

"Please forgive us for stealing a shovel and then hiding it."

"We ask for your forgiveness for all of our sins."

"We also thank you for the many blessings you have given us."

"If it's in your will that we find that shovel, we ask for your help in finding it."

"We also pray for your continued love and help."

Together, Rose and Travis said, "In Jesus' name we pray, Amen."

They turned around and started walking back down the pathway. Before they had gone too far, Rose said, "This might be the spot."

"How do you know?" Travis looked around and then added, "It doesn't look familiar to me."

"See?" Rose pointed slightly to their left. "Right over there is a line of crushed plants on the ground. You probably did that yesterday by dragging the shovel through them."

Travis climbed over the fence and then helped Rose. They followed the line of crushed plants. Rose said, "Hopefully, these plants will grow back okay."

"None of them look too bad. I'm sure they'll be okay."

Suddenly, Rose stopped walking and asked, "What if the employees yesterday noticed the same line that we're following? Would they have found the shovel?"

Travis stopped walking, frowned, and then started walking forward again. "They probably wouldn't have noticed this line through the undergrowth. And even if they did, the line will probably stop at the clearing. That's where I put the shovel on my right shoulder."

When Rose and Travis reached the clearing, the line in the undergrowth was no longer visible. They went up to the oak tree and then over to the bush. With a smile, Travis picked up the shovel from under the bush.

Rose said, "I wonder if they noticed this missing shovel yesterday."

"If they noticed, they probably guessed we were the thieves."

"So, Travis, once we're done, how will we get the shovel back to them?"

"We'll just leave it next to the fence. If it's in the spot where they'll be planting flowers, they'll be sure to see it."

"Should we leave them a note or anything?"

"I don't know. What do you think, Rose?"

"I think we should. We can even apologize and ask for their forgiveness. It will make them happier to know there are still some honest people in our world today."

Travis put the shovel over his shoulder and then said, "Okay. Right now, let's try to find the treasure—if there is a treasure."

Rose took the sampler out of her purse. "So, we should probably go back to the trail first."

"Then we can just follow the shoreline until we get to the right spot."

Rose followed Travis back to the trail. After they had climbed over the fence, they started walking up the path. Within a few minutes, they were at the point where the sampler's arrow seemed to be pointing. Rose pulled out her picture of her grandmother's watch case. She and Travis looked at the circle of rocks and compared them to the shovel on the sampler.

"Should we look in the forest and try to find something that looks like these items?" Travis asked.

"Okay." Rose and Travis walked to the fence. They climbed over, went into the forest, and walked past some trees, vines, bushes, and wild flowers. In front of a juniper tree, Rose said, "This is the kind of wood that the Pilgrims first brought back to the *Mayflower*."

"Did they use it for cooking?"

"They used it for freshening up the smell of the *Mayflower*, as well as for cooking and heat."

Travis and Rose stopped walking, turned around in circles, and gazed at different parts of their surroundings. Rose said, "I don't see anything that looks like a circle of rocks."

"Neither do I."

"Maybe the rocks are small." Rose's eyes fell to the ground as she searched for circles of pebbles.

"If the rock circle is really small, Rose, we'll never be able to find it anyway."

"You're right. Perhaps we're too far away from the shoreline."

"Possibly."

"So, Travis, do you think we should look on both sides of our current position?"

"Yeah. It also would be a lot faster if we separated."

Rose's face looked surprised as she turned to Travis and asked, "So, do you really want to be separated from me?"

Travis lay his hand gently on Rose's shoulder. "There's no way that I want to be separate from you. I wasn't thinking when I said that."

Rose hesitated and then said, "Well, you were right—it would be faster if we separated."

"Being fast isn't always the best thing."

Rose laughed, "You're saying the opposite thing, but you're completely right again."

Rose pulled out the picture of the watch case from her purse. "The shovel seems to be slightly to the right. Let's try going to the right for a little bit and then heading back toward the shore."

"That sounds like a plan."

They walked under several trees and through some vines. Travis suddenly stopped and pointed toward his right. "That might be a path over there."

They walked over to the path and then followed it as it curved several times. "Is this path going in a circle?" Rose asked.

"I think so."

"There's a good-sized rock over near that tree."

They went over to the rock, looked around, and found three other large rocks. Travis walked forward about five feet. "If all of the rocks were here, this spot would be where the center of the circle was."

Rose joined Travis. "Okay. So what do we do now?"

Travis put the shovel that he was carrying on the ground. "Where do you think we should try and dig first?"

Rose looked around at the ground near their feet. "I have no idea. What do you think?"

"Logically, if something had been buried somewhere, the dirt would have been looser for a while."

"Should we look for an area where the plants are growing worse or better?"

"When someone digs a hole and then replaces the dirt, it will be a better place for plants to grow. There will be fewer problems, like roots from other plants." Travis walked over to a small area that seemed to have slightly greener and thicker vines. He started digging. After about ten minutes, he still had not found anything.

Rose said, "You've probably dug deep enough. I don't think anything's there."

Travis sighed, scooped dirt back into the hole, put the shovel down next to his feet, and replanted several of the plants. "Where else should we try?"

"Well, maybe something that's buried in the ground would give the plants less room for their roots, so there would be fewer plants."

"Okay." Travis looked around and then started to dig in an area that appeared to be mostly grass. Almost immediately, his shovel hit something. He dug more carefully around the object, which turned out to be a rock. As he started to scoop the dirt back over the rock, Rose said, "That rock seems to be a part of a circle with the other four rocks. And there were eight rocks on the watch's case. Maybe the treasure is under one of the rocks."

Travis began to dig up the dirt again from around the edges of the rock. After enough of the dirt was removed, he and Rose both pulled upwards on the rock. It moved slightly and then gradually slid toward them as they pulled it out of the hole. The empty hole only contained dirt. Travis dug into the dirt some more until the hole was another foot deep. There still was no treasure. After resting for a minute, he put the dirt, grass, and rock back so that the hole was covered up.

Travis asked, "Should we try another rock, or do you want to try to find a different circle of rocks?"

"There probably aren't too many circles of rocks in this forest. Perhaps we should try to dig around another rock."

"Okay. Which one should we try?"

"I don't know." Rose looked at the sampler. "Perhaps the shovel on the sampler is actually a bell, and the musical note on the sampler is telling us where to ring the bell."

"That sounds like something we could try."

Rose showed Travis the sampler. "So where do you think the musical-note spot is?"

Travis walked over to one of the rocks. "This one has a musical note carved into it."

"Really?" Rose went over to stand next to Travis and the rock. They both moved the rock, and then Travis began to dig. After only a few shovelfuls of dirt were removed, a scraping noise was heard. Travis carefully moved dirt from the top of the object in the ground. Finally, he lost his patience. He dropped the shovel, knelt down on the ground, and felt the object with his hands. "It feels like metal."

Rose knelt down and touched the object. Then she and Travis both used their hands to scrape dirt away from it. The top part of a black metal box became visible. It didn't have any designs on the outside part of its top section.

Travis asked, "Should we try to open the top of the box now, or do you want to wait until we take the whole box out of the hole?"

Rose laughed. "Let's try to see what's inside now."

Travis motioned with his hand that Rose should open it. She tried pulling off the top part of the box, but it wouldn't come off. Travis then tried to open up the top part of the box, but it still wouldn't come off. He sighed and began to dig around its sides. Finally, he and Rose pulled the box out of the hole and set it on the ground between them.

"Rose, this must be from your great, great grandfather. You should be the one to open it."

"Okay, you talked me into it." Rose picked up the box and tried to pull off the top lid. "It doesn't want to come off."

Travis took out his key chain and opened up his tiny pair of scissors. "These might help."

Rose watched as Travis wedged one blade of the scissors between the lid and one side of the box. He pushed, and the top lid moved upwards and off of the bottom metal section. He handed Rose the box.

Inside was another smaller metal box that was wrapped in a rubber cloth. Rose opened the second box. She pulled out a gold watch and then caught a key that fell off of the top of the watch. "So, he really did have a railroad chronometer."

"Is that what that watch is?"

"Yeah."

"Is it worth anything?"

"Probably, but I think I should give it to my grandmother."

"The one who owns the watch case?"

"Yeah."

"Is there anything else in there?"

Rose pulled out a folded-up piece of cardboard. When she unfolded the cardboard, three bills fell into her lap.

Travis asked, "Those can't actually be $10,000. bills, can they?"

Rose slowly looked at the front and back of each bill before placing one in front of Travis's face. "It's a real $10,000. bill. It's not counterfeit."

"$30,000. is a nice inheritance."

"Actually, the bills are worth quite a bit more than their face value."

"Really, Rose?"

"Yeah. $10,000. bills haven't been printed since 1946."

"So how much are they worth?" "If we sell them online, we can probably get at least $60,000. for each bill."

Travis laughed. "With that much money, we won't be fighting over money anymore. At least not for a day or two."

Rose laughed as she stared at the back of one of the bills. She then handed it to Travis and said, "All three of these bills are the 1918 series. If you look at the back of the bill, you'll see the Reverend John Robinson in the picture of the Pilgrims."

"Who's this on the front of the bill?"

"It's Salmon P. Chase."

"Who's that?"

"He was the Secretary of the Treasury under President Lincoln. He later became the Chief Justice on the Supreme Court."

Rose looked at the picture of Salmon Chase and then flipped a bill over again to look at the picture with the Reverend John Robinson in it.

Travis gave a $10,000. bill back to Rose; he then asked, "What do you think we should do with these bills? Are all three of them legally ours?"

"Maybe or maybe not. I'll have to talk to my parents, but I don't know if it's okay for us to take even one of these bills. My great, great grandfather had other descendants who are still alive."

"We are the ones who found the bills, so we should be able to have at least one of them," Travis said with a thoughtful look on his face.

"Granny and my parents owned the watch case and the sampler that got us here. My parents also paid for my train fare to see Granny."

"That means your parents and grandmother need some of the money."

"I'd feel funny, Travis, if we only gave some money to my relatives. Your family also needs some of it."

Travis shook his head in agreement and then said, "Thanks so much for thinking of my family, too."

"You're welcome, Travis."

"What about giving money to Plimoth Plantation? They supplied us with the shovel."

Rose smiled. "It's wonderful how everyone has been helping us so much."

"You're so right about that."

"What do you think the Pilgrims would have done if they had found money like this?"

Travis was silent for a moment. "Obviously, they would do what they thought would be correct according to God."

"We need to donate ten percent to our church."

"Of course. We'll always be tithing everything."

Rose looked at Travis; they read each other's eyes and sighed at the same time together. Rose then said, "So, we're sure that we'll be sharing the money. It's just a question of how much and with whom."

Travis shook his head in agreement and then asked, "Is there anything else in the box?"

Rose laughed. "I didn't even look." She picked up the box and looked at the bottom. "It's empty."

"Are you sure? It seems strange that your great, great grandfather would just leave a watch, a key, and some bills in the box."

"You're right. It would make sense for him to have left a note or a letter."

"Rose, how about if we look at the boxes and the wrappings again?"

"Okay." Rose handed the larger box to Travis. He looked at and pulled at the different sections of the box, trying to see if anything was stuck. Rose looked at the smaller box. Neither one of them found anything, so they switched boxes. They still found nothing, so they tried looking at the rubber and cardboard wrappings. Again, they found nothing.

Rose said, "I don't think there is anything else."

Travis picked up the shovel and started to replace the dirt that he had removed from the hole.

Rose suddenly said, "Wait a minute! Let's look in the hole some more to see if there are any other boxes."

"That's a good idea." Travis started to dig more dirt out of the hole. After just a few shovelfuls, he found another box. It contained three more $10,000. bills. However, there still was no note or letter.

Rose voiced both of their thoughts when she said, "I wonder if there's a third box."

Travis started shoveling again and quickly found a third box. This box also contained three $10,000. bills, as well as a piece of paper.

Rose silently read the paper and then said to Travis: "The paper explains that the $10,000 bills were earned legally through the stock market. There's even information about the stocks here."

"Is there anything else on the paper?"

"Yeah. It says that people should share their abilities, money, and other treasures with those in need." Rose smiled before adding, "There is also a verse of scripture: 'To do good, and to distribute forget not: for with such sacrifices God is pleased'" (Heb. 13:16 GNV).

"So the note is telling us to share the money, right?"

"Yeah, it is. The note also says how we should share it: ten percent should be given to churches/charities, thirty percent should be kept by us, thirty percent should go to Robinson descendants, and thirty percent should go to our closest relatives and friends."

Travis said, "I guess that partially answers our question about what to do with the money."

"Only partially?"

"We'll have to pay taxes. And we'll also have to pay for a lawyer and maybe an accountant."

Rose laughed. "We'll definitely be sharing this money with many other people."

Travis and Rose looked at each other. When Travis kissed her, Rose's pulse sped up. On her left wrist, her watchband seemed to move with each pulsing motion. Finally, the watch itself seemed warmer and aligned with her pulse. The second hand was moving more quickly. Rose wondered if her ancestors were now a part of her watch's reality, as well as a part of her dreams. If genes of her ancestors were still alive within her body, then they might be connected to her watch through the band around her wrist.

When Travis and Rose had finished their kiss, they put the dirt back into the hole. The note and $10,000. bills were placed in Rose's purse. Since the boxes were all different sizes, they fit into each other. While there was now only one box to carry, it was fairly heavy. Travis carried both the box and the shovel, while Rose carried her purse and their lunch; they walked out to the pathway. They put the shovel and a note in the spot where the employees would be planting the perennials. They then walked up the pathway toward one of the gates in the fence that surrounded the English Village.

Before they walked through the gate, Rose asked, "Travis, do you really want to carry that nest of boxes around?"

Travis shifted the box he was holding. "If we put the box down somewhere, someone might think it's trash and throw it out."

"Perhaps we could hide it somewhere close by and then get it as we're leaving."

They hid the box under a bush at the edge of the forest and then went back to the gate at the entrance to the village.

A PILGRIM WEDDING

Rose and Travis walked through the South Gate of the seventeenth century English Village about ten minutes before noon. They went over to where the dance lesson was supposed to take place. No one was there yet, so they walked over to the center part of the village and looked at some of the people who were dressed like Pilgrims. Even though it was over ninety degrees outside, the Pilgrim actors were all wearing hats, long-sleeved shirts, and multiple layers of clothing. Only the skin on their hands and faces was visible. The women had long skirts, aprons, and sometimes scissors or other items hanging down on strings from their belts. The men also had items hanging down from their belts, such as knives and leather pouches.

Travis and Rose stepped into the doorway of one of the houses and then watched as a Pilgrim lady started a fire in a fireplace inside of the house. As the home became warmer and the Pilgrim started to sweat, Travis said to Rose, "These Pilgrim actors are working really hard to try and act like seventeenth century Plymouth Pilgrims."

Rose said, "I know. I've been reading about the Puritan work ethic. It connects many of their activities to their God."

"I've heard of the Puritan work ethic before, but I've never really known exactly what it is."

The Pilgrim lady, who was standing next to the fire, turned around and looked at Travis. "A visitor left some papers for me about doing tasks appointed to us by our God." The Pilgrim Fire Lady walked away from the fire to the opposite end of the room. She opened up a chest, took some papers out, and handed them to Travis. "Thou mayest keep these." The lady then walked back to the fire and continued to stir the pot.

"Thanks." Travis started to read one of the pieces of paper. He then said to Rose, "This is an article with the title 'The Original Puritan Work Ethic.'"

"What does it say?"

Travis read a sentence from the article: "[T]he Puritan view that God calls all workers to their tasks in the world dignifies all legitimate kinds of work."[102]

"So, the article talks about how the Puritans viewed God's connection to workers and their tasks."

"I think the article defines the Puritan work ethic as someone serving God by working hard in any kind of legal work."

Rose read one of the pages that Travis was holding. She then said, "This article quotes Thomas Gouge as saying Christians should 'so spiritualize our hearts and affections that we may have heavenly hearts in earthly employments.'"[103]

"So we should be happy and stop complaining so much."

The Pilgrim lady looked at Travis and smiled. "I am most happy to be cooking food for my family. 'Tis a godly pursuit."

Travis looked at the Pilgrim. "You're doing a great job. The physical labor is tough enough; the mental labor of being a Pilgrim must be tough, too."

The lady continued to stir the pot as she asked, "What do you mean by 'mental labor'?"

"Something that takes a lot of mental ability. Pilgrim actors like yourself need to know the history and language of real Pilgrims." Travis watched as the lady took the spoon out of the pot and tasted the soup that she was making.

"'Tis easy for me to learn about history and to speak English. However, at times, the words of a visitor are very difficult to understand."

Rose said to the lady, "You are really wonderful! You look, talk, and act just like some of the Pilgrims in my dreams."

"Thou art dreaming about Pilgrims?"

"Yes, I am."

"Thy dreams must be merry."

"Yeah, my dreams about Pilgrims have made me very happy. I have learned a lot about my ancestors."

"Thou doth have Pilgrim ancestors?"

"Yeah, I do. My dreams about them have been so very exciting. I even imagined myself as a part of your voyage on the *Mayflower*."

"That voyage brought us to this goodly place."

"So you like Plymouth?"

"Ay. We used to work for other people."

"In New England, haven't you paid off some of your debt to the Merchant Adventurers?"

"Ay, now there are times when we work for ourselves. And we are not persecuted for being Godly. We are of good cheer." The lady stirred the soup some more.

Music from a flute began to sound from an open field in the English Village. Rose and Travis thanked the Pilgrim lady and walked over to where the music was playing. There were four Pilgrim ladies. One of them was playing a flute. Another of the ladies was showing a group of visitors how to move their feet.

Rose and Travis joined the group of people. As they learned the steps together, they talked to other people in the group. A man in blue shorts, who was standing next to Travis, said, "I've never danced before today."

Travis said, "You're doing a great job."

Rose nodded her head in agreement and then said, "I never would have guessed that this is your first day of dancing."

The Pilgrim ladies showed them a new step, and they all concentrated on repeating the motions.

A few minutes later, Rose found out that a married couple in the circle was from Holland. The Dutch people talked about some of the Leiden tourist attractions, including the Leiden American Pilgrim Museum. The Dutch wife said, "It is so wonderful to visit this Plimoth Plantation living museum. I never knew what a living museum was before today."

The Dutch couple moved toward the other end of the field. Rose said to Travis, "Don't you just love to hear their Dutch accent?"

"It's so neat, especially in combination with the British accents of the Pilgrim role-players."

The Pilgrim dancing ladies had everyone join hands in a big circle. Rose and Travis followed the directions they were given and quickly learned how to do a few more steps. Rose said to Travis, "This is easier because we can already do some ballroom dance steps."

"Yeah, it is. But look at that guy in the blue shorts—the one who was next to me a while ago." Travis pointed to the man who was now across from them in the other half of the circle. "He's never danced before, but he's doing all of the steps correctly."

"He's even dancing in time to the music."

"That's something you've always been good at, Rose."

"Thanks. You're good at setting up a rhythm, so it's easy for me to follow along with you."

They paused in their dancing for a few seconds to look at each other's faces, but they were still holding hands with other people in a big circle. The dancers on either side of them let go of their hands and pushed them forward into the center of the circle.

As Rose moved forward, she said, "I've so much missed dancing with you, Travis."

"I've missed doing everything with you, Rose."

"Me, too, Travis."

Rose and Travis were alone in the center of the circle, holding hands with each other, as the circle of other people turned around them.

Travis and Rose lifted up their now-free hands in front of each other. As if they were reading each other's minds and inner clocks, at the same time, they each grabbed onto the other's hands and began to turn around in a small circle. They were moving much faster than the bigger circle that was still circling around them.

When the song was over, Travis kissed Rose's right hand, let it go, and still held onto her left hand. They said "good-bye" to the people in the circle before slowly walking into the forest. Travis placed a blanket on the ground; he then took some sodas, turkey sandwiches, and chips out of the picnic bag.

"This was such a great idea, Travis."

"Thanks." He passed some of the food items over to Rose. They began to drink some of their soda.

"I've loved that picnic bag for years. It does such a great job of keeping things cold when it's hot outside."

"You're so right. It's one of the things you've bought that I completely love."

Rose sighed. "So you sometimes like me to spend money."

"Of course I do. You're the best shopper I know."

"If you think I'm such a great shopper, why do you get mad sometimes at what I buy?"

"Well, I guess we sometimes just disagree about how to spend our money."

"You're right." Rose paused before adding, "Occasionally, I do buy what I want, rather than what you want."

"On the plus side, sometimes, we completely agree with each other."

Rose smiled. "I often don't think enough about when we agree with each other. I think too much about our fights."

"I think about the fights, too. We should just talk to each other more often, like we've been doing out here in Plymouth."

"Yeah, we've been getting along so well on this trip. It's like a second honeymoon."

"It is." Travis opened up the picnic bag and brought out a box of candy. "Does this look familiar to you?"

Rose's eyes opened in surprise. "That's the same kind of candy you brought in your suitcase on our first honeymoon."

"Yes, it is."

Rose sighed. "You know how much I love dark chocolate. I'm as happy now as I was on our first honeymoon."

"I'm so glad." After Travis and Rose kissed, he opened up the box of candy. They both reached for the same caramel pecan piece of chocolate. As soon as Travis realized that Rose was reaching for the same piece of chocolate that he was, he picked it up and put it close to her mouth. Rose bit off half of the chocolate and then moved the remaining half over to Travis's mouth.

Rose said, "I love having lunch in the same location where the Pilgrims used to eat."

"So do I. And I've had so much fun while learning about the Pilgrims with you, Rose."

"I've been having fun learning about the Pilgrims, too." Rose smiled at her husband. "It's interesting that they didn't even know the full importance of what they were doing for future generations."

"Do you really think so?"

"Yeah." Rose thought for a moment before adding, "Before my Thanksgiving dream last night, I read about the first Thanksgiving."

"What did you read?"

"I looked at a few sections of the book *A Great and Godly Adventure The Pilgrims and the Myth of the First Thanksgiving.* I've been thinking about something the author said."

"What did the author say?"

"I think I can remember some of his exact words." Rose looked up into the sky, rubbed her forehead, and slowly recited this quote from the book: "The Pilgrims lived in their own time, children of that time, quite unaware of the vast superstructure of patriotism and ideology that would be balanced on their shoulders."[104]

"That's an interesting quote. Even though the Pilgrims didn't have any clocks or watches, they were still children of their time."

"It's possible that one or two of the Pilgrims in 1620 had a watch or a clock, but they didn't really need to know the time as precisely as future generations did." Rose laughed. "In some ways, I think our own generation is too concerned with time."

"We have to be. Otherwise, we wouldn't meet up with so many other people as well as we do."

"Yeah, we often have to travel miles to get to our jobs and our homes; time is needed to make a connection with people from distant locations."

Travis shook his head in agreement. "It's interesting that, at Plimoth Plantation, the cultures of different times and places can meet at the same time in the same place."

"Yeah, it is."

Travis took another piece of chocolate and gave it to Rose, who ate it and then finished drinking her soda. Travis collected the trash, put it into a pocket of the picnic bag, and stood up. When Rose stood up next to him, he said, "I love you more today than ever before."

"I love you more than you love me."

"No, I love you the most."

"I love you more than the most."

Travis bent forward and kissed Rose. Their breaths danced in each other's airways. At first, they were doing a slow waltz. Then their breathing became faster, sounding like a Hustle. Finally, the air was jumping around between them as if it were doing a Jive. After an eternity of enjoying this single kiss, Rose and Travis slowly walked back to the English Village.

Once inside the gate, they walked up the hill toward the meetinghouse. When they were almost there, Rose said, "I think we're going to the wrong place. The Puritans didn't get married in church."

"Really?"

"Yeah. They believed marriage was a civil ceremony."

"That means the wedding might not be taking place here in the meetinghouse."

Rose looked down the hill and then pointed to a group of people as she said, "It must be over there, where all those people are."

Rose and Travis walked down the hill and joined the people waiting for the bride and groom. Rose said, "We're early."

"Yeah." Travis smiled at her before continuing, "You're getting better at being on time."

Rose laughed. "I'm also getting better at arriving early."

"Do you know why you're suddenly better at being on time?"

"I think our second honeymoon has helped."

"Really?"

"Yeah, I've been a lot happier, so I'm moving around faster when I'm getting ready to go somewhere."

"That makes sense."

"I think learning about the Pilgrims' history has helped me, too."

"Learning about history is making you better at how you use time?"

"When I realized that even the Pilgrims were late, I felt better about myself."

"When were the Pilgrims late?"

"They wound up leaving Southampton, England in September, 1620, which was much later than they had initially planned. Because of the late crossing, they encountered many storms. Crossing the Atlantic took them a fairly long time: sixty-six days. When the *Mayflower* went back to England in April 1621, the same crossing only took thirty-one days."

"Because they were late in leaving England, they took too long to cross the Atlantic Ocean, which made their arrival in New England even later."

"The Pilgrims then had to explore the coastal area to find a place to anchor their ship, build their homes, try to find more food,..." Rose sighed. "On the days when I've been late, I've still been able to go into nice buildings and eat good food."

"Our lives are so easy when compared to the lives of the Pilgrims."

"Learning about history has helped me to think about my own use of time. I'm less anxious about how I look and act, so I've stopped doing things that will make me late."

"You're multi-tasking, which I also do. Sometimes, though, multi-tasking makes me late."

"You're just saying that to be nice, Travis. You're very rarely late."

"Thanks, Rose."

"You're right, though, about multi-tasking. I used to look at my knee, change my clothes, and sometimes start limping. Occasionally, I'd even start crying. I'd then have to redo my make up."

"Has your knee injury gotten better on our second honeymoon?"

"No, but the way I look at my knee has gotten better. I'm no longer scared or anxious about it." Rose looked down and pointed to her left knee. "See? I'm wearing shorts for the first time since the robbery."

Travis looked at her knee. "Oh, I never realized before that you were always trying to hide your scar."

"I'm not anymore." Rose raised her knee, looked at the scar, and ran a finger over it. "Your love and support on this trip, Travis, have helped me to get better."

"Thanks. I should have helped you more when you were first injured."

"You didn't know how to help me, and I didn't tell you about all of the problems I was having."

"What's important is that we're happy now."

"I love you, Travis."

"I'm even more in love with you, Rose."

Travis looked like he was about to kiss Rose, but the people around them started to move forward. One man brushed against Rose's purse as he walked past her.

Rose opened up her purse and looked inside to make certain the $10,000. bills were still there. They were. She and Travis then moved forward a few steps; a large number of people were already in front of them. Because they were standing on an incline, though, they could still see what was happening.

A group of role-playing Pilgrims started to re-enact the 1623 Pilgrim wedding of Robert Bartlett to Mary Warren. A role-playing Governor William Bradford was conducting the ceremony. There were at least six other role-playing Pilgrims present at the wedding.

On top of the bride's head was a ring of flowers. The bride had on a black long-sleeve jacket with white lace on its wide collar and cuffs. Also on her jacket were white buttons and some pink vertical embroidered lines. Her long gray skirt fell to just a couple of inches from the ground. Her shoes and socks were hidden beneath her skirt. Her long white apron had lace around its edges.

The groom was wearing a black felt hat with a wide brim. His suit was a matching reddish-brown jacket and breeches. The collar and cuffs of the white shirt under his jacket were visible. His shoes were brown, and his socks were gray.

All of the other Pilgrim actors were wearing hats, long skirts or breeches, and long-sleeve shirts or jackets. Most of them also had a small wedding bow with three loops in it; the bow was attached to the actors' right shoulders. Surprisingly, even though the temperature was over ninety degrees, they did not appear to be too hot in their layers of clothing.

The Pilgrim actors raised their hands and closed their eyes. Even though Rose could not hear their words, their body language clearly showed that they were praying. Because of her experience with the Puritans, she knew that a part of the prayer would include words about being thankful to God for his many blessings.

The role-playing Governor Bradford continued to read the wedding ceremony from a piece of paper. Before the ceremony was complete, the groom picked up and held onto the bride's hand. The bride was not wearing an engagement ring; neither the bride nor the groom put on wedding rings during the ceremony.

Once the wedding was finished, everyone went down the hill to an area that had been set up for a wedding feast. A real cow was in the fenced-in yard next to the wedding feast area. It was peacefully eating the grass and swatting bugs away with its tail. Rose walked over near the cow, and Travis followed her. After a minute of being bitten by the mosquitos swarming around the cow, Rose said, "I think this cow is almost as cute as the *Mayflower* cow statue in the Visitor Center, but I can't stand all of these bugs. Let's move over there." They both walked over to the other side of the wedding feast area.

Two tables were set up with white linen tablecloths on them. One of the tables was a tall one that was off to the side; it already had some food items on it. The other table was surrounded by different chairs, stools, and a bench.

Soon, the Pilgrim actors brought more food items out from different houses, and some of the Pilgrim men sat down. Several of the women served the men who were already seated at the main table. The meal included some round loaves of bread, salad, meat items, a casserole, and cheesecake. Only the Pilgrim actors ate the food; Travis, Rose, and the other visitors watched as the wedding feast progressed from its beginning to its ending.

After the feast was over, the actor who was role-playing William Bradford stood up. He looked around at the crowd that was watching him, walked over to Travis, and asked, "Art thou and thy wife ready?"

Rose looked at Travis, and he smiled awkwardly at her. She turned to the role-playing Bradford and asked, "Are we ready for what?"

Bradford cleared his throat and waved at Travis, who took in a deep breath, knelt down in front of Rose, and asked, "Will you marry me again? If you want to, which I really hope and pray you do, we can renew our vows—right here and right now."

Rose's face showed her surprise and then her happiness. She embraced Travis with her happy eyes. "I'd love to marry you again, Travis."

He kissed her hand, stood up, and then kissed her on the mouth. Before their kiss got too lengthy, the Role-playing Bradford said to them, "Some children are watching you."

Travis glanced briefly at the Role-playing Bradford, the children, and then turned back to look at Rose's happy face. He said to her, "I was thinking of asking you about renewing our vows for our third anniversary next month, but with the wedding here at Plimoth Plantation, today just seemed like the right time."

"Today is the perfect time for us to renew our vows." Rose looked at Travis's wedding ring and said, "Besides, I need you now. I can't wait for another month to renew our vows."

"Neither can I."

"There's one problem, though, Travis."

"What's that?"

"Our relatives and friends will want to be with us when we renew our vows."

"Have you looked behind us?"

Rose turned around. Behind them were their parents, Granny, some other relatives, and many of their friends. Rose waved at the people behind her and then hugged Travis. Cameras were snapping pictures; the noises blended in nicely with the sounds of people talking to each other.

Rose asked Travis, "What wedding vows should we use?"

He took two pieces of paper out of his billfold and gave one of them to Rose. "Here are some of the words we spoke at our wedding. Do you think these would be okay?"

Rose read the paper and smiled. "They're perfect."

She handed the paper to the Role-playing Bradford, who looked at the words. He then said, "These words are most loving, but some are wrong for our English in this most modern year of 1627. Dost thou want me to revise these words, so they will be corrected?"

Travis said, "Even though some of the words might sound strange, can you read them the way they are written on the paper?"

"To make thee happy, I will read the words as thou hast written them."

"Thanks," Travis and Rose said at the same time.

The Role-playing Bradford put the paper into a leather pouch that was hanging on his belt. He then told Travis and Rose, "You are very blessed to have so much love between you."

Travis and Rose shook their heads in agreement. After a moment of silence, Rose asked, "Is it possible for us to renew our vows right here and right now?"

The Role-playing Bradford said, "Most often, people have weddings in the building that standeth near the Visitor Center, but thy husband hath planned a different festival that he thought thou wouldst like."

"Really?"

"Ay. Thy husband hath already planned everything. If thou wantest me to, I will do the ceremony right now. It can take place in the most formal building in our village, which is where these events are most often done, or it can be held somewhere else. Thy husband told me about a nice place in the forest."

"What spot were you thinking of, Travis?"

"In the forest opposite the meetinghouse. When people take pictures of us, the meetinghouse will be in the background."

"That sounds like a perfect spot. And I'm sure the pictures with the meetinghouse in them will remind us about this wonderful second 'meeting' of ours."

Travis held out his hand to Rose; she took a step forward, stood next to him, and slid her hand gracefully into his. They then walked up the hill toward the meetinghouse. The Role-playing Bradford, their relatives, their friends, and even some tourists followed them.

Next to the meetinghouse, Travis, Rose, and the Role-playing Bradford walked through the gate and left the English Village behind them. A crowd of a hundred and two—or perhaps it was a hundred and three—people followed them out of the gate, around the wooden fence, and over toward the edge of the forest. Travis asked Rose, "Are you okay with strangers, as well as our family and friends, watching us?"

"Yeah, I am. It will be sort of nice to have some 'strangers' watch our ceremony. We'll feel more connected to the Pilgrims."

"That's right—I remember you told me about the 'strangers'— the English people who joined some of the Leiden separatists on the *Mayflower*. You also told me that the Separatists were called 'saints.' So who will be the 'saints' at our ceremony?"

"There are many wonderful people here who could be saints." Rose looked around at the large group of people before adding, "We'll also need crew members and Native people."

The Role-playing Bradford had stopped walking. The two-story wooden meetinghouse stood tall behind him. In front of him was a stack of boxes; Rose immediately recognized the boxes as the ones that had contained the Robinson $10,000. bills. A picture from Travis and Rose's first wedding sat on top of the boxes.

Travis asked Rose, "Do you want me to see if one of the 'strangers' will use my camera to take pictures of us?"

"We have two cameras. We could have two strangers take our pictures."

A man and a woman from the audience immediately stepped forward. Rose recognized them as the couple from Holland. The husband said, "We loved learning how to dance with you two Americans. Now we need to be the ones to take your pictures."

Rose said, "Oh, I'm so happy that you're going to help us out. I completely love your accents, too."

"We're from Leiden," the Dutch wife said.

"Really?" Travis asked.

"Yes. We came to Plymouth to visit the place where some of our ancestors now live."

"So, are you related to any of the Pilgrims?"

The Dutch wife said, "Actually, I'm a descendant of the Reverend John Robinson."

Rose's face lit up in joy as she said, "So am I." The Dutch wife and Rose hugged, looking as if they had just found each other after centuries of being apart. Travis and the Dutch husband watched in fascination as their wives embraced. Then all four of them shook hands with one another. Travis and Rose gave their cameras to the Dutch couple, who positioned themselves in the first row among the relatives.

Travis held onto Rose's hand as they walked over to stand in front of the meetinghouse. The Role-playing Bradford asked, "Is everyone ready for the wedding of Travis and Rose Hopkins?"

"Yes" was said at the same time by many different people.

The Role-playing Bradford looked at Travis and Rose as he read from his piece of paper, "We have gathered here today to renew the wedding vows of Travis Hopkins and Rose Hopkins. They were first married on August twenty-fifth, almost three years ago. At their first wedding, they said the following words in unison."

Travis and Rose read together from their copy of the paper: "May we be patient, kind, loyal, and loving to each other. May we be thankful to our Lord for our love, for our strengths, and even for our weaknesses. In times of weakness, we promise to keep helping and loving each other. May our love continue to grow for as long as we both shall live."

The Role-playing Bradford next asked Travis, "Do you take Rose to be your lawful wife, to have and to hold, in sickness and in health, for better or worse, for richer or poorer, through good times and bad, from this day forward and into the future—as the one you will love for the rest of your life?"

Travis said, "I do." He removed his wedding ring and gave it to Rose. She kissed the ring before placing it back onto his ring finger. Travis then moved his left hand high above his head, swirled his ring finger in circles, and showed everyone how happy he was to be wearing his wedding ring.

The Role-playing Bradford next asked Rose, "Do you take Travis to be your lawful husband, to have and to hold, in sickness and in health, for better or worse, for richer or poorer, through good times and bad, from this day forward and into the future—as the one you will love for the rest of your life?"

Rose said, "I do." She then opened up her purse, took her wedding ring out of her billfold, and let Travis put it onto her ring finger, right next to her engagement ring that was already shining brightly in its correct spot. He then kissed her hand before she raised it up high, so everyone could see it.

Speaking out loud together and sounding almost like a single voice, Travis and Rose next read the following quote from the Bible: "And now faith, hope, and love abide, these three; and the greatest of these is love" (1 Cor. 13:13 RSV). While holding hands, they then said together, "May our love for each other and for our Lord and Savior, Jesus Christ, endure forever."

The Role-playing Bradford then raised his hands high and said, "Travis and Rose are now husband and wife. Travis, thou mayest kiss thy bride."

Standing in the light of the sun, Travis and Rose kissed while an ever-growing audience of people watched them. There were now at least a hundred and thirty visitors and staff members. More children seemed to arrive every second until nearly every couple had at least one child standing nearby. A spot of sweat moved from Travis's forehead onto Rose's face, moving down her nose and landing between their two pairs of lips. The moisture only seemed to glue them together even closer as they continued to kiss each other. When a baby in the audience started to cry, Travis stepped back from Rose and asked, "Was the timing of our kiss enough to make you happy?"

Rose laughed. "Yes, that was the best time for the longest kiss that I've ever had."

Travis took his cell phone out of his pocket and turned it on. The song "Miracles Happen" began to play. Travis held his hand out to Rose. While an audience of Plimoth Plantation employees and visitors continued to watch them, they danced together, using the steps that the Pilgrim dance instructor had shown them earlier that day. As the song progressed, Travis and Rose speeded up. They no longer were dancing according to the timing of the beats of the song, but rather were dancing within the beats of their own time frame. They didn't notice that close to two hundred people were watching each of their joyful dance steps.

A gentle breeze began to blow. Travis and Rose slowed down and paused to look at each other's faces. Rose noticed that Travis's hair was moving. She thought that the breeze was making his hair move; she also felt her own hair move and assumed it was caused by the same breeze. She didn't realize that two role-playing Pilgrim ladies were attaching red, white, and blue ribbons into their hair. One of the ladies had a feather in her hat and was known to be a descendent of one of the *Mayflower* Pilgrims.

Near the end of the "Miracles Happen" song, when Travis and Rose heard the line "You showed me dreams come to life,"[105] they kissed again. During that moment, they did not notice their audience of historical role-players, American families, European families, Native people, and *Mayflower* descendants clapping their hands in time to the music. Some were singing the song's lyrics, and some were humming. All of them saw that Travis and Rose were happily in love with each other. At the end of the song, a voice that sounded strangely like the Feather-hat Lady's called out, "Heaven hast brought them good fortune!"

Pilgrim Language

Language is one way people are connected to their culture. When a culture changes, the language also changes. For example, before cell phones were invented, people would not have understood that a "cell phone" was a portable phone. They might have thought that a "cell phone" was a prison phone used by criminals in a jail cell or a living phone composed of biological cells.

In *Mayflower Dreams,* the use of Pilgrim language shows different aspects of Pilgrim culture. Two of these aspects are religious content in the vocabulary and social class in the second-person pronouns:

> In Pilgrim vocabulary, religious content can be seen with the use of many religious phrases, such as "God be with thee" and "Bless thee." A Pilgrim would say "Pray pardon me," rather than "Excuse me."

> In Pilgrim second-person pronouns, social class can be seen in the use of different pronouns for different situations and audiences. The words "thou," "thee," "thy," "thine," and "thyself" were used in informal situations (when speaking to a friend or to someone of a lower social class). The words "you," "your," and "yourself" were used in formal situations (when speaking to more than one person, to a stranger, or to someone in a higher social class).

Mayflower Dreams uses some—rather than all—of the Pilgrim linguistic structures. The intent is to show realistic Pilgrim dialogue while maintaining readability for modern readers. To make the words more readable, many of the spellings of words have been modernized. Pilgrim verb endings were not modernized because these spellings enhance the distinctions between such words as the informal "thou" and the formal "you."

PILGRIM LANGUAGE IN LITERATURE

Pilgrim language structures can be found in the letters, journals, books, and other writings of seventeenth-century authors, such as William Bradford, the Reverend John Robinson, Edward Winslow, and Captain John Smith. Early Pilgrim-era language can also be seen in the 1599 edition of the *Geneva Bible* and the 1611 edition of the *King James Bible*. The Plimoth Plantation Webpage "Talk Like a Pilgrim" has some examples of Pilgrim dialogue that are used by the role-playing actors in their living museum.[106]

Even though the Pilgrims were in contact with French and other languages while in Amsterdam and Leiden, their language background was primarily English. Thus. the literature of most British authors of the same time period show the same linguistic structures used by the Pilgrims. For example, the prose dialogue sections of Shakespearean plays illustrate many Pilgrim language components.

PHRASES AND CLAUSES

The Pilgrims often used long sentences with multiple phrases and clauses: *The Pilgrims came to the New World on the Mayflower, which had a gun deck floor, which is the level where the Pilgrims usually stayed.*

Double Negatives

Extra stress or emphasis was achieved in Pilgrim communications by using double or triple comparatives, superlatives, or negatives: *Nothing in this world hath not never been so fast; our ship is sailing the most fastest ever.*

Compound Subjects

Compound subjects joined by the word "and" used either a singular or a plural verb: *God and Jesus giveth many wonders to me in my present life; also, they give hope to me for a wonderful future.*

Countable Nouns

A few nouns that were countable in the early seventeenth century are uncountable now, including *music, courage, information, thunder, money,* and *revenge.*[107] *She playeth two musics* means *she plays two musical items.*

Pronouns

Most of the pronouns used by Pilgrims were the same kinds of pronouns that we use today: nominative (I, he, she, it, we, you, they), objective (me, him,…), possessive (my, his,…), reflexive (myself, himself,…), relative, interrogative, indefinite, intensive, demonstrative, and personal. There were a few differences in usage, though. For example, the relative pronouns "which" and "that" were used for people, as well as for objects and animals. Another difference in pronoun usage was second-person pronouns ("thou" versus "you"). When talking to someone else, a Pilgrim would use either singular/informal ("thou") or plural/formal ("you") pronouns, depending on the situation.

For singular or informal situations, the Pilgrims used "thou," "thee," "thy," "thine," and "thyself." These situations included speaking with a friend or with someone in a lower social class:

> *Thou art a Pilgrim.*
> *I thank thee for helping me with my tasks.*
> *Thy most favorite book is the Bible.*
> *That picture belongeth to thine aunt.*
> *Thou wouldst pray by thyself whenever thou wast alone.*

In plural or formal situations, the Pilgrims would use "you," "your," and "yourself." These situations would include speaking to more than one person, to a stranger, or to someone in a higher social class. In the following example, "your" is used by the speaker while talking to someone who is wearing very expensive clothing: *Your beaver hat hath diamonds that have been attached to it; my linen hat only hath dirt on it.*

Verb Tenses

A verb tense shows when the action of a sentence "happens" (simple present), "happened" (simple past), or "will happen" (simple future). Depending on the verb tense and the point of view, the spelling of a verb will change. The following list describes verb spellings of regular Pilgrim verbs. (Irregular verbs, such as "to be," often had different verb endings.)

- In the present tense, second person singular/informal verbs (with "thou" pronouns) ended in "st" or "est": *Thou lovest thy family.*

- In the present tense, third person singular verbs (with "he/she/it" pronouns) ended in "th" or "eth": *He loveth his family. He is a person who doth great work.*

- In the past tense, second person singular/informal verbs (with "thou" pronouns) ended in "dst," "edst," or "st": *Thou prayedst to our Lord. Thou didst sail to the New World.*

- In the future tense, second person singular/informal verbs (with "thou" pronouns) ended in "t": *Thou wilt pray to our Lord.*

- A modal *(can, may, must, shall, will, should, would, could)* helps the main verb to convey its meaning. Second person singular/informal modal verbs (with "thou" pronouns) had "st" or "est" endings: *Thou shouldst sail on the boat.*

Present Tense Pilgrim Verbs

	Thou (singular/ informal)	He, She, It	I, We, They, You (plural/ formal)
to pray	prayest	prayeth	pray
to run	runnest	runneth	run
to have	hast	hath	have
to be	art	is	are
to say	sayest	saith	say
to do (active)	dost	doth	do
to do (auxiliary)	dost pray	doth pray	do pray

Past Tense Pilgrim Verbs

	Thou (singular/ informal)	He, She, It	I, We, They, You (plural/ formal)
to pray	prayedst	prayed	prayed
to run	runnedst	ran	ran
to have	hadst	had	had
to be	wast	was	was, were
to say	sayedst	said	said
to do (active)	doest	doeth	did
to do (auxiliary)	didst love	did pray	did pray

Future Tense Pilgrim Verbs

	Thou (singular/ informal)	I, He, She, It, We, They, You (plural/formal)
to pray	wilt or shalt pray	will or shall pray
to run	wilt or shalt run	will or shall run
to have	wilt or shalt have	will or shall have
to be	wilt or shalt be	will or shall be
to say	wilt or shalt say	will or shall say
to do (active)	wilt or shalt do	will or shall do

Pilgrim Greetings

Phrase	Meaning
Good morrow.	Good morning.
Good day or evening.	Good day or evening.
How now?	How are you feeling now?
How dost thou?	How are you doing?
What cheer?	What is making you happy?
How do you fare?	How are you doing?
Fare thee well.	Be well.
Farewell.	Good-bye.
Peace.	May peace be with you.
Pray remember me.	I pray you'll remember me.
Good.	Okay.

Pilgrim Common Sayings

Phrase	Meaning
God be with thee.	May God be with you.
Bless thee.	May God bless you.
I thank thee for	I thank you for . . . .
Many good thanks.	Thanks a lot.
I am blest.	I am blessed by God.
I beseech thee.	I beg you to . . . .
What sayest thou?	What are you saying?
Pray pardon me.	Please excuse me.
Huzzah!	Hurray!
Ay	Yes
Nay	No

ENDNOTES

1. NetworkMedia.com, Inc., *Ancestry.org*, "Mayflower Ancestors," http://ancestry.org/mayflower-ancestors/ (accessed August 13, 2012).

2. Karen Petit, *Banking on Dreams* (Mustang, Oklahoma: Tate Publishing and Enterprises, LLC, 2012), 83.

3. Edward Johnson (1910), qtd. in Nick Bunker, *Making Haste from Babylon* (New York: Alfred A. Knopf, 2010), 19.

4. Society of Mayflower Descendants in the Commonwealth of Pennsylvania, "Pilgrim Fun Facts," *Sail 1620* (sail1620. org, 2012), http://www.sail1620.org/educational/48-materials/131-pilgrim-fun-facts.html (accessed June 22, 2012).

5. John Robinson, quoted in Walter H. Burgess, *John Robinson Pastor of the Pilgrim Fathers A Study of His Life and Times* (London: Williams and Norgate, 1920), v.

6. Francis Dillon, *The Pilgrims Their Journeys & Their World* (Garden City, New York: Doubleday & Company, Inc., 1975), 98.

7. William Bradford, *Of Plymouth Plantation,* ed. Samuel Eliot Morison (New York: Alfred A. Knopf, 1970), back cover.

8. NetworkMedia.com, Inc., *Ancestry.org,* "Mayflower Ancestors," http://ancestry.org/mayflower-ancestors/ (accessed August 13, 2012).

9. Samuel Eliot Morison, ed., "Footnote 9" in Chapter 1 of William Bradford's *Of Plymouth Plantation* (New York: Alfred A. Knopf, 1970), 7.

10. *Columbia Electronic Encyclopedia,* 6th ed. (2011): 1. *Academic Search Complete,* s.v. "Dream," http://0-search. ebscohost.com.helin.uri.edu/login.aspx?direct=true&db=a 9h&AN=51475659&site=ehost-live.

11. Ibid.

12. Jessica Hamzelou, "The Secret of Consciousness: Reinterpreting Dreams," *New Scientist* 206, no 2764 (June 12, 2010): 39, in *Academic Search Premier,* EBSCO*host* (accessed 9 August 2012).

13. William Bradford, *Of Plymouth Plantation,* ed. Samuel Eliot Morison (New York: Alfred A. Knopf, 1970), 15.

14. Jeremy Bangs, "Leiden American Pilgrim Museum," *Ancestry.com,* http://www.rootsweb.ancestry.com/~netlapm /Page12.htm (accessed August 6, 2012).

15. Kelly Clarkson, "What Doesn't Kill You (Stronger)," *AZLyrics.com,* accessed December 22, 2012, http://www. azlyrics.com/lyrics/kellyclarkson/whatdoesntkillyou stronger.html.

16. Ibid.

17. Orleans, "Dance with Me," *LyricsMode,* accessed August 24, 2012, http://www.lyricsmode.com/lyrics/o/orleans/ dance_with_me.html.

18. Guess Who, "No Time," *elyrics.net,* accessed December 20, 2012, http://www.elyrics.net/read/g/guess-who-lyrics/no-time-lyrics.html.

19. Ibid.

20. Nick Bunker, *Making Haste from Babylon* (New York: Alfred A. Knopf, 2010), 219.

21. Godfrey Hodgson, *A Great and Godly Adventure The Pilgrims and the Myth of the First Thanksgiving* (New York: Public Affairs, 2006), 64.

22. Samuel Eliot Morison, ed., "Introduction," in *Of Plymouth Plantation*, William Bradford (New York: Alfred A. Knopf, 1970), xxv.

23. Walter H. Burgess, *John Robinson Pastor of the Pilgrim Fathers A Study of His Life and Times* (London: Williams and Norgate, 1920), 234-35.

24. "Morning Prayer," *1599 Geneva Bible Patriot's Edition,* (White Hall, West Virginia: Tolle Lege Press, 2010), 1340.

25. Jeremy Bangs, "The Pilgrims' Leiden," *Ancestry.com,* 1997, http://www.rootsweb.ancestry.com/~netlapm/Page31X.htm (accessed August 6, 2012).

26. Dr. Marshall Foster, "The History and Impact of the Geneva Bible," *The 1599 Geneva Bible, Patriot's Edition* (White Hall, West Virginia: Tolle Lege Press & White Hall Press, 2010), xv-xvi.

27. Footnote for 2 Corinthians 5:9, *1599 Geneva Bible Patriot's Edition* (White Hall, West Virginia: Tolle Lege Press & White Hall Press, 2010), 1195.

28. Jeremy Bangs, "Pilgrim Occupations in Leiden," *Pilgrim Life in Leiden A Summary Account of the Pilgrims' Stay in Leiden,* ISBN 90-76317-01-1, *Ancestry.com,* first published 1997, revised, http://www.rootsweb.ancestry.com/~netlapm/Page31X.htm (accessed August 6, 2012).

29. Waldo Selden Pratt, *The Music of the Pilgrims* (Boston: Oliver Ditson Co.), http://ia700208.us.archive.org/13/items/musicofpilgrimsd00pratuoft/musicofpilgrimsd-00pratuoft.pdf (accessed August 16, 2012), 7.

30. Edward Winslow, Hypocrisie Unmasked, 1646, quoted in Waldo Selden Pratt, *The Music of the Pilgrims* (Boston: Oliver Ditson Co.), http://ia700208.us.archive.org/13/items/musicofpilgrimsd00pratuoft/musicofpilgrimsd-00pratuoft.pdf (accessed August 16, 2012), 6.

31. John Robinson, "John Robinson's Farewell Letter to the Pilgrims," quoted in Walter H. Burgess, *John Robinson Pastor of the Pilgrim Fathers A Study of His Life and Times* (London: Williams and Norgate, 1920), 253-56.

32. William Bradford, *Of Plymouth Plantation*, ed. Samuel Eliot Morison (New York: Alfred A. Knopf, 1970), 47.

33. Samuel Eliot Morison, ed., "Footnote 4" in Chapter 7 of William Bradford's *Of Plymouth Plantation* (New York: Alfred A. Knopf, 1970), 47.

34. Thomas Gibson, "The Leiden Separatists, (Saints) and London Investors, (Strangers)," York College of Pennsylvania, April 8, 2008, http://faculty.ycp.edu/~tgibson/gibson/Genealogy/ListOfMayflowerPassengers.html (accessed December 30, 2012).

35. Ibid.

36. Ibid.

37. Pilgrim Hall Museum, "Peregrine White Cradle," 2012, http://www.pilgrimhallmuseum.org/CE_funiture.htm#Peregrine_Cradle" (accessed December 30, 2012).

38. Thomas Gibson, "The Leiden Separatists, (Saints) and London Investors, (Strangers)," York College of

Pennsylvania, April 8, 2008, http://faculty.ycp.edu/~tgibson/gibson/Genealogy/ListOfMayflowerPassengers.html (accessed December 30, 2012).

39. Godfrey Hodgson, *A Great and Godly Adventure The Pilgrims and the Myth of the First Thanksgiving* (New York: Public Affairs, 2006), 60.

40. Nick Bunker, *Making Haste from Babylon* (New York: Alfred A. Knopf, 2010), 23.

41. Duane A. Cline, "The Pilgrims and Plymouth Colony: 1620," Hosted by *rootsweb*, an *ancestry.com* community, 2006, http://www.rootsweb.ancestry.com/~mosmd/ (accessed August 20, 2012).

42. Ibid.

43. John Robinson, "John Robinson's Farewell Letter to the Pilgrims," quoted in Walter H. Burgess, *John Robinson Pastor of the Pilgrim Fathers A Study of His Life and Times* (London: Williams and Norgate, 1920), 253.

44. Ibid, 256.

45. Hannibal Hamlin, "Psalm Culture in the English Renaissance: Readings of Psalm 137 by Shakespeare, Spenser, Milton, and Others (*), *Renaissance Quarterly* 55.1 (2002): 224+, in *Literature Resource Center*, Gale Document Number: GALE A84722725, http://0-go.galegroup.com.helin.uri.edu/ps/i.do?id=GALE%7CA84722725&v=2.1&u=ccri_main&it=r&p=LitRC&sw=w (accessed December 21, 2012).

46. Henry Ainsworth, "Psalm 100," *The Music of Henry Ainsworth's Psalter,"* Lorraine Inserra and H. Wiley Hitchcock, eds., I.S. a.m. Monographs: Number 15 (Brooklyn, New York: Institute for Studies in American Music, 1981), 115.

47. William Bradford, *Of Plymouth Plantation*, ed. Samuel Eliot Morison (New York: Alfred A. Knopf, 1970), 58.

48. Ibid.

49. Ibid, 59.

50. Ibid.

51. Ibid.

52. Francis Dillon, *The Pilgrims Their Journeys & Their World* (Garden City, New York: Doubleday & Company, Inc., 1975), 129.

53. Collins, Ron, "A Brief History of the Pilgrims," *mayflowerfamilies.com*, 2012, http://www.mayflowerfamilies.com/colonial_life/pilgrims.htm (accessed August 16, 2012).

54. Duane A. Cline, "The Pilgrims and Plymouth Colony: 1620," Hosted by *rootsweb*, an *ancestry.com* community, 2006, http://www.rootsweb.ancestry.com/~mosmd/ (accessed August 20, 2012).

55. Grand Funk Railroad, "Locomotion," *youtube.com*, accessed January 9, 2013, http://www.youtube.com/watch?v=6j_I5ndxI28.

56. Henry Ainsworth, "Psalm 8," *The Music of Henry Ainsworth's Psalter,"* Lorraine Inserra and H. Wiley Hitchcock, eds., I.S. a.m. Monographs: Number 15 (Brooklyn, New York: Institute for Studies in American Music, 1981), 46.

57. Francis Dillon, *The Pilgrims Their Journeys & Their World* (Garden City, New York: Doubleday & Company, Inc., 1975), 229.

58. *Desperate Crossing The Untold Story of the Mayflower*, produced by Lone Wolf Documentary Group for the History Channel, directed and produced by Lisa Quijano

Wolfinger, written by Rocky Collins, edited by Tony Bacon and Jed Rauscher (A&E Television Networks, 2006), DVD.

59. Ibid.

60. *The Mayflower Compact.* Quoted in Walter H. Burgess, *John Robinson Pastor of the Pilgrim Fathers A Study of His Life and Times* (London: Williams and Norgate, 1920), 264-65.

61. Walter H. Burgess, *John Robinson Pastor of the Pilgrim Fathers A Study of His Life and Times* (London: Williams and Norgate, 1920), 265.

62. Winston S. Churchill, quoted in Society of Mayflower Descendants in the Commonwealth of Pennsylvania, *Sail 1620* (sail1620.org, 2012), http://www.sail1620.org (accessed August 15, 2012).

63. *The Mayflower Compact.* Quoted in Walter H. Burgess, *John Robinson Pastor of the Pilgrim Fathers A Study of His Life and Times* (London: Williams and Norgate, 1920), 264-65.

64. William Bradford, *Of Plymouth Plantation,* ed. Samuel Eliot Morison (New York: Alfred A. Knopf, 1970), 68.

65. *A Journal of the Pilgrims at Plymouth Mourt's Relation,* ed. Dwight B. Heath and consulting editor Henry Bamford Parkes. (New York: Corinth Books, 1963), 27.

66. "A Godly Prayer to be Said at All Times," *1599 Geneva Bible Patriot's Edition,* (White Hall, West Virginia: Tolle Lege Press, 2010), 1342.

67. *Mourt's Relation Or, Journal of the Plantation at Plymouth,* ed. Henry Martyn Dexter (Boston: John Kimball Wiggin,1865), in The Lambertville Archive, http://

catalog.lambertvillelibrary.org/texts/American/winslow_
edward/mourt/mourt.htm (accesssed August 29, 2013),
24.

68. Ibid.

69. Ibid.

70. Ibid.

71. Ibid, 25.

72. Ibid.

73. Steve Miller Band, "Fly Like an Eagle," *elyrics.net,*
accessed August 30, 2012, http://www.elyrics.net/read/s/
steve-miller-band-lyrics/fly-like-an-eagle-lyrics.html.

74. Nathaniel Philbrick, *Mayflower* (New York: Viking,
2006), 110.

75. Ibid.

76. Ibid.

77. "A Prayer to be Said before a Man Begin His Work,"
1599 Geneva Bible Patriot's Edition, (White Hall, West
Virginia: Tolle Lege Press, 2010), 1343.

78. Maine Historical Society, "Wadsworth Longfellow
Genealogy," *hwlongfellow.org,* (2013), http://www.
hwlongfellow.org/family_genealogy.shtml (accessed
May 29, 2013)

79. Department of Conservation and Recreation, "Pilgrim
Memorial State Park," *mass.gov,* http://www.mass.gov/
dcr/parks/southeast/plgm.htm (accessed 2 January 2013).

80. Megan Gambino, "The Story Behind Plymouth Rock,"
Around the Mall, (November 22, 2011), *smithsonian-
mag.com,* http://blogs.smithsonianmag.com/aroundthe-

mall/2011/11/the-story-behind-plymouth-rock/ (accessed April 6, 2012).

81. John Patrick McCaffrey, "John Alden," *Geni.com*, (2013), http://www.geni.com/people/John-Alden-Mayflower-Passenger/6000000003454509677 (accessed May 31, 2013).

82. Megan Gambino, "The Story Behind Plymouth Rock," *Around the Mall*, (November 22, 2011), *smithsonian-mag.com*, http://blogs.smithsonianmag.com/aroundthe-mall/2011/11/the-story-behind-plymouth-rock/ (accessed April 6, 2012).

83. Nathaniel Philbrick, *Mayflower* (New York: Viking, 2006), 105.

84. Ibid, 92.

85. *A Journal of the Pilgrims at Plymouth Mourt's Relation,* ed. Dwight B. Heath and consulting editor Henry Bamford Parkes. (New York: Corinth Books, 1963), 56.

86. Ibid, 56-57.

87. Ibid, 57.

88. John Smith, "To the right Worshipfull Adventurers for the Countery of New England, in the Cities of London, Bristow, Exceter, Plimouth, Dartmouth, Bastable, Totneys, &c. and in all other Cities and Ports, in the Kingdome of England," *A Description of New England (1616): An Online Electronic Text Edition,* Ed. Paul Royster, (1616), *Electronic Texts in American Studies,* Paper 4, http://digitalcommons.unl.edu/etas/4 (accessed December 21, 2012).

89. John Smith, *A Description of New England (1616): An Online Electronic Text Edition,* Ed. Paul Royster, (1616),

Electronic Texts in American Studies, Paper 4, http://digitalcommons.unl.edu/etas/4 (accessed December 21, 2012).

90. Nathaniel Philbrick, *Mayflower* (New York: Viking, 2006), 105.

91. E.W. [E.W. is defined by the editor Dwight Heath as probably being Edward Winslow], "A Letter Sent from New England to a friend in these parts, setting forth a brief and true declaration of the worth of that plantation; as also certain useful directions for such as intend a voyage into those parts," in *A Journal of the Pilgrims at Plymouth,"* ed. Dwight B. Heath and consulting editor Henry Bamford Parkes. (New York: Corinth Books, 1963), 82.

92. Abraham Lincoln, "Lincoln's Thanksgiving Proclamation" (October 3, 1863), in *Infoplease.com,* http://www.infoplease.com/spot/tgproclamation.html (accessed March 21, 2013).

93. Henry Ainsworth, "Psalm 23," *The Book of Psalms," The Music of the Pilgrims,* Waldo Selden Pratt, ed. (New York: Russell and Russell, 1971), 10.

94. E.W. [E.W. is defined by the editor Dwight Heath as probably being Edward Winslow], "A Letter Sent from New England to a friend in these parts, setting forth a brief and true declaration of the worth of that plantation; as also certain useful directions for such as intend a voyage into those parts," in *A Journal of the Pilgrims at Plymouth,"* ed. Dwight B. Heath and consulting editor Henry Bamford Parkes. (New York: Corinth Books, 1963), 82.

95. Ibid, 84.

96. Ibid, 82.

97. Ibid, 81.

98. Ibid.

99. William Bradford and Edward Winslow, "Mourt's Relation," in *The Mayflower Papers Selected Writings of Colonial New England,* eds. Nathaniel Philbrick and Thomas Philbrick. (New York: Penguin, 2007), 142.

100. Ibid.

101. Billy Ocean, "Caribbean Queen (No More Love on the Run)," *AZLyrics.com,* accessed January 19, 2013, http://www.azlyrics.com/lyrics/billyocean/caribbeanqueennomoreloveontherun.html.

102. Leland Ryken, "The Original Puritan Work Ethic," *Christian History & Biography* no. 89 (Winter2006): 33 in *Academic Search Complete,* http://0-search.ebscohost.com.helin.uri.edu/login.aspx?direct=true&db=a9h&AN=20005750&site=ehost-live (accessed January 10, 2013).

103. Ibid, 34.

104. Godfrey Hodgson, *A Great and Godly Adventure The Pilgrims and the Myth of the First Thanksgiving* (New York: Public Affairs, 2006), 58.

105. Myra, "Miracles Happen (When You Believe)," *AZLyrics.com,* accessed January 20, 2013, http:http://www.azlyrics.com/lyrics/myra/miracleshappenwhenyoubelieve.html.

106. *plimoth.org,* "Talk Like a Pilgrim," *Plimoth Plantation,* 2012, http://www.plimoth.org/learn/just-kids/talk-pilgrim (accessed October 11, 2012).

107. David Crystal, *'Think on my Words' Exploring Shakespeare's Language* (Cambridge, UK: Cambridge University Press, 2008), 185.

9 781629 942933